# RESISTANCE
## THE GATHERING STORM

# RESISTANCE
## THE GATHERING STORM

# William C. Dietz

**BALLANTINE BOOKS • NEW YORK**

A Del Rey Books Mass Market Original

Copyright © 2009 by Sony Computer Entertainment America Inc.

Published in the United States by Del Rey Books, an imprint of The Random House Publishing Group, a division of Random House, Inc., New York.

DEL REY is a registered trademark and the Del Rey colophon is a trademark of Random House, Inc.

RESISTANCE is a trademark of Sony Computer Entertainment America Inc.

ISBN: 978-0-345-50842-3

Printed in the United States of America

www.delreybooks.com

OPM   9  8  7  6  5  4  3

To my dearest Marjorie . . .
Thank you for going to the dance instead of studying,
for believing that I could,
and for every second of our time together.

# ACKNOWLEDGMENTS

I would like to thank Ted Price, who is President and CEO of Insomniac Games as well as Creative Director on *Resistance;* Cristian Cardona, Sony Marketing; Jefferson Dong, Sony Marketing; Greg Phillips, Sony Product Development; Brian Hastings, Chief Creative Officer of Insomniac Games; and Ryan Schneider, Insomniac Games Community Director, for all of their help and advice.

Special thanks go to TJ Fixman and Marc Mailand of Insomniac Games for their creation of the Stillman character, and TJ's initial draft of the Stillman section of Chapter 9, which he wrote to order.

And finally, I am especially indebted to my editors, Keith Clayton, Tricia Narwani, and Steve Saffel, and to Sony Senior Producer Frank Simon, for his tireless efforts to coordinate all of the moving parts, and track down the answers to at least a hundred writer-type questions. Thank you one and all! I couldn't have done it without you.

# CHAPTER ONE
# HIDE AND SEEK

The snow-clad hill didn't look like much, but the granite that lay just a few feet below the topsoil had been strong enough to hold its own against a retreating glacier thousands of years before, and was likely to be there for millennia yet to come. Of more importance to the men hidden on top of the hill was the vantage point their position provided, giving them the ability to watch enemy troop movements and, God willing, defend themselves if attacked.

The daytime temperature should have been about forty this time of the year, but it was ten degrees lower than that, a grim reminder of the way the alien Chimera had altered Earth's atmosphere to their advantage. As a result, Lieutenant Nathan Hale's breath fogged the air as he lay on his belly and trained a pair of binoculars on the highway below. He wore a winter white parka and matching pants over a wool uniform and thermal underwear. And yet he was *still* cold.

Something Hale forced himself to ignore as he studied the scene that lay in front of him.

He remembered the familiar white ribbon of road as the one that he and his family had traveled each year on their way to the South Dakota State Fair in Huron. The memory made his heart ache, because even though he'd been back in the United States for months, Hale hadn't been allowed to contact his foster parents or his sister. Unanswered questions plagued him. Had they fled south into Nebraska? Or remained on the ranch? Three generations of the family had battled the elements, the economy, and the land itself—and won. But the invasion would have been too much, even for them.

If they were still on the ranch, they were in terrible danger. Having conquered most of Asia and Europe, the Chimera had turned their attention to North America. Chicago already had fallen to the invaders, in October, quickly followed by key cities in Wisconsin and North Dakota. Now, as the enemy continued to move south, the United States Army and the Marine Corps had been forced to pull back into an ever-shrinking "Fortress America."

But the Chimera could be stopped. As Hale peered through a thin veil of steadily falling snow he knew that a ring of defense towers were being built to the south, constructed for the sole purpose of blocking the Chimeran advance. But would they be enough?

Hale had his doubts, because he'd been a member of the ill-fated 3rd Ranger Regiment, and seen firsthand the atrocities that had occurred in England. So Hale knew that no matter how many defense towers the government put up, the Chimera wouldn't stop until they had overwhelmed their foes.

Hale's thoughts were interrupted by Sergeant Marvin Kawecki.

"We have company, sir . . . Ten o'clock."

Kawecki crouched to Hale's left, his right eye at the 10× scope of an L23 Fareye. Particles of dry snow were rapidly accumulating on the back of his parka.

Hale had been looking south, and as he panned the

binoculars to the left, he saw that Kawecki was correct. Three Chimeran Attack Drones emerged from the veil of snow, following the ribbon of highway, high-intensity beams of light knifing out in front of them. Each one flew about six feet off the ground, and they darted about like hunting dogs following a scent.

Their presence in and of itself was revealing, because even though most of the civilian population had fled south, Hale knew that nonmilitary resistance groups like Freedom First continued to operate behind enemy lines, where they had met with some success. The arrival of the drones most likely indicated that the stinks were concerned about the possibility of an ambush.

The presence of Chimera on Highway 281 was exactly the sort of Intel that Hale, Kawecki, and Private Jim Jasper had been ordered to obtain. Too little was known about the invaders, and with each new piece of data the Intel specialists could build a matrix of information that would be very valuable indeed.

Suddenly Hale felt his stomach muscles tighten as one of the drones left the edge of the road and began to move straight in their direction! It dropped slightly, until it was flying about four feet off the ground, and seemed determined to reach the top of the hill. Snow sleeted down through the beam of light that swept the ground in front of it. Had they been spotted? Or had the machine been programmed to examine hilltops?

"I have it," Kawecki said tightly. "Just say the word."

But Hale didn't *want* to say the word, because if Kawecki brought the drone down, all hell would break loose. And given the fact that the team was three miles inside the gray zone, it would be impossible to escape.

But as the construct continued uphill toward their position, there seemed to be few options.

Hale opened his mouth, and was about to give the

necessary order, when a white-tailed jackrabbit broke cover and the drone came to an abrupt stop, its light swiveling in the direction of the fleeing animal. The rabbit hadn't traveled more than ten feet before there was a single shot and it tumbled head over heels, blood spraying everywhere. Finally it came to rest on the snow.

The Chimeran scout hovered menacingly for a moment, then pivoted back toward the road, following the slope downhill.

Hale was surprised to discover that he'd been holding his breath, and released it as silently as he could.

"Jasper," he said softly, "how's the back door? We may need to pull out soon."

Jasper was lying in the prone position five feet behind the other two men. He was facing west, his M5A2 Folsom carbine at the ready, providing security for Hale and Kawecki. Just because some of the Chimera had chosen to travel south on 281 didn't mean *all* of them would have.

"The back door's wide open, sir," Jasper replied. "We're good to go."

Hale was about to acknowledge the report when he felt the ground tremble beneath his chest.

"Holy shit," Kawecki swore. "What's *that*?"

Hale thrust the glasses back into position, and watched as a phalanx of forward-leaning Steelheads emerged from the curtain of swirling snow to his left. That was bad enough, but he knew that while the heads were dangerous, something far worse would be following along on their heels. Sure enough . . .

The thing was a smudge at first, an amorphous mass that could barely be seen through the swirling snow. But a few moments later the Mauler came into focus. The beast stood about thirty feet tall, and each step spanned twenty feet of highway. The earth shuddered with a teeth-rattling *thump* as each enormous three-toed foot hit the ground. A grotesquerie such as this one could spew something akin to napalm, and launch corrosive-filled pods that exploded on contact. While a couple of well-placed rounds from a rocket launcher might bring the beast down, the lightly armed recon team wasn't carrying that kind of firepower.

Then he saw the huge pack that was strapped to the creature's back, and let out a sigh of relief. The pack meant it was currently being used to transport supplies.

There was no way to know what was in the packs, where the Chimera were headed, or to what end. But those were questions for Intel to wrestle with.

The vibrations increased as two additional Maulers appeared, their sloped backs covered with snow and jets of lung-warmed air shooting out of their nostrils as they followed the first behemoth south.

As they disappeared into the obscuring snow, Hale put the binoculars down and began to take notes. He was careful to jot down the time, the direction that the Chimera were traveling, and how many of each form there were. Chimera came in various forms, and Intel would want to know which ones were involved in the North American assault.

Then as the last of the stinks disappeared into the white haze, he buttoned the book into his breast pocket.

"Okay," Hale said, just loud enough for both men to hear. "I don't know about you, but I could use a hot shower and some of that slop they serve in the mess hall. So let's get the hell out of here . . . But remember, those bastards have six eyes—so don't break the horizon."

Kawecki had seen lots of action, and knew Hale's comment was directed at Jasper, who had been in a dustup or two but was relatively inexperienced, especially for a Sentinel. Most members of the elite combat organization were ex-Army or Marine Corps ground pounders with lots of special ops experience—Hale being an excellent example. And while the serum developed by the Special Research Projects Administration (SRPA) enabled Sentinels to recover from what would otherwise have been fatal wounds, the "bug juice"—as some of the men called it—couldn't counter the effects of a direct hit from a Chimeran mortar.

So casualty rates remained high, and newbies like Jasper were increasingly common. They had plenty to learn.

Jasper was fully aware of the fact that the veterans were watching him like hawks as he elbowed his way forward and slid headfirst down the slope. Snow slipped through his open collar and chilled his skin as he brought his feet around and used them to brake. Reaching the bottom of the incline, he took cover behind a group of snow-capped rocks.

A quick look around told him that the horizon was clear, and he raised a thumb.

Kawecki descended the hill next, quickly followed by Hale. They retraced the path they had followed earlier, down into a dry ravine. Hale was on point, with Kawecki in the two-slot, and Jasper bringing up the rear. Walking drag was a tough job that required Jasper to pause from time to time, in order to eye the team's back-trail, before running to catch up.

Though dry now, the ravine would be half-filled with runoff come spring. It led them to a half-frozen stream where running water could be seen through holes in the ice. It produced a cheerful gurgling sound which served as a suitable accompaniment to the *crunch, crunch,*

*crunch* made by their boots, and the occasional crackle of broken ice.

The landing zone was still a good two miles to the south, but Hale knew it would take the pickup plane some time to get there, so he triggered his radio.

"Bravo-Six to Echo-Three . . . Do you read? Over."

"This is Three," came the immediate reply. "I read you Five-by-Five. Over."

"We're about forty-five minutes out," Hale responded, "And we're tired of walking. Over."

"Say no more," Echo-Three replied cheerfully. "*Marilyn* and I are on the way. Over."

Hale grinned as he jumped from one sheet of ice to the next, careful to stay away from the holes. Echo-Three's much patched VTOL bore a beautifully rendered likeness of a scantily clad Marilyn Monroe on the left side of the fuselage.

"Can't wait to see her," he replied sincerely. "Over."

After that the journey to the LZ became a seemingly endless obstacle course as the three men were forced to cross and recross the partially frozen stream to avoid reaches of deeper water, large rock formations, and sections of thin ice.

As smaller tributaries flowed in from the left and right, the banks rose higher, and the stream became a river. That was a mixed blessing from Hale's perspective, because while the thirty-foot banks allowed them to travel relatively unseen, they would make it almost impossible to escape if they were attacked.

Still, everything seemed to be going well, until Hale rounded a bend, and froze as a wall of snow and dirt exploded away from the embankment ahead. Tons of soil slumped into the river, where it formed a momentary dam, before being washed away.

Close on his heels, Kawecki came to a sudden halt. "Jeez, Lieutenant, what the hell . . ."

Hale shook his head, and held a finger to his lips. "Listen!" he hissed urgently.

They didn't hear anything at first, but then came a faint rumble, a vibration beneath his boots. That was when Hale shouted, "Burrower!"

A fraction of a second later Jasper hollered, "Contact!" and began firing his carbine behind them.

But there was no time to see what he was referring to, as even more earth slid down into the river and a whirling drill head broke through the embankment, and a cylindrical machine roughly the size of a locomotive thrust up out of the ground. It lurched heavily to a stop with half its length hanging out over the river. As snow landed on the Chimeran construct it was immediately transformed into steam.

Hale had seen machines like this before, back in England, and knew they had been used to flood London. A hatch clanged open and at least a dozen heavily armed Hybrids clambered out and dropped into the shallow water below thereby blocking the humans' escape route. Hale scanned the area for a way to retreat, but it was too late. Behind them, Jasper continued to fire bursts upstream.

"It's an Attack Drone, sir!" he shouted. "I can't make a dent in it."

*Were we spotted by that first drone?* Hale wondered. *Are the Burrower and the Attack Drone working in concert?* Or was the team in the wrong place at the wrong time?

That was the problem with the Chimera—there was no way to know. Not that it mattered, because they were out of options, other than to fight back. Geysers of snow, dirt, and water shot up into the air as the drone opened fire and the Sentinels scrambled for cover behind a cluster of water-smoothed boulders.

"I'll deal with the drone," Hale said grimly, as he put his shotgun aside. "You take care of the Hybrids."

As the other men nodded and turned their attention toward the still steaming Burrower, Hale readied his Bellock Automatic. The grenade launcher had been slung across his back, and qualified as the heaviest weapon they had.

The drone consisted of a central housing, sensor arrays, and a pair of weapons pods. Muzzle flashes sparkled as the machine fired and projectiles *pinged* off the boulders Hale was hiding behind. In order to engage the target Hale would have to expose himself momentarily. He knew from experience that there was only one way to defeat the machine—he'd have to hit its heavy-duty shield and beat it down.

Between enemy rounds Hale fired, took cover, then emerged to fire again. Most of the flaming projectiles hit home, and each hit yielded an explosion and a puff of black smoke, which took an inexorable toll on the drone's shield.

As he twisted out of the line of fire, something hit Hale's left arm. It hurt like hell, but Hale threw a grenade before taking cover again.

It was a battle of attrition that seemed to last forever, though only moments had passed. Finally a thin stream of black smoke appeared, and the machine began to lose altitude. But it continued to fire, forcing Hale to seek cover as his Bellock *clacked* empty. He dropped the grenade launcher and grabbed the Rossmore 236 shotgun. It wasn't high-tech, but it packed a wallop, and had saved his life more than once back in England.

The 12-gauge was barely in position when Hale heard a loud *thrumming* noise as the drone appeared directly over his head. He swung the shotgun up and fired both barrels. The recoil punched into his shoulder, and there was a loud *BOOM* as the Chimeran machine took two loads of double-ought buck from less than six feet away. Lurching backward, the drone exploded and peppered Hale with small pieces of shrapnel. They stung in a dozen places, but Hale saw with satisfaction that the threat had been neutralized.

Kawecki heard the explosions behind him, but focused on dealing with the Hybrids, so he didn't have time to look.

One of the most numerous Chimeran forms, Hybrids were tenacious and adaptable. Standard Hybrids were vaguely humanoid, boasting six eyes and a mouthful of needle-sharp teeth fangs—the result of an alien virus that broke human bodies down into their constituent parts, creating new forms appropriate to a wide variety of purposes.

"There's a bunch of stinks hiding behind that ledge!" Jasper shouted. "I'll drop a grenade on them."

"Don't let the bastards tag you!" Kawecki warned, but Jasper was head and shoulders above the rocks by then. He fired the carbine's under-barrel grenade launcher, and as the projectile hurtled toward its target, one of the Hybrids fired a Bullseye tag. It hit Jasper, but did no visible damage as the Sentinel took cover.

But in the second before the exploding grenade blew its head off, the Hybrid managed to trigger a dozen Bullseye projectiles, all of which ripped through the air, looking for the tag that had been fired moments earlier.

"No!" Kawecki shouted desperately, but it was too late.

The sparkling swarm circled above Jasper's head, then all twelve of the projectiles slammed into Jasper in rapid succession. It was more damage than even a Sentinel could sustain and Jasper jerked spasmodically as the slugs tore him apart.

Hale rejoined them just as Jasper went down. He reloaded the Bellock, and loosed a barrage of explosive projectiles against the enemy position. Hybrids screamed hideously as some were blown apart and others began to burn. They ran every which way, batting at the flames, and became easy targets for Kawecki to pick off. Then an eerie silence settled over the much trampled section of riverbed. After what seemed like an eternity the battle—which had lasted only minutes—was over.

Hale knelt next to Jasper's mangled body, somberly removed the young Sentinel's dog tags, and dropped them into a pocket. Then, with a quickness born of grim experience, he stripped Jasper of any items he and Kawecki might be able to use.

As much as he wanted to take the body back for a proper burial, they were still half a mile short of the LZ, and had to assume that more Chimera were on the way. Rather than leave Jasper's remains to be picked over, however, Hale pulled the pin on a thermite grenade, dropped the cylinder next to the body, and backpedaled away. Kawecki followed suit.

There was a flash as the device went off, followed by an eye-dazzling glow as powdered aluminum combined with iron oxide to produce molten iron and aluminum oxide. Even from where he paused, a good thirty feet away by then, Hale could still feel the wave of intense heat as half a dozen rounds of loose ammo cooked off.

Hale wanted to say something, to thank Jasper for his sacrifice, but there wasn't any time. Shots rang out again as Kawecki fired his Fareye upstream.

"We got Howlers, Lieutenant . . . Six, make that five, all southbound."

Hale sighed.

"Okay," he said as he dropped the empty Bellock in favor of Jasper's carbine. "Let's haul ass."

They took off at a fast jog, and caught a whiff of ozone as they passed under the Burrower, splashed through knee-deep water, and emerged on the other side. Hale spoke into the lip mike of his radio as he ran. Each burst of words was interrupted by the need to suck some air.

"Bravo-Six to Echo-Three . . . We have one man down . . . Five Howlers on our tails . . . Southbound in the riverbed . . . ETA about ten minutes . . . Over."

"This is Three," the pilot replied grimly. "You keep a-coming, Six . . . We'll take care of those Howlers. Over."

The pilot sounded confident, but Hale had his doubts. They increased as the Howlers—lion-sized Chimeran quadrupeds—uttered the long, bloodcurdling cries from which their name had been taken. From the sound, he could tell that they were closing the gap.

"Let's slow them down!" Hale shouted as they came to a bend in the river, and he skidded to a halt. The now discarded shotgun would have been effective at close range, but Hale didn't want to get up close and personal with any Howlers if he didn't have to. Kawecki watched as the lead Chimera fell, and managed to get back on its feet again. Then, dragging a wounded leg behind it, the beast continued to advance as another Howler took over the lead. Meanwhile, having slowed the Chimera down a bit, the humans turned and ran.

The ground was uneven, the ice-covered rocks treacherously slippery, and freezing water splashed away from their combat boots as the two of them zigzagged back and forth across the riverbed in order to avoid rocks and patches of slick ice.

Then the VTOL shot into sight, coming straight at them and traveling only ten feet higher than the top of the riverbank. *Marilyn*'s engines roared as she passed overhead, and Hale could feel the plane's prop wash.

The pilot opened fire. He turned to look back, and saw a curtain of spray appear as hundreds of high-velocity bullets chewed their way through both the water *and* the oncoming Howlers. They went down screaming their defiance, and the river ran red with their blood, as the resulting waves broke around his boots.

"Tell *Marilyn* I love her," Hale said appreciatively into the mike, as the aircraft flashed overhead.

The VTOL turned upstream and waggled its wings as it roared overhead in search of a secure landing spot. Ten minutes later what remained of the team was safely on board and strapped in.

The mission had been successful—but had the trade-off been worth it? Had Jasper died for something? Or was his death just one more sacrifice in an unwinnable war?

The Sentinel closed his eyes and allowed his head to rest against the bulkhead. He was exhausted, but sleep refused to come. In his hand, clutched so tight that the metal cut into his flesh, was a pair of dog tags.

# CHAPTER TWO
# BANDIT DOWN

**Near Valentine, Nebraska**
**Friday, November 16, 1951**

The chasm was hundreds of feet deep, and as Hale made his way out onto the flexible conduit, he was careful to keep his eyes fixed on the far side of the canyon. If he looked down, he would almost certainly lose his balance and fall.

So Hale placed one foot precisely in front of the other, and felt the conduit start to sway.

Suddenly someone knocked on the door. The bottom fell out of his stomach, and he was snatched into the *real* world, where he lay panting on a sweat-soaked sheet.

"Lieutenant Hale?" a voice inquired from the hallway outside. "Sorry to wake you, sir . . . but the major wants you in the briefing room by 0400."

Hale peered at his wristwatch. It was 0325.

"Okay," he croaked. Swallowing, he added in a firmer voice, "What's up?"

"Don't know, sir," the voice answered. "It's above my pay grade."

Hale swung his feet off the metal rack, planted them on the cold floor, and began the process of making himself look halfway presentable. Less than twelve hours had elapsed since he and Kawecki had returned from the field. Two of those hours had been spent telling a team of debriefers the same things, over and over again. Finally, having been wrung dry, he'd been released, and used his freedom to eat some chow, and grab some much needed shuteye. He had fallen into bed without even hitting the showers.

Now Hale stripped down to his boxers and took a turn in front of the mirror that was mounted over the sink. Only a slight trace of redness could be seen where enemy fire had sliced his left arm open. The puncture wounds caused by the exploding drone were completely healed, and he felt better than he had any right to. Ironically he had the Chimeran virus to thank for his quick recovery, although if left to its own devices, the alien bug would likely turn malevolent.

Fortunately, frequent inhibitor shots kept the virus in check, and were supplemented by aerosolized doses he took into the field in his I-Pack. But everything depended on access to a military treatment center. Without regular inhibitor treatments his cells would begin an inexorable transformation.

That was a possibility Hale preferred not to think about.

He wrapped a towel around his neck, slipped his feet into a pair of moccasins, and carried his shaving kit out into the hall. From there he followed a line of naked light bulbs down a windowless corridor toward the communal showers. The SRPA base wasn't equipped with a lot of amenities, but there was plenty of hot water, and Hale was determined to get his share.

The countenance in the mirror was pale and thin. It was the face of an ascetic, rather than a man of action. He'd been teaching classes at MIT only six months earlier, had never fired a weapon until he entered Officer Candidate School, and was scared shitless. But Captain

Anton Nash *knew* things, important things that had to do with physics, which was why he had been given the brevet rank of captain.

Now he was going to lead soldiers into combat.

A lot of men had been called up under President Grace's Emergency Mobilization Order, and placed in jobs they weren't qualified for. But what made Nash different, or so he assumed, was the fact that he was absolutely terrified. Not only of the Chimera, but of his own weaknesses, of which there were many. So as Nash looked himself in the eye he wasn't very impressed. Was this the day he was going to die?

*Yes,* Nash thought to himself, *it probably is.* And with that he made use of a washcloth to wipe the beads of sweat off his forehead, buttoned his jacket with palsied fingers, and took one last look at the photo that was sitting on top of a utilitarian dresser. The woman in the picture was beautiful, *very* beautiful, and more than a man like him deserved. Above all else he wanted to make her proud.

With that thought in mind Nash went to meet his fate.

Each SRPA base was different, but all of them had certain things in common, including underground bays in which aircraft and vehicles could be maintained and stored. Subsurface levels were dedicated to administration, medical, and food services. Typically, living quarters were located even deeper underground, where they were protected by a matrix of passageways in which prepositioned explosives offered a defense against incoming Burrowers.

Nevertheless, Hale was armed as he made his way through the maze of corridors and boarded an elevator that would take him up to the admin deck. Standing orders called for *every* Sentinel to be armed while on duty, so Hale was carrying an HE .44 Magnum in a cross-draw holster, plus two six-shot speed loaders in quick-release belt pouches. Though not fully combat-ready he was wearing thermals and a cotton shirt, with a waist-length gray jacket. It would do in a pinch.

The gold bars on Hale's collars drew salutes from the enlisted people he passed, and having only recently been promoted to second lieutenant, he was self-conscious about returning the courtesy. As the elevator door started to close, a sergeant darted in and, finding Hale there, quickly tossed him a salute.

There was no such thing as central heating in a SRPA base, so the air was chilly and Hale was glad of the wool uniform as the elevator lurched to a stop and he followed the sergeant off.

Before Hale could enter the briefing room, it was first necessary to pass through a security checkpoint manned by three heavily armed soldiers. Having shown his SRPA ID card and the number that had been tattooed onto the inside surface of his left arm, he was allowed to make his way down the spartan corridor to the point where a table was loaded with coffee, orange juice, and thick ham and egg sandwiches.

It was simple food, but Hale knew better than to take it for granted, because as the planet's atmosphere grew colder and the Chimera took more and more land, food shortages were becoming increasingly common. It made him feel slightly guilty as he carried a heaping plate into the briefing room and looked for a place to sit down. A corner preferably, where he could maintain a low profile while consuming his breakfast.

Any such hopes were quickly dashed, however, as Major Richard Blake spotted him from the front of the room and gestured for him to come forward. There were about thirty officers and other SRPA officials in the room, and at least a dozen heads turned as Hale made his way forward, partly because he was in motion, but mostly because of who he was. He'd had a hard time maintaining a low profile since he'd come back from the battle for Britain—one of the few who had survived.

He was also one of the first Sentinels, *and* a key member of the Search and Recovery team that was slated to leave the base at 0630.

Captain Nash, who was already seated at the mission table at the front of the room, watched Hale approach. There was no question about the lieutenant's identity. After being infected with the Chimeran virus in England, and somehow surviving the normally fatal experience, Hale's eyes had changed color. They were yellow-gold, and therefore reminiscent of the Chimera, despite the fact there were only two of them.

Hale's hair was little more than stubble on the top of his head, and there was something hard about his features, as if he was a man who didn't suffer fools gladly. As Hale set his food and a steaming cup of coffee on the table and prepared to take a seat in the front row, Nash rose to greet him "You're Lieutenant Hale . . . It's a pleasure to meet you. My name is Nash. Anton Nash."

As the gold eyes came up to meet his, Nash saw a good deal of intelligence there, as well as what might have been caution—which was understandable, given the circumstances.

"Glad to meet you, sir," Hale replied, his voice neutral. He might have said more, except Blake chose that moment to begin the meeting.

Blake was a big man with prominent brows, cavelike eyes, and a pugnacious jaw. His gray SRPA uniform was immaculate, and it was well known that he expected *every* SRPA uniform to appear that way, regardless of who was wearing it. His parade-ground voice carried to every corner of the room.

"Please take your seats . . . As many of you know time is of the essence—so let's get this briefing underway."

There was a scraping of chairs, followed by a rustling sound as everyone got settled. Hale found a seat, and grabbed the opportunity to take a big bite out of his sandwich, then wash it down with a swig of hot coffee. Peering around, he noticed that there seemed to be a heightened air of expectation, and wondered what the source might be.

"Okay," Blake said, making his way past the mission table to the podium beyond. It was located next to a large white screen. "We've got something unique today, and we need to move quickly. But before we begin, there's something you need to see." The lights dimmed and the projection system came on. The quality of the video footage wasn't very good.

It looked as if it had been taken late in the day, when the light level was low, and snow swirled in front of the camera, making it even more difficult for the viewer to tell what he was looking at. Centered in the middle of the screen was what many people would have called a hill—and a rather unremarkable one at that, except for the way it towered over the surrounding plain. Most of that area was flat as a pancake.

Being a native of South Dakota, Hale recognized the geological feature, which, according to his seventh-grade science teacher, was a laccolith, a juncture where molten magma had been injected between two layers of sedimentary rock, forcing one to bulge upward.

"You're looking at Bear Butte," Blake confirmed as the camera began to move, indicating that it was airborne. "A little more than 1,200 feet tall, and located near the town of Sturgis, South Dakota."

Hale shifted in his chair, and wondered why the major was wasting their time on a relatively unremarkable piece of landscape. He reached for his food as Blake spoke again. "And *here,* as we come around the other side, we find the wreckage of a Chimeran shuttle."

*That* got Hale's attention. As the video froze he put the rest of his sandwich down.

The Chimeran aircraft was positioned high on the hillside, just below the snow-capped top. And while the fuselage was intact, large pieces of debris could be seen. There were no signs of an explosion or post-impact fire, however, and that was promising.

"This footage was taken late yesterday. We don't know what happened to the shuttle," Blake said, as his pointer tapped the image of the crash site. "Perhaps it suffered a mechanical problem of some sort, or given the weather conditions late yesterday—when we think the incident occurred—it's possible the pilot didn't see the hillside until it was too late. Whatever the reason it was a stroke of good luck for us, because if we can put a team in there fast enough, we can search the wreckage for Chimeran tech. The kind of stuff that will help us to defeat the bastards.

"But we'll have to be quick," he added, "because the stinks are onto our SAR strategy and will probably put some sort of freak show on the butte to secure the crash site."

At that point Blake turned to gesture toward the two men seated at the mission table. "Please welcome Captain Anton Nash to the team . . . He'll be in overall command of the mission—and I'm sending Lieutenant Hale along to provide backup. The rest of the team will consist of two squads, each led by an NCO. You'll leave at 0630. Are there any questions?"

There *were* questions, at least one that Hale could think of, though he didn't give voice to it. *Has the major lost his mind?* Nash was green as grass. Anyone could see that. And lives were at stake.

So Hale waited for the staff officers to stop peppering each other with questions and comments. When the hubbub died down, and the group made ready to leave, he sidled up to Blake. "Sir?" Hale said. "Do you have a moment?"

Blake smiled grimly. "Don't tell me—let me guess. You're pissed off at the prospect of reporting to Nash."

A muscle twitched in Hale's left cheek. "Permission to speak freely?"

Blake sighed. "I'll probably regret it, but yes, go ahead."

"I think it's bullshit, sir . . . My men deserve an officer with combat experience."

"And they have one," Blake replied pointedly. "*You!* As for Nash, you're lucky to have him. Rather than swoop in and secure a location so the techies can sweep it for artifacts, the way you have in the past, this mission is going to be different."

Hale started to speak, but the major raised a hand to silence him.

"Think about it. Let's say you're one of our guys, rummaging around in the Chimeran shuttle, and it's loaded with fancy-looking equipment, but your men are under attack. Which thing would you take? The box with the most knobs? If so you might come home with the Chimeran equivalent of a toaster! We've had that happen too many times, because we weren't prepared to take advantage of the situation.

"This is serious business, Hale . . . The freaks are way

ahead of us where technology is concerned, so we're always playing catch-up. Nash may not look like much, but he's smarter than you and me. He knows more than we'll ever forget about the enemy's tech, and if push comes to shove he'll know which box to take. So he goes, and you will make the best of it. Do you read me?"

"Sir, yes, sir," Hale replied stiffly.

"Good. Now get going. You're on the clock," Blake replied. Then his tone eased. "Be careful out there . . . You may not be as smart as Nash, but you come in handy from time to time."

The mech deck, as the Sentinels referred to it, was a huge space in which banks of bright lights stood in for the sun, and the frigid air was thick with the combined odors of Avgas, oil, and exhaust fumes. Engines roared, chain hoists rattled, and power tools screeched, as the ubiquitous public address system produced a nonstop flow of incomprehensible gibberish. It was a chaotic atmosphere to anyone who wasn't used to it, and that included Captain Anton Nash.

In his eagerness to do everything right, Nash was already standing next to the big, twin-engine VTOL transport when Sergeants Kawecki and Alvarez arrived, each leading a squad of Sentinels. All of the soldiers wore I-Packs over white winter gear, and were armed to the teeth. Each one carried two firearms, a variety of grenades, and as much ammo as they thought they could get away with. It was a balance that had developed through practical experience, since too much weight could slow them down.

Nash hoped to score points by being early, but Kawecki and Alvarez seemed to interpret his presence as a lack of trust, since it was their job to have the men ready *before* officers arrived on the scene. The NCOs didn't say anything, but Nash could sense their resentment, even though no slight had been intended.

So all he could do was stand next to his utility bag and feel useless as containers of climbing equipment, C rations, and other equipment were loaded onto the plane. Every now and then a soldier would glance up and smirk. Nash followed one man's gaze and realized he was standing directly below a likeness of the big-eyed cartoon character called Betty Boop. Before he could move, however, Lieutenant Hale arrived.

Having been a sergeant himself, Hale understood the theater involved in getting ready for a mission, and knew the part he was supposed to play. So at exactly 0615 he strolled across the oil-stained concrete toward the point where an awkward-looking Anton Nash stood waiting. Hale directed a glance at the blank-faced NCOs, felt pretty sure he knew what the situation was, and was careful to approach Nash first. The salute was parade-ground perfect.

"Good morning, sir . . . It looks like we're ready to go. If it's okay with you—let's take a look at the team."

Nash gave off a tangible sense of relief. He returned the salute.

"That would be fine, Lieutenant. Thank you."

Nash watched with interest as the soldiers were ordered to pair off and check each other's gear while Hale strolled among them, closely followed by both sergeants. With the exception of a man who was carrying too much ammo, and a soldier who was equipped with a potentially faulty I-Pack, all the Sentinels passed inspection.

So by 0628 the SAR team was boarding the plane, the soldier with the I-Pack malfunction was donning a new one, and the rest of the Sentinels were strapped into their seats.

Nash felt an intense need to yawn, and tried to hide it as he did so, and more than once. He should have been amped—should have been high on adrenaline—but for some reason he felt sleepy. Maybe that was a good sign. Maybe it meant that he wasn't as tense as he thought he would be. And maybe it would cause him to appear calm, even confident. He hoped so.

In someone else, the yawns might have been the sign of a cool customer, the sort of officer who could take a nap on the way to a firefight. But Hale knew better. In part because he felt a strong desire to yawn himself, and knew it was a sign of fear.

Which—all things considered—was a logical reaction to the situation.

A sudden jerk caused him to brace himself as the motorized tug towed the *Betty Boop* out onto one of four large elevators located at the center of the mech deck. Then, freed from the transport, the little tractor hummed away. There was a loud *clang* as machinery engaged, a door whined open high above, and the platform began to ascend. The light dimmed as they entered the shaft, away from the artificial suns.

A loud clatter was heard as the VTOL's starters went to work, quickly followed by a throaty roar as both of the radial engines came to life, and the entire ship began to vibrate. Light and cold air flooded into the cargo compartment as the lift delivered the *Betty Boop* to the surface.

Operating under the top secret charter conceived by General Arthur L. Pratt, Senator Robert Crowe, and Dr. Fyodor Malikov in 1934, SRPA Base 6 had been constructed near the original site of old Fort Niobrara in

Nebraska. Hundreds of thousands of tons of soil and rock had been taken out of the ground to make room for the underground base, and rather than being trucked away, the material had been used to construct a fifty-foot-tall wall that surrounded the base and was home to all manner of defensive weapons.

Recently, in response to SRPA Directive 1140.09, work had begun on an outer moat. A deep ditch that could be flooded with Avgas and set on fire should it become necessary. It didn't take a whole lot of imagination to figure out why.

The VTOL's engines were tilted upward for takeoff, and as the pilot fed them more fuel, the plane began to shake with greater intensity. Then, as the landing gear parted company with the ground and snowflakes blew in through the side doors, Hale caught a glimpse of the meager surface base as the *Boop* rose. But not his *last* glimpse, he hoped, as the engines tilted forward and the plane pulled itself north with a lurch.

Bear Butte was about 120 miles away, so given the VTOL's top speed of 300 miles per hour, Hale expected to be boots on the ground in about half an hour. With a low ceiling and poor visibility the *Boop* was fairly safe from above, but the need to fly low over an area the Chimera had already begun to infiltrate meant the ship would be vulnerable to ground fire. It was a chance they'd have to take, since there was no other way for them to reach the butte quickly enough to beat the enemy to the punch.

As it was, he hoped they weren't already too late.

Hale peered across the center aisle to where Captain Nash was sitting, saw the other man's eye close in response to an involuntary tic, and hoped none of the men would notice. The VTOL shuddered as a crosswind hit the fuselage, the port door gunner wrapped a long scarf around his neck, and the seconds ticked away.

The mission clock was running.

It was clear that Hale didn't expect much from him. In a way that was better, since it meant he wouldn't need the type of supervision Nash couldn't provide.

Rather than dwell on his own lack of military expertise, the scientist chose to focus his thoughts on the mission. They were going to secure technology that would help the United States win the war.

And if they found what they expected to find, it wasn't just *any* technology. Judging from what they could see of the downed craft, they hoped to scavenge what SRPA called "alpha artifacts," Chimeran equipment that would help the scientists in New Mexico unravel the secrets of nuclear fission, perhaps even fusion, thereby paving the way toward unbelievably powerful new weapons.

Such were Nash's thoughts when he was startled out of his reverie by an unfamiliar voice that spoke to him via the plug in his ear.

"This is the pilot speaking . . . We're five from dirt. Be sure to take everything with you, the obvious exceptions being women of ill repute, and any cases of Schlitz beer which may happen to be on board."

The announcement elicited laughter, a few catcalls, and some loud whistles, until Kawecki and Alvarez reined in their men, then ran through the checklist to make sure they were combat-ready. Having found everything to their liking, they reported to Hale.

"The first squad is ready, sir," Kawecki said crisply.

"Ditto Squad Two," Alvarez reported.

"Thank you, gentlemen," Hale replied. "Let's lock and load."

A series of clacking, clicking, and hissing sounds followed Hale's order as a variety of human and Chimeran weapons were readied for combat. They had been doled out to take advantage of each individual's skills and the team's need to cope with a wide variety of potential adversaries.

That thought weighed upon Nash as he checked the carbine he had propped, muzzle up, between his knees. Would he have to fire it? Would he even remember how? There hadn't been time for him to receive anything more than the most basic training. He lifted the weapon, worked a round into the chamber, but left the safety on as he put it down again.

Nash peered across the aisle at Hale, and thought he saw an almost imperceptible nod, the beginning of what could have been a smile. It might have been taken as a sign of condescension, but Nash didn't think it was meant that way. The other officer didn't seem to work like that. So he responded with a boyish grin.

Suddenly, for the first time, Nash felt like a member of the team. But his blood ran cold when he heard the pilot's next words.

"Uh-oh, it looks like the stinks got here first! The top of the butte is swarming with Hybrids."

Nash released his harness and came up off his seat without really thinking about it. As the VTOL entered a wide sweeping turn, the starboard door gunner made room and Nash stuck his face into the frigid slipstream.

He could see the snow-covered butte, the point where the aircraft had slammed into the rocky slope, and the large group of Chimera rappelling down to it as quickly as they could, given the conditions. The shuttle had come to rest in a spot that offered no easy access point. There was no sign of whatever aircraft had delivered them to the top of the butte, but it seemed safe to assume they had one on call.

"Put us on the ground directly below the wreck," Nash instructed, and he was surprised by the certainty in his own voice. "Next to that cluster of trees."

Hale peered over Nash's shoulder and nodded. The VTOL couldn't land on top of the butte, and it couldn't land on an incline, so the instructions made perfect sense. The problem being that the Chimera not only had the advantage of arriving first, but they currently held the high ground, which would allow them to fire down on the Sentinels with near impunity.

But it couldn't be helped, Nash realized, as the Chimera opened fire on the VTOL. They sent long strings of tracers up in the attempt to find the aircraft and bring it down.

Meanwhile, the pilot was dropping toward the landing site. Projectiles began to *ping* and *bang* off the fuselage as the VTOL's engines went vertical and it fell into place. All of the Sentinels had released themselves from their harnesses by that time—and hurried to disembark the moment they felt the landing gear hit solid ground. Kawecki was there to urge them on. "What the hell are you waiting for?" the NCO bellowed. "A frigging *invitation*? Let's get off this bucket of bolts and find some cover."

Nash was about to follow the rest of the team out onto the frozen landscape when he suddenly realized that he couldn't move. His legs knew what they *should* be doing, but it didn't matter. They refused to obey his commands.

He watched helplessly as the men just ignored him and passed him by. As the last one exited, a Chimeran projectile slammed through the VTOL's skin and passed within an inch of Nash's nose. That scared him even more, enough to start his feet moving, and get him out the door.

But not before he had grabbed a heavy duffel and thrust it out ahead of him.

Hale was one of the first troops through the door. He crouched and took a quick look around as projectiles kicked up geysers of dirt around him. Spotting a cluster of trees, he gestured to the men. "Over there!" he shouted, pointing to the tightly bunched evergreens. "Take cover!"

One member of the team, a private named Lang, took a hit, and was half carried, half dragged into the relative safety of the trees. A medic immediately went to work on a leg wound that had already begun to heal.

Hale was about to make a dash for the trees when he saw Nash throw a bag out of the VTOL's cargo compartment. Instead of being one of the first off the plane Nash was the last to leave, and Hale swore angrily as he ran over to grab the heavy bag and escort his commanding officer to the cluster of trees.

Engines roared, and the *Boop*'s propellers created a momentary blizzard as the ship lifted off.

"Let me know when the fun is over," the pilot said in his ear, "and I'll come back to get you." Then with a tilt of its engines, the VTOL was gone.

Hale and Nash finished their sprint to the trees. By then the rest of the team was busy setting up defensive positions.

"What's in this thing, anyway?" Hale demanded, dropping the bag next to Nash. "A load of rocks?"

He didn't bother with the honorific "sir," but Nash didn't seem to notice. Rather than correct Hale, he chose to answer the question. "Tools," he replied. "Chimeran tools. If we find something valuable we'll have to disconnect whatever it is from the shuttle, and as quickly as we can."

That made sense, Hale thought, and he felt stupid for asking, but pushed the thought aside and assessed the situation.

The wreck was about eight hundred feet above them. The Chimera were damned near on top of it, and pretty well in charge. There was a loud *crack* as a large-caliber projectile hit the tree Hale was standing next to, spraying him with splinters of wood and showering him with snow. "Sergeant Kawecki . . . Sergeant Alvarez," Hale said, using the radio now. "Let's put those Fareyes to work. Or do you *like* being shot at?"

That produced some chuckles, and the team's best marksmen went to work. Within moments the enemy barrage was being countered by the steady *crack, crack, crack* of outgoing sniper fire.

Hale went forward to get a better look at the butte, and Nash followed. Once there Hale discovered a long line of boulders that marked the bottom of a scree-covered slope and offered good concealment. Bringing his binoculars up to his eyes, he followed the slope up to the wreck and its debris field. Already half a dozen dead Chimera lay sprawled on the bloodied snow. The surviving Hybrids had taken cover by then, but every now and then one of them would pop up to take a pot shot at the humans, and most paid a high price for their audacity.

"So," Nash said, from his position next to Hale's right elbow. "You have experience at this sort of thing . . . What do you think we should do?"

Hale bristled at the question because Nash was wearing the railroad tracks, and it was tempting to force him to lead. But that would be suicide, and there were the men to think of, not to mention the mission, so he chose his words with care.

"I don't think we have much choice," he said deliberately. "It looks like we'll have to fight our way uphill. It won't be easy though—and we're going to take a lot of casualties."

Nash flinched as a stray projectile hit one of the rocks and made a zinging sound as it whipped past his ear.

"You know best of course," he said, lowering his own binoculars. "But there might be another way."

"Really?" Hale said sarcastically. "And what would that be?"

Nash's eye twiched spastically and he battled to keep his voice steady.

"You've seen the wreck, Lieutenant . . . It's sitting on a bed of snow-covered scree. The snow is slippery, as are all those chunks of loose granite, which could work in our favor. What if you had the men fire those LAARK things at a point immediately *below* the wreck? That could precipitate a landslide which would bring the remains of the shuttle at least halfway down the slope."

Hale just stared at him. There was a moment of silence, broken only by the intermittent *crack* of a sniper rifle—and the occasional *ping* of an incoming projectile. He wrestled with the idea for a full five seconds. "It seems like a long shot, sir," he said tentatively, "but it's worth a try."

Nash smiled weakly as another involuntary muscle contraction caused him to wink. *I wish he'd stop that,* Hale thought.

"Good . . . I'm glad you think so."

The team was equipped with two L209 LAARK rocket launchers. It took the better part of ten minutes to collect the soldiers who were in possession of the weapons, position them at the foot of the slide area, and give them their instructions. It was snowing more heavily by then, which made the already misty crash site even more difficult to see, so Hale felt a sense of urgency as he knelt between the men.

"Aim for a spot fifteen feet *below* the wreck," he told them, "and fire on the count of three. Once the first rockets are on the way, reload quickly—and prepare to fire again. But don't do it unless I say so. Got it?"

"Yes, sir," both soldiers responded, their voices overlapping.

"Good," Hale said. "Now acquire your targets . . . Tell me when you're ready."

About ten seconds passed as both men took careful aim.

"Ready, sir," the one on the left said, quickly echoed by the soldier to the right.

"On the count of three, then," Hale said. "One, two, and *three.*"

There was a loud *whoosh*, followed by another just a fraction of a second later, as two rockets sped uphill. Moments later they struck the slope. Twin explosions produced what sounded like a single *boom*, geysers of snow and pulverized rock shot up into the air, and Nash felt the resulting vibration through the soles of his boots.

But once the smoke cleared the scene was unchanged.

Hale glanced at Nash, saw the look of uncertainty on his face, and turned back again.

"Let's try again," he said levelly. Both men had already reloaded. "Same spot as before—on the count of three. One, two, and *three*!"

There was another stereo *whoosh* as two more rockets roared away, followed by overlapping explosions. But this time Hale heard another sound as well.

It began with a throaty rumble, followed by the *clatter* of loose rock, which increased to a muffled roar as the entire hillside began to move. And not just the hillside, but the Chimeran wreck as well, which was beginning to edge downhill. Metal screeched, rocks exploded as additional weight bore down and pulverized them.

A reedy cheer went up from the Sentinels when their objective came down as if to meet them.

Hale lifted his glasses to watch the shuttle's progress, and was just in time to spot one of the Hybrids who had been hiding in the rocks downslope from the wreck. The creature popped up and tried to run, but seconds later it threw its hands into the air and mouthed a silent scream as it disappeared under the advancing beetle-shaped wreck. Instantly it was lost from sight altogether.

Hale turned toward Nash and saw a wide grin spread across the officer's face. Involuntarily, he grinned back.

"We need to hurry, sir," he said quickly. "Your plan took the stinks by surprise, but it won't take them long to recover. I suggest that you board the shuttle as quickly as possible. I'll send Private Unver along to provide security and carry your tools.

"Thirty minutes, sir . . . That's the most I can give you . . . So make them count."

The rock slide had stalled by then, and while the wreck hadn't slid all the way down the hill, it was at least four hundred feet closer. Nash could have taken offense to the way in which Hale had given him orders but knew the other officer was correct. "Thank you, Lieutenant," Nash replied. "I'll get right to work."

Hale briefed Unver, and sent both men scrambling uphill, then turned his attention to Kawecki and Alvarez. They placed some of their men in strategic positions just below the wreck, where Chimeran projectiles couldn't reach them.

"Kawecki . . . take First Squad, and half of Second uphill, past the wreck, and prepare a primary position plus two fallbacks. I don't expect you to kill every Chimera on the butte. Just slow the freaks down. Once you fall back to the third position, the one immediately above the wreck, be sure to pull Nash out." Kawecki nodded, his features set.

"As for you," Hale said as he turned to Alvarez, "I want you to take four of your men down to secure the back door and guard the LZ. Be ready to provide covering fire for Kawecki and his people as they pull out. Questions?"

"How 'bout some command-detonated mines, sir?" Kawecki asked. "We could place them upslope from position one."

"Good idea," Hale said approvingly. "That'll give the Hybrids something to think about as they come down. Don't blow more than one at a time though . . . We don't want another landslide.

"Anything else?

"No? Then let's do this thing."

The shuttle was roughly the size of two city buses sitting side by side, and had come to rest nose down—or was it tail down? The badly battered hull was shimmery black, boasting knifelike wing extensions and protrusions that were unlike any aircraft Private Mike Unver had ever seen before.

More important, given the nature of the assignment, the gull-wing-style main hatch was open and apparently unguarded. But Unver knew that the wreck had been home to half a dozen Chimera not an hour earlier, so he entered first, his Bullseye assault rifle at the ready. *Take care of Captain Nash.* Those were the orders Lieutenant Hale had given the Sentinel, and Unver was determined to do his best.

The main power was clearly off, but judging from some glow panels and dozens of indicator lights, some sort of backup system had kicked in. So it was dark and gloomy, but not pitch black, as Unver turned to his right and climbed a steeply sloping deck.

The tiny control compartment was about a third of the way back from the badly crushed bow. It consisted of a control panel and two chairs—both of which were occupied by dead Hybrids. Or that's how it appeared anyway. But Unver knew better than to make assumptions, so he shot each pilot in the back of the head, just to make sure. A mixture of blood and brains splattered the instrument panel.

"Unver?" Nash inquired over the radio. "Are you okay?" He was still crouched outside.

"I'm fine, sir," Unver replied. "Just tidying up, that's all. Let me check the stern. Then you can board."

Two minutes later, having carried out a quick check of the small cargo area in the ship's stern, Unver returned to the main hatch.

"Everything's okay," he said confidently, and he gestured to the captain. "Come on in." The Chimera had recovered from the initial shock of having the ship slide out from under them by that time, and they were streaming down the butte. Fareyes cracked as Kawecki's group engaged them, and the aliens fired back.

But such was Nash's eagerness to enter the shuttle and see what lay within that he forgot his fear. He pushed the tool bag onto a scimitar-shaped section of wing, placed his foot on a support strut, and hoisted himself up. Unver was there to grab the tools and give him a hand. From there it was only a few steps to the open hatch.

The first step, according to protocol, was to carry out a quick inspection of the so-called setting before zeroing in on specific items or groups of items. That procedure was intended to make sure field investigators didn't become so enamored of a particular object that they missed something that might be of even more importance.

In order to carry out the initial survey, Nash had to call upon carefully memorized images of the Chimeran tech that had already been captured, evaluated, and in some cases reverse-engineered. He saw several things he recognized, but the whole point of a SAR mission was to find *new* tech. As Nash made his way forward he saw very little to get excited about, and disappointment began to seep in.

The blood-drenched scene in the control compartment made his stomach lurch, and he might have thrown up had he been able to get anything down earlier that morning. But Nash forced himself to stand behind the pilots and scan the instrument panel to make sure it matched the photos he'd seen. Everything appeared to be normal. So he left the Chimeran cockpit and kept his eyes peeled as he made his way back to the stern.

When he arrived in the small cargo area aft of the main hatch, he spotted a case that was secured to ring bolts set into the deck. Not recognizing the design of the case, he was curious as to what might be inside. Leaning his carbine against the bulkhead, Nash knelt next to the box, undid a series of latches, and lifted the lid.

Light splashed the officer's face. His eyes went round, and his heart began to beat faster. It was the most beautiful thing he'd ever seen.

The Chimera had taken casualties, *heavy* casualties, but they'd still managed to push what remained of First Squad into position two. And Hale was worried. Not just because of the snarling Hybrids—who fought as if possessed—but due to the fact that something even more dangerous was prowling the battlefield. Something so stealthy that two of his Sentinels had been decapitated without anyone seeing what had killed them.

Sergeant Kawecki had made the gruesome discoveries. But rather than broadcast the news to the entire team, he'd made it his business to tell Hale face-to-face, mikes off. Based on the evidence, it appeared as though a Chameleon was stalking the Sentinels.

And that was bad news indeed. Hale glanced around involuntarily.

Chameleons were ugly brutes with heads set low between their massive shoulders, and long claw-tipped arms. That was bad enough, but what made the creatures worse were the high-tech field generators they wore on their backs. Machines capable of rendering the Chameleons invisible. This capability was dangerous in and of itself, and it had a profound psychological impact as well. Because soldiers who worried about what might be standing immediately behind them had a tendency to fire at shadows.

So as Kawecki went about keeping the level of outgoing fire up, Hale readied the Rossmore and followed a set of large footprints that led away from the blood-splattered boulder where Laraby had been decapitated. Even though the Chameleon could make itself invisible, it still had mass, and couldn't hide its tracks.

The trail led downhill, past the point where Laraby's head had come to rest, toward the shuttle. It would have been nice to have a couple of Sentinels with him, but they were needed on the hillside, which left Hale to track the Chameleon alone.

He felt something heavy land in the bottom of his stomach as he rounded the shuttle's badly crushed bow, and spotted the body that lay on top of a blood-splattered wing. Bullets *pinged* off the ship's hull as he climbed up onto the flat surface and knelt next to Unver. Judging from appearances, the private had been standing with his back to the hatch, sucking the aerosolized serum commonly referred to as I-Gas through his mouthpiece, when the Chameleon ripped his abdomen open. At least a yard of purplish intestine had spilled out through the wicked gash, yet judging from the vapor that issued from his nostrils, the Sentinel was still alive.

Hale switched his radio from the team freq to the command channel.

"Alvarez! I'm on the shuttle. Unver is down by the main hatch. Send two men to bring him out, and alert the medic. Tell them to keep their eyes peeled . . . We have a Chameleon on the loose."

Nash was on his knees with his back to the main hatch when he heard what sounded like a scraping footstep. "Unver? Come here . . . There's something I want to show you."

After a couple of seconds without a response, Nash swiveled toward the hatch, wondering if he had imagined the footfall. The sounds of fighting were coming closer—so close that the Chimeran projectiles sounded like hail as they rattled against the hull. He had been distracted up until then, fascinated by the object in the box, and oblivious to the situation around him.

Now the hairs on the back of his neck rose and a bad smell invaded his nostrils.

There *had* been a footstep, he was certain of it. So where was Unver?

He realized that his earpiece had come loose, and he hurried to fumble it back into place. That was when he heard Hale.

"Captain Nash? Can you hear me? If so, listen carefully . . . I have reason to believe that a Chameleon is on board the ship. Put your back to something solid, keep your weapon ready, and slide along the bulkhead toward the hatch. I'll be there to cover you. Please confirm."

Nash attempted to reply, but produced a croak instead. So he swallowed, cleared his throat, and managed a "Roger, that." Then he came to his feet.

By that time he was aware of a shallow rasping noise that seemed to originate from a few feet away, though it was impossible to pinpoint the exact source. Was it the sound of breathing? Or just his own fear-fed imagination?

The carbine was right where he had left it, leaning against a bulkhead, but would the Chameleon allow him to touch it? Or would it take his head off the moment he moved?

There was only one way to find out.

Nash turned as if to orient himself to the hatch, and found the assault weapon with his right hand. Slowly, working by touch, he flicked the safety to the off position, as his eyes scanned the cargo area. Then, having pressed his back to the bulkhead, he brought the rifle up and pointed it toward the spot where he thought the Chameleon might be.

There was a scritching noise, and being too afraid to do anything else, Nash opened fire. One of his bullets must have hit the Chameleon's field generator, for where there had been nothing, suddenly a hideous creature appeared, and it was only four feet away. Its right arm was poised to slash at him when one of Nash's bullets passed through the Chimera's open mouth and blew the back of its skull out.

The Chimera staggered as more bullets hit it, but stubbornly refused to fall, and even managed to lurch forward. That was when Hale arrived and opened fire. Two blasts from the shotgun were sufficient to blow a hole in the Chimera's barrel chest and bring the monster down.

Nash was out of ammo by that time, but still pulling the trigger, as Hale slowly pushed the carbine down. "Good work, sir . . . You nailed the bastard."

Nash stared in astonishment at the body on the floor. "I did?"

"Yes, you sure as hell did," Hale confirmed. "And that's saying something, because Chameleons are damned hard to kill. Now let's get out of here."

"Not without this!" Nash said triumphantly, and turned to retrieve the box. "I think we stumbled across something extremely valuable. We can't be sure, of course, not until experts examine it, but I'm pretty sure it's what we've been looking for. That's why the Chimera fought so hard to protect the wreck."

"Good," Hale responded, but the tone of his voice indicated that his mind was elsewhere. "Follow me."

Thirty seconds later Hale was through the hatch, and immediately he hit the ground, bullets whipping around him, as Nash made his way out onto the blood-slicked wing. There was no sign of Unver.

Nash had both arms wrapped around the metal box and there was still a look of triumph on his face when the energy bolt hit him between the eyes. His head jerked back, and the box tumbled free as he fell backward, landing with a meaty *thump* as his body struck metal. The cube bounced off the wing, and Hale rushed to catch it.

He wanted to climb up to get Nash's dog tags, but there wasn't enough time.

"Come on!" Kawecki yelled, "the *Boop* is two minutes out!"

Hale, with the cube clutched in his arms, turned to

make sure that the rest of the team had begun to withdraw.

The Chimera were streaming down the hill at that point, intent on overrunning them. But at the last moment one of the Sentinels—Private Budry, Hale thought— stepped out from his cover. He was a big man, and very muscular, which was a good thing because it took a lot of strength to hold the Wraith minigun and fire it.

Budry's lips were pulled back into a snarl, and his white teeth made a stark contrast to his dark skin, as the machine gun growled and sent 1,200 slugs per minute racing upslope.

The hail of lead caught half a dozen Hybrids in midstride, cut them down, and sent the survivors scuttling for cover as Hale took advantage of the momentary lull and threw an air-fuel grenade into the shuttle. There was a loud *whump* as the bomb detonated, and a gout of flame shot out through the hatch.

Budry was out of ammo by then, but it would take the Chimera a few minutes to regroup as the Sentinels withdrew to the LZ.

Ten minutes later all the surviving soldiers, Unver included, were aboard the VTOL as it lifted off and Hybrids streamed into the LZ. Machine guns rattled and empty casings arced through the air as the door gunners swept the area below with a hail of bullets.

Finally, as the *Betty Boop* leveled out, the men had time to suck I-Gas out of their packs, and wonder why they were still alive while others were dead.

Meanwhile, Hale stared at the box positioned between his boots, and thought about Nash.

"So what's in it?" Kawecki inquired, as he toed the box.

Hale didn't have an answer. So he opened the latches,

flipped the lid back, and was surprised to watch the sides fall away.

There, sitting on the deck, was a roughly twelve-by-twelve-inch cube made of a translucent material. Deep within the gelatinous mass thousands of sparkling lights could be seen. They looked like stars in a miniature galaxy and were beautiful to behold.

"What does it do?" Alvarez wanted to know.

"I don't know," Hale replied soberly, as he restored the cube to its container. "But Captain Nash thought it was worth dying for—and that's good enough for me."

# CHAPTER THREE
# RED, WHITE, AND BLUE

Washington, D.C.
Friday, November 16, 1951

It was still dark outside as President Noah Grace awoke at exactly 5:58 A.M., and reached over to silence the alarm clock before it could go off. What little light there was came from the streetlamps beyond the curtains or slid in under the door from the hallway.

Careful not to disturb his wife, Grace rolled off the bed. His bare feet were silent as he padded across the soft carpet, entered the bathroom, and closed the door behind him. At that point he could flick the lights on without bothering Cora.

He blinked at the sudden brightness, made his way over to the commode, and lifted the seat.

Having emptied his bladder, Grace stepped in front of the pedestal-style sink, opened the medicine cabinet, and laid his implements out on the shelf above the basin. The array included a toothbrush, a tube of Ipana toothpaste, a nearly new Gillette Super Speed safety razor with an aluminum handle, a can of Mollé shaving cream, and a pair of tiny scissors, all laid out like surgical instruments.

Ten minutes later the President used a warm washcloth to wipe the last traces of shaving cream off his face and took a moment to survey the person reflected in the mirror. His hair was black, except for a little gray at the temples, and it was parted on the right. A broad fore-head suggested intelligence, he thought, two perfectly shaped eyebrows served to frame his large brown eyes, and a long straight nose conveyed a sense of strength and purpose. All anchored by a firm jaw.

There were imperfections of course, like the hairs that threatened to sprout from his nostrils and ears, but a snip here and a snip there left Grace ready to go.

Satisfied with what he'd seen, Grace returned each im-plement to its rightful place. Then he checked the time on his Rolex Royal Stainless Steel Oyster wristwatch. It was 6:26 A.M., which meant Grace was running a minute late as he slid his arms into a white bathrobe.

The lonely wail of an air raid siren could be heard off in the distance as Grace entered the bedroom and paused for a moment.

A Chimeran attack? No, more likely a false alarm, triggered by a nervous volunteer out in the suburbs.

There was a soft knock, and Grace opened the door to the hallway. Bright light gave Bessie a halo of white hair, framing her kindly face, and there was so much starch in her gray and white uniform that it crackled as she moved.

"Good morning, Mr. President," she said respectfully. "Here's your coffee." And with that she extended a tray loaded with a coffeepot, creamer, a bowl of sugar, two cups, and two spoons. It was a ritual the two of them had shared for eleven years.

"Thank you, Bessie," Grace said, and he turned to carry the tray over to the big bed. He heard the door close behind him.

Cora was sitting up by then, and by long-standing tra-dition the next half-hour belonged to her, as another day in the White House began.

Then, at precisely 7:30 A.M., President Grace made the journey downstairs.

Presidential Chief of Staff William Dentweiler awoke with a headache, a bad taste in his mouth, and the cloying scent of Eau d'Hermès perfume in his nostrils. His left arm was numb, and no wonder, since someone was lying on top of it.

But who?

Then he remembered the party at the French embassy, the desperate gaiety as two hundred guests sought to drink the war away with bottles of Taittinger champagne. The wine was increasingly hard to come by, yet many American officials seemed to have quite a bit of it. Most of Europe had fallen to the Chimera, and just about all the foreign diplomats wanted to bring someone into the United States before communications were severed.

This also explained why a stone-faced German military attaché had turned the other way when Dentweiler had left the party with his beautiful wife. A willowy blonde, who, though less than fluent where the English language was concerned, certainly knew how to please a man. She was snoring softly as Dentweiler pulled his arm out from under her bare shoulders, swung his feet onto the floor, and eyed the clock next to the bed.

It was 8:12 A.M.! *Damn.* And the cabinet meeting was scheduled for 9:00. Not 9:05, 9:10, or—God forbid—9:15.

Not while Noah Grace was President.

Dentweiler swore under his breath, made his way into the bathroom, and stepped into the tub. There was a rattling noise as he pulled the shower curtain closed, followed by the shock of cold water, which gradually turned warm. Once it reached body temperature Dentweiler was free to pee and shower at the same time. A rather efficient practice that continued to serve him well.

Fifteen minutes later Dentweiler was freshly shaved, dressed in one of his tailor-made gray suits, and ready to go. The German woman was still asleep—but he left her a note with a name and telephone number on it. *If* her husband's parents were still alive, and *if* they could make it to a pick-up point near Bremen on a certain date, they would be brought to America. "A deal," as Dentweiler liked to say, "is a deal."

A long black town car was waiting in front of Dentweiler's apartment building as he turned up the collar of his sleek Brooks Brothers overcoat and entered the crisp November air. There weren't many Christmas decorations to be seen, and weren't likely to be. Not with thousands dying every day.

Dentweiler stepped into the car, and it pulled away.

Having heard Dentweiler leave, the German woman opened her eyes. Then, softly, she began to cry.

The Cabinet Room was located in the West Wing of the White House, on the first floor. It had been completed in 1934 and was positioned to look out on to the Rose Garden through French doors topped with lunette windows. A painting titled *The Signing of the Declaration of Independence* hung over the fireplace at the north end of the room, while a row of portraits personally selected by President Grace lined the west wall. The floor was covered by a custom-made burgundy-colored carpet. And that's what Secretary of War Henry Walker was looking at as he completed the last of his twenty-five push-ups. It was a ritual he performed frequently throughout the day.

Having regained his feet, the sixty-three-year-old retired colonel was in the process of putting his blue pin-striped jacket on as President Grace entered the room, closely followed by the other members of his cabinet.

"There you are," Grace said cheerfully. "I should have known . . . *Military men are always on time*. Especially when the budget comes up for discussion!"

That was sufficient to elicit a chorus of chuckles from the coterie of toadies, sycophants, and ass kissers with whom Grace had chosen to surround himself. The group didn't care for Walker any more than he cared for them. But he was—insofar as they were concerned—a necessary evil, due to the fact that he was popular with the top brass. A group upon whom Grace was *very* dependent.

So as everyone took their seats, Walker knew he was deep inside enemy territory, and largely on his own. His only potential ally was Vice President Harvey McCullen, who, in his own scholarly way, served to put the brakes on Grace's worst excesses.

Walker scanned the group. Grace sat halfway down the long oval table with his back to the Rose Garden. Chief of Staff Dentweiler and Secretary of the Interior Farnsworth sat to his right, with Secretary of Commerce Lasky and Secretary of State Moody on his left. Presidential Counsel Hanson, Attorney General Clowers, Vice President McCullen, Secretary of Agriculture Seymore, and Secretary of Transportation Keyes were seated opposite the President.

That left Ridley, the Director of the Office of Special Projects (OSP), and Walker himself to man opposite ends of the table, where their flanks were open to attack. Or that was the way Walker thought about it as he took his seat.

As was his habit, Grace said a prayer once everyone

was seated. But if God had been listening during the last eight-plus years, there weren't any signs of it.

Secretary of the Interior Farnsworth was the first to give a report. Walker had a hard time taking him seriously, since he wore carefully brushed shoulder-length hair at a time when most men cut theirs short. His prow-shaped nose extended out over a handlebar mustache so prominent it was impossible to see his lips. His department was responsible for the Protection Camps that thousands of displaced Americans had been forced to enter after being driven from their homes by Chimeran forces.

Yet despite the relative safety of the camps, many people who entered them rebelled against the highly regimented lives they were forced to live within the fenced enclaves. In fact many were leaving to take up residence in the sprawling shacklands that were growing up around the larger cities. Slums really, which Farnsworth described as "breeding grounds for crime and disease."

"So," Grace responded once the report was complete, "what would you suggest?"

"We need armed security guards, Mr. President," Farnsworth said. "And we need to require all displaced persons to demonstrate a verifiable need before they can leave the camps. For God's sake, the United States is under attack! We can't have people running around like lunatics."

Grace nodded thoughtfully.

"What you say makes sense. Homer, do you see any problem with Larry's suggestion?"

The Attorney General's head was covered by an explosion of frizzy white hair and he had eyebrows to match. His mustache was unexpectedly dark, however, and it bobbed up and down as he spoke.

"You have the necessary authority, Mr. President. It's

implicit in the Executive Protection Act of 1950. Should you wish to create the sort of security force that Larry mentioned, you could tuck the new organization in under the Domestic Security Agency. That would lay the groundwork to use the Protection Camps as a place to house agitators, dissidents, and anarchists until the cessation of hostilities."

"Which is just a fancy way of saying that people who attempt to exercise their civil liberties—including the right of free speech—will be imprisoned," Walker put in cynically. Walker had a countenance that one wag had likened to Mr. Potato Head, which was a reference to the toy that enabled children to create funny faces by attaching plastic ears, noses, and lips to an Idaho spud. Now, as blood suffused his already homely features, he became even less attractive. "Or, put another way," the Secretary of War growled, "I think Larry's full of shit."

A pained expression appeared on Grace's face, and he sighed audibly.

"I know the Secretary is accustomed to rough language—but I would appreciate a semblance of civility here in the White House. And, while I applaud the Secretary's love of *liberty,* I feel it necessary to remind him that our freedoms extend from the rule of *law.* Not protest, not chaos, but law. We *will* have order in this country—or we will have nothing at all.

"So," Grace continued as his eyes shifted to the Attorney General, "Larry's proposal is approved. Homer . . . please prepare the necessary paperwork for my signature." Then, having turned his attention to Seymore, Grace spoke again.

"George?" Grace inquired. "How's the Department of Agriculture doing?"

Seymore was a long-faced man with a receding hairline and the demeanor of an undertaker. And for good reason. Crops had begun to fail due to changes in the weather, food shortages were becoming alarmingly common, and the price of even the most basic foodstuffs was spiking. Seymore noted that while the Victory Garden program had met with some success, it wasn't going to be enough.

For the moment, however, there was one glimmer of hope. The administration's decision to stop shipping food abroad was helping to ameliorate the shortfall.

And so it went as the Secretaries of Commerce, Transportation, and State all weighed in with reports that were unrelentingly grim. Ironically, the only person with anything even remotely positive to say was Walker, who gave a report regarding a successful commando raid into Chimera-occupied Britain, and a high-altitude fly-over of enemy headquarters in Iceland. Where, based on aerial photography, it was clear that some sort of construction program was underway. But, in spite of a few isolated victories, Walker had to admit that the future looked bleak.

Grace nodded somberly. "That brings us to the last item on today's agenda," he said. "A contingency plan I don't believe we'll have reason to use—but which I feel obligated to put in place. I call it Project Omega. Simply put, it would be a process by which to conduct negotiations with the Chimera."

After a moment of stunned silence, Walker opened his mouth to object, but Vice President McCullen beat him to it.

"Surely you can't be serious, Mr. President . . . Why, just last month you gave a speech in which you swore that the United States would fight to the last man, woman, and child! Were the news of such a plan to get out, there would be political hell to pay."

Thanks to the efforts of SRPA, knowledge gleaned

from the Chimera had been applied to all sorts of things over the last few years, including audio technology. And as Secretary of War, Walker had access to all the latest products, including the pocket-sized wire recorder he used for taking notes. Walker reached into a pocket to turn the device on as Grace formed a steeple with his fingertips. The recorder made a soft whirring noise, but thanks to Walker's position at the end of the table, no one else could hear it.

"I hear you, Harvey," Grace said tolerantly. "And, as I said before, I continue to believe that we *will* win a military victory. But I think you'll agree that the government has a responsibility to examine every alternative, no matter how unpleasant.

"Furthermore," Grace added, as his eyes swept those around him, "if there is to be any chance of a successful negotiation with the Chimera, it would have to take place while the country is in a position of strength, or the enemy won't have a reason to enter into talks with us."

Another long moment of silence followed the last statement.

Walker was tempted to speak but wanted to get *all* of the traitors on the record before he told them what assholes they were.

The Director of the OSP spoke. Because Ridley's famously large head sat atop a relatively small body, his detractors sometimes referred to him as "the troll." He was also known for the colorful bow ties he wore, a surprisingly beautiful wife, and his ability to play pool. His voice was smooth and cultured.

"I agree with the notion that all of the possible alternatives should be explored . . . But I would like to share some observations about the Chimera."

He was famous for his mini-lectures, and Farnsworth rolled his eyes. Ridley continued, undeterred.

"As all of you know, the Chimeran forms have one thing in common," he said. "They are constructs—tools, if you will, created by an alien virus that arrived on our planet in June of 1908. As such, the Chimera don't have a government, military, or culture as we think of such things. In fact, as far as our experts can tell, they have no formal hierarchy whatsoever. Everything they do flows from common instincts, shared desires, and biological imperatives.

"So," Ridley continued carefully, "taking those realities into account, it's difficult to know who we would talk to . . . And more importantly, to what end? It would be like trying to negotiate hurricane season with the wind. Besides they already have most of Europe and Asia. There isn't much incentive for them to negotiate at all."

Grace had a lot of respect for Ridley, even if he didn't like having his programs subjected to criticism, but he nodded tolerantly.

"Thank you, Tom. You make some excellent points. Still, just because some difficulties appear to block the way, it doesn't mean we shouldn't try."

Dentweiler had been silent up to that point, and now he cleared his throat.

"We *might* be able to contact the Chimera through an infected soldier named Jordan Shepherd. He had already begun to change when he escaped from SRPA custody in Iceland, and by the time he was recaptured a couple of months ago, the reports I read described him as a new form of Chimera. Part-human and part-Angel. Yet, interestingly enough, one that is still capable of communication."

Grace could see where Dentweiler was headed and hurried to seize upon the opportunity.

"Good thinking, Bill . . . This could be the opportunity we're looking for!"

"Not so fast," Ridley countered soberly. "I'm sorry to inform you that Shepherd—now referred to as Daedalus—is no longer in custody. He was being transferred from a temporary holding facility at Offutt Air Force Base, to a specially built maximum security lab in Florence, Colorado, when the convoy he was riding in was attacked by a force of what we would classify as Chimeran commandos. Half of the stinks were killed, but Daedalus escaped, and remains on the loose."

"How long ago was that?" Farnsworth inquired doubtfully. "I didn't hear about it."

"Three days ago," Ridley answered tightly, "and no, you *didn't* hear about it. The report went to those with a need to know . . . The SRPA people are very upset by the way . . . They claim they should have been given responsibility for the transfer rather than the DSA. Which is ridiculous, given the fact that they were the ones who lost Daedalus to begin with!"

Grace had a need to know, or thought he did, but chose not to say anything, fearing that the relevant report was somewhere in the stack of papers on his desk. As for Ridley's complaints regarding SRPA, he agreed. The people in charge of the organization had become increasingly combative of late. The Sentinels would be a critical part of any military victory—which made it difficult to rein them in. But that was a problem he would deal with later on.

Dentweiler smiled bleakly. His dark hair was combed straight back, his round wire-framed glasses sat high on his nose, and his prominent cheekbones gave his face a gaunt appearance. "That's a tough break," he said smoothly. "But it serves to support my point . . . Because if the Chimera chose to free Daedalus, it implies that he can call on them. Or that they *need* him."

"Daedalus may provide a channel for negotiations!" Grace put in brightly. "See? We *can* accomplish anything if we put our minds to it."

Then, turning to Dentweiler, Grace said, "Bill, please follow up on the Daedalus thing, and report back as soon as you have something. This could be a real opportunity, and we need to be ready to take advantage of it."

He stood, and the meeting would have come to an end at that point, except that Walker couldn't remain silent any longer. He brought a fist down onto the table so hard that a pen jumped into the air and landed with a clatter.

"Are you *insane*?" he demanded loudly. "Didn't you hear what the Vice President said? What you propose is treasonous! What about Congress? And the American people? Shouldn't *they* have a say?"

Grace just stared at him across the table. Finally he responded.

"Congress had its say when it approved the Emergency War Powers Act of 1946," Grace replied stiffly. "As for the American people, you'll recall that they elected me to an unprecedented third term in November of '48.

"That being said," the president added tightly, "I take exception to the notion that anyone who doesn't happen to agree with your idealistic nonsense is a traitor!" He paused, and seemed to relax. "For the moment, Henry, I choose to believe that you're overworked and distraught about our losses."

Then his voice hardened again. "But if I'm wrong, and you wish to resign, you know where to send the letter." He stood, and addressed the room. "This meeting is over."

Vice President McCullen was the only person to direct a sympathetic look at Walker as Grace led the rest of the cabinet out of the room.

Once they were gone, Walker put his head back, closed his eyes, and battled the overwhelming sense of despair that threatened to drown him. The recorder still was running—but it stopped when a button was pushed.

The rest of the world continued to spin.

# CHAPTER FOUR
# A STROLL IN THE PARK

### East of the Badlands National Park, South Dakota
### Monday, November 19, 1951

A miniature snowstorm billowed up around the *Party Girl's* hard angular lines as the battle-scarred VTOL descended out of the grayness above.

There was a *thump* as the transport's landing gear came into contact with the ground, and Hale came to his feet. He was wearing four layers of clothing, counting the winter-white parka and matching trousers. And, in spite of the viral inhibitor shot he had received prior to takeoff, he was wearing a combination combat harness and white knapsack over his I-Pack. The emphasis was on health, food, and ammo. Everything else having been eliminated to keep the weight down.

He was armed with a Rossmore 236 shotgun for clean-up work, and an L23 Fareye for use on targets up to six hundred yards away. Although it was Hale's hope to avoid enemy contact if at all possible.

Last, but not least, were ski poles plus a pair of snowshoes that Hale would don once he left the plane. His thoughts were interrupted as the *Party's Girl's* pilot—a long, lean officer named Harley Purvis—appeared at his side. Purvis sported a New York Yankees baseball cap, a well-worn leather jacket, and a pair of fleece-lined boots. He had dark brown skin, even features, and had been given the call sign "Hollywood" in flight school.

"You are one *crazy* bastard," Purvis said as he slapped Hale on the shoulder. "You know this could cost you your bars." The pilot had to yell in order to be heard over the sound of the engines.

Hale knew that what Purvis said was true, but he didn't care. He was tired of being dead.

Like all the soldiers in the Sentinel program, he was officially listed as "Killed in Action," which meant his family believed him to be dead. It was a precaution intended to prevent information about the top secret SRPA program from leaking out.

But as the Chimera continued to push down into his home state of South Dakota, most people fled or were killed. As a result, Hale had no idea what had happened to his mother, father, and sister. Were they still alive?

The question had haunted Hale ever since his return from overseas—and repeated attempts to obtain information had been fruitless. None of them was listed as having entered one of the government-run Protection Camps. Was that because they weren't willing to take what his father would regard as a handout? Or was it because they were dead? Like millions of other people around the world.

Hale was determined to find out.

"Yeah," he responded, "if they catch me, I'll have to call you 'sir,' and *that* would be ridiculous."

"Actually, given the fact that I'm a *first* lieutenant, and you're a butter bar, you should call me 'sir' anyway," Purvis responded loftily. "And I plan to *keep* my bars . . . So if you get caught roaming around the countryside, be sure to lie about how you got here."

"You can count on it," Hale assured him. "And you

can consider that IOU paid in full. Where did you learn to play poker anyway? The Girl Scouts?"

"At UCLA," Purvis answered with mock indignation. "But having lost to a lowlife like you, it looks like I need a refresher course." Then he turned serious. "Remember, thirty-six hours, that's all I can give you! And one more thing . . ."

"Yeah?"

"Watch your six . . . It'd be a shame if a Hybrid blew your ass off and ate it for lunch."

Hale just grinned, gave a wave, and left the plane through the rear hatch. After a one-foot jump his boots sank four inches into the soft snow—a sure sign that snowshoes would be needed.

Hale knew Purvis had a mission to complete, so he hurried to clear the LZ quickly so the *Party Girl* could take off. Once he had waded out to a point where he could be seen from the cockpit he waved again, and saw the pilot give him a thumbs-up in return. There was a dark-skinned beauty painted on the VTOL's nose, and Hale noticed that one of her eyes was closed in a sardonic wink. Then the engines roared, snow swirled, and the ship went straight up.

Hale watched it go, but it wasn't until the plane had disappeared into the lead gray sky, and the drone of its engines died away, that he felt the full weight of his decision. Maybe he *was* crazy, but what else could he do?

If his family was dead, well, the reality of it would be hard to take. But *not* knowing was even worse. Frank and Mary Farley weren't his *real* parents. They had been killed during the influenza epidemic of 1924. But the Farleys had raised Hale as if he was their biological son, and now it was his duty to do what any son would, which was to help his mom and dad if such a thing was possible.

So Hale found a spot where the wind had blown away most of the snow, sat down, strapped the snowshoes to his boots, and got back on his feet with help from a ski pole. Then, having checked his compass, he set off.

The surface of the snow was frozen, so each time Hale brought one of the snowshoes forward and shifted his weight to it, there was a soft *crunch* as the shoe broke through the top crust. Hale had used snowshoes throughout his childhood, but it had been a while. The key was to maintain the correct distance between his feet, because if he placed them too far apart he would consume more energy than was necessary. And if he brought them too close he would bark his shins.

It took a while to find the old rhythms again, but once he had, Hale made much better time. Good thing, too, because the Rocking F Ranch was still fifteen miles away.

It would have been nice if Purvis had been able to put him down in the front yard of the family home, of course, but that would have forced the pilot to enter prohibited airspace. "Prohibited," meaning airspace that had been ceded to the Chimera. It was off-limits to any aircraft not on an authorized mission.

So he had to do it the old-fashioned way. Still, Hale was confident that he could make the round-trip with time to spare, so long as the weather held and he didn't encounter any of the enemy. The low cloud cover would keep most of the Chimeran aircraft on the ground, and the steady snowfall would obliterate his tracks as well.

That was the theory anyway.

But as Hale topped a rise and made his way down the opposite slope he discovered that he was unexpectedly tired, and welcomed the opportunity to rest next to a group of trees. After less than an hour of walking his thigh and calf muscles were already sore. He knew they would hurt even more the following morning. The weight of his food, weapons, and ammo was a factor as well.

The break offered him an opportunity to eat a hard Hershey bar and scan the whiteness that lay ahead. He knew he would be easier to spot out in the open, and if forced to defend himself, he'd have no place to hide. With that in mind he panned the binoculars across the rolling prairie, looking for even the tiniest hint of movement, a color that shouldn't be there, or a feature that wasn't consistent with its surroundings.

Between the misty haze that hung like a backdrop across the land, a veil of thinly falling snow, and the dim winter light, visibility was poor. But Hale spotted some movement off to the right and felt a sudden surge of adrenaline, only to discover that he was looking at three gaunt horses. Left on their own by the war, they stood huddled next to the building where they had once been fed.

Satisfied that the way was clear, Hale left the relative protection offered by the trees and slip-slid out across the unmarked snow. Lung-warmed air jetted out in front of him, the snowshoes made a consistent *swish-thump* sound, and the Rossmore thumped against his chest. The alternative was to carry the weapon across his back, along with the Fareye, but that would open him up to a sudden attack by Leapers. The dog-sized creatures could jump six feet in the air and had a lethal bite. It required quick reflexes and a powerful weapon to bring them down, so having a shotgun at the ready increased one's chances of survival.

So the shotgun remained where it was as he crossed the open area, passed the barn on his right, and spotted some snow-blurred tracks that ran down through a gully and up the other side. Some of the impressions had been made by various types of livestock, but there were others as well, including impressions left by splay-footed Hybrids.

As Hale sidestepped his way up the slope, he was careful not to pop up over the top, knowing that just about anything might lie in wait beyond. But his fears were groundless, and when he brought the binoculars up, all he saw was open prairie.

No, not all. Some of the tracks wandered off to the right and left, but the rest led to a point where a dark smudge could be seen, about a hundred yards in front of him. There were no sounds other than the measured rasp of his own breathing, the soft rustle of his parka, and the insistent sigh of the wind.

Hale's tracks overlaid all the rest as he made his way out toward the dark thing—and he was momentarily startled when a flock of crows took to the air.

A moment later he realized he was looking at a dead Titan. Judging from the sizable cavity where its abdominal organs should have been, the carcass had been lying there for days. The variety of tracks in the blood-tinged snow indicated that scavengers of every possible description had been feeding off the carcass for some time. But what was responsible for the monster's death?

Certainly it hadn't been a band of civilians, even if any remained in the area. Titans were twenty feet tall, carried powerful cannons, and were notoriously difficult to kill. Hale knew firsthand, because he'd been forced to tackle the beasts in England, and had no desire to do so again.

So what brought the Titan down, Hale wondered, as he circled the body. A strafing attack by a Sabre Jet? Had a VTOL happened by on its way back from a mission? Hale figured it had been something of that sort, although he would never know for sure.

The next three hours were spent slogging across the gently rolling prairie. Hale was forced to cut his way through a barbed wire fence on one occasion, and came across others that, judging from the tracks in the snow, had been torn down by a Chimeran Stalker. A patrol perhaps? If so it was one more thing he had to worry about.

There were other signs of the enemy presence as well, including piles of frost-glazed Hybrid dung, a dead steer that had been riddled with projectiles from a Chimeran Bullseye, and the remains of an encampment littered with partially gnawed human bones. All of which forced Hale to slow down lest he inadvertently walk into a Chimeran emplacement.

By that time he knew he was nearing the White River. It ran roughly east and west, a few miles south of the main highway that ran between Rapid City and Sioux Falls. The Rocking F Ranch was located in the strip of land south of the highway and north of the river.

In order to get there Hale would have to cross the river via one of the local bridges. The span he had in mind was a modest affair that had been put in place to serve ranchers who needed to move livestock back and forth across the waterway. Hale had spent the first two decades of his life in the area, so he knew exactly how to reach the bridge. But would it still be there? If so, was it being used by the Chimera? There was only one way to find out.

At that point Hale decided to remove the clumsy snowshoes, bundle them with the ski poles, and tie all of them to his pack. Then, boots sinking into the snow, he fought his way up the side of a low-lying hill to an outcropping of rock at the top. A spot where a much younger Hale had spent many an hour while his horse grazed below. It was a fairly simple matter to circle around, find cover, and examine the bridge through his binoculars.

The good news was that the structure was still in place, but the bad news was that four stinks were guarding it. Two of the Hybrids were stationed at the north end of the span, one carrying a Bullseye, and two of them paced back and forth at the south end, one of them wielding an Auger.

The Chimera had smooth skulls, six eyes each, and mouths filled with needle-sharp teeth. None of the stinks were equipped with the sort of cool packs Hale had seen in England, suggesting that the cold weather was to their liking, and sufficient to keep their core temperatures down.

This was a disappointment, since it had been Hale's hope to carry out his self-assigned mission entirely unnoticed. But he wasn't about to let four Hybrids prevent him from reaching his goal. So he shrugged off the pack, put the Rossmore aside, and brought the Fareye around to where he could use it. Then, placing his right glove on a rock, he set the rifle on top of it.

With that accomplished, Hale brought his eye down to the telescopic sight and began the not altogether unpleasant process of deciding which stink to kill first.

He needed to drop all four of the aliens one right after the other, if possible, both to clear a path across the bridge and to prevent them from spotting him before he had finished taking them down. Had the targets been human, Hale might have chosen to kill an officer or noncom first, but with no way to determine which freak was in charge, he had to rely on speed. So he made the decision to drop the sentries located at the north end of the bridge first, because they were farther away and had quicker access to cover.

Then would come the ticklish task of swinging the Fareye to the right and acquiring his other two targets, both of whom would probably be firing on him by then. Thanks to the distance, he would retain the advantage, however, so he couldn't allow them to come closer. Because the last thing he wanted was for the alien with the Bullseye to tag him and send a dozen projectiles to seek him out. Or for the stink with the Auger to shoot *through* the rocks, and kill him that way.

Judging from the drift of the snowflakes the wind was blowing west to east, something Hale would need to take into consideration along with the ambient air temperature and the way the slug would drop slightly while in flight. With all of those factors in mind, he placed the crosshairs over the first Chimera's head, made a tiny adjustment for the wind, and tilted the barrel up a fraction of an inch. Then, having taken a deep breath, he let most of it out. The trigger seemed to squeeze itself.

The Fareye nudged Hale's shoulder, but thanks to the cylindrical silencer, the report was no louder than a baby's cough. Hale saw a halo of blood appear as the Chimera's head exploded, but resisted the desire to watch the body fall, knowing that every second was precious.

Target number two was turning circles at that point, trying to figure out where the bullet had come from, and that was when the second slug hit. The Hybrid went facedown in the snow and slid for a good two feet before finally coming to rest.

Swinging the rifle to the right in an attempt to acquire the third and fourth targets, he saw only one of his opponents. An object blurred past his telescopic sight, and Hale brought the rifle back, noting with a grim sense of satisfaction that one of the Hybrids was hiding behind a bridge support.

Time seemed to slow as Hale poured his entire being into making the critical shot. Slowly but surely the crosshairs drifted into place, Hale sent the necessary message to his right index finger, and felt it tighten on the trigger. The rifle coughed and a sudden spray of blood marked a hit as the third Chimera fell. It was only wounded, however, and a pink smear marked its progress as it began to drag itself through the slush.

Hale wanted to finish the Hybrid—*needed* to finish him—but there was the fourth one to consider. So he swung the rifle away, quartered the ground below, and came up empty. That was when the breeze flew a rank odor into Hale's nostrils and the hairs on the back of his neck stood up.

He felt the Hybrid's foul breath wash across the left side of his face, and swore as long needle-sharp fangs sank into his shoulder. There wasn't enough time in which to bring the Fareye around, and the Chimera was too close for him to shoot it with the long-barreled weapon, anyway, so Hale made a grab for the double-edged commando knife that was fastened to his forearm. As he did, the stink lost its grip, but leaned in to press its advantage.

The Fairbairn Sykes fighting knife had been a gift from Lieutenant Cartwright in England, and as he jerked the weapon free of its sheath, Hale leaned away from his attacker. Then, bringing the double-edged blade around with his right hand, Hale drove its six inches of steel through one of the Chimera's yellow-gold eyes.

Something warm squirted onto Hale's fist as the Hybrid opened its jaws, screeched in pain, and reeled backward. Since it was still moving he guessed that the sliver of steel had missed the Chimera's brain, but it was sticking out through the spot where a human nose would be. So it *should* have been dead, but bounced off the rock face behind it.

Having regained a momentary advantage, Hale threw himself to the left. The Rossmore was there, leaning against the pack, and he made a desperate grab for it, but the Hybrid was on him by then. Its skeletal fingers were wrapped around his throat as it pressed down with all its weight.

Hale felt dizzy, knew he would lose consciousness soon, and sought to push the stink away with his left hand while exploring the ground with his right. His fingers found and rejected two smaller rocks before finally closing around a chunk of granite that had the right amount of heft.

Then, as the world began to fade to black, Hale brought the rock up with all of his strength. There was a loud *thok* as the makeshift weapon found its mark, and a sudden loosening of the creature's grip as all of the alien's remaining eyes rolled back in his head. Suddenly the weight was gone as the Chimera fell over sideways and allowed Hale to scramble clear.

Within seconds he was back on his feet. There was a loud *boom* as Hale put a load of double-ought buckshot into the unconscious stink. The blast blew a hole the size of a dinner plate through the creature's chest.

It was tempting to fire *again,* just for the emotional satisfaction of it, but Hale knew he had to conserve ammo. So he stood there for a moment, chest heaving, his shoulder throbbing, as he fought to regain his composure.

Still in pain but functional once more Hale bent to retrieve his knife. There was a certain amount of suction, but having secured a good grip on the handle, he managed to jerk the weapon free. After cleaning the blade, and returning the weapon to its sheath, he reloaded the Fareye and slung both it and the pack over his good shoulder.

That accomplished, and with the shotgun at the ready, Hale went hunting.

The third stink wasn't hard to find. Having made his way down onto the bridge deck, he picked up the Auger he had seen earlier. Then all Hale had to do was follow a trail through the blood-tinged slush to the north side of the span, where the badly injured Chimera was still dragging itself away. The 'brid snarled and snapped its teeth, but having left its weapon behind, there wasn't anything it could do as Hale fired half a clip of Auger rounds into the alien.

The body jerked convulsively as the projectiles passed through both it *and* the bridge deck to splash into the river below.

The weapon was too heavy to carry given the combined weight of his other armament, so Hale dropped it into the river, and followed the well-churned road north. Unlike the pristine whiteness of the prairie, this was a dangerous way to go, since a group of Chimera could come barreling down the road at any moment, yet there was a method to Hale's madness.

Even a Native American tracker would have found it difficult to pick his bootprints out of the muck that covered the road and Hale doubted that any of the Chimera possessed such skills. Plus, with solid cement only four or five inches under the slush, he could move faster.

And, as Hale topped a rise and followed the highway down to the point where it crossed a streambed, he had the opportunity to get off the road without leaving tracks. Which he proceeded to do.

Once in the half-frozen stream, Hale followed it west.

Twenty minutes later he was within the borders of the Rocking F Ranch. But the light had started to fade, and by now the bodies of the Hybrids would have been found. If a massive search wasn't already underway, it soon would be.

Which was why Hale forced himself to maintain a brisk pace until he spotted a four-foot-tall pine tree that lay within reach of the streambed. It took a moment to wrestle the tree out of the frozen soil and fill the hole with snow, but two minutes later Hale had what amounted to a broom.

With the tree in one hand and the shotgun in the other, he followed the creek uphill to the point where he could see the rocky hill that he and his family called Prospector's Knob, named after the rusty tools his father had found there.

Backing out of the stream, he used the tree to obliterate his tracks, and worked his way up to the point where the windswept hillside was clear of all but a thin dusting of snow. At that point it was safe to toss the tree in a ravine and continue on until he arrived at what a ten-year-old version of himself had called the Fort. A collection of car-sized rocks that had been the scene of many an imaginary battle, and still stood guard over a boyhood secret. One which, if it remained intact, might save Hale's life.

He entered the small clearing behind a screen of snow-frosted rocks and immediately made his way over to the base of the hill. Many years had passed since the slab of rock had been put into place, but it was still there. Having placed his pack and the Fareye off to the side, Hale lifted the slab out of the way.

That produced a jab of pain as he got down on hands and knees. A combination of dirt and loose gravel had filtered into the cavity from both sides, but once he scooped the material away, a small opening was revealed. Hale's boyhood dog had discovered the hole and immediately scuttled in, forcing the youngster to follow. He was pretty sure he could still fit through the aperture, and was determined to give it a try.

Grabbing his pack, Hale shoved it into the cave, followed by the snowshoes and his weapons. He used the ski poles to push everything further in, then he lay down on his back and stuck his head into the blackness.

There was a slight dip that had to be negotiated before he could wiggle his way up into the main cavern. It had been a negligible obstacle when he was ten, but it represented a more significant barrier now as Hale kicked with his feet and swore when some dirt fell on his face. His shoulders scraped both sides of the hole as he reached up to push and pull on the rock face within. Progress was incremental, but after a three- or four-minute battle, Hale was inside.

It was pitch black, but Hale was ready for that. He took a flashlight out of a pocket, and as the torch came on a blob of light splashed against one of the walls. He scrambled to his feet and discovered that there was just enough room to stand.

The beam took him on a journey into the past as it roamed the walls of the cavern.

The makeshift shelving was still there, as were the supplies a younger Nathan Hale had considered to be important, including a beat-up kerosene lantern, a box of safety matches, a jar of what had once been peanut butter, a spoon borrowed from his mother's kitchen, a stack of well-thumbed Red Ryder comic books, a box of .22 shorts, half a roll of toilet paper secured with a rubber band, a mousetrap, the bottom half of a broken shovel, and an Ovaltine decoder ring.

That brought a smile to Hale's face, because he could

remember sending for it, and running all the way down to the mailbox every day for two weeks before it finally arrived.

Life had been simple then, and in retrospect very special, because even though the Chimera had already arrived on the planet, the people of South Dakota had remained blissfully unaware of them.

*If only we had known* . . . Then again, he realized, even if they *had* known, it's unlikely anything could have been done.

There were more artifacts of the past, including a blackened fire pit, the pile of desiccated wood stacked next to it, a crude likeness of a Neolithic cave painting Hale had seen in *National Geographic* magazine, and lots of overlapping sneaker prints left by the young explorer.

There was a narrow aperture over the fire pit that was just big enough to carry smoke up and out of the cavern. Normally, a soft whistling noise could be heard as wind crossed over the natural chimney. But now, as Hale heard a thrumming sound, he knew something mechanical was nearby.

A Chimeran drone? Yes, that was a strong possibility, and he felt his stomach muscles tighten as the noise grew louder, then softer again.

Seconds later the airborne machine was gone, causing Hale to breathe easier. Had the drone discovered him, it would still be lingering above. But there would be other hunters, some of whom would be a lot more dangerous than drones, so Hale hurried to move his belongings farther away from the entrance and rolled a rock in to block it.

What had been difficult for a ten-year-old was easier for an adult.

Then it was time to light the kerosene lamp and set up

housekeeping. It was tempting to start a fire, both for additional warmth and psychological comfort, but Hale had reason to believe that at least some of the Chimeran constructs could sense heat. If so, a column of smoke and warm air would function as a beacon, and lead them right to his hiding place.

So rather than take that chance, Hale lit a military-style fuel tab and placed a can of beans and franks over the tiny flame. Rather than bring entire C rations, Hale had pilfered components from six of the cardboard boxes prior to departing the base, taking only the items he wanted. Beans and franks being his favorite.

While dinner was cooking Hale took a few swigs from his canteen, followed by three long drags from the I-Pack before turning his attention back to the now bubbling brew. Humble though the dinner was, Hale enjoyed both it and the chocolate bar he had for dessert. That made him thirsty though, and with only half a canteen of water left, he had to limit himself to tiny sips.

Feeling refreshed, he stripped off the parka and two layers of clothing underneath, to inspect the damage the Hybrid had done earlier. His T-shirt was thick with clotted blood, but thanks to the regenerative powers of the Chimeran virus, Hale knew the puncture wounds would already be closed and would soon be healed.

It was a few degrees warmer inside the cave than outside, but it was still chilly, so he hurried to put his clothes back on. Having left his bulky sleeping bag behind, Hale planned to curl up on the floor, and not for the first time. He had slept there as a boy, though not during the winter.

But first, before Hale could take care of his own needs, there were two weapons to clean. That took the better part of forty-five minutes, but was extremely important since both had been exposed to moisture all day long.

Eventually, after completing his chores, Hale positioned his pack for use as a pillow and took the Rossmore into a lover's embrace. The lantern remained on—which was fine, since there was sufficient fuel to get him through the night. And while it provided no real heat, the light would serve as a source of psychological comfort.

Hale could see the glow through his eyelids, as he thought about his family and the long happy days of his youth. Before he knew it he was far, far away.

The ground shook.

The vibration woke Hale immediately, but he wasn't sure why, and lay with the shotgun at the ready until a *second* tremor caused tiny particles of rock to rain down from above. And that was when Hale realized that something extremely large was stalking the land.

A Titan? Like the dead Chimera he'd come across earlier? Or maybe a Mauler, like the ones spotted during the recon mission.

Or perhaps a three-hundred-foot-tall Leviathan— possibly the largest creature to ever walk the surface of the planet. There were mechanical possibilities, too— including heavily armed Stalkers and Goliaths.

Whatever the case, a full minute passed before the earth-shaking footsteps faded away, leaving Hale to try and go to sleep again. That took a while, however, as memory chased memory, and the hours ticked away.

It was an urgent need to take a piss that caused Hale to awake at what his wristwatch said was 0632. His shoulder felt fine, but his rarely used snowshoeing muscles were aching, and there was a bad taste in his mouth.

So he got up, urinated in a corner, and brushed his teeth. That process consumed what remained of his water.

Having rolled the barrier rock out of the way, and with empty cup in hand, Hale lay down on his back and pushed his head and shoulders out into the open. It was cold, *very* cold, and as the thickly falling snowflakes kissed his upturned face Hale grinned happily. Because bad weather was *good* weather—for him anyway— since visibility would be limited to a few feet.

Securing a mugful of snow, Hale wiggled his way back inside the cave, and went to work. Breakfast consisted of three drags of aerosolized inhibitor from the I-Pack, followed by *more* franks and beans, plus the mugful of snow-water in the form of some hot chocolate. Then it was time to clean up out of respect for his younger self, push his gear out into the open, and follow it into near-whiteout conditions.

Minutes later Hale had both his pack and snowshoes on. With both weapons positioned for traveling, and the ski poles in hand, he set off for home.

Thanks to his knowledge of the local terrain Hale felt confident that he could find the ranch house regardless of the weather, but was careful to check his compass every now and then just to make sure he was still on course.

He did his best to keep his head on a swivel, but the parka made that difficult, as did all the gear he was carrying. After the first half-hour or so, the endless snowfall combined with the steady *swish, swish, swish* of snowshoes threatened to dull his senses and leave him open to attack.

To counter that possibility, Hale made it a habit to pause every ten minutes or so and conduct a 360-degree scan of his environment as far as he could see—which wasn't very far. But with the exception of a forlorn steer and a briefly glimpsed white-tailed deer, he saw no signs of life until he topped a rise and spotted a line of enormous footprints that cut across his path. Each pod-print was so deep that not even the heavy snowfall had been sufficient to fill them in, although there had been enough to obscure the shape. Given the configuration, though, the vibrations he had experienced the night before must have been caused by a Chimeran battle mech, possibly a Goliath.

There were other signs of the machine's passage as well, including shattered boulders, trampled trees, and a black scorch mark off in the distance. Something—or someone—had the misfortune to be in the wrong place at the wrong time.

The thought made him pick up the pace. He needed to get home.

His progress was generally uneventful, although a pack of feral dogs followed him for a while until eventually turning away to follow a more promising scent. He began to see familiar landmarks, like the frozen pond where both cattle and the local wildlife came to drink in the summer, and the tumbledown line shack his foster father's father had built, and the windmill that brought deep-lying water up to fill a metal tank.

The windmill was still now, its metal blades hung with icicles, its purpose lost—along with an entire way of life.

After the first inclination to rush ahead, Hale forced himself to slow down again. Because if his parents had left, and the ranch house still stood, it could serve as a haven for almost anything. Chimera included.

With that in mind Hale took cover in a cluster of trees. He removed both his pack and snowshoes, and stuffed everything under some low-hanging branches.

Then, carrying only the I-Pack plus weapons and ammunition, Hale worked his way forward.

The house had been built in a hollow where it and the outbuildings were sheltered from the prairie winds, so it wouldn't be visible until he was practically on top of it. He traveled the last few feet of the journey on his belly with the Fareye at the ready and the Rossmore slung across his back.

As his head inched up over the top of the rise his heart beat faster.

The house was intact!

The snow fell like a lacy curtain around the two-story structure. It looked as it always had, and could have been featured on a Christmas card. It was so quiet that the sudden pistol-shot sound caused Hale to jump.

A quick scan of the terrain revealed that an overloaded branch had snapped under the weight of the snow.

Having slowed his breathing, Hale turned his attention back to the house. He knew better than to rush in, and made use of the Fareye's scope to examine every inch of the structure's facade. That was when he saw details that caused his spirits to plummet.

There wasn't any glass left in most of the windows, the walls were riddled with bullet holes, and the front door was ajar.

There was no sign of life, so Hale made the decision to trade weapons, knowing that if he was forced to fight *inside* the house the Rossmore would be the better weapon. Then he rose, and began to advance.

Snow crunched under his boots and deep drifts made it necessary to lift his feet high as he angled down the slope. Once on flat ground he took momentary cover behind the ranch's snow-encrusted propane tank before dashing across the parking area to crouch by the pump house, where he paused to eyeball his surroundings.

Then, as certain as he could be that there weren't any nasty surprises waiting for him, Hale left the shelter of the pump house and made his way up the snow-drifted walkway. His boots made a hollow thumping sound as he climbed the front steps to the wraparound porch. The screen door had been holed, and hinges squeaked as Hale pulled it open.

A nudge from the Rossmore was sufficient to push the wooden front door out of the way to reveal a devastated living room. Hale's heart sank as he stepped inside. A .30-30 Winchester casing rattled away as a snow-encrusted boot hit the brass cylinder and sent it skittering across the wooden floor. Photos from the Farley family album, bloodied bandages, and broken crockery lay everywhere.

As Hale looked around he saw that the walls were riddled with bullet holes and blast marks. Pictures hung askew, the world map over the couch had been half-obliterated by an Auger blast, and blood splatter could be seen on the floor. Based on the medical paraphernalia that sat on the sideboard, it looked as if the wounded had been laid out on the dining room table. Hale could imagine his mother bent over a bloodied ranch hand, doing what she could to prolong his life for another few minutes, as the battle raged around her.

Judging from the hundreds of empty .30-30, .45, and even .22 casings that littered the floor, plus the red, green, and yellow shotgun shells scattered around the house, it appeared that the Farleys and their employees had put up one helluva fight. It had been a losing battle however, or that's the way things appeared. But where were the bodies? Had the Chimera taken them away? Or was there some other explanation?

Although it was only mid-afternoon, little sunlight pierced the clouds and the snow, so the room was dark and gloomy. Hale removed the flashlight from his pocket and began to play the beam across the walls and floor in an effort to find some clue as to what had taken place after the battle. That was when he spotted the familiar scrawl on the living room wall.

To friends and family,

Farleys don't run. That's what dad said. So we stayed. They came the day before yesterday . . . And I'm proud to say that we killed every damned one of the bastards!

But Sam went down, and Red, and Pete. Then mom died, followed by dad, and I should have been next. But it didn't turn out that way. So I scooped out a grave with the tractor and buried them out back. Right next to mom's garden.

I'm heading south with Ruff. Pray for me.

Susan

Ruff was the family's mastiff—and Susan was Hale's sister. Not his *real* sister, but she might as well have been, because the two of them were as close as any blood relatives had ever been. Susan was one of the few people who could shoot a rifle as well as Hale could, and given her knowledge of the outdoors, she might have been able to escape Chimera-occupied territory alive. That possibility made Hale feel a little better as he passed from the dining room and badly ravaged kitchen to leave the house through the back door.

The snowfall slowed by then, making it a little easier as he took a look around. The barn stood off to his left, the tractor she had mentioned was straight ahead, and the garden was off to the right. A wonderful sight in the spring and summer, but fallow now, and buried under the snow.

And something new had been added, a mound that could only be the mass grave Susan had referred to, adjacent to the garden.

Each footstep made a dry crunching sound as Hale made his way over to the mound and stood with his chin on his chest. Tears trickled down his stubble-covered cheeks as he thought about the battle that had been fought, and how hard the burial must have been for Susan. These were the people who had raised him—not because they had to, but because they *wanted* to.

Frank and Mary Farley had been good people, who, like so many others, had been killed by the stinking invaders.

As Hale's head came up he felt stronger, more determined than ever to eradicate the alien menace, no matter what the effort might cost him.

That was when Hale heard metal *clang* on metal, he brought the Rossmore up, and swiveled toward his left. Someone or something was moving around in the barn.

# CHAPTER FIVE
# LIAR, LIAR

President Grace stood in the Oval Office and looked out into the Rose Garden. It was pouring rain, just as it had been on the morning when he was born.

His father had chosen to name him Noah after the man selected to rescue all living things from the Great Flood. It was one of many decisions that had been made without any input from his wife, who was treated as a member of her husband's staff, and given very little authority over anything other than her garden.

Perhaps that was why Grace actually *liked* the rain, because it was in a way symbolic of the role reserved for him, although the deluge he faced was far worse than the events described in the book of Genesis. A time when people had doubts about the first Noah, even though he was correct about the coming flood, and how to best prepare for it.

That thought made Grace feel better as he turned his back on the garden, stepped out into the hall, and followed it to the Cabinet Room. Most of the cabinet members were present, including Director of Special Projects Ridley, Secretary of Commerce Lasky, Secretary of State Moody, Secretary of War Walker, Secretary of Transportation Keyes, Vice President McCullen, and Attorney General Clowers. And last, but not least, Grace's Chief of Staff, William Dentweiler.

Secretary of the Interior Farnsworth and Secretary of Agriculture Seymore were both in the country's heartland dealing with a multitude of issues related to the Protection Camps, the ever-growing shacklands, and persistent food shortages.

Some of the officials already were on their feet, chatting with one another, and those who weren't rose as the President entered. Grace knew how important appearances could be, so he was careful to shake each man's hand as he made the rounds. And with the exception of one man Grace felt good about his team.

Choosing Henry Walker as Secretary of War had been a mistake—one that Grace was planning to correct as soon as a suitable replacement could be found.

But there was no sign of what Grace planned to do as he slapped Walker on the back, then made his way to the chair located at the center of the table. The back of the chair was two inches taller than the rest, and fitted with a brass plaque that proclaimed, "The President."

The meeting began with the usual prayer, followed by a series of reports, the most interesting of which came from Secretary of State Harold Moody. He had a receding hairline, a bulbous nose, and a well-trimmed mustache. His bright blue eyes darted around the table as he spoke.

"Many of you will remember Operation Overstrike, during which a force comprised of United European Defense troops, also known as the Maquis, and British forces went after a number of Chimeran targets in Paris. During the assault Major Stephen Cartwright, of the British Royal Marines, led a successful attack against the enemy's central hub tower. Its destruction resulted in a disruption of the entire Chimera power grid in Western Europe."

Many of those present nodded approvingly.

"What most of you weren't aware of was the fact that Overstrike was a diversionary attack," Moody continued. "The actual purpose of Overstrike was to deploy a retrovirus designed to infect Carriers, the Chimeran creatures that collect humans for conversion. And I'm happy to announce that the plan was successful. Carrier corpses have been found on the ground everywhere from Ireland to Spain. And without Carriers to supply them with bodies, Chimeran Conversion Centers have shut down all over Western Europe."

That announcement produced a couple of "Hear, hears" and a round of light applause.

"Unfortunately," Moody went on gloomily, "the Chimera have already begun to adapt. New forms—unofficially called Spinners—have been reported. The new creatures bypass the Crawler/Carrier conversion process by cocooning victims in whatever nook or cranny may be available. A process that makes both the victims and the Chimera more difficult to find. Obviously these new reports are troubling," Moody added, "and all available information has been channeled to the Secretary of War and the Pentagon."

Moody's somewhat downbeat report was followed by updates from the Secretaries of Commerce, Transportation, and War. The latter being of most concern because Chimeran battleships had been sighted over the English Channel, off the Atlantic Seaboard, *and* in Canada as well.

The good news was that weapons of all sorts were coming off American assembly lines, and at a record pace. The draft had been expanded to include all males between the ages of eighteen and fifty, and the United

States would soon have another million men under arms.

Grace had to acknowledge that Walker had done a truly remarkable job of bringing the U.S. military onto a wartime footing, and Vice President McCullen led the rest of the cabinet in a round of applause.

But the show of confidence was quickly swept away as Grace cleared his throat.

He eyed the faces around him, then turned his attention to Chief of Staff Dentweiler. "And now it's time for an update regarding the Omega Project. Bill? If you would be so kind . . ."

Dentweiler was ready. He nodded and light reflected off of his glasses as he looked down at his notes.

"I'm sure you'll recall that during our last meeting I raised the possibility that a missing soldier named Jordan Shepherd, aka Daedalus, might represent our only realistic channel of communication with the Chimera." He paused, and several men nodded.

"Since that time I've met with various experts, including SRPA's Dr. Malikov. All the people I met with were told that the purpose of the interview was to obtain information regarding the circumstances under which Daedalus was freed from custody, and to assess what kind of threat he might pose. At no time was any information given regarding the Omega Project.

"There were several different opinions, of course," Dentweiler said, as his eyes flicked from face to face, "but there were areas of agreement as well. Especially where the subject's medical history was concerned.

"As part of a top secret program called Project Abraham, Private Shepherd received an experimental vaccine intended to counter the effects of the Chimeran virus. After Shepherd was inoculated, a genetic recombination took place. In retrospect Dr. Malikov—who was in charge of the program—believed that Shepherd was immunocompromised at the time of the vaccination.

"In any case, the genetic recombination altered both Shepherd's physical and mental state far beyond projected parameters, and produced what most of us would regard as a monster. *But,*" Dentweiler added meaningfully, "according to those who had an opportunity to interact with Shepherd-Daedalus before his escape, it was determined that he *can* communicate with humans. Although the process is often difficult.

"That's partially due to the fact that Daedalus seems to be in what amounts to telepathic contact with hundreds, if not *thousands,* of Chimera at any given time. As a result he has been known to pause in mid-sentence for up to three or four minutes before resuming the conversation.

"Making the situation even more difficult," Dentweiler continued, "is the fact that Daedalus can be totally incomprehensible at times. He seems to be especially inclined toward obscure rants which even the experts are hard-pressed to follow. Some of the people with whom I spoke claim that Daedalus can impinge on their thoughts, although the evidence of that is rather thin.

"With all of those considerations in mind," Dentweiler concluded, "I came away with the impression that Daedalus could indeed serve as a go-between, if we can find a way to motivate him."

He took his seat, and after a few moments of silence, McCullen was the first to speak up.

"All right," he said evenly, "let's say Bill is correct. Let's say there *is* a way to communicate with the Chimera. That still leaves a very important question unanswered. What kind of offer would we make?"

But if McCullen hoped to lead the discussion into a

dead end, he was quickly disappointed, because the President had given the matter considerable thought.

"Good question, Harvey," Grace responded approvingly. "And the answer is clear. If the Chimera agree to leave what remains of the United States alone, we will withdraw our forces from other countries, and allow them to rule the rest of the world unimpeded."

"That's *outrageous*!" Walker interrupted, his face beet red. He stood to address the group. "Such an offer would run counter to what we promised the citizens of the United States—and it would violate mutual defense agreements with more than a dozen governments!

"Not to mention the fact that it wouldn't work. Would the Chimera honor such an agreement? Or would they use it to buy time? I say they'll use it to buy time, and turn on us like the monsters they are!"

Grace remained unperturbed.

"The Secretary of War may be surprised to learn that I agree with him," he said calmly. "Only a fool would trust the Chimera. However, the notion of buying time cuts two ways—because we may need to do so as well. And remember, Henry, the Omega Project is an *option*, not a formal policy statement. So there's no need to get your boxers in a knot."

The comment produced a round of chuckles, just as it was intended to, and Walker took his seat. But nothing in his appearance suggested he was going to let the matter go.

The meeting ended a few minutes later. McCullen approached Walker in an attempt to mollify him, but the Secretary of War was in no mood for compromises. When the Vice President reached out to touch Walker's arm, he jerked it away.

Walker took his hat and raincoat off the rack in the

hallway outside, and made the long walk from the Cabinet Room to the front lobby alone.

There was no one to see Walker off, but had the Secretary of War glanced back over his right shoulder as he stepped out into the rain he would have seen Dentweiler standing inside the press room looking out. He was smoking a cigarette—and the expression on his face was anything but friendly.

But Walker's attention was elsewhere as he entered the back seat of the black town car.

"The office, sir?" the uniformed driver wanted to know. "Or home?"

"Home," Walker said. "And step on it."

Having pulled the recorder out of his pocket, Walker pressed the stop button.

There was a definitive *click* as the recording ended.

Henry Walker and his wife, Myra, had rented the large house near Dupont Circle because neither one of them liked Washington, D.C., nor had any intention of remaining there once Grace left office or Walker was replaced.

But as the town car pulled into the circular drive in front of the three-story building, it was still home—if only for a few more hours.

A servant with an umbrella hurried to open the door, and rain rattled on the taut fabric as the man escorted Walker to the formal entry where a maid stood waiting to take his hat and coat.

"Mrs. Walker is in the library, sir," the young woman said. "Would you like some coffee?"

"Yes, please," Walker replied, and he made his way down the first-floor hallway to the library. It was the one thing that Myra liked most about the house. The pocket doors were halfway open, and she was sitting in her favorite chair next to the bay window. She rose to collect a kiss.

Though well into her fifties Myra was still slender, fit, and pretty. *Too* pretty for a grizzled old warrior like Walker, some said, but Myra was in love with the inner man, and one look at her husband's homely face told her everything she needed to know.

"So nothing has changed? Grace still plans to negotiate with the Chimera?"

Walker scowled.

"He says that the Omega Project is an *option*, not a policy, but that's a crock. Things are going poorly, dearest . . . *Very* poorly. And it's only a matter of time before he tries to contact them. He says we could use the negotiations to buy time. I think Grace has something else in mind."

The maid entered the room at that point, so Myra was forced to wait for her to serve the coffee and go out before she could ask the obvious question.

"You said Grace has something else in mind . . . What would that be?"

Walker took a sip of coffee and put the cup down.

"I don't know for sure, but if I had to guess, I'd say he hopes to cut a deal for himself."

Myra shook her head sadly.

"The rotten bastard. So this is it? We're leaving?"

"Yes," Walker said soberly, "assuming you agree. I have all of it on the recorder. We'll make our way to Chicago and link up with Freedom First. Then, once they broadcast the recordings for the American people to hear, Grace will be forced out of office."

Although the Walkers' hometown of Chicago had been overrun by the Chimera, a few hundred brave men and women still lived there, hiding in basements, sewers, or any other spot they could find. Places from which lightning-fast strikes could be launched against the Chimera, even as uncensored radio broadcasts went out over the airwaves.

Something which, ironically enough, would have been almost impossible to accomplish in government-controlled areas.

So Myra knew that what her husband proposed to do verged on suicidal, but she also knew it was important as well, and she smiled bravely.

"Yes, Henry, of course I agree. All of the preparations have been made. I can be ready in an hour."

He stood and took Myra's hand as she came to her feet.

"I love you," he said.

"Yes," Myra answered softly, as his lips met hers. "I know."

As Walker and his wife left the house they knew they had about eight hours—twelve at most—before they would be missed. Although the couple normally made use of a chauffeur, they had been careful to take outings on their own as well, so the servants would think nothing of it as their employers drove away.

Later, once the truth was known, each staff member would receive a full month's severance pay.

Walker took the wheel of the black Bromley and guided the car out into traffic. Their destination was in the southeast quadrant of the city, but rather than head there directly, he chose a meandering route which provided him the opportunity to make sure they weren't being followed. Not so much by the police, but by members of the Domestic Security Agency, the increasingly aggressive arm of government tasked with identifying dissidents and taking them off the street.

When he was confident that no one was following

them, Walker drove the car to a working-class district where they parked behind a church, then walked the last three blocks to a small one-bedroom apartment that had been rented under a false name. That was where two suitcases were waiting, along with a selection of equipment, all of which would come in handy once they made it to Chicago.

An hour later, with the recorder in one coat pocket and an Army-issue Colt .45 semiautomatic in the other, Walker was ready to go. Myra was right behind him as he carried both suitcases down three flights of shabby stairs and out to the street, where it was still raining. A battered station wagon was parked at the curb. Having loaded the suitcases into the back, Walker opened the passenger-side door, waited for Myra to get in, and circled around to get behind the wheel.

The engine caught on the third try, the wipers slapped from side to side, and a siren could be heard off in the distance. No one was present to see them off, other than the local postman—and he was busy delivering the mail.

After years spent living in a city which neither one of them enjoyed, it felt good to be free. Even if their next home was likely to be a good deal less pleasant.

The car pulled away.

# CHAPTER SIX
# HOME SWEET HOME

Snowflakes continued to swirl down out of the pewter gray sky as Hale stood in front of the mass grave, and paid his last respects to his parents and their ranch hands. Then came the *clang* of metal on metal, which caused him to pivot toward the barn, Rossmore at the ready.

But rather than the sudden burst of gunfire he half expected, the only sounds were the gentle tinkle of the wind chimes hanging from the porch of his childhood home, the rasp of his own breathing, and the steady *crunch, crunch, crunch* of his footsteps as he made his way over to the barn.

There was a yawning black hole where the big doors hung open. Hale entered cautiously, shotgun at the ready, but saw nothing other than what he expected to see. His father's office was located at the near end of the cavernous building, the workshop was next to it, and stalls lined the west wall. Stalls Hale had been responsible for mucking out each day along with all the other chores his father insisted on. He'd been resentful then, but those duties didn't seem so bad now, and Hale would have been glad to return to that carefree time.

The north end of the barn was stacked high with bales

of hay intended to get the family's livestock through the winter.

Hale's father had purchased sheets of steel and laid them just inside the entrance, where they would protect the wooden floor from the wide range of abuses that the entryway would otherwise have suffered. Now, as Hale took a step forward, he saw a hunting knife lying in the middle of the metal ramp.

His head went back and his eyes focused on the half-loft located directly above his father's office. A central walkway led across the rafters to the point where the hay was stacked. All of which had been an indoor play-ground for Susan and himself.

*Is someone up there now, concealed by the darkness?* Yes, Hale thought so, and he felt certain that the knife's owner was human. Because had any of the Chimera been present they would have attacked.

"I know you're here!" Hale shouted. "Come on out . . . I won't hurt you. My name is Hale . . . Lieutenant Nathan Hale. And this is my parents' ranch."

There was a long moment of silence, followed by a vague rustling, and the sound of footsteps somewhere over Hale's head. Then he heard what sounded like a boy's voice. "Don't shoot! We're coming down."

Moments later the end of a rope slapped the steel ramp, and a boy in his late teens slid down, followed quickly by a younger girl. The boy hurried to retrieve the knife—leaving the girl to speak for both of them. She had big brown eyes, a slightly upturned nose, and a wide mouth.

"My name is Tina. That's my brother, Mark . . . He's the one who dropped the knife. I told him not to play with it, but he did."

Hale saw that both youngsters were dressed in multi-ple layers of clothing, and both were armed. The boy had a lightweight Reaper carbine slung across his chest and carried at least half a dozen extra magazines stored in a modified Chimeran battle harness. The girl was wearing some sort of semiauto pistol in a shoulder holster and had what Hale recognized as a sawed-off .410 shotgun as well. The weapon dangled from a lanyard.

"I recognize you," Tina added. "Except for the eyes . . . They look Chimeran."

"You *recognize* me?" Hale inquired incredulously. "Have we met?"

Tina shook her head.

"No, Mark and I are from Pierre. We were going south when a Chimeran fighter strafed the road. Mommy and Daddy were killed, but we got away. That was four— no, wait—five weeks ago, and we've been on our own ever since. The house was empty when we got here, but there were pictures all over the floor. That's how I knew you."

Mark had brown eyes, just like his sister, and the beginnings of a fuzzy beard. Hale noticed that the teen's right index finger was extremely close to the Reaper's trigger as he spoke. The boy followed his gaze.

"No offense, mister," he said skeptically, "but what about your eyes? They don't look right."

"All of the Chimeran forms are the work of a virus," Hale explained. "I was infected while fighting the Chimera in England. That caused my eyes to change color. But I take shots and breathe a special aerosol mist that keeps the virus in check."

Mark still looked skeptical but Tina's thoughts were focused elsewhere.

"Did Susan make it out?" The question had a plaintive quality, as if Tina identified with Susan, and thought that if the older girl had been able to escape, then maybe she could, too.

"I don't know," Hale replied honestly. "I hope so. But we have more immediate things to worry about. I'm going back now. Will you come with me?"

Tina looked at her brother as if to get his blessing, and received a curt nod by way of a response.

"Yes," Tina said, as her eyes swung back to make contact with Hale's. "We've been stuck here for the better part of two weeks now. We made two attempts to leave, but ran into Chimeran patrols both times, and were forced to return."

"That's right," Mark agreed. "We were going to head out last night when a couple of drones came sniffing around."

"That was my fault, I'm afraid," Hale confessed. "I was forced to kill some Chimera on the way in, and they came looking for me. But the search seems to have died down—so maybe we should head out tonight. Before the weather starts to improve."

The youngsters looked at each other, then back again. "Maybe tomorrow," Mark said dubiously. "But not tonight."

"Why not?" Hale wanted to know.

"Because the zombies are coming tonight," Tina answered soberly. "That's what we call them anyway . . . They come through here every four days, and tonight is the night."

Hale frowned. "What do they look like?"

"They look kind of human," Mark replied cautiously. "Only they have eyes like yours. And they always arrive in large groups. They're dangerous," he added, "but not very smart."

Tina nodded. "Maybe that's why we've seen other types of Chimera herding them along."

Hale guessed that what the youngsters referred to as zombies were officially classified as Grims, not that the name mattered if one of the horrors got close enough to attack. Because once a Grim sank its teeth into a victim, it was difficult—if not impossible—to escape. The grotesque, naked horrors had been seen to emerge from Spinner pods, but beyond that very little was known regarding the creatures.

That other Chimeran forms would herd the Grims from one place to another was something new, and would be of interest to Intel. Assuming, of course, that he could figure out a way to tell them without being court-martialed.

"Okay," Hale agreed. "We'll hole up for the night."

He turned to look out through the open doors at the gray skies beyond. It was getting dark, and the temperature was dropping.

"I left my pack under some trees. I'll get it and be back in half an hour."

Mark nodded gravely. "We'll be here."

When Hale returned, Mark and Tina hurried out to brush the tracks away as all three of them backed into the barn.

"Do you have packs?" Hale asked. "And snowshoes? Because you're going to need them."

"Yes we do," Tina answered brightly. "We found a lot of stuff up around Draper. The whole town was deserted."

"And the Reaper?" Hale inquired mildly. "How did you get that?"

"From the Chimera," Mark answered proudly. "We followed one of them to a clearing, saw he was getting ready to butcher a corpse, and shot him in the back. I had a bolt action hunting rifle then—and the bullet went right through him!"

"I shot him, too," Tina added earnestly. "Six times."

"Good for you," Hale said, though he wondered at the enthusiasm with which she spoke. "This would be a good time to gather your things, so we'll be ready in the morning. Just necessities, mind you," he added sternly. "That means one change of clothes, food for three days if you have it, and all your ammo. If we run into trouble I'll expect you to help out." Both youngsters nodded agreeably.

"So where do you sleep? Up in the loft?"

"No," Mark replied. "We found a better place! Come on . . . We'll show you."

He followed Mark toward the huge pile of hay, but he already knew where the youngsters had been sleeping. By removing bales of hay, and taking advantage of tunnels intended to conduct cool air into the center of the pile, Hale and his sister, Susan, had been able to create hidden rooms inside the enormous stack.

And sure enough, after following Mark up some stair-stepped bales of hay, he watched the boy drop his gear down a vertical shaft and follow it down. Tina stood off to one side and aimed a flashlight into the depths as Hale worked his way down through the chimneylike hole, then turned to crawl the length of a horizontal tunnel. The passageway delivered him into a generously sized chamber that had clearly been occupied for some time.

Mark's flashlight provided what illumination there was. Two sleeping bags were laid out on the floor, back-packing gear was piled in one of the corners, and various odds and ends sat perched on ledges and protrusions. Thanks to the insulation provided by the surrounding hay, it was at least ten degrees warmer inside the hide-away. "We can't use lanterns," Mark said as Hale put his weapons down, "for obvious reasons."

Hale nodded silently, and regarded their surroundings

with some concern. As comfortable as it might be, in an emergency it would be very difficult to escape from the refuge quickly. And that could prove fatal.

"Tell me something," he said, as Tina entered the room. "When the Grims come—that's what we call the zombies—do they stop at the ranch, or just keep going?"

"Oh, they stop," Tina answered quickly. "Sometimes they use the hand pump to bring up some water, and sometimes they just walk around."

That was troubling news. Hiding in the cave had been iffy enough, but hiding in the middle of the haystack, knowing that a whole lot of Chimera were going to gather around the barn, seemed nothing short of crazy.

"This place is really nice," Hale said tactfully, "but I think we should sleep somewhere else. Fully dressed and ready to fight, if necessary. It won't be as comfortable, but it will be a lot safer."

"Can I take this?" Tina inquired as she picked up a book and handed it to Hale. "It's really good—but I'm only halfway through it."

Hale took the book and aimed his flashight at the cover. That was when he saw the title *Treasure Island,* and knew it was his. "Yes," he said kindly, "you can. And I agree. It's a wonderful book."

The youngsters packed up after that, and all three of them moved up to the loft, where Hale made use of his father's brace and bit to drill a line of head-high holes in the outside wall. It wasn't the best place to be, not in Hale's opinion, but the light had started to fade by then and he had doubts about finding a better place to hide before darkness fell.

Dinner was cooked over Army fuel tabs in an old metal wash tub, with candles for light, and a jar of Mary Farley's strawberry jam for dessert. Then, with all their gear packed and ready to go, it was time to take turns sleeping on a pile of horse blankets. They smelled to high heaven, but were softer than the wood floor, and provided some much needed insulation.

Hale noticed with admiration that Tina lay with her shotgun nearby, and was still wearing the pistol and shoulder holster as she slid into her bag.

Mark volunteered to take the first watch and Hale agreed, knowing that even if the trip back went flawlessly, he would need all his strength and have all his wits about him.

"They're here."

Hale was awake instantly.

"There's fifty-three of them, if you include the escorts," Mark whispered.

It should have been pitch black, but there was light coming from somewhere, and it was moving. Hale nodded, got up, and tiptoed over to the east wall.

Tina was awake as well, and sat crouched next to her pack.

Conscious of the fact that one or more of the Chimera could be directly beneath him, Hale put his right eye to one of the holes made earlier, and looked out onto a scene that made his skin crawl. There was plenty of illumination, thanks to the Chimeran battle lamps that had been placed here and there, and the shadows they threw loomed large on the snow and the house beyond.

The Grims were lined up in front of the old hand pump, which produced a squeal each time one of them worked the handle. Cold water gushed out of the spout and the Grims drank their fill. They could have eaten snow of course—Lord knows there was plenty of it— but the Chimera did lots of things he didn't understand.

Meanwhile, as the Grims took turns at the pump,

Hale turned his attention to their escorts, and was disturbed by what he saw. Because rather than regular Hybrids, a trio of Steelheads had been sent to herd the Grims along. They were larger than the Chimera Hale had killed the day before, more powerful, and armed with Augers. Weapons capable of firing through concrete walls, never mind wooden ones.

So all Hale could do was stay as quiet as possible, and hope the Grims would leave soon.

The first hint of trouble came when one of the Steelheads raised his Auger and aimed it at the ranch house. But rather than fire at a target, the Chimera swung his weapon from left to right, as if scanning for something.

*Damn.*

Sensors built into each Auger could pick up the least bit of heat, even *through* solid walls. There was no way to know *why* the Chimera had chosen to scan the house—boredom, perhaps, or an abundance of caution. But whatever the reason, Hale felt adrenaline trickle into his bloodstream as the Auger swung around to point directly at him.

"Get ready," he said grimly, as he backed away from the peephole. "They're onto us. They could shoot through the walls, but I'm hoping they'll come inside, so I can drop a grenade into their laps. So stay back . . . The key is to keep the Grims off the platform.

"Mark, you defend the walkway . . . Tina, you take the top of the ladder. I'll work the gaps. And remember what the Chimera did to your parents. Shoot to kill. Understand?"

It was too dark to see their expressions, nor was there time for a reply as two Steelheads stormed into the barn and opened fire. Bolts of lethal radiation hit the wood flooring, accelerated through it, and went on to punch holes in the roof.

Having readied a hand grenade, Hale pulled the pin and tossed the explosive over the side. There was a flash of light as the grenade went off, followed by a resonant *boom* and at least one scream as razor-sharp shrapnel flew in every direction. A piece of metal hit the floor near Hale's right boot, tore a hole in it, and continued on to bury itself in a rafter.

He felt certain that at least one of the Steelheads was down—but what about the others? It was risky to peer over the side, but he did so anyway, just as a Grim entered the barn holding a Chimeran battle lantern high.

Thanks to the sudden spill of light Hale could see that *two* Steelheads were down, but there was no time to celebrate as more Auger projectiles stuttered through the walls. Some of the bolts missed Hale by a matter of inches as he threw himself backward.

Mark and Tina were flat on the platform, but they didn't seem to have been injured.

A follow-up shot by the remaining Steelhead outside might have been successful at that point, but more than a dozen Grims had entered the barn by then, and the Hybrid had no way to know who it was shooting at. So the incoming fire stopped.

The battle *inside* the barn was just getting started at that point however, as three Grims succeeded in scaling the mountain of hay bales, and began to cross the walkway that led directly to the loft. Consistent with Hale's orders Mark was there to meet them, and as he fired short bursts from his Reaper, the first Grim staggered and crashed into the rail. It shattered, allowing the body to fall to the floor below, where *more* of the shambling creatures were looking for a way up.

Meanwhile, twenty feet away, there was a muted *boom* as a Grim made it to the top of the wooden ladder and Tina fired her shotgun. Though not as powerful as a Rossmore, the smaller-gauge .410 was deadly at close range and blew the top of the Grim's head off. A bloody mist rained down on the creatures below as battle lanterns threw grotesque shadows onto the west wall, and the air was filled with a cacophony of inarticulate growls.

Hale was pleased to note that the youngsters were holding their own, so far at least, but then another problem presented itself. Even though they weren't very bright, the Grims were active, and those not already on the walkway or the ladder came swarming up the walls! As with most barns, the studs and crossbeams were fully exposed on the inside, and that was all the purchase the Grims needed.

So Hale shouted, "Grenade!" and dropped another bomb onto the floor below. The explosion knocked most of the creatures loose from their handholds, then it was time to go to work with the Rossmore. The shotgun made regular *boom, clack, boom* sounds as double-ought buck tore into the Grims still climbing the east wall and dumped what remained of their bodies into the charnel house below.

That was when Hale heard a scream, and turned to discover that, having been unable to reload her shotgun quickly enough, Tina was in trouble. Having successfully gained the platform, one of the horrors had wrapped its scabrous arms around the girl, and lifted her off the floor. Hale couldn't fire without hitting Tina, so he lurched forward, knowing he wouldn't arrive in time.

The Grim opened its jaws wide.

That was when Tina surprised both the Grim and Hale as she pulled the Browning Hi-Power 9mm semi-auto pistol out of its shoulder holster and pressed the muzzle against the monster's lumpy skull. The Browning jumped in her hand, and a long rope of bloody goo shot out from the other side of the Grim's head and splashed the floor beyond.

Tina landed on her feet as the Chimera released her, and had the presence of mind to shoot a *second* Grim in the stomach. But it wasn't enough, as even more of the blood-crazed horrors flooded onto the platform.

Hale was at Tina's side by then, blasting the ferocious Grims to bloody bits. Empty shotgun shells arced through the air, bounced off the floor, and rolled off the platform. There was no time in which to think or feel. All Hale could do was fire, reload, and fire again, in a desperate attempt to stem the grotesque tide.

Then, as if by magic, it was over. The last of the creatures was dispatched, and the only sounds that could be heard were a liquid gurgling noise as a badly wounded Grim choked on its own blood, and the repetitive *snick, snick, snick* as Hale fed shells into the shotgun.

"We did it!" Mark proclaimed jubilantly, as he slid a fresh magazine into the Reaper. "We killed them all!"

"Don't count on it," Hale replied darkly. "There were *three* Steelheads, and as far as we know, one of them is still on the loose. Grab your packs . . . We're getting out of here."

Then as if to confirm Hale's assessment, an air-fuel grenade came flying into the barn, landed ten feet away from the haystack, and went off with a loud *whump!* Hale and the two youngsters were outside the immediate blast zone, but the explosion set fire to the hay, and it went up quickly. Air-fuel grenades had been invented by humans, but just as humans made effective use of Chimeran weapons, the reverse was true as well. Hale theorized that the surviving Steelhead was planning to drive the humans out of the barn and silhouette them against the flames.

"Come on," Hale said, having shouldered his pack. "Follow me." Mark and Tina obeyed as Hale half slid down the ladder to the floor below. The fire was spreading, and the heat was intense.

Auger rounds began to probe the inside of the barn.

"Over there!" Hale shouted, as he pointed to the east wall. Having stopped by his father's workshop long enough to snatch a sledgehammer off its hooks, Hale hurried over to where Mark and Tina were waiting. There was a loud *bang* as the first blow made contact with the wall. The key was to land each blow squarely between neighboring studs, and the weight of the pack, snowshoes, and Fareye made that difficult, but after three solid hits a section of siding gave way. That was progress, but not enough, as Hale put the sledgehammer down in order to kick at the loose boards.

"Mark!" Tina shouted. "Behind you!"

Hale turned and saw that one of the Grims was on fire. Whether it had been wounded previously, or was simply lurking in a corner at the moment when the air-fuel mixture detonated, didn't really matter. What mattered was that the fiery apparition was just six feet away, and staggering forward with arms spread wide.

Mark shot the Grim repeatedly, but the monstrosity kept on coming. Hale was about to fire on it when the Steelhead who was lurking outside unknowingly put an Auger projectile into the Grim. That knocked the monster off its feet, and the fire crackled noisily as all six of its eyeballs began to boil. Its heels drummed against the floor, then stopped abruptly.

The Sentinel turned his attention back to the wall.

"There!" he exclaimed as a hole finally appeared in front of him. Peering through it, he saw no sign of the Steelhead, and judging from its last shot, Hale figured it was on the opposite side of the barn. "Tina, you first, then Mark."

There was no need to tell the youngsters to hurry as the stack of hay collapsed, flames clawed at the walls, and the roof caught fire. The moment Mark disappeared Hale entered the hole, swore when one of his snowshoes got caught, and had to wrestle it loose.

Then they were free, as the entire barn was engulfed in flames. Thankfully, it was snowing again, which would help conceal their tracks, but Hale knew that wouldn't prevent the Steelhead from following them. The Chimera was close, *too* close, and would have to be dealt with before the threesome could make their way south.

So Hale ran, breaking a trail for the others as they passed along the west side of the house and crossed the parking area beyond. There was plenty of light, thanks to the brightly burning barn and the battle lamps, which were still in place. Hale rounded the propane tank and angled up the slope beyond. Once on top of the low-lying hill he shrugged his pack off and motioned for the others to get down.

Having positioned the pack for use as a gun rest, Hale laid the Fareye across it and lowered himself into place. With his eye to the scope, Hale waited for the Steelhead to appear and it didn't take long. Less than thirty seconds later the hulking stink rounded the northwest corner of the house and began to follow the human tracks south. That was to be expected, but what Hale *wasn't* expecting were the three Grims who trailed along behind. He'd have to bag the 'brid *and* the Grims.

So Hale settled on a plan, smiled grimly as the Chimera crossed the parking lot, and put the Fareye's crosshairs on the very center of his target. Then, as the Steelhead passed the propane tank, Hale fired. The high-velocity armor-piercing bullet passed through the tank and caused a spark. That was sufficient to trigger a flash of light, a rising ball of flame, and a loud explosion.

There were no bodies to be seen in the wake of the massive blast, just a large circle of blackened ground, and a cloud of hot steam.

"That was awesome!" Mark said admiringly. "What's next?"

"One helluva long walk," Hale answered, as he stood up. "It's time to put your snowshoes on."

Ten minutes later the threesome were ready to hit the trail.

The barn's roof had collapsed by then, sending thousands of glowing sparks up into the air. Some of them fell onto the house and set it on fire as well. Hale was standing there, watching his childhood home start to burn, when Tina took his free hand.

"I'm sorry," she said simply. "But we're still alive—and we have you to thank for that."

Hale turned to look down at her solemn face. "Let's get going."

It was pitch black once they put the house and barn behind them, and like it or not Hale and his companions were forced to use their flashlights. Thanks to the thickly falling snow they weren't likely to be seen unless they had the bad fortune to pass within fifty feet of their pursuers.

As they slogged along, Hale assessed what lay ahead, and how to deal with it. The most pressing problem was time, because if they hadn't reached the LZ when Purvis put the *Party Girl* down, the pilot would be forced to leave them behind. If that happened, could they make it all the way back to Valentine, Nebraska? Maybe, but the odds were against it.

Then there was the bridge across the White River to consider. Even more stinks would be standing guard on the span, in the wake of the first attack, and given the time constraint, Hale couldn't afford to try one of the bridges up- or downriver. So what to do?

Bit by bit a plan came to mind. A *crazy* plan, but one that might catch the Chimera by surprise, and enable Hale and his charges to cross the first span.

Old Man Potter had been something of a recluse, especially after his wife's death, which was when Hale had gotten to know him. Potter's ten-acre spread lay just south of the Rocking F, and years earlier, while out riding his horse and searching for strays, an eighteen-year-old Nathan Hale had come across the old man lying unconscious at the bottom of a ravine, right next to the wreckage of the old Triumph motorcycle.

Potter had loved that bike.

Hale brought him around with water from his canteen, lifted him onto Blacky, and led the horse two miles east to Potter's old farmhouse. The old man was more of a dreamer than a doer, always coming up with wild new business schemes, none of which bore fruit. His house was surrounded by the brooding remains of possibilities that had passed him by.

The collection included a rusting grader which was part of Potter Paving, a snow-shrouded drilling rig that had once been the pride and joy of the Potter Well Company, and a fifty-two-foot fishing boat the old man planned to haul cross-country to Seattle, where it would become the flagship of the Potter Fishing Company.

And the broken dreams were still there, sleeping under a blanket of snow, as Hale and his two companions approached the ramshackle house. It was growing lighter by then, the snowfall had slowed, and it felt significantly warmer. All bad signs insofar as they were concerned, but what was—*was*, so all Hale could do was keep a sharp eye out for tracks in the snow, and hope for the best.

"Potter's Junkyard," as the locals called it, wasn't harboring any Chimera, not unless you counted the five skulls arranged directly in front of the house, each sitting atop its own carefully planted pole. Each trophy wore a cap of white and an extra eye socket, where a bullet had passed through—tributes to Potter's stalking skills and his prowess with the Mauser bolt action rifle he treasured so highly. It was a weapon that employed the high-powered 6.5 × 68mm Von Hofe Express cartridges favored by German hunters in the Alps.

"Wow," Mark said, as he examined the skulls. "That was good shooting."

"Yes," Hale agreed soberly, "it was. Even though it was my dad who taught me how to shoot, Mr. Potter took my education to the next level. He didn't believe in scopes, he thought semiautos were for sissies, and when he went deer hunting he took *one* bullet with him."

"So where is he?" Tina inquired pragmatically, as she looked around.

"I have no idea," Hale replied. "Dead most likely. He was like my parents, like a lot of folks around here, which is to say stubborn. So when the Chimera came, chances are he fought them. Five lives for one . . . That isn't bad."

"So what are we going to do?" Mark wanted to know. "Hide here?"

Hale shook his head.

"No, we have a plane to catch, and about eight hours to reach the landing zone. What we're looking for is a ride." He glanced around, then turned toward them again. "Wait here and keep your eyes peeled. I'll be back in a minute."

Hale's boots produced a hollow sound as he made his way up onto the porch, opened the door, and entered Potter's living room. And that's where the old man was, rifle across his lap, sitting in a rocking chair. He was dead of course, and had been for weeks, judging from the condition of his mummylike corpse. A few hanks of white hair still hung from his leathery scalp, his eyes were gone, and his tobacco-stained teeth were bared in a permanent grin. Potter's bib overalls were intact however, as were his lace-up boots, which could be seen below a length of bright bone. Surprisingly there were no signs of violence, leading Hale to suppose that Potter had died of natural causes, while sitting in his shabby parlor waiting for the Chimera to come. Hale nodded respectfully as he circled the chair and went back to the 1920s-style kitchen. The homemade key rack was hanging right next to the back door. Would the vehicle Hale had in mind start? There was no way to know for sure, but he took the keys to the Lyon dump truck, and passed out through the living room.

Out front, Mark and Tina were eating oatmeal patties they had fried up the evening before.

"Come on," Hale said, "let's see if we're going to walk or ride."

It had been years since Hale had been back to visit Potter, but he wasn't surprised to find the truck where he'd last seen it, parked next to the old man's rickety workshop. The outlines of the vehicle were plain to see in spite of the snow, including the Lyon's considerable bulk, the flat two-panel windshield, the softly rounded cab, and the chromed lion that stood on the hood with one paw lifted as if in mid-step.

Would the engine start? Although Potter wasn't much

of a housekeeper, he had always been meticulous as far as his machines were concerned, even going so far as to fire up the fishing boat's diesel on a regular basis. So there was reason to hope as Hale circled the snow-encrusted rig and confirmed that all of the truck's six tires were inflated.

With that established he put a foot on the driver's-side running board, opened the door, and climbed into the cab. The flat bench-style seat squeaked under his weight as he pushed the clutch all the way to the floor, checked to make sure the stick shift was in neutral, and turned the key.

The starter produced a weak *ur-ur-ur* sound, but nothing happened. The battery was low, the engine was cold, and Hale could feel his hopes starting to slip away.

"Come on, baby," he muttered. "Do it for Mr. Potter."

The starter produced the same *ur-ur-ur* sound, followed by a loud *bang* that caused Hale to jump. Then came a friendly rattle as all six cylinders began to fire.

"That's right!" Hale said exultantly, as he revved the engine. "I *knew* you could do it."

The fuel gauge was down to a quarter-tank, so the next fifteen minutes were spent searching for gas, and then pouring it in. Hale let the engine run throughout the process fearing that the Lyon would refuse to start a second time.

The cab was far too small for three people and their gear, so they put most of their equipment in back, and kept only weapons and ammo up front. Hale placed both the Fareye and the Rossmore in the bed of the truck and used some cord to tie everything down.

Finally with the sawed-off .410 shotgun lying across his lap, Tina sitting astride the gear shift, and Mark on the passenger side, they were ready to go. He shifted into low, let the clutch out, and stepped on the gas. The engine roared, ugly black smoke belched out of the Lyon's twin stacks, and the dump truck began to roll.

Heat was pouring into the cab by that time and the snow had stopped. Frank Sinatra was singing "April in Paris" as Mark turned the AM radio on, and a familiar voice was heard as the song came to an end.

"Hello, fellow citizens, this is Jack Peavy, welcoming you to the *Jack Peavy News Hour.*" The announcer's voice was deep and resonant, and he spoke with the authority of a man who knew things other people didn't.

"Contrary to information put out by the so-called Freedom First party," Peavy said, "we have reports that the Army is battling the Chimera in South Dakota, and has recently won a major engagement near Rapid City. Once the hard-fought battle was over, thousands of enemy bodies lay on the bloodied snow . . ."

"That's bullshit!" Mark exclaimed, as he clicked the broadcast off. "Do you see any god-damned soldiers here?"

"Lieutenant Hale is here," Tina replied tartly, "and Mom doesn't like it when you swear."

"Mom's dead," Mark replied bleakly. "Hell, just about everybody's dead, so far as I can tell, and Peavy is lying."

Peavy *was* lying, or that's how it appeared to Hale, as he downshifted and caressed the brake, careful not to put the truck into a skid. The main road lay just ahead, and judging from the way it looked, it was heavily used. With his heart beating faster, he made a right-hand turn onto the pavement. They were committed at that point, because the bridge was only two miles away, and there was nowhere else to go.

He upshifted, put his foot down, and upshifted again. Within minutes the truck was doing its top speed of sixty and rattling like a can full of marbles as it charged down the middle of the road and threw waves of slush to both sides.

They were approaching the bridge when a Chimeran Stalker lurched out onto the road ahead of him, repositioned its turretlike body, and fired on the truck. Hale was familiar with the big crablike machines, having piloted one in the past. So he knew how dangerous they could be.

His eyes narrowed as a steady stream of machine gun projectiles kicked up geysers of dirt and snow. Fortunately, the gunner hadn't latched on to them yet, as Tina covered both eyes. Was there enough room? Yes, Hale thought there was, and proceeded to bet all their lives as he swerved to the right, then left again.

The Chimeran pilot attempted to respond, but the dump truck was more agile than it was, and managed to swerve around the mech, before it could be repositioned. Machine gun bullets followed the truck south, but the pilot couldn't fire missiles without hitting the bridge *and* the guards that had been positioned to defend it.

Metal barriers had been erected at the north end of the span and two automatic weapons were half-hidden behind piles of sandbags on both sides of the road. The gun on the left began to fire, quickly followed by the one on the right, as the truck barreled toward them.

"Pull the pin!" Hale ordered, and Mark obeyed. The passenger-side window was already down, so all the teenager had to do was keep a firm grip on the safety lever, or "spoon," while waiting for the right moment.

Projectiles made a persistent *pinging* noise as they hit the truck, the windshields shattered—front and back— as a projectile passed between Hale and Tina, and the Lyon hesitated slightly as it hit the barricade and smashed it aside. That was when Mark stuck his arm through the window and let go of the grenade. It hit the ground, bounced high into the air, and exploded. Shrapnel cut down one of the stinks as it sought to swivel its machine gun around.

The truck itself slammed into another Hybrid and killed it instantly. Hale heard a soft *thump* and knew that at least one Chimera had dropped from the superstructure above to land on the roof. Seconds later a skeletal hand shot through the already shattered rear window and caught hold of Tina's hair. She screamed and tried to pull away. That was Hale's cue to reach forward and pull on the red knob that protruded from the dashboard.

The Hybrid let go of Tina's hair when the dump box began to tilt upward, thereby exposing it to fire from behind. The stink's body jerked spastically as it took multiple hits before being dumped out onto the bridge deck where it rolled away.

With the box in the raised position, the cab was protected from behind. Bullets ricocheted away as they hit solid steel. One of the rear duals was flat by then, but with five tires left there was no stopping the truck as it began to close with the barrier at the south end of the bridge.

The disadvantage of having the box raised was that the truck's speed was cut in half, and Hale was busy downshifting when a stink jumped up onto the driver's-side running board. The Chimera roared angrily as it tried to stick its head in through the open window. Hale could taste the creature's foul breath as he let out the clutch, stomped on the gas, and brought the .410 level with the window.

There was a satisfying *boom* as the tightly focused cone of birdshot blew half of the Hybrid's face away. The three eyes on the other half registered what might have been surprise as the horror fell away, hit one of the upright supports, and broke in two.

Tina accepted the shotgun and hurried to reload it as Mark fired the Reaper out the passenger-side window. A 'brid standing on the other side of the barricade fell, and the big bumper hit the metal obstruction and sent pieces of steel flying through the air. That cut even more Chimera down.

Hale knew it was going to be necessary to abandon the truck and hike cross-country, so he wanted to reduce the number of Chimera who could follow them. With that in mind he braked, shifted into reverse, and backed onto the bridge again, killing two more stinks in the process.

He shifted into low, lowered the box, and drove forward until it was time to stop the Lyon and bail out. Missiles were landing all around. The Stalker was too large to cross the span from the north, but the pilot still could lob missiles over the bridge.

As columns of dirty snow shot into the air and pattered down all around them, the trio went around to the back of the truck and scrambled up into the dump box. At least half of the gear had fallen out during the crossing, including both Hale's pack and the Fareye. Fortunately the Rossmore and all three sets of snowshoes were still lashed to the bottom of the box. "Grab your snowshoes," Hale shouted as another missile hit nearby, "and follow me!"

Having secured the shotgun and his snowshoes, Hale led the others up the hillside toward the jumble of now familiar rocks. Once they passed over the crest, they were out of range and there was nothing the Stalker could do but pace back and forth and lob rockets at the truck. The Lyon took a direct hit, exploded into a ball of flame, and sent a pillar of black smoke up toward the gray sky.

Ten minutes later Hale and his companions had their snowshoes on and were slip-sliding cross-country in a desperate attempt to reach the landing zone in time. The detour to the Potter homestead had consumed valuable time, and now they were paying for it.

The warmer temperature was causing the snow to melt, but it was still too deep to abandon the snowshoes. Despite the hard going, Hale was suddenly grateful for the snow, when they paused on a rise to look back. Three Hybrids, summoned from Lord knows where, could be seen half a mile back, but lacking snowshoes, the stinks were struggling.

One of the 'brids paused to fire an ineffectual shot from his assault rifle, causing Hale to yearn for the missing Fareye. All three of the Chimera would have been easy meat for it. "Come on," he said grimly. "We'll outwalk the bastards."

But as the next couple of hours came off the clock, the youngsters began to slow, and the Hybrids were catching up. That meant it was no longer a choice of whether to fight, but of *where* to fight, and Hale tried to remember a pile of rocks, a cluster of trees, or a ravine where they could lie in wait for the pursuers.

It was no good. That section of the gently rolling prairie was almost featureless. Or so it seemed until Hale spotted a dark smudge in the distance.

"We're going to ambush the stinks," Hale announced confidently. "Come on, Mark . . . Let's help Tina. We need to hurry."

The lead Hybrid paused at the top of a slight rise, saw the snow-frosted corpse laid out on the ground ahead, and wondered who or what had been able to bring the big form down. But it was a passing thought, because like all 'brids the Chimera lived in the eternal now, it being left to higher forms to contemplate the past and plan for the future. His task was to catch up with the humans, kill them, and eat his fill.

The tracks led past the Titan and over the next rise, indicating that the humans were still on the move, but they were slowing. It wouldn't be long before he and his fellows would be able to savor the coppery taste of human blood. So he waved the others forward, and led them past the horribly ravaged corpse, confident that the chase was about to end.


"Now!" Hale yelled. He and Mark burst from within the hollowed-out corpse already firing, Hale with the Rossmore and Mark with the Reaper. The stinks never had a chance.

Tina had gone ahead, thereby creating a fresh set of tracks that led over the next rise, where she had strict orders to stay out of sight.

The stinks tried to turn, tried to defend themselves, but a hail of close-range projectiles tore them apart. Blood sprayed the snow beyond the Hybrids as they jerked this way and that before collapsing in heaps.

Hale started to reload, discovered that he was out of shotgun ammo, and scrambled up and out of the Titan's abdomen. A Bullseye lay next to its previous owner.

"Come on," he said cheerfully as he bent to retrieve the weapon. "We're almost there." They moved to rejoin Tina.

And forty-five minutes later they *were* there when the drone of engines was heard, and the *Party Girl* settled into the soft snow. Two minutes later Hale lifted Tina up into the cargo compartment, climbed in beside her, and turned to give Mark a helping hand.

"Congratulations," he said as the hatch began to close. "And welcome to what's left of the United States of America."

Having convinced Purvis to drop the three of them outside Valentine, Nebraska, Hale was determined to make sure that Mark and Tina would have a place to stay before returning to the SRPA base. The so-called Protection Camps were somewhat controversial because, even though hundreds of thousands of people had decided to enter them, an equal number of people had refused on philosophical grounds, or because they didn't want to subject themselves to the strict, almost military-like discipline required of the internees.

Like all members of the military, Hale was used to strict discipline, and thought of the Freedom First people as whiners. Still, as the delivery truck paused a quarter-mile short of the main gate to let them jump down, he had to admit that the razor wire fences, and the evenly spaced watchtowers, looked a lot like the prisons he'd seen.

Nevertheless there was a long line of people waiting to get in, some pushing wheelbarrows stacked high with belongings, while others wore packs or carried suitcases. Unfortunately many of those in line had nothing more than the clothes on their backs. Babies cried, dogs barked, and old folks looked grim as they waited for the queue to jerk forward.

Eventually, after an hour or so, Hale and his companions drew even with a uniformed guard who confiscated the children's weapons, and would have taken Hale's as well, if the Sentinel hadn't opened his parka to reveal his uniform.

Mark hated to part company with the Reaper but there was nothing he could do about it.

There was a good deal of wailing at the next checkpoint, where people were forced to surrender their pets, all of which were taken away to be euthanized.

Finally, having been allowed to enter the camp's processing center, Hale, Mark, and Tina were shunted into another line intended for orphans. And there were hundreds of them, most of whom were unaccompanied, and trying to help one another as best they could.

The sight of it brought a lump to the back of Hale's throat as a matronly-looking woman welcomed Mark and Tina to the facility, gave them prepacked bags filled with toiletries, and took down their information. She smiled brightly in spite of the fact that the people standing in front of her smelled to high heaven.

"Don't worry, Lieutenant . . . they'll be well cared for. They'll have to be separated, of course, since we can't have boys and girls living in the same dormitory, but I can assure you that they will receive three square meals a day, good medical care, and be back in school on Monday!"

Neither of the teens looked very happy, but there was nothing any of them could do, so Hale shook hands with Mark and gave Tina an awkward hug. His smile was forced.

"Take care of yourselves, you two . . ."

Mark gave a jerky nod, and Tina wiped a tear away. Then they watched Hale leave.

Once outside the processing center he saw a square that was obviously used for ceremonial purposes, and beyond that some of the hundreds of identical six-story wooden buildings, all thrown up over the last year or so. Everything was neat as a pin, but there was something depressing about the place, as Hale followed a neatly kept path toward the main gate. A guard nodded politely. "Good afternoon, Lieutenant . . . Have a nice day."

It was too late for that, but as Hale exited the camp, the sun appeared. The warmth felt good on his face—and there was a hot shower to look forward to. And, all things considered, that was as much as Hale could reasonably hope for.

Now if only he could stay out of prison.

# CHAPTER SEVEN
# THINGS THAT GO BOOM!

**Near Valentine, Nebraska**
**Friday, November 23, 1951**

"Report to my office at 0900 hours 11/23/51." Signed, "Maj. Richard Blake."

The message was waiting in Hale's SRPAnet inbox when he returned to Base 027 and went online. The meeting could be about anything of course, but the brevity of it and Hale's guilty conscience combined to make him uneasy.

Blake's office was located on the admin deck a few doors down from the briefing room in which the officer spent so much of his time. His door was open, and Hale could see him sitting within, but knew better than to enter without an invitation. His knuckles made a rapping sound as he knocked three times.

"Come."

As Hale took the prescribed three steps forward, he could feel the tension in the air. His boots thumped as he came to attention, his eyes were fixed on the wall over Blake's head, his back was ramrod straight, and his thumbs were aligned with the seams on his carefully pressed trousers. "Lieutenant Hale, reporting as ordered, *sir*!"

There was a series of rapid clicking sounds as Blake completed an email message and hit send. Then he swiveled his chair around to face Hale and made eye contact. It was like looking down a couple of gun barrels. No "At ease," or invitation to have a seat.

"Well," Blake said flatly, "how was your three-day pass? Did you have fun?"

Hale's mouth felt dry, so he did what he could to muster some saliva, and then swallowed. All he could do was let the situation play itself out.

"Sir, yes, sir."

"That's good," Blake growled. "That's *real* good . . . Because your little vacation cost a great deal of money. First there's a full load of Avgas for the VTOL you rode in, then there's the Fareye you took with you, but failed to return, plus three grenades and various other pieces of government property. All of which are going to be deducted from your pay. Do you read me, Lieutenant?"

Hale's eyes remained focused on the spot directly above Blake's head.

"Sir! Yes, sir."

"I guess you think we're *stupid,*" Blake continued. "And maybe your plan would have worked, except I sent people to find you, and guess what? You weren't in your quarters, and you hadn't checked out through the main gate, which meant you had left some other way. Aboard the *Party Girl* as it happens."

Blake paused, and made a point of taking a document from a stack of papers and studying it silently. "By the way, Hale," he added ominously, "you might find it interesting to know that Lieutenant Purvis will be flying every shit detail his CO can come up with for the next thirty days. So you might want to avoid him. I don't imagine he'll be pleased." He returned the document to its stack.

"Now," Blake continued, as he leaned back in his chair, "enough about Purvis . . . Let's talk about *you.* I could have your bars, but court-martials involve a lot of paperwork, and I *hate* paperwork. And why bother? Because I have a rather challenging mission lined up for you—and the odds are you won't make it back. That will save me a lot of aggravation. So be in the briefing room at 1100 hours, and see if you can avoid getting lost along the way."

"Sir, yes, sir," Hale responded, his face wooden.

Blake nodded. "Dismissed."

Hale did a neat about-face, took two steps, and was almost out the door.

"And Hale . . ."

Hale paused to look back. "Sir?"

There was something like sympathy in the major's eyes. "I'm sorry about your family."

Hale nodded. "Thank you, sir. They were good people."

And with that he left.


The briefing room was packed when Hale arrived at 1050 hours. A sure sign that something big was in the offing. Senior officers and SRPA officials were seated toward the front of the rectangular room leaving captains, lieutenants, and half a dozen NCOs to find chairs farther back. Which was fine with Hale.

All the doughnuts were gone, but there was plenty of coffee, so Hale filled a mug and took it back to a seat located between a portly supply officer and a square-jawed sergeant major. Both could see his nametag—not to mention the color of his eyes.

Hale was worried that he might have to make conversation with one or both of the men, but he was granted a reprieve when Blake called the meeting to order.

"Good morning . . . And welcome to Operation Iron

Fist. We've been taking a lot of shit from the Chimera lately, and this will be an opportunity to hit back.

"Iron Fist will be a combined forces operation involving the 5th Ranger Battalion, under Lieutenant Colonel Jack Hawkins"—he nodded in the direction of a man in the front row—"and a Sentinel SAR team, under the command of Lieutenant Nathan Hale." He acknowledged Hale with a similar gesture. "Besides killing as many freaks as we can, the objective of this little outing will be to locate and retrieve what could be some very important tech."

Hale felt a combination of pride, embarrassment, and fear. The sergeant major grinned knowingly. "The good news is you'll be in command of a team," he whispered. "And the bad news is that you'll be in command of a team!"

Hale smiled. That was the strange thing about being an officer. The simultaneous desire to be in command and the fear of what might happen as a result of a lack of preparation, poor judgment, or bad luck.

"Before we review the details of the mission, Dr. Linda Barrie will provide you with some important background information," Blake continued. "For those of you who haven't met her, Dr. Barrie is a graduate of MIT and a member of SRPA's technology assessment team. They're the folks who study the items the SAR teams bring back, assess their potential, and tell us how to exploit them. Dr. Barrie?"

Barrie was one of only three women in the room, which by itself was enough to make her stand out, but the fact that she was stunningly beautiful guaranteed that every eye was on her as she took the podium. Her black hair was short and straight, her brown eyes were partially hidden by bangs, and her lips displayed only a trace of red lipstick. She wore a plain leather jacket and khaki pants that couldn't be considered glamorous. She cleared her throat and began to speak.

"Thank you, Major. As a result of missions like the one Captain Anton Nash led a few days ago, SRPA has been able to reverse-engineer technology developed by the Chimera, and make incredible advances in a relatively short period of time. And now, because of an artifact recovered by Captain Nash and his men, we have what may be an opportunity to take another leap forward."

At that point Barrie removed a remote from the podium and aimed it at the wall screen. Video swirled and locked up into an image that Hale recognized right away. Thousands of lights glittered deep within the gelatinous cube, and as the camera zoomed in, Hale could see tiny sparks jumping the gaps between them. *It wasn't doing that before,* he mused silently. *They must have figured out how to turn it on . . .*

"Beautiful, isn't it?" Barrie inquired of no one in particular. "But this is beauty with a purpose. What you're looking at is an optical computer . . . Meaning that it uses photons rather than electrons to store and manipulate information. We're still in the process of figuring out how to replicate it, but we've been able to retrieve a great deal of data from it, and screen that information for importance.

"The best way to think of the cube is as a filing cabinet," Barrie added, as she turned back toward the audience. "And, like most filing cabinets, it's stuffed with all manner of things, some of which are useful and some of which are not. One of the items that *is* of value could be described as a fuel inventory. And by fuel I don't mean gasoline." She leaned forward for emphasis.

"I mean *nuclear* fuel, like the plutonium that was recovered from Great Britain and taken to our research facility in New Mexico. Unfortunately, we haven't been able to get the necessary yields out of the plutonium, and at the rate things are going, it could be years before we have nuclear weapons that can be used against the Chimera."

That comment elicited a rumble of conversation because if there was one thing the men and women in the briefing room knew, it was that the United States was running out of time.

Barrie nodded, and continued. "According to the fuel inventory we've deciphered, the stinks are storing nuclear fuel in a recently completed base near the town of Hot Springs, South Dakota. So we're going to attack in force, draw most of the defenders into a pitched battle, and send a SAR team in to snatch what we need. Once the people in New Mexico have a chance to analyze it, there's a very good chance that they'll be able to achieve the necessary breakthrough, and produce the nuclear weaponry we need.

"I guess that's about it," she concluded. "Thank you."

As Barrie returned to her seat, Hale already was thinking about the mission ahead. Nash had been correct, the storage cube *was* important, and Hale wished that he had lived long enough to learn *how* important.

The familiar emptiness began to form in the pit of his stomach as he considered the coming battle. Clearly, the 5th Ranger Battalion would have a major role to play, but it would be up to his team to recover the fuel, and that—Hale realized—made him understand what he and Nash had in common.

A fear of failure.

Operation Iron Fist was going to involve nearly two thousand people, including support personnel, all of whom had to be pre-positioned, equipped for the mission at hand, and in some cases trained for specific tasks. So once the larger briefing was complete, the participants were directed to various conference rooms where topics such as logistics, matériel, and tactics would be discussed.

Hale was directed to a door with a "Command" placard on it.

Once inside, he saw that dozens of aerial photos had been taped to one wall while a detailed map of South Dakota took up most of another. As a former NCO only recently promoted to second lieutenant, he found himself nervous at being included in a meeting attended by the likes of Lieutenant Colonel Hawkins, his XO, Major Murphy, and a half-dozen other people, including Dr. Barrie. The glasses had disappeared for the moment, and as the two of them shook hands he was struck by how serene her eyes were. When Barrie smiled, Hale saw that a gap separated her two front teeth. A tiny imperfection that was endearing somehow—although he wasn't sure why.

"It's a pleasure to meet you, Lieutenant," Barrie said coolly. "Shouldn't you give my hand back?"

"Sorry," he mumbled as he let go, and hurried to escape as Major Blake brought another officer over to meet the scientist.

Having made a fool of himself, Hale was glad to take his place at the long conference table, only to discover that the same sergeant major was seated next to him.

"The name's Guthrie, sir," the noncom said genially. "It's nice to know that the SAR team will be led by a Ranger. Even if he is wearing a funny-looking uniform."

Hale laughed, and felt better now that he had a sergeant to protect his right flank. The two of them continued to chat until the meeting began.

"Time to get down to business," Blake said from the head of the table. "Now that all of you are aware of the general outlines of what we're going to do, it's time to review the specifics. Colonel Hawkins . . ."

Hawkins was tall and lanky, so when he stood it took a while, and two steps were sufficient to carry him to the map. He had a collapsible pointer which made a series of clicking sounds when he extended it. Hawkins had brown hair that was starting to gray, a deeply lined face, and an eternally downturned mouth.

"We're here," he said brusquely, as the end of the pointer tapped the town of Valentine, Nebraska. "And the assembly point will be here."

Hale followed the pointer to Chadron, Nebraska, which looked to be forty or fifty miles south of Hot Springs, South Dakota. "The plan calls for us to send a tank company north along the main highway," Hawkins continued. "They will be supported by Lynx All-Purpose Vehicles, and by two infantry companies.

"That should bring most of the freaks out of the woodwork. Then, as they stream south to meet us, we'll engage them from the east and west using troops dropped into position by VTOLs. And that's when the fist will close," he said grimly. "With any luck at all, we'll kill at least a thousand of the bastards."

Although Hawkins was technically senior to Blake, the Sentinel officer was part of the SRPA leadership team, which was responsible for the SAR aspect of the operation. So no one thought it strange when Blake spoke approvingly. "I think all of you will agree that it's a good plan," he said, "and one that's likely to catch the stinks by surprise."

"However, as important as the conventional part of the operation may be," Blake added tactfully, "the primary reason for pulling the enemy forces south is so that

Dr. Barrie and Lieutenant Hale will be able to successfully penetrate the Chimera base near Hot Springs. And more than that, to find a fuel cell, and bring it out. Dr. Barrie?"

Hale was startled to discover that the civilian would accompany the SAR team, and the announcement set off alarm bells he needed to squelch. Having accompanied Captain Nash to the crash site on Bear Butte, he knew why Barrie was being sent. Still, the prospect of entering a heavily defended Chimeran complex with a female civilian in tow didn't sit well.

Barrie was on her feet, glasses back in place, standing next to the montage of aerial photos. "This is the complex where the fuel is stored," she said evenly, and pointed her pen at a cluster of cylindrical constructs, all viewed from above. "These pictures were taken by the pilot of a specially equipped Sabre Jet on a clear day *before* we made the find on Bear Butte. So things may have changed a bit since then. The complex was built to exploit energy from a geothermal tap. It's fed to a standard tower over *here*—and from that location to a hub tower located near Rapid City."

Having dealt with the system of Chimeran towers in England, Hale knew that they were often located near sources of geothermal energy, and were used to funnel the power to larger hub towers via physical conduits. Where, if scientists were correct, the energy was used to cool the Earth's atmosphere, and for some other purpose that was still being studied.

"The tower complex near Hot Springs has another function as well," she said. "The structure next to the geothermal tap, and adjacent to a building about which we have very little information, is almost certainly used to store nuclear fuel. Because only thirty feet of the facility extends aboveground, we assume that most of the fuel cores are located deep below, where they are safe from air attacks." Then she paused. "Any questions so far?"

There was a brief moment of silence before Hale raised his hand. "Yes, ma'am . . . I notice that there appear to be four small structures positioned on those roofs. What are they?"

"You have a good eye," Barrie said, as she touched each of the tiny blocks with the tip of her pen. "Those are antiaircraft weapons. Some fire missiles, others fire explosive projectiles, and all of them are dangerous."

Hale didn't like the sound of that. Not if he and his team were slated to arrive in a VTOL. But rather than voice his misgivings then and there, he decided to hold back and give the matter some thought.

The meeting—which was to be the first of many— came to an end shortly thereafter. Lieutenant Colonel Hawkins, Major Murphy, and Sergeant Major Guthrie left the room in order of rank. And as Hale rose to follow them, Barrie appeared at his side. The glasses had disappeared again. "Lieutenant Hale, do you have a moment?"

"Sure," Hale replied. "What can I do for you?"

"You frowned when Blake announced that I'll be coming with you," Barrie said seriously. "You're unhappy with that decision, aren't you?"

Hale shrugged.

"No offense, Doctor, but it would help if you were a soldier."

Barrie's brown eyes locked with Hale's yellow ones. "Like Captain Nash?"

"Yes," Hale answered honestly. "Like Captain Nash."

"You were with him when he was killed?"

"Yes," Hale replied soberly. "I was there."

"And he died bravely?"

It was a strange question, or so it seemed to Hale, and his eyebrows rose.

"Yes, *very* bravely."

"That would have pleased him," Barrie said evenly.

"I suppose it would," Hale agreed. "Why do you ask?"

"We were engaged," Barrie answered simply. "Don't worry, Lieutenant . . . I may be female, and I may be a civilian, but I'm not helpless."

And with that she was gone.

# CHAPTER EIGHT
# A FAMILIAR FACE

Denver, Colorado
Monday, November 26, 1951

After three days of on-again, off-again snow, the clouds had finally been blown away by a wind out of the west, and bright sunlight was streaming through the top portion of the tall narrow window on the east side of Cassie Aklin's bedroom.

The sun hit Cassie in the face, and when she tried to open her eyes, it forced her to close them again. She brought one hand up to block the light as the other fumbled for the alarm clock. A quick peek confirmed what Cassie suspected. It was only 7:10, and she wasn't due to get up until 7:30.

But there wasn't any point in going back to sleep for such a short period of time, and the prospect of feeling the sun on her face as she walked to work made her want to get up. So Cassie turned off the alarm, swung her feet over the side of the bed, and began the process of getting ready for another day.

Cassie shared the tiny one-bedroom apartment with a woman two years older, who was in charge of the clerks working the night shift at the Denver Federal Center. So the twin bed next to hers was empty as Cassie showered, put on her makeup, and got dressed. As a psychologist employed by the Army and assigned to support SRPA, it was important to look professional.

So even though Cassie would have preferred to wear something more casual, she chose a dark blue suit from the three hanging in the closet. The jacket ended at her waist, and the long, slightly flared skirt fell below her knees. A crisp white blouse, plus some hard-to-find hose, completed the outfit. A pair of black high heels went into her leather briefcase and would replace her galoshes once she arrived in the office.

Breakfast consisted of tea, made from a bag that had been used twice before, and two pieces of toast smeared with a tiny bit of butter and some strawberry jam. Due to persistent food shortages the scrambled eggs and bacon she had once enjoyed almost every morning were a special treat now, and would constitute a good dinner if she could afford them. All of which seemed to run counter to what Secretary of Agriculture Seymore had said on the radio the day before.

He had referred to the shortages as "temporary allocation problems," then "seasonal commodity anomalies," and finally "transitory market fluctuations." Not that it mattered much since the result was the same.

Cassie finished her second piece of toast and chased it down with the last of the weak tea, before washing the dishes and putting them in the rack to dry. Then it was time to put on her overcoat, slip her feet into a pair of galoshes, and pick up her purse and briefcase as she passed the table in the hall.

Locking the door behind her she made her way down two flights of stairs, through the small lobby and out the front door. It was only a few blocks from the apartment house located on Virginia Avenue to the sprawling Denver Federal Center where she worked. There was still a lot of snow on the ground, but stretches had been shoveled, making it easier to walk.

Even though it was a residential neighborhood, subtle signs of the war and its effects could be seen all around. Both sides of the street were lined with cars because, as people had been displaced from the northern states, many came south to stay with family or friends, filling Denver to the bursting point. Renters like herself added to the pressure, which left thousands with no choice but to enter one of the hastily constructed Protection Camps, or make a place for themselves in the shacklands in and around Aurora to the east.

Reports from the shacklands painted the picture of a slum where people built shelters out of anything they could buy, salvage, or steal, and raw sewage ran through open ditches while people were forced to burn anything they could find for heat. Food was scarce, and medical care was nonexistent. The situation had led to a restriction intended to force as many people as possible into the Protection Camps.

Other signs of the war's impact could be seen in the snow-covered vegetable gardens that had been planted on the parking strip, the gold stars displayed in the windows of families that had lost a father, son, or brother in the fighting, and the American flags that hung limply from porches, drooped from poles, and were tied bannerlike between houses.

In order to reach the Center, as employees referred to it, Cassie had to cross Alameda Avenue. It was busy as usual—and she had to wait for a fifteen-vehicle military convoy to pass before she could hurry over. The two-and-a-half-ton six-by-six trucks threw waves of slush to both sides as they rolled by. The last five were open, with warmly dressed soldiers sitting in back, and some of them whistled.

Cassie waved as the convoy pulled away.

There was a great deal of construction going on beyond the center's twelve-foot-high, six-foot-thick outer walls. Defensive towers had been erected at the corners and midpoint along each stretch of wall. They bristled with weapons, and at night there were high-powered rotating spotlights that the civilian neighbors hated.

Dozens of buildings made up the Federal Center, and she had even heard that a top secret facility was under construction at the very heart of the complex. There were lots of theories about what the new building would be used for, but those who knew weren't talking, and guards had been posted to keep the curious away.

Regardless of the reason, hammering, sawing, and other construction-related din could be heard around the clock.

There were a number of gates, and because all the guards knew her, Cassie was permitted to enter with little more than a wave of her ID card. The Center employed hundreds of women, but they were outnumbered ten to one by the men, so Cassie drew some admiring looks as she made her way to what was called Central Hospital. It was much more than that, however, since it also housed the medical facilities required to support the burgeoning Sentinel program.

She belonged to a team of civilian psychologists who were paid to make sure all the Sentinels remained mentally stable—a task made all the more difficult by the fact that the soldiers were prone to medical issues associated with the inhibitor shots. Most were struggling to cope with combat-related stress, and were entirely cut off from their families—all of whom believed them to be dead.

Having passed all the checkpoints, Cassie approached her building. The brick and masonry structure had an art deco sensibility about it. Metal-clad doors opened into a large lobby with mural-covered walls and a wraparound reception desk with a stern-faced matron behind it. She sat under three clocks, each of which was associated with a different city. It was 12:00 in New York, 10:00 in Denver, and 9:00 in San Francisco.

Cassie breezed past the desk, followed a hallway to a bank of sleek-looking elevators, and was in her cozy third-floor office five minutes later. It was barely large enough for two people, but it was all hers, and a haven of privacy.

Her first client was already seated in her guest chair, and his name was Sergeant Marvin Kawecki.

Hale hated the Denver Federal Center, the hospital, and everything that went with it. Especially since the trip to Denver required him to leave the base where the preparations for Operation Iron Fist were well underway. But, as Major Blake pointed out, it was a good idea to get an inhibitor shot prior to going out on a major mission, and sitting down with one of the shrinks was part of the process.

The spinal injection was old hat by that time, and given the number of Sentinels in town to receive it, the procedure was rather impersonal as well. Just like everything else the military did. One by one the soldiers were taken into an operating room where they were ordered to strip to the waist. They sat on a metal stool while a nurse painted a wide swath of cold antibacterial solution over the injection site.

Then a balding doctor plopped himself down on a stool and injected small amounts of a local anesthetic into the area around the site. Moments later, having checked to make sure that the area was numb, he removed a 10cc syringe from a Mayo stand and positioned the needle between the L-4 and the L-5 vertebrae. As the needle went in, a fluoroscope allowed the doctor to monitor his progress via a black-and-white screen.

"Hold still," the doctor admonished gruffly as he depressed the plunger, "or you'll be sorry."

Hale felt the pressure as the inhibitor was injected into his body, and was glad when the needle was removed. A nurse gave him a list of possible side effects, which the Sentinel wadded up into a ball and threw into a trash can on the way out. He'd experienced many of the symptoms in the past, and survived them. That was all he needed to know.

With the shot out of the way it was time to head up to the third floor for his interview with Dr. Alan McKenzie, an elflike man who was forever peppering Hale with questions about his childhood, interpersonal relationships, and sexual fantasies. Much of which Hale made up as he went along, thereby causing McKenzie to emit puffs of cherry-flavored smoke from his pipe, as he scribbled notes in a spiral-bound notebook.

The elevator doors parted and Hale stepped out into the hall, only to see someone he knew standing among those waiting to board. It had been a long time since Project Abraham and the first experimental inoculations, but the sight of Cassie Aklin's face brought memories rushing back. The sterile environment, the interviews, and something more. A physical attraction most certainly, but another connection as well, and one he hadn't experienced before. And certainly missed.

Cassie's expression brightened.

"Nathan? It *is* you! I saw Sergeant Kawecki earlier this morning and he said you were here. I was about to go down to the clinic to see if I could find you."

Hale smiled and reached out to take both of her hands in his.

"Cassie . . . This is a surprise! And a pleasant one. You look wonderful."

Hale looked tired, and a bit worn, but Cassie didn't want to say that, so she lied. "So do you!" she said brightly.

Hale glanced at his watch.

"I'm supposed to see Dr. McKenzie in a few minutes . . . Is there any chance that you're free for lunch?"

"I was hoping you'd ask," she replied, "and I am. I'll meet you at the Alameda Diner . . . It's two blocks east of the Center on Alameda." She looked left and right. No one else was close enough to hear. "And Nathan . . ."

"Yes?"

"I'd rather you didn't mention our lunch to Dr. McKenzie."

Hale grinned.

"What lunch?" And then he was gone.

Hale left the Denver Federal Center via the gate that led to Alameda and took a left. A corporal saluted him, he returned the courtesy, and sidestepped a puddle of snowmelt. By keeping his answers short—and thereby giving Dr. McKenzie very little to work with—Hale had managed to escape the hospital in record time. It had been a while since he had spent time with a woman, never mind such an attractive one, and he was looking forward to the lunch with Cassie.

The truth was that Hale had mixed emotions about the psychologist. He was attracted to her, and had been from the beginning, but he had never been sure of how she felt about him. She had been decidedly cool toward him during Project Abraham. But had that been a matter of professionalism? Or a signal for him to back off?

He had never been sure.

Then there was the fact that she had a Ph.D. in psychology, while he merely had a high school diploma, which raised the question of whether he would be biting off more than he could chew where Cassie was concerned. Still, she had clearly been eager to see him, and that was worth something. Wasn't it?

Hale spotted the diner up ahead. It looked like what it was—a railroad dining car that had been taken out of service, refurbished for use as a small restaurant, and plopped down next to Alameda Avenue. Judging from the number of cars in the parking lot, the eatery was quite popular.

Hale followed a man wearing a business suit inside, where he looked for Cassie, but didn't see her. So as a couple got up to leave, Hale took possession of their window booth and a harried-looking waitress arrived to bus the dishes. "Sorry, soldier," she said. "I'll clear this stuff away and come back for your order."

About five minutes passed, and Hale was beginning to wonder if he'd been stood up when he looked out the window and saw Cassie hurrying up the street. She saw him, waved, and entered the restaurant a minute later. She was pretty, so lots of men took notice, but once they'd seen her most turned back to their meals.

"I'm sorry," Cassie said apologetically, as she allowed him to take her overcoat. "My boss walked into my office just as I was trying to leave."

"I understand," Hale assured her. "You're a busy lady."

They chatted for a few minutes, Hale about life with his fellow Sentinels, Cassie about her tiny apartment and roommate, and the waitress brought their menus. When she walked away, Hale turned to face Cassie and asked something he had been wondering about. "So did they send you to Denver? Or did you request it?"

"The latter," she replied. "I have trouble staying in one place for very long—and I was tired of Alaska."

"Maybe you should see a psychologist about that," he suggested dryly.

She had short blond hair, direct eyes, and full lips that broke into a wry smile. When she laughed it had a full-throated sound.

"If you're suggesting that I have a problem with commitment, you're probably correct . . ." She paused, then said, "They make a really good chocolate shake here if you're interested."

Hale was, and when the waitress returned both of them ordered cheeseburgers, fries, and chocolate shakes. All of which cost 30 percent more than six months earlier.

"You're a lieutenant now," Cassie said brightly as their orders went in. "Congratulations."

"Thank you," Hale replied. "I'm still getting used to it. After complaining about officers for years, it's weird to be one."

"Well, it appears as if you're good at it, or at least so I'm told," Cassie responded. "And who would know better than your men?"

It hadn't occurred to him that Cassie might have been assigned to monitor the psychological well-being of some of his subordinates, and Hale wondered if it was proper for her to talk about it that way. Not only that, but he felt embarrassed at the compliment, and looked away. "Yeah, well, I've been lucky so far."

She must have seen his discomfort, because she changed the subject. The next forty-five minutes passed quickly, as their food arrived and they discussed a wide range of topics, including the war, the economy, and the latest Bob Hope–Bing Crosby movie: *Road to Rangoon*.

He hadn't seen it, but she had, and said it was very funny.

Then, having paid the bill, the couple suddenly found themselves outside. "I'll walk you back," Hale said.

"Thank you," Cassie replied, "but I don't think that would be a very good idea."

Hale's eyebrows rose.

"It isn't? Why not?"

Cassie looked down, then up again. "The truth is that I probably shouldn't be spending time with you. You're seeing McKenzie now, and you and I had a clinical relationship during Project Abraham, so any sort of outside relationship might be considered unethical."

"Which means we can't see each other again?"

"No," Cassie replied evenly, as a wisp of vapor drifted away from her mouth. "It means we shouldn't see each other as long as we're both working for SRPA."

Hale grinned. "Okay, problem solved," he announced. "I quit! Now, will you go to dinner with me?"

She didn't laugh, as he had hoped she would, and she was silent for a moment. He realized then that he had no idea what was going through her head. Finally, she spoke.

"When do you have to return to Nebraska?"

"Thirty of us came down together," Hale replied. "We were told to report to Stapleton by 0300. Knowing how long some of them have been waiting for a drink, I imagine the MPs will deliver at least half of them to the airport."

"Then it's clearly my duty to save you from a similar fate," Cassie said, as she removed a small notebook from her purse and scribbled on one of the pages. "So rather than go out—let's eat in. Here's my address . . . Dinner will be at seven. My roommate will have left for work by then."

Hale felt a sense of elation, but tried not to show it as he accepted the scrap of paper. He didn't want to screw this up.

"What can I bring?"

"Bring yourself," she replied as she glanced at her watch. "Yikes! Sorry, I have to run! See you at seven."

Hale watched her walk away, thought about how lucky he was, and turned in the opposite direction.

There was a bus stop one block east and on the other side of Alameda. He had an afternoon to kill—and a mission to accomplish.

The administrator watched as the couple left the diner, spoke with each other, and parted company. The lunch wasn't a big deal, not really, but it was currency of a sort. The kind of deposit which, when combined with similar payments, would eventually add up to a promotion.

The thought made him feel cheerful as he left the diner, tucked the *Post* under his arm, and returned to work. The world might be going to hell in a handcart, but his life was good.

It was necessary to transfer once before arriving in downtown Denver—and both of the electric trolleys were crowded. So Hale stood, as did most of the men aboard, allowing women and elderly people to sit. Based on information gleaned from the driver, he knew that the Customs House was located on Broadway, and that the trolley would stop across the street from it. So he was ready as the trolley came to a halt.

"Customs House, post office, and main business district," the driver intoned. "Please watch your step."

The bi-fold doors opened, Hale took two steps down, and hurried to get out of the way so that other people could board. Having cleared the back end of the trolley, he could see the Customs House on the far side of the street. It consisted of two matching five-story buildings, divided by a long, gently sloping flight of stairs that led into the courtyard between them. And, much to Hale's surprise, a long line of people stretched from the inner courtyard out onto Broadway, where it turned the corner and ran down 19th Avenue.

There was no way to tell what the people were lined up to do, and based on how diverse they were, it was impossible to guess.

He went down to the corner, waited for the light to change, and crossed the street. A whalelike blimp could be seen in the distance, propellers turning slowly as it patrolled the western suburbs. A staff sergeant stood in front of the Customs House. He had a round face and his cheeks were a ruddy red. The noncom saluted as Hale approached. If he was curious about the officer's golden yellow eyes, he managed to hide it.

"Good afternoon, sir . . . Can I help you?"

"Yes," Hale replied, having returned the salute. "I was hoping to visit the Bureau of Displaced Persons. Could you tell me where it is?"

"It's at the other end of that line," the sergeant replied, as he jerked a thumb back over his shoulder. "It seems like everybody's looking for somebody," he added soberly.

That was true. And he was one of them. Now that Hale knew Susan had survived the attack on the Rocking F Ranch, he was hoping to find her. According to the newspapers he'd read, a central registry had been established by the Department of the Interior's Bureau of Displaced Persons. The problem was that there were millions of people to keep track of—many of whom were suspicious of the government-run program. In fact, the group called Freedom First had gone so far as to suggest that rather than trying to help family members find each other, the registry was simply one more effort by the Grace administration to strip the population of its freedoms.

Hale had no way to evaluate the truth of that allegation, but he was determined to find out if Susan was alive. "Yeah," Hale said as he glanced at the line, then back again. "I guess there are a lot of folks in that position. I'm looking for my sister."

"I hope you find her, sir," the noncom said, and he sounded sincere. "I'll have Private Yano take you to the head of the line."

Hale shook his head.

"No, that wouldn't be fair. I'll wait like everybody else."

"Okay, sir," the noncom replied doubtfully. "But you might want to bleed your tanks first."

It was good advice, so Hale entered the Customs House via another door and paid a visit to the men's room before returning outside. After following the line all the way around the corner onto 19th and down the block, he fell in behind a woman in a tattered overcoat. He stuck his hands into the pockets of his overcoat to keep them warm.

As they began to notice him, those around Hale peppered him with questions about the fighting, as if expecting everyone in uniform to know everything that was going on. Some of them had been listening to broadcasters like Peavy, and believed that the Chimera were on the run, while others had been tuning in to clandestine broadcasts by Radio Free Chicago, which was operated by Freedom First. They held the opinion that the stinks had crossed into Nebraska, and were pushing south.

Hale tried to set the record straight as best he could without revealing anything he shouldn't, but he soon discovered that both groups were wedded to their beliefs, and unwilling to budge.

He had now been there for a couple of hours. Time passed slowly, and the line moved ahead in a series of spasmodic jerks, as a steady trickle of people were processed at the other end. The air grew steadily colder as the sun fell toward the mountains. After another hour and a half or so, a pair of women pushed a cart along the line. It was loaded with a big urn, and as the two handed out cups of hot coffee, they did what they could to cheer people up. Hale wanted to pay, but one of the women shook her head, and smiled.

"It's what we can do, Lieutenant. I hope you find the person you're looking for."

But if the line attracted nice people, it attracted others as well, including all manner of salesmen, beggars, and fanatics. At one point a wild-eyed man waving a Bible walked the length of it. "Listen to me!" he demanded loudly while bits of spittle flew from his purplish lips. "The truth about President Grace can be found in Revelation 13:9–10: 'If any man have an ear, let him hear. He that leadeth into captivity shall go into captivity: he that killeth with the sword must be killed with the sword!' "

The man might have said more—no doubt *would* have said more—if three men in plainclothes hadn't arrived to take him away. Which was good riddance in so far as Hale was concerned. He was inside the courtyard by that time, and glad that he wouldn't have to depart prematurely to keep his date with Cassie.

Fifteen minutes later the main line split into three shorter lines, each of which led to a wooden table with a computer terminal sitting on top of it. The man waiting to greet him wore a tag with the name Crowley on it. He had dark hair, a badly rumpled white shirt, and a potbelly. The light from the screen made his face glow. He didn't bother to look up. "Name?"

"My name is, Hale . . . Nathan Hale."

"Not *your* name," Crowley replied irritably. "The name of the person you're looking for."

"Oh," Hale said. "That would be Susan Farley. That's spelled F-A-R-L-E-Y."

The keyboard rattled as Crowley entered the name. His eyes blinked as words appeared. "I have five of them . . . You got a birthday?"

"March 7, 1920."

"Nope," Crowley replied. "Not even close. Next!"

"Wait a minute," Hale objected. "She's from South Dakota. Do you have any Susan Farleys from South Dakota?"

"Yes, I do," Crowley answered insolently. "But she's sixty-three years old. Now step out of the line, or I'll call security."

So after waiting for more than five hours, Hale was forced to leave the Customs House empty-handed. It appeared that either Susan had been killed during the trip south from the ranch, or had chosen to keep her name off the national registry, which wouldn't be surprising, given the Farley family's fierce sense of independence.

It was dark as Hale made his way to a southbound trolley stop, and joined the crowd there. He had slightly less than an hour in which to reach Cassie's place, but figured he could make it as long as the trolleys were running on time and he was able to board the first one to come along.

Fortunately, they *were* running on time, and he was able to board the first one, which put him back at the Federal Center with fifteen minutes to spare. Just enough time in which to stop at a neighborhood store and buy a bottle of wine, since flowers weren't available. Then with a cold wind nipping at his face he followed the grocer's directions over to Virginia Avenue and Cassie's apartment house.

As Hale entered the lobby he was nervous. Because no matter what he told himself, he knew Cassie was smarter than he was, and it would be easy for him to make a fool of himself. So with a sense of dread he climbed a flight of stairs and knocked on her door.

There was the *click* of high heels on hardwood, followed by a momentary rattle as she turned the knob and opened the door. Suddenly all of Hale's fears melted away when she smiled and planted a kiss on his cheek.

"Nathan! Please come in."

She was wearing pearls, a black cocktail dress, and matching heels. It was an elegant yet sexy look that took Hale's breath away. Ella Fitzgerald could be heard singing "How High the Moon" in the background as Cassie took Hale's overcoat, thanked him for the bottle of wine, and preceded him into a cozy living room that was lit by a standing lamp and half a dozen candles.

"Thank you for the wine—that's very sweet of you," she said. "How 'bout a drink? We can open the bottle, or I can offer you a bourbon on the rocks, a gin and tonic, or a screwdriver. Amazingly enough they had orange juice at the market."

"I'll take the bourbon," Hale replied as he looked around. Although the furnishings weren't fancy, a good deal of thought had gone into the way they were arranged, and there was very little clutter. "I like your apartment."

"It is nice, isn't it?" Cassie said brightly, as she went over to the side table where a selection of glasses and bottles stood. "It's very difficult to find a place to live here in Denver, so I was lucky to hook up with Vicki. She's my roommate. Please, have a seat. Your drink will be ready in a minute. We're having pot roast by the way. I hope that's okay . . . I went looking for steaks, but they didn't have any. That's how it is in stores now. You take what you can get."

"I love pot roast," Hale said truthfully, "and I haven't had any in years."

"I like it, too," she agreed as she brought his drink over. "Although it takes quite a while to cook. That gives us time to talk though." She sat next to him on the sofa. "So, what did you do with your afternoon?"

Hale took a sip of his drink and told Cassie about the line, the people he'd met, and his failure to learn anything regarding Susan's fate. That led him to the trip back to the ranch, what he had discovered there, and the journey with Tina and Mark. They were on their second drink when a slow dance by the Ink Spots came on the radio.

Cassie stood and held out her hands. "You're a nice man, Nathan," she said as he put his drink down. "A lot of people would have left those children to fend for themselves. Now, come here . . . I want to dance."

Dancing of any kind was at the top of the list of things that terrified Hale the most, but the opportunity to hold her in his arms was too good to pass up. So he got up from the chair and took her hands.

Moments later he was somewhere else, lost in the fragrance she wore, and the softness of her body. His feet moved, but not very much, as the two of them swayed to the music. Hale nuzzled Cassie's hair, reveled in the soap-smell of her, and held her close.

Then, when Cassie looked up into Hale's golden yellow eyes, it was as if an unspoken agreement had been reached. He kissed her, her lips melted beneath his, her hands came up to caress the nape of his neck, and their bodies seemed to meld.

At some point the dancing stopped, as hands explored, and important discoveries were made.

"*Please,*" Cassie whispered into Hale's ear, "please."

Hale swept Cassie off her feet, carried her into the bedroom, and was about to lay her on a single bed when she said, "No, Nathan . . . The other one."

Which bed made no difference to Hale, who lowered her onto the white bedspread, and took up where he'd left off. Women's clothes—especially evening clothes— were something of a mystery to him, and it was necessary for Cassie to help from time to time. But the process was very enjoyable, and by the time the black dress lay on the floor, Hale was half-naked himself.

"You aren't my first," Cassie said softly. "But it's been a long time."

Hale understood and kissed her concerns away as he removed the last of her clothing. Then he paused to look at her. The only light in the room came from candles, and one half of her face was in flickering shadow as she peered back. Her coral-tipped breasts were small but pert. He reached out and drew a line between them down to her belly button. She smiled dreamily.

"Do you like what you see?"

Hale answered the question with a series of kisses that wandered from place to place until Cassie's breathing quickened and her fingers began to fumble with his belt buckle. Then it was Hale's turn to help as he stood long enough to get rid of the uniform trousers before taking his place between Cassie's long slender legs.

The bed was too narrow for them to lie side by side, but that was fine with Hale as Cassie's hand found him and pulled him in. It had been a long time for *both* of them, so Hale was careful to take his time, nudging his way into her wet warmth, their mutual passion building. Cassie made little sounds in the back of her throat and wrapped her legs around his torso as she urged him on.

"I want you, *all* of you," she growled softly as the age-old rhythm began to build. Then they were there, climbing to the very peak of passion, before falling into an ocean of pleasure.

The intensity of the moment was beyond anything Hale had experienced before, and once it was over, Cassie continued to shudder beneath him. Then she began to cry.

That was a development Hale wasn't prepared for and he felt a wave of concern.

"Cassie? What's wrong?"

"Nothing's wrong," Cassie replied softly, as her chest heaved. "Women cry for all sorts of reasons."

"Oh," Hale replied. "I understand."

But he didn't, not really, and he was glad when the crying stopped. They lay there for a while, happily entwined in each other's arms, as the afterglow gradually faded away. Then came a shower, which they chose to take together, and it might have led back into the bedroom, had there been more time.

After toweling herself off, Cassie threw on a terry-cloth robe, and went into the kitchen. The candlelit dinner was consumed at the kitchen table. Hale had thrown on an olive drab tank top and his uniform trousers, but his feet were bare. The wine was good, the pot roast and vegetables were delicious, and he thought it was the best meal he had ever been lucky enough to eat.

But time passed quickly, and suddenly it was 0200 hours, which left Hale with only an hour to summon a cab, and make the trip to the airport. Both of them did what they could to keep the conversation light as Cassie put in a call for a taxi and Hale finished dressing.

Fifteen minutes later the cab was waiting in the street below, Hale was kissing Cassie goodbye, and the magical evening was over.

"I'll come back as soon as I can," Hale promised as he looked into her eyes.

Cassie smiled, or tried to, as she straightened his tie. "I'll be here."

But both of them knew that nothing was certain, that everything was in doubt, and that the evening together might well be the only such time they would ever have. Cassie stood at the window and watched as Hale went out the front door and entered the spill of light from a nearby streetlight. He turned to wave.

Then he was inside the taxi, it was pulling away, and Cassie was alone.

"I'm sorry, Nathan," Cassie said, as she thought about what had been done to him. And *was* being done to him. "So very, very sorry."

Cassie went to bed after that—and sought to lose herself in sleep.

But when the sun rose, and sent streamers of light down into the bedroom, Cassie was still awake.

# CHAPTER NINE
# ROLLING THUNDER

The skies were clear, and a cold wind was blowing in off the Atlantic, as President Grace's Chief of Staff, William Dentweiler, climbed the narrow stairs that led to a small one-bedroom apartment on the third floor of a nondescript apartment building.

An FBI agent was there to greet him. His name was Milt Wasowitz. He wore a gray snap-brim fedora, a dark blue trench coat, and a pair of very shiny shoes. He had heavy brows, a broad face, and pendant jowls. The two men had been working together for the better part of a week by then, and were on a first-name basis.

"Morning, Bill," Wasowitz said cheerfully. "You look like hell warmed over."

Dentweiler winced. "And I feel worse than I look. Older women can be extremely demanding, Milt. They know what they want, and won't give up until they get it."

Wasowitz smiled sympathetically. "I'll have to take your word for that, Bill. Maggie and I have five kids, and by the time I get home, the only thing she wants is a back rub and a glass of wine."

Both men laughed as they entered the apartment. It was furnished with pieces of mismatched furniture, and bereft of personal photos, knickknacks, and personal items. Dentweiler had seen hotel rooms with more personality.

"This is how you found it?" he inquired.

"That's correct," Wasowitz acknowledged. "It was clean as a whistle. There wasn't so much as an empty beer bottle in the trash."

"Fingerprints?"

The FBI agent nodded. "Plenty of them . . . Most of which belonged to Secretary Walker and his wife. The rest were a match to the building manager, the maintenance man, and previous tenants."

Dentweiler nodded thoughtfully. Originally, when the Walkers were reported missing, everyone assumed that the couple had been kidnapped. But without a ransom note, speculation turned to the possibility of a double homicide, or a murder-suicide, as an all-points bulletin went out to street cops everywhere.

Then, as the investigation continued and photographs of the couple appeared in the papers, a man reported that a woman who looked a lot like Mrs. Walker had purchased a used station wagon from him. Except that she gave a different name, paid for the car with cash, and was tight-lipped about her plans.

As more details emerged, the likelihood arose that the power couple had fled Washington voluntarily. A possibility that was of considerable concern inside the Grace administration, due to Walker's knowledge of and his opposition to Project Omega. If Walker went public with his allegations, it would feed the flames of public discontent already being fanned by Freedom First.

All of which explained why Dentweiler had been ordered to work with authorities to find out what had taken place, and report back to President Grace. The secret hideaway was the latest piece of a larger puzzle.

"So they took off," Dentweiler concluded as he polished his glasses with a white handkerchief.

"That's the way it looks," Wasowitz agreed soberly. "We have an APB out for the car . . . But no luck so far."

"Okay," Dentweiler replied, settling the glasses over his ears. "But if you find the station wagon and/or the Walkers I want to hear about it immediately. And no leaks to the press. Understood?"

"Understood," Wasowitz replied solemnly.

"Good," Dentweiler said as he turned toward the door. Then he turned back.

"And Milt . . . When you go home tonight, try taking some flowers with you. Who knows? You might get lucky."

President Grace didn't like the British ambassador, and never had. Mostly because Lord Winther was an aristocrat and Grace didn't trust aristocrats. So as Grace circled his desk to greet the diplomat, he had what his staffers referred to as "the number one smile" firmly in place.

"Ambassador Winther," he said warmly, "it's a pleasure to see you! Please, have a seat . . . Some tea perhaps? I know how Englishmen love their tea."

Winther was an austere-looking man, with gray hair that was parted in the middle, wintry blue eyes, and a carriage reminiscent of the Army officer he had once been. He was wearing a three-piece Savile Row suit, complete with a restrained bow tie and a gold watch chain that formed the letter V across a flat stomach.

"Thank you, Mr. President," Winther replied gravely. "A cup of tea would be nice."

The two men were joined by members of their staffs, including Secretary of State Moody for the Americans, and Canadian Ambassador Pimm on behalf of the beleaguered Commonwealth. A world-spanning organization which was more imaginary than real in the wake of so many Chimeran victories.

The first fifteen minutes of the meeting were spent on tea, pastries from the White House kitchen, and small talk. Then Winther launched into what was clearly a carefully rehearsed plea. The essence of which was that rather than have the allies remain on the defensive, the British government hoped to interest the Americans in a joint task force which would attack Chimeran assets in Canada before the aliens could settle in there. Then, if successful, the effort could be extended to England and beyond.

It was a good idea, or might have been years earlier, before the death of 150 million people in Russia, 450 million in Europe, and untold millions in Asia. But like many governments around the world, the United States had been slow to react to the Chimeran menace, and the British plan was no longer realistic.

It was something Winther and Pimm already knew, deep down. Grace could see it in their eyes. So he heard them out, promised to give their proposal serious consideration, and was grateful when the pair left.

Grace's secretary had an office that adjoined his, and once the visitors were gone, and Moody with them, Dentweiler entered from there. Grace was back behind his desk by that time and nodded as his Chief of Staff appeared.

"Good afternoon, Bill. What were you up to last night? You look tired."

"I had to work late," Dentweiler lied smoothly. "How did it go with Ambassador Winther?"

Grace made a face. "I can't stand the man, but I still feel sorry for him. And the other displaced diplomats as well. The city's full of them. How about you? Any progress on the Walker thing?"

Two guest chairs were positioned in front of the antique desk, which was made of timbers from the British vessel *Resolute*. Dentweiler chose the seat to the right. "Yes, Mr. President, I have. Based on all the available evidence, it's clear that Walker and his wife left voluntarily. And given the way they went about it, I think it's safe to assume that they mean us harm."

"*Damn* the man!" Grace said as he brought his fist down hard onto the surface of the desk. A photo of Mrs. Grace jumped and fell flat, and Dentweiler could see the anger in his eyes. "What will Walker do?" the chief executive demanded.

Dentweiler shrugged. "I suspect he's been in touch with the Freedom First people, who will be eager to take him in. Walker is from Chicago, and Freedom First's radio broadcasts originate there, so that's a likely destination. Once he arrives, my bet is that he'll be on the air fifteen minutes later."

"But Chicago is occupied by the Chimera," Grace objected.

"True," Dentweiler agreed, "but that's where the Freedom Firsters get their credibility. They live underground, in basements and sewers, and come up to fight. The stinks have made repeated efforts to root them out, and so far they've failed to do so."

Grace looked thoughtful. "Even if Walker goes on the air, so what? No one would believe him . . . Especially after we accuse him of treason."

"Unless Walker has something we don't know about," Dentweiler put in. "Detailed notes from the cabinet meetings, perhaps. That might be credible enough to do some real harm."

"Then we need to stop Walker *before* he can reach Chicago," Grace said darkly.

"He's got a healthy head start," Dentweiler cautioned.

"Then what are you waiting for?" Grace wanted to know. "Get ahold of the FBI, the Domestic Security Agency, and all branches of the military. Put them to work. I want Walker arrested, and failing that, I want him dead! Do I make myself clear?"

Light glinted off Dentweiler's glasses as he nodded.

"Yes, Mr. President. *Very* clear."

"Good," Grace said, as he came to his feet. "My schedule says we're due at the Lincoln Memorial in half an hour—and you know how I feel about punctuality."

The Lincoln Memorial was intended to resemble a Greek temple, and thanks to tons of Yule marble and thirty-six Doric columns, it succeeded. That—plus the brooding presence of the statue within—made it a favorite with tourists and politicians alike. And now, after a million-dollar-plus renovation, President Grace himself stopped by to inspect the repairs and say a few words.

Which was why radio reporter Henry Stillman and freelance cameraman Abe Bristow were waiting outside, and they weren't alone. About thirty other journalists were present as well, along with a crowd of roughly fifty tourists, all of whom hoped to catch a glimpse of the President.

Stillman had a long gaunt face, a no-nonsense chin, and was dressed in a well-cut gray suit. He flamed another in a long chain of Camels he had smoked that day, clicked the Zippo closed, and dropped the lighter into his coat pocket.

"So, Abe," Stillman said as he sucked the rich smoke

deep into his lungs. "What do you think Grace is doing in there? Asking Lincoln for some advice?"

Bristow was short and squat, as if God had taken a normal-sized man and squashed him like clay. He was fiddling with his huge flash camera.

"God knows the bastard could use some," he replied sourly. "Not that he'd listen." Stillman might have said something more, but there was a sudden stir at the top of the steps leading up to the memorial and the crowd surged forward.

Stillman and Bristow went with the flow, but were soon forced to stop as half a dozen uniformed police officers rushed to block the way. A man dressed in civilian attire appeared immediately behind them and stepped up to a microphone. His voice boomed through speakers set up two hours earlier.

"Good afternoon . . . My name is William Dentweiler, the President's Chief of Staff. There's no need to push and shove. President Grace will take questions for about ten minutes. Then it's back to the White House for some important meetings.

"Mr. President?" At that point Dentweiler took two steps to the right, which gave Grace access to the microphone.

Grace flashed one of his trademark smiles as he stepped up to the microphone and a coterie of Secret Service agents came with him. It was a sunny day, so there were no flashbulbs for the President to contend with as Bristow and his fellow photographers began to click away.

In the meantime Stillman pushed his way forward in an attempt to get his new Minifon battery-powered recorder as close to the President as possible. Most of the journalists shouted questions, but it was one of the veteran radio reporters who managed to make himself heard.

"Mr. President! Arthur Norton, WDC News. There are rumors that sections of the Liberty Defense Perimeter have been breached. Is the government concerned that citizens may panic?"

Grace frowned. "Panic? Do me a favor, Arthur . . . Everyone . . . Look up."

Stillman, recorder extended, looked up. The rest of the crowd did as well.

"Now," Grace said. "What do you see?"

Norton was a balding man in his early thirties. He looked confused. "Nothing."

Grace nodded knowingly. "Exactly. *Nothing.* And the reason you see nothing is that taxpayers such as yourself have been gracious enough to put their confidence in my administration. Law and order is the reason our country remains safe while those overseas have fallen."

Stillman had successfully elbowed his way forward by the time Grace stopped speaking. "Henry Stillman for USA News, Mr. President . . . Our reporter in Montana says that a Protection Camp located outside the defense perimeter was overrun by thousands of aliens the day before yesterday."

At that point Dentweiler leaned in to speak. There was undisguised anger in his voice. "That camp would have been located *inside* the defense perimeter if it hadn't been for all of the raw materials appropriated by the Freedom First people! They forced the government to limit the size of the perimeter."

"Bill's right, I'm afraid," Grace put in reasonably. "The so-called Freedom Firsters are a greater menace than the stinks are."

Apparently Dentweiler wasn't all that thrilled with

the line of questioning because he stepped in to shut the press conference down.

"All right," the Chief of Staff said, "the President has a busy schedule to keep. Let's wrap this up."

Suddenly a high-pitched whistling sound was heard, and something fell out of the clear blue sky and hit the roundabout behind the crowd. A taxi was thrown into the air. There was a loud crash as it smashed into the ground and burst into flames. A cloud of black smoke enveloped the scene as women screamed, policemen shouted conflicting orders, and the President was half carried toward a waiting limo.

As the smoke began to clear, Bristow pointed at the spire. It was shaped like a huge spear, the head of which had penetrated the concrete, and was lodged underground. But unlike a normal spear, this one was made of metal, and thousands of times larger. Vapor out-gassed from the object, the air shimmered around it, and Stillman heard pinging sounds as the missile began to cool.

"Henry . . . What *is* that thing?"

Stillman shook his head. "I don't know, Abe . . . But it wasn't made by humans. That's for sure."

Some people were lying on the ground where Good Samaritans tried to assist them as sirens sounded and the presidential motorcade pulled away. Meanwhile, like the newsmen they were, Stillman and Bristow went over to examine the spire. The cameraman snapped shot after shot as they got closer.

"Thank God it didn't explode," Bristow said, as he lowered his camera. "But maybe we should—"

Bristow never got to finish his sentence. An ominous hum was heard as a series of plates were pushed out and away from the spire's fuselage. Then, without warning, hundreds of softball-sized eggs began to tumble out onto the street. Stillman felt something cold enter his bloodstream as the yellowish globes bounced and rolled in every direction. "I don't like the look of those things," he said. "Run!"

Both men turned back toward the memorial and started to sprint up the stairs as the eggs began to hatch. A cacophony of bloodcurdling squeals was heard as thousands of Spinners were born. Within seconds of breaking out of their soft-shelled containers the horrible-looking creatures began to morph and were the size of house cats by the time they swarmed the slowest members of the crowd.

People screamed as they were borne to the ground by five or six Spinners. Each stink was equipped with fangs and hollow barbs through which chemicals could be injected into their victims, all of whom instantly began to thrash about.

Having escaped the initial onslaught, Stillman and Bristow were halfway up the stairs, right behind a mixed group of journalists and tourists. Both men heard something howl, and Bristow felt one of the creatures land on his back as more of them swept up the stairs. He stopped, and was trying to reach back and get a grip on the Chimera when Stillman took hold of the squirming stink and ripped it away. The Spinner was hot to the touch, and it snapped angrily when the reporter heaved it down toward the street.

Hundreds of additional Spinners were flowing up the stairs by then, so both men turned and ran. People had been trampled and Stillman felt something give horribly as he was forced to step on a man's chest. The building was equipped with steel gates, and as a quick-thinking security guard hurried to secure the last one, the duo managed to slip inside.

There was a loud clang behind them when the door closed, followed by a persistent rattling noise as hundreds of frustrated monsters hit the barrier. It consisted of closely set vertical bars that allowed those inside to see out as the pimply-faced guard emptied his .38 revolver into the squealing mass. Each bullet killed at least two or three Chimera, but there were plenty more, and it wasn't long before the guard's pistol clicked empty.

Then, as if in response to some unseen signal, the tidal wave of alien flesh broke and fell away. That was when Stillman saw a horrible sight as a man stumbled up the last few steps with half a dozen Spinners clinging to his body. But the creatures weren't stinging him. Not yet anyway.

"Oh, my God," Bristow said. "It's Norton!"

The WDC newsman reached the top and grabbed the bars with both hands, then began to rattle them. His eyes were wide—and his pupils were dilated.

"Let me in! For God's sake, let me in!"

The security guard produced a large ring of keys and was on his way to the gate when Stillman grabbed an arm.

"Wait! You can't do that."

The security guard attempted to break Stillman's grip but Bristow was there to restrain him as well.

"Are you crazy?" the young man demanded. "There's an innocent man out there!"

"And there's twenty innocent people in here," Stillman responded urgently. "They're using him as bait! They want you to open the door so they can get in."

"What do you mean?"

"I mean, he's dead already," Stillman answered soberly. "And there's nothing we can do about it."

The security guard had stopped struggling by that time and stared in horror as the Spinners allowed Norton to plead.

"Please! I have a family . . . Don't let me die." Norton

tugged at the bars as his eyes went from face to face. "Why?" he wanted to know. "Why won't you let me in?"

Then, as the Chimera realized that Norton was of no further use to them, they took him down. A man began to retch and a woman sobbed pitifully as the Spinners went to work. Norton screamed while the Chimera wound layer after layer of glistening pinkish brown webbing around his body, but it wasn't long before the sounds were silenced, as it became impossible for him to breathe. Then all the struggling came to a stop as a large group of Spinners bore the newly cocooned body away.

The gibbering sounds continued unabated, but the gate held, so most of the people pulled back from the bars as the security guard put in a call to the police. A waste of time, in Stillman's opinion, since there were bound to be other spires, and the police sure as hell had to know about them.

"Hey," Bristow said. "Have you seen my camera? I lost it."

"No," Stillman said matter-of-factly, "I haven't."

"Then how 'bout a smoke?" Bristow inquired.

Stillman removed a pack of Camels from his pocket, shook one of them loose, and offered it to Bristow. "You smoke? Since when?"

"Since five minutes ago," Bristow said, as he accepted both the cigarette and the light. Then, having pulled some smoke into his lungs, he began to cough.

Stillman was putting the pack back into his pocket when he felt the recorder—and realized he had tucked the device away prior to the desperate run up the stairs. He pulled it out, turned the recorder on, and held the microphone to his lips. "This is Henry Stillman . . . Today, during a tour of the newly refurbished Lincoln Memorial in Washington, D.C., the President of the

United States paused for a moment to reassure reporters and citizens alike as to the integrity of the much vaunted defense perimeter.

"No sooner had the President concluded his remarks than a huge spire fell out of the sky, landed about five hundred feet from the memorial, and killed at least a dozen people. Soon—within a matter of minutes—thousands of eggs poured out of the missile. They hatched quickly, releasing hundreds of vicious creatures, which are outside the memorial now.

"I'm approaching the gate as I speak, and the next thing you will hear is the sound of screeching, as the Chimeran horde tries to get in. It's a horrible sound, ladies and gentlemen—and one I hope none of you have occasion to hear in person."

The Spinners grew more agitated as Stillman neared the gate, the intensity of the gibbering sound increased, and the reporter extended the microphone in an attempt to capture the sound for the benefit of his audience.

But suddenly there was the roar of a diesel engine from somewhere just out of sight. Moments later, the Spinners fell away from the gate like a wave being sucked back into the sea, as an armored personnel carrier bucked its way up the stairs. Spinners screeched angrily as they were crushed by the half-track's metal treads, and a vehicle-mounted machine gun began to yammer madly, with hundreds of Chimera disappearing into a blood-mist cloud.

Orders were shouted as a dozen soldiers wearing black hoods jumped down from the half-track to battle the Chimera with shotguns, Bellocks, and flamethrowers. Stillman heard a flurry of gunshots followed by a loud *whump* as a gout of flame consumed more than fifty Spinners and filled the air with the throat-clogging stench of burned flesh.

The battle ended five minutes later when the last stink was hunted down and dispatched with a blast from a Rossmore.

Keys rattled as the security guard unlocked the gates and swung them open. Stillman was one of the first to leave and found it difficult to walk without stepping on a body. The stairs were slick with blood and littered with hats, purses, and other debris. By placing each foot with care, he was able to make his way halfway down the stairs to the point where a badly mangled camera lay. As Bristow arrived, he bent to pick up the object. "Here," he said, "I believe this belongs to you."

Bristow accepted what remained of his camera and took a long slow look around. "We're lucky to be alive."

Stillman was silent for a moment as sirens wailed in the distance, a woman sobbed as she cradled a dead child in her arms, and a flight of Sabre Jets roared overhead.

"Maybe," Stillman replied somberly, "or maybe the lucky ones are already dead."

# CHAPTER TEN
# PAYBACK IS A BITCH

The shimmery blue Stalker crawled crablike up over a rocky ridge. Then, having successfully crossed the barrier, its articulated legs made *whine-thud-whine* sounds as they spidered down the steep slope toward the ravine below.

Occasional bursts of static, fractured sentences, and the sounds of fighting could be heard over the headphones Hale wore, but there was no way to tell who was winning the battle miles to the east. Two additional machines, both of which had been captured months earlier, followed along behind his.

The notion of using Chimeran vehicles to penetrate the enemy base near Hot Springs, South Dakota, had been Hale's idea, yet now as he and his team battled the rough terrain, he was beginning to doubt the wisdom of the plan.

The goal had been to surprise the Chimera by arriving in three of their own vehicles—thus avoiding the antiaircraft batteries located on top of the target building. But after hours of tedious cross-country travel, their slow progress was eating up valuable time, and Hale was worried lest he and his team miss the narrow window of opportunity created by Lieutenant Colonel Jack Hawkins and the 5th Ranger Battalion.

Hawkins's job was to advance up the main highway from Chadron, Nebraska. Then, as the stinks located in and around Hot Springs streamed south to engage the invaders, pre-positioned American troops would sweep in to crush them from both sides. Which was why the attack had been code-named Operation Iron Fist.

Meanwhile, as the battle took place, Hale and his team were supposed to sweep around to the west in an effort to bypass the action. If all went as planned, they would enter Hot Springs unopposed, break into the storage building, and snatch one of the fuel cores before the Chimera could bring a large force back to oppose them.

It was all dependent on good communications and perfect timing. Except that the radio link to Battalion Command was spotty at best, and according to Hale's wristwatch, the team was running fifteen minutes late. Hale glanced to his right.

Despite the way the Stalker was lurching up, down, and sideways, Dr. Barrie appeared to be completely unruffled.

"I've been studying the map," Barrie said, "and I have a suggestion."

Hale sent the Stalker sideways to avoid a cluster of boulders, and did his best to sound casual. He still wasn't entirely clear whether she was his superior, equal, or subordinate. "Yeah?" he said. "What's that?"

"The top of the next ridge is one of the highest points between us and our objective. Once we hit the top of this slope, let's park the Stalkers just below the skyline, and take a look. Then if everything looks okay, we'll commit."

That made sense. According to his own calculations,

and the map-board strapped to his right thigh, they were coming up on the separation point. Beyond that spot, the Stalkers would pass the Rangers off to the east, and be entirely on their own.

A meaningless exercise unless the overall plan was working.

"Okay," he said. "That makes sense, but only if we can't reach BatCom, since we're running fifteen minutes late."

Hale made two attempts to contact BatCom subsequent to that, received nothing but gibberish in return, and was forced to conclude that the Chimera were jamming Ranger communications. So with no other course open to him, and having found a ledge on which the Stalkers could pause, Hale brought his machine to a halt.

Fortunately the highly localized squad-level frequency that connected him with the other two machines was working fine.

"Echo-Six, to Echo-Five, and Echo-Four . . . Here's your chance to take a break. The doctor and I are going to take a look over the ridge. I want one unit manned and ready to fight at all times. So take turns. Do you read? Over."

"This is Five . . . Roger that," Sergeant Marvin Kawecki replied. "Over."

"This is Four . . . I read you Five-by-Five," Corporal Tim Yorba echoed. "Over."

Five minutes later all three of the Stalkers were parked as Hale opened the hatch and allowed Barrie to precede him. She was wearing trousers, and he couldn't help but notice how well they fit as she disappeared through the hatch.

Once outside, Hale was pleased to see that the civilian

had remembered to take a Bullseye assault rifle with her as she dropped onto one of the machine's massive legs and jumped to the snow-covered ground. With the exception of Hale's .44 Magnum pistol, the entire team was equipped with Chimeran weapons because, once they arrived, there wouldn't be any American ammo lying around to scavenge. And they were likely to need more than they could reasonably carry. Hale was carrying a Marksman rifle as he jumped to the ground. Though manufactured by humans, the weapon was based on Chimeran tech, and chambered to eat enemy ammo. It could fire twenty-one rounds in three-round bursts and was devastatingly accurate.

The moment they left the confines of the Stalker, they could hear the muted sounds of the distant battle as they rolled across the land. Once in position both flopped onto their stomachs and brought binoculars up to their eyes.

The ridge ran southwest to northeast, allowing a clear view of the snow-covered grasslands that lay between them and the north–south highway. A pall of gray smoke hung over the scene, but there were places where the fog was less dense, and the battlefield could be seen. It extended at least a mile to either side of the badly cratered road and was carpeted with the carcasses of burned-out M-12 Sabertooth tanks, smoking Stalkers, and the skeletal remains of Lynx APVs.

And there were bodies, too—*thousands* of them, representing both sides—which lay in drifts on the bloodied snow. Hale could read the lines of casualties the way a fortune-teller might read a palm. The northernmost line, the one that zigzagged west to east, was comprised of dead Rangers. Judging from the way they lay, like successive waves of flotsam on a beach, they had been the first ones to make contact with a southbound tsunami of Chimera.

The stinks had literally rolled over the Rangers, in some cases stomping their vehicles under enormous feet while they rushed forward to collect what looked like a certain victory.

But as Hale panned his binoculars across the smoke-drifted battlefield, he could see the points where the freaks had been hit from both flanks. The Chimeran bodies were piled high there, where they had been forced in on themselves, and had been slaughtered in the hundreds.

Beyond the field of the dead, the survivors were preparing to continue the carnage. As Hawkins sent his reserves forward, another colossal confrontation was about to take place. American shells arced over the battlefield and threw columns of dirt and snow into the air when they exploded. Heard from a distance, the artillery fire made a low muttering sound.

A squad of gigantic bipedal Titans plodded their way south, launching fireballs as they went. The monstrous aliens seemed immune to the automatic weapons fire that sleeted their way. They were supported by Stalkers, though precious few, since dozens had been destroyed earlier.

Slightly to the rear of the widely spaced Titans, and positioned to defend them from infantry attacks, there was a company-sized force of Ravagers. Their nearly impervious energy shields had been raised to protect both themselves and the horde of Hybrids following along behind. The incoming artillery shells blew holes in their ranks, but those gaps were quickly filled as more stinks came forward.

Suddenly there were Steelheads pushing to the front of the shambling pack, their Augers at the ready, with at least a thousand standard Hybrids close behind. Meanwhile, out along both flanks, dozens of Howlers were visible, dashing this way and that and baying like wolves.

It was a terrifying sight, and from the safety of the ridge, Hale felt a combination of thankfulness and guilt as the Rangers fought back. Tanks targeted the Titans, quickly blowing half of them into bloody hamburger, as LAARK-equipped hit teams rushed in on Lynx APVs to deal death to the Ravagers, all of which were vulnerable from behind. And Hale's fellow Sentinels were present as well, their uniforms making them distinguishable from the rest as the infantry swept forward to engage the bloodthirsty Hybrids.

Nor were the skies empty as a flight of three Sabre Jets roared in to fire rockets at the Chimeran horde and hose them with cannon fire. Their presence made a difference at first, but was quickly neutralized as two knife-winged enemy fighters appeared and immediately sent one of the American planes spiraling into the ground. The ensuing explosion produced a muted *boom*, which rolled across the prairie like thunder.

"Damn," Hale said, lowering his binoculars. "Did you see that? The poor bastard never had a chance."

"Yes," Barrie replied bleakly, "and that's why we need nuclear weapons. Come on. This is our chance to slip past them." With that she stood and moved back toward the Stalker.

He was impressed by her grim determination as he got up to follow her. Together they slip-slid down the reverse slope to the point where the vehicles were waiting. As they approached he could see Yorba and Pardo on the ground, taking the opportunity to stretch their legs, while Kawecki and Gaines were on standby inside their unit, ready to fight if necessary.

"This is Echo-Six," Hale said into his lip mike. "Let's saddle up. We're going in."

Yorba spun in his direction, offered a grin and a quick thumbs-up before turning to follow his partner up into the machine that loomed above them. Kawecki signaled his understanding by clicking his mike on and off twice.

Ten minutes later Hale was piloting the Stalker up and over the ridge, watching carefully to make certain an alert Sabre Jet pilot didn't spot the machines and try to take them out. The last thing they needed was to be attacked by an American plane. But if any of the flyboys were still alive, they had their hands full off to the east, and the Stalkers were able to proceed unimpeded.

Once in the ravine below all he had to do was follow it to the point where it emptied out into a low-cut channel that meandered east. That was the point where he led the other Stalkers up onto a gently rolling prairie and began a high-speed run toward the town of Hot Springs.

"High-speed" being a relative term, because while extremely agile—especially over rough terrain—the Stalkers weren't very fast. In fact, any tank or APV could outrun the Chimeran machines on a reasonably flat surface. But that couldn't be helped, so all Hale and his companions could do was grit their teeth as they lurched along, and hope for the best.

Half an hour later they closed with the main highway and began to follow it north. Given the volume of southbound traffic it appeared that the battle was still underway, which was excellent news.

Their situation presented a new danger however, because no one really understood how the Chimeran command structure functioned, and Hale was worried that the equivalent of an officer would take notice of the fact that three Stalkers were headed north, rather than south into the battle, and attempt to turn them around. If that occurred they would have no choice but to fight, thereby attracting all sorts of lethal attention and compromising the mission so many had given their lives to support.

But the Chimera didn't question such things, or so it appeared, as the Stalkers were permitted to pass through a heavily defended checkpoint approximately one mile outside Hot Springs. Or what was left of the town, since most of it had been reduced to little more than blackened rubble. Almost all the buildings had been gutted by fire, bullet-riddled cars lay every which way, and the only sign of human habitation was the bird-picked remains of a corpse that dangled from a lamppost.

It was a sight that filled Hale with both anger and determination.

"Okay," Barrie said as she consulted an aerial photo, "take a right here, and follow this street to the main gate."

As the Stalkers spidered their way along the side street, Hale saw that a strip of land around the Chimeran base had been leveled with heavy machinery, creating a free-fire zone through which attackers would have to pass before they could assault the nine-foot-high metal walls encircling the installation. All of which raised an interesting question.

Who where the Chimera afraid of? Conventional forces like the Rangers to the south? Or resistance fighters like the Freedom First group? The second possibility seemed more likely—since the U.S. forces had been primarily on the defensive until earlier that morning.

"This should be interesting," Barrie said grimly as the Stalker marched toward a pair of heavy-duty gates.

"That's one word for it," Hale agreed as he eyed the towers to either side of the entryway. "Echo-Six to Five and Four . . . Watch those towers. If they fire, take them out. I'll take care of the gates. Over."

There were two double-clicks by way of a response. Moments later Hale felt a profound sense of relief as the huge doors parted and began to rumble in opposite directions. "We're in!" Barrie said jubilantly, as the Stalker passed through the opening.

"Yeah," Hale agreed soberly. "But will we be able to get *out*?"

The question went unanswered as the Stalkers passed through a narrow corridor, took a left, and entered the open area that lay beyond. A scattering of Hybrids could be seen, but no more than fifty, thanks to the battle still raging south of Hot Springs. A watchtower soared above all else, with lesser structures clustered around it, one of which was the storage facility they hoped to enter.

But before they attempted that, there was something else they needed to do.

"This is Echo-Six," Hale said grimly. "Once we enter the storage complex the Chimera will know we're here and they'll come after us with everything they can muster. So before we go after the fuel, let's do some housecleaning. Every stink you kill will be one less problem to deal with later. I'll take the towers, while you tidy the grounds. Over."

Again two sets of clicks as the Stalkers split up and went to work. Kawecki fired first, using his machine gun to mow down a file of unsuspecting 'brids crossing the open area in front of him. The weapon made a loud rattling noise as tracers sought the aliens and tore them apart.

Meanwhile Hale turned his machine to face the nearest tower. It was about fifty feet tall. The top consisted of a reflective metal ball which housed two gang-mounted machine guns that could clearly be brought to bear on aerial or ground targets. It was impossible to see the gunner through the chrome surface, but Hale could imagine a Hybrid ensconced in some sort of powered seat, surveying the area. From the 'brid's perspective, the Stalkers would have been part of the usual scenery, and of little or no interest.

There was a red reticle on Hale's heads-up display, and the moment it centered on the top of the tower, he triggered the missile launcher mounted on the left side of the Stalker's turretlike body. He felt the machine shudder as the weapon took to the air. It paused for a fraction of a second and gave birth to a sub-munition which accelerated toward the target.

There was a flash of light, followed by a muted explosion as the gun turret took a direct hit. The half-blackened gun-ball swiveled toward the Stalker, but didn't fire, as if the gunner was trying to figure out what to do. Was it taking friendly fire? Or had the attack been intentional? There was no way the 'brid could be sure.

The answer came in the form of a *second* missile, which blew a hole in the gun-ball, and detonated the ammo within. The secondary explosion blew the top of the tower clean off and left a blackened stump in its place.

Before Hale could enjoy his success, the gunner in the adjacent tower opened fire on his Stalker. Bright green tracers found the machine and converged on it. The Stalker shook madly as Hale sent it crabbing sideways in an effort to escape the incoming fire. Hale knew that if he turned, thereby exposing the back of his machine to the enemy, it would only be a matter of seconds before the incoming slugs tore through the mech's power core and blew the Stalker apart.

"I'll operate the turret," Barrie said as she flipped a

cover out of the way and slapped a switch. Hydraulics whined as the turret containing two auto-cannons extended upward and she released her harness.

Hale felt conflicting emotions while she climbed up into the turret above. He was supposed to be in command, but it was difficult to pilot the machine and operate all of the weapons, too, so her willingness to act as gunner was welcome.

Plus it was nice to know that Barrie would fight when the need arose.

Meanwhile, as he took partial cover behind a pumping station, and Barrie poured cannon shells into the second tower, the other Stalkers prowled the Chimeran base, killing anything that moved. Then, having put dozens of Hybrids down, Kawecki and Yorba went after the gun towers on the other side of the base. Their combined fire proved to be more than any one tower could withstand, and it was only a matter of minutes before the rest of the gun-balls were out of action.

As Kawecki and Yorba returned to the area in front of the storage facility, Hale and Barrie won their engagement and were rewarded as the top half of tower two broke free and toppled onto a flat one-story structure, thereby crushing it. A cloud of dust rose, quickly followed by smoke when something caught fire.

"Nice one, Echo-Six," Kawecki said admiringly. "That was good shooting! Over."

"Thanks," Barrie replied. "And Lieutenant Hale deserves some of the credit, too."

The others were too smart to laugh with their microphones turned on, but Hale knew they were, as he brought the Stalker to a stop in front of the target building.

"This is Six," Hale said. "It's time to bail. Don't forget to bring your gear with you. Place charges on all three machines. Do you read? Over."

"Roger," Yorba replied. "I'm going to need ten minutes. Over."

"The clock is running," Hale answered as he hit the harness release. "Out."

One of the reasons Hale had chosen to enter the Chimeran base on the ground rather than by air was the antiaircraft guns located on top of the storage building's flat roof. But the Stalkers weren't tall enough to attack the batteries, and the Chimeran guns weren't set up to fire on ground targets, so a stalemate was in effect.

The Hybrids stationed on the roof could use their Bullseyes and Augers to fire down on the invaders, however, and they hurried to do so, as Yorba went from Stalker to Stalker placing demolition charges on each machine.

So the moment Hale's boots hit the pavement he was forced to take refuge behind a huge crablike leg and return fire with the Marksman rifle. The idea being not only to kill as many Hybrids as possible, but to force the rest of the stinks to keep their heads down, thereby allowing Yorba to complete his task, without enemy fire to stop him. The rest of the team took cover in the building's entryway, where the Chimera couldn't see them.

Not directly anyway, although that didn't prevent the Hybrids from directing Auger fire down through the intervening structure.

Hale followed suit and began to pick off Hybrids like targets on a rifle range. They were head shots mostly, each of which was marked by a cloud of blood as the high-velocity projectiles flew straight and true. Soon the Chimera drew back, rather than accept more casualties. That allowed Hale to grab his gear, dash across open ground, and join the others as they completed their preparations.

Kawecki was armed with an Auger, while Gaines, Pardo, and Barrie carried Bullseyes. The latter had requested two of the small Reaper carbines as well, which she wore pistol-style in specially designed clamp-holsters.

A choice which, like so many other things having to do with Barrie, left Hale mystified. Were the weapons an affectation? Intended to make her look more danger-ous? Or were they the sensible choice for someone who wasn't very good with a pistol?

There was no clear answer.

"The charges are set, sir," Yorba said, joining the group. He, too, carried an Auger. "They'll go off when anything larger than a cocker spaniel passes by. So don't go back for anything! You'll be sorry if you do." He had black hair, brown skin, and a round face, and he was eternally cheerful, which was one of the many things Hale liked about him.

"Good work, Corporal. And thanks for the warning. Okay, let's get in there, find the fuel core, and get the hell out. Remember, the pick-up point is on the roof, and there's a whole lot of stinks up there. Corporal Yorba, please feel free to open that door for us."

Yorba grinned happily, removed what he liked to refer to as a "door knocker" from the satchel at his side, and slapped a wad of plastic explosives onto one of the double doors.

"You'd better move back," he suggested gleefully, and promptly took his own advice. As soon as he reached an appropriate distance, he turned and gestured.

"Open sesame!" With that, he triggered the charge. There was a sharp *bang* as the door knocker went off, the right panel sagged, and smoke poured out through the newly created gap.

That was a sufficient invitation for Gaines, who tossed a grenade into the space beyond, and waited for the resulting explosion. It came quickly, after which he gave the bottom of the door a kick. It fell outward, missing him by a matter of inches and landing with a crash.

He was the first inside, with Hale right behind him. Both darted to the side to avoid defensive fire, yet there was no resistance. The lighting was dim—so dim that it was impossible to see the ceiling—and what illumination there was came straight from spots located high above.

The rest joined them in the open area beyond. There were two doorways separated by a twenty-foot-long section of wall. That, according to the plan agreed to back in Nebraska, was the point when Barrie was supposed to assume overall command. And she was quick to do so.

"We're looking for an elevator, stairs, or a ramp," she announced confidently. "The fuel cores are probably stored in the lowest level. Let's go through the left-hand entrance and keep our eyes peeled."

Hale nodded. "Gaines will take the point, followed by me, Dr. Barrie, Yorba, Pardo, and Kawecki. Be sure to watch our Six, Sergeant . . . I don't like surprises."

"Sir, yes, sir."

Gaines was six foot six. He had a big head, thin, nearly nonexistent lips, and a pugnacious jaw. Like all Sentinels, he was a good shot, and he possessed an almost spooky ability to spot Chimeran ambushes. Some people credited him with exceptional eyesight, others claimed he could smell the malodorous stink they exuded better than anyone else.

Whatever the reason, he was good at it. And that was all Hale cared about as they proceeded down a corridor flanked by seven-foot-tall transparent tubes. Each cylinder contained a Hybrid. They were hard to see, due to the pearly gas that surrounded them, but judging from a complete lack of activity, they were asleep. Or unconscious. Not that it mattered, so long as they stayed that way.

"I think they were damaged, and are being reconditioned," Barrie offered. "Although they could be in storage, too . . . Especially if this is the equivalent of a warehouse."

Hale hadn't seen anything like the facility before, but didn't like the feel of the place, which was eerily silent except for the soft *whir* of pumps. Some of the tubes were empty, but Hale figured that at least fifty of the life-support chambers were occupied, which equated to one hundred stinks, assuming the next aisle over was home to the same number.

His thoughts were interrupted as Gaines's voice came through his earplug.

"I see what looks like an elevator up ahead. Over."

Hale saw that Gaines was correct, and more than that, an open platform was descending from above! Four Hybrids became visible as it cleared the ceiling— some of the surviving AA gunners most likely, sent down to intercept the invaders.

Gaines tagged one of the beasts, sent a burst of projectiles after it, and heard a screech as it went down.

But that gave the stinks time to begin firing back, and Gaines took a hit, which spun him around and dumped him on the floor. Hale and Yorba opened fire, and thanks to the way the Hybrids were bunched up, they were dispatched in a matter of seconds.

"Get control of that elevator!" Hale shouted. "We're

going to need it—and I don't want any more visitors from above."

Pardo ran forward to secure the blood-splattered platform as Hale knelt to check on Gaines. The shoulder wound, which would have taken most soldiers out of the fight, had already begun to close.

"You were lucky," Hale said as he helped the other Sentinel up. "Duck next time." Gaines grinned.

"Yes, sir."

"Okay," Hale said as he waved the rest forward. "We're going down. Stay sharp. There's no telling what's waiting for us on the level below."

Dr. Linda Barrie felt slightly nauseous as she followed Kawecki onto the elevator. Firing auto-cannons at a chromed gun-ball was one thing—but wading through a pile of dead bodies was something else. In part because of the throat-clogging smell, which was like that of rotten meat, and worse than anything she had encountered before. Part of it could be explained by the fact that one of the Hybrids had been eviscerated, but the rest of it was due to the Chimera's typically rank body odor, which brought new meaning to the sobriquet "stink."

One of the 'brids gave a convulsive jerk, and was in the process of sitting up when Hale blew its brains out. That was too much for Barrie, who immediately threw up.

There wasn't much food in her stomach, so the episode was over quickly. She lifted up her head to discover that Hale's golden eyes were waiting to meet hers.

"Sorry about that," he said sympathetically. "We've all been through it. But they aren't human. Not anymore. Try to remember that."

Barrie brought the back of a hand up to wipe the bile off her lips. Was this how Anton felt the day he died?

Sick to his stomach, afraid to fail, yet determined to go on?

*Yes,* Barrie thought, *now I know. Hale was correct. Anton was a brave man.*

Then there was a whirring noise and the elevator began to drop.

Hale and his men stood with weapons at the ready as the platform dropped down into the level below and came to a smooth stop. Again the light was dim, but when Hale looked out into the room beyond, he could see row after row of sturdy storage units.

"Don't tell me," he said out of the corner of his mouth, "let me guess. You want to go shopping."

Barrie was fully recovered by that time. "Yes," Barrie replied firmly. "I do. The fuel cores could be anywhere."

"Roger that," Hale replied stoically. "Kawecki and Pardo will guard the elevator while the rest of us walk the walk. I'll be on point, the doctor will fill the two-slot, and Yorba will walk drag. Let's go."

Hale's rifle wasn't equipped with a light, not normally anyway, but that deficiency had been corrected by the simple expedient of taping a black flashlight to the barrel. So he slid the switch into the on position, and a blob of white light sprang into existence.

Barrie slung the Bullseye across her back so her hands were free to use a small video camera. It had a light of its own, and the two sources of illumination enabled them to examine the objects on the shelves. None of the items on display looked familiar to him until Barrie stopped to examine a chunk of machinery.

Before he could warn her, the insectoid-looking Patrol Drone came to sudden life. All Hale could do was reach out and jerk her backward as the machine fired from inches away. The blast missed, and as the drone wobbled up off the shelf, Gaines put a burst of automatic fire into it. The machine exploded, peppering everyone with tiny bits of shrapnel, all of which stung.

That was when all hell broke loose.

Having been "awoken" by the destruction of a fellow machine, more than a dozen drones came to sudden life and darted into the air. They produced an ominous humming sound which seemed to come from every direction at once, and they fired on the intruders. The blackness made them almost impossible to see as Hale, Gaines, and Yorba fired up at them.

"Take cover!" Hale shouted, launching one of the Marksman's small semiautonomous drones. "Then we can pick them off."

Large cargo modules were stored against the adjacent wall, and offered the only alternatives. So as the rifle-launched drone began to fire on its larger counterparts, thereby drawing them away from the humans, Hale led the team across the open area. There were spaces between some of the containers, and a couple were empty, giving the humans a place to hide.

"This is Echo-Five," Kawecki said over the radio. "Do you want us to stay where we are? Or come a-running? Over."

"Maintain control of that elevator," Hale replied as projectiles pinged the modules around him, "but find cover. It won't be long before they attack you as well. Over."

Hale heard two clicks as Kawecki acknowledged the order. Yorba was using the heat-activated reticle to find targets and fire *through* the module he was hiding in. Striking up a rhythm, he began to destroy the drones with machinelike efficiency. Some of them exploded, strobing the big room with momentary light, while others crashed into storage units, cargo modules, and the floor below.

Hale managed to bag a couple of Patrol Drones with well-placed shots from the Marksman. Then the battle was over, and an uncanny silence spread through the room.

Barrie was the first one who crawled out into the open. "Come on," she said. "I don't think the cores are stored on this level, but we need to make sure, and the clock is running."

Hale gestured, and the team followed her over to the vertical storage units, where the inventory continued. It took about ten minutes to check the rest of the shelves and confirm what she had predicted. "The fuel cores are located somewhere else," she announced. "Probably on a lower level. We need to get back on the elevator."

Kawecki and Pardo were waiting for them by the time the rest of the group arrived. They gathered together, and Gaines took the controls.

"Check your weapons," Hale said grimly, as the platform began to drop. "Because if there are a bunch of stinks on the next level down, they sure as hell know we're coming."

But once again there were no Chimera waiting to shoot at them. The only illumination came from regularly spaced pools of light, and they could see that this room was quite different from the one above.

The floor consisted of gratings that crisscrossed a large open space. Below them, and located to either side, a maze of large storage chambers could be seen. They were open to each other and filled with what looked like water. Vertical boxes occupied each chamber, some of which were empty, and others of which contained cylindrical objects.

Above the storage chambers a system of rails could be

seen, along with the chain hoists that rode them, and could be positioned anywhere in the room.

"This is it!" Barrie said excitedly, as the platform came to a stop. "They store the fuel rods in those water-filled chambers in order to keep them cool." From what Hale could see, it looked as if the rods came in several different sizes.

Barrie was gone after that, and he had to jog to keep up with the scientist as she hurried out onto one of the walkways. Kawecki and Yorba remained behind to guard the elevator. Gaines and Pardo followed Hale.

"There!" Barrie proclaimed, as she came to a halt. "See the smaller ones? That's what we want."

Hale followed her pointing finger down to a section of storage silos and saw that roughly half of them were filled with silvery canisters. Each was about the size of a standard oxygen tank. That meant they were larger than he would have liked, and no doubt heavier as well, which explained the need for chain hoists.

"It's my guess that the actual fuel rods are about the same diameter as a milk bottle," Barrie said, "and twice as long. Each canister probably contains three or four of them, all protected by a steel cylinder and at least three inches of shielding. Inside, nestled between them, is some form of neutron absorber. What we need to do is jerk one of them out of there, load it into one of the shipping containers stacked against the far wall, and take it up to the roof."

Hale met her eyes.

"Is that all? For a minute there I thought the process might get complicated."

Barrie's eyes narrowed.

"The clock is running, Hale . . . Shouldn't we get going?"

"All right," he conceded, turning to Gaines. "Go get

one of those chain hoists and slide it over here. Pardo, jump down there, and get ready for the hookup."

"Gotcha, Lieutenant," Pardo responded as he laid his weapon on the grating. "We'll jerk that thing outta there in no time at all," he said confidently.

The Fury lived in the ever present now.

It didn't think, not the way humans do, nor did it have a need to. Because its purpose was simple—to execute a carefully prescribed set of activities which, when combined with the functions carried out by other Chimera, would enable the virus that had created them all to conquer the planet.

*Any* planet.

In this circumstance it meant living where the Fury was designed to live, in a body of water that it considered its own, defending it against anything not Chimeran. So when the not-Chimera appeared on the gratings above, the Fury could hear their discordant speech-sounds, and followed them to a point it knew as a unique water-taste.

Stealth came naturally to the Fury and it propelled itself through the water with its flexible tail, making barely a ripple as it swam through the shadowy depths.

The chain hoist ran along a rail, and made a loud rattling sound as Gaines towed it into place. Then, having positioned it directly above Pardo, he lowered a pair of cargo hooks.

Pardo took control of them and bent to make the necessary connections. Gaines, who was watching from above, took hold of the control unit that dangled from the hoist. The moment he touched a delta-shaped button a loud whine was heard, chains rattled again, and the canister began to rise.

Pardo was crouched down, waiting for the canister to clear the surface, when a pincer shot up out of the water to grab his throat. His features contorted, and he made a horrible gargling sound as both hands went to the sinewy arm that held him.

As soon as he saw what was happening, Hale opened fire. Gouts of water jumped into the air as the projectiles sought their target, but the creature was extremely tough. Barrie's Bullseye was slung across her back, and she couldn't fire the Reapers without spraying Pardo, so she looked as if she was about to jump down when Hale beat her to it.

The thing was pulling Pardo under by that time, and as Hale landed on the concrete chamber wall, he drew the .44 Magnum in a last-ditch attempt to save the Sentinel. The two-handed grip came naturally but the pistol was still difficult to control due to its massive recoil. He put all six of the explosive rounds into the Chimera's brown sea lion–sized body.

There was blood in the water, *lots* of it, as what remained of Pardo floated to the surface. He arrived belly-up, and when Hale saw that the Sentinel's face was missing, he triggered the revolver's secondary-fire mode. That detonated all five of the bullets that were buried in the monster's muscular body and blew it in half. A series of closely overlapping *thuds* were heard, the water heaved, and chunks of raw meat boiled to the surface.

The kill brought Hale no pleasure as he emptied the revolver's spent casings into the water, replaced them via one of the two speed loaders that he carried on his belt, and flipped the cylinder closed. The handgun went back into the cross-draw holster.

The canister had cleared the walkway by then, and as Gaines towed it toward the elevator, Barrie knelt on the grating.

"I'm sorry," she said softly, "but we have to go."

"Yeah," Hale replied. "I know."

Then, as he'd been forced to do so many times before, he had to leave a fallen comrade where he was. Adrift in a cooling tank, his face gone, and no longer recognizable as human.

By the time he and Barrie arrived at the elevator, Kawecki, Yorba, and Gaines had already dropped the canister into a rolling cargo module. It was equipped with both a cradle and clamps to hold the cylinder in place. Once the lid had been closed and secured, all they had to do was transport the module to the roof. And that, based on the earlier battle, was where Hale figured the team would run into trouble.

More than an hour had elapsed, which meant Chimeran reinforcements were on the way, or had already arrived.

So as the elevator began to rise, there was a series of clicks, clacking sounds, and a loud whine as Hale slipped a full magazine into what had been Pardo's Bullseye. While the Marksman was ideal for some tasks, a free-for-all melee wasn't one of them.

No sooner had that thought passed though Hale's mind than he heard a chorus of guttural growls, screeches of rage, and incomprehensible stink-speech, and an army of Hybrids rushed the humans. Someone, or something, had released them from their vertical coffinlike storage tubes, and the air was thick with their rank odor as dozens of the raging beasts surged forward.

Fortunately, none of them was armed, but the strength of their charge was sufficient to instantly put six of the hideous creatures on the platform, where one threw itself at Gaines. The Sentinel fired *through* the Hybrid's abdomen, thereby killing the stink immediately behind it in the process, but not before the Chimera managed to sink its fangs into his throat. Bright red blood sprayed the surface of the elevator as Gaines went down, his neck ripped open, his eyes already glassy in death.

Meanwhile, the platform continued to rise and Hale, Kawecki, Yorba, and Barrie poured automatic weapons fire into the ravening horde from point-blank range. The mad chatter of their weapons, combined with the screams of dying Hybrids, created a cacophony of sound.

Having emptied her Bullseye, Barrie drew both Reapers and fired them into the mob. Chimera fell like wheat before a combine, their bodies effectively blocking the beasts behind them while the elevator made its way upward.

Hale lobbed two grenades into the crowd just before it disappeared from sight, heard two slightly muffled explosions, and took pleasure in the knowledge that another half-dozen Chimera were dead.

But then the body-strewn platform delivered the team and their hard-won prize onto the building's flat roof. The AA batteries were still operational, and even though there were fewer 'brids than there had been before, those that remained began firing on the elevator as soon as it surfaced.

The closest Chimera were only a dozen feet away, and scored hits on both Kawecki and Yorba, but they were unable to put either Sentinel down before being killed themselves. That gave the humans control of one AA gun and the northwest corner of the roof. Though wounded, Kawecki and Yorba were still functional, and already starting to heal as they took cover behind the gun mount and shield.

Hale crouched next to Barrie, and they were protected by the metal cargo box as projectiles continued to slam into it. He put the Bullseye down, and was prepping the Marksman for use when the radio transmission came in. "Hollywood to Echo-Six. We're inbound from the south. Do you read me? Over."

The voice was familiar.

"Purvis? Is that you? Over."

"Who the hell else would they send to retrieve your miserable ass?" the pilot replied. "I'm still on the shit list for making that drop north of Valentine. Over."

"I'm sorry about that, I really am," Hale said sincerely. "So how 'bout I buy you and your crew a drink? Or a couple of drinks? Assuming you can pluck us off this roof that is. Over."

"Consider it done," Purvis replied confidently. "And it'll be more than a couple. Over."

"Don't bring the *Party Girl* in yet, though," Hale advised. "We've got some stinks to deal with first—not to mention some AA batteries. Over."

"Roger that," Purvis replied. "How's the neighborhood? Over."

"Nasty by now," Hale answered. "Can you give me a couple of gun runs? Over."

"Your wish is my command," came the response. "I have two Sabre Jets circling at Angels five. They'd like nothing better than to hose that place down. Over."

"Just keep them off the building," Hale replied. "Echo-Six out."

There was still a single Hybrid located at the southwest corner of the roof. It couldn't bring the AA gun into play because mechanical stops kept the weapon pointed skyward—but it could plink away at the humans from behind the weapon's shield. Hale solved the problem by launching a drone toward the stink. It flew *over* the AA battery, fired down on the 'brid, and killed it.

That ceded control of the entire west end of the roof to the humans as the first Sabre Jet roared in from the south. Rockets jumped off wing rails and sleeted in to hit a group of Steelheads on the ground as they jogged toward the building. Body parts were still cartwheeling through the air when the pilot fired his .50 caliber machine guns. The fighter was equipped with six of the weapons, and the hail of shells carved a path of destruction through the base. The plane was so low that they caught a glimpse of the pilot's helmeted head as he passed the building.

Meanwhile there were still two antiaircraft cannons operating, and as the stinks turned to watch the jet flash by, one of them brought its AA gun around in an attempt to fire on the Sabre, and exposed his back in the process. Hale saw the Marksman's reticle flash red, and fired. Blood sprayed the AA gun's shield as the 'brid slumped forward—and Yorba nailed another Chimera with his Auger. "That's for Pardo!" Yorba shouted.

Only one AA gun remained as another Sabre Jet made its run across the base. However, the pilot had a Chimeran fighter on his tail and barely managed to get off a flight of rockets before being forced to pull up in a desperate attempt to escape.

It was at that moment that Barrie got up and began to sprint toward the last AA battery, firing all the way.

"No!" Hale shouted and took off after her, but it was too late as a hail of Chimeran projectiles brought her down. That prompted Kawecki and Yorba to fire on the surviving stinks, both of whom ducked.

Hale paused next to Barrie's body, then pulled a grenade and pitched it in under the gun's shield. There was a flash of light as both Hybrids were blown apart.

Moments later the *Party Girl* was there, throwing its shadow over the roof, and Hale scooped Barrie up. She was surprisingly light. There was blood on the front of her shirt and her eyes were open.

"Am I going to die?"

"No," Hale said firmly, and even though he knew he couldn't be heard over the roar of the VTOL's engines, he could tell that she understood.

"You're a liar, Hale," she said, as he leaned in close to hear. "*All* of us are going to die. The only question is when."

She passed out as medics rushed to take charge of her, and the rest of the survivors entered the plane. Kawecki and Yorba made certain that the box of fuel rods was securely fastened to the D rings set into the deck. They took off seconds later with the port gunner firing like mad as a pair of Titans arrived from the north.

As the *Party Girl* turned toward the south, Hale knew that the mission had been successful. So why did it feel like a failure? That question, like so many others, went unanswered.

# CHAPTER ELEVEN
## DEAD END

It was pitch black, with only the car's headlights to show the way.

The man called Twitch was behind the wheel, and had been ever since Henry Walker and his wife, Myra, had left Indianapolis two days earlier. Twitch was a runner, one of a very small group of men and women who dared to transport mail, medical supplies, and occasionally people back and forth between the government-controlled heartland and Chimera-occupied territory to the north.

Their destination was the city of Chicago, where the Walkers planned to join Freedom First and give that organization the recordings in which President Grace could be heard discussing what Walker viewed as treason.

The three of them had slept in the station wagon the day before, because they were well into what Twitch referred to as "the stink." Chimera-occupied territory. So there was nowhere else to sleep except in a cold car, parked in an old barn, a hundred feet off the highway.

Now, as they listened to radio station WLK, and Twitch hummed along with Tony Bennett's "Cold, Cold

Heart," Walker sat in the seat next to him, and Myra was propped sideways in the back seat.

Twitch had thinning hair, beady eyes, and a hatchet-shaped nose. A two-day growth of beard covered his gaunt cheeks. His incessant humming was starting to drive Walker crazy, and Twitch had a bad case of body odor, which was one of the reasons Myra had chosen to remain in the back seat.

*Of course, we'll smell like Twitch soon,* Walker mused, *and it won't seem so bad then.*

It had been snowing on and off for days, so they had put chains on the tires, which rattled against the inside of the wheel wells as the vehicle followed the road northwest past the remains of Lowell off to the east. There weren't any tire tracks to follow, which was why Twitch was keeping the speed down to twenty-five miles per hour. It was a precaution Walker approved of.

The wash of the car's headlights provided Walker with occasional glimpses of empty houses, burned-out vehicles covered in snow, and clusters of improvised crosses. Drainage ditches were frequently used as makeshift graves because they were both handy and the right depth.

The journey rolled by rather peacefully, with only the soft murmur of the radio, the incessant whir of the heater, and the steady rattle of chains to keep Walker from falling asleep. But then, as the station wagon started up a long sloping hill, Twitch swore. He wasn't a talkative man, which made anything he said important enough to pay attention to.

Walker sat up straight. "What's wrong?"

"Lights," Twitch said laconically, as his head gave an involuntary jerk to the left. "Behind us."

Walker felt a heavy weight land in the pit of his stomach as he looked back over his shoulder, past Myra's sleeping form, stretched out across the back seat. Twitch was right. There, about a quarter of a mile behind, two headlights could be seen through the filthy rear window. "Who are they?" he wondered out loud.

"Don't know," Twitch answered grimly. "But I can tell you who they *aren't* . . . And that's friends of ours. You'd better wake your wife and get ready to bail out. If it's a car that belongs to human jackers, that's bad, 'cause they'll take everything we have and leave us to die, but if it's being driven by the Chimera, then we might as well blow our brains out and save them the trouble."

It was a long speech for Twitch, and Walker knew the runner was serious. So he reached back to wake Myra.

"Wake up, hon . . . And lace up your boots. We have company."

Myra sat up quickly, looked back, and saw the lights just before they disappeared into a dip. She made no response, but Walker knew she was scared, and had every right to be.

"It *could* be a coincidence," Twitch said tersely, "but I doubt it. We can't turn off, because they'd just follow our tracks. And odds are they have a roadblock waiting for us up ahead, so I'm going to pull over. Grab your packs, get out, and run like hell . . . Then, assuming you get clear, make your way north. Sorry, folks, but that's the best I can do."

"But what about you?" Myra wanted to know, as she pushed her husband's pack over the seat. Both of them secured their heavy winter coats, and put on thick gloves. "What will *you* do?"

"I'm going to turn the lights off, turn around, and run straight at them," Twitch replied grimly. "They won't be expecting that. And, if I'm lucky, I'll squeeze past to the left or right."

Walker had doubts. Was this some sort of an elaborate hoax? A way for Twitch to rid himself of his clients, without having to drive all the way to Chicago? The lights might belong to a friend of his, a person who had been paid to show up at that point, and would accompany Twitch back to Indianapolis.

Such a thing was possible, Walker knew that, but he didn't think so. Why go to so much trouble when Twitch could shoot his human cargo instead? So after accepting his pack, Walker unbuckled one of two money belts that he wore around his waist and laid it on the seat between them. The pockets were filled with gold double Eagle coins. The only kind of payment runners would accept anymore.

"There you go, Twitch . . . The second half of your fee."

Twitch looked down, then straight ahead again.

"Thank you, Mr. Paulson . . . And one more thing . . ."

Walker's eyebrows rose.

"Yes?"

"If the stinks close in, shoot Mrs. Paulson right away."

Walker felt a cold, clammy hand clutch at his intestines, and never got a chance to reply as the car skidded to a halt.

"Now!" Twitch said urgently, and he pointed. "Run east, that way!"

So Walker hopped out and opened the passenger-side door for Myra. She handed her husband the pump-action Winchester shotgun purchased in Indianapolis, and got out of the car.

They shut the doors in quick succession, and true to his word Twitch made a U-turn, skidding around until the tires found traction and the car headed back the way it had come. A few seconds later it was gone, as a pair of beams appeared to the south.

Having already shouldered his pack, Walker helped position Myra's, and led his wife up off the road. There was a three-foot bank, and no sooner had they climbed it than a flash of light strobed the wintry landscape and a clap of what sounded like thunder rolled across the land.

"The bastards got Twitch," Walker said bitterly while a fireball floated up into the night sky. "God damn them to hell!"

There was no time to wonder who—or what—the bastards were, or to mourn Twitch, as the headlights quickly grew brighter. The two of them turned and ran.

The snow was deep, however, and it was slow going. They hadn't made much progress when a loud thrumming noise filled the air. It came from above, some sort of aircraft. Suddenly a bright spotlight shot down to sweep the ground in front of the fugitives.

They changed course and ran north, both gasping for breath by that time, but to no avail. The spotlight—or the Chimera who were operating it—seemed to know exactly where they were as a circle of white light washed over them.

Walker pumped a shell into the shotgun's chamber, and was about to shoot Myra in the back of the head when a ball of blue light hit him from above. His muscles seized up and he fell helpless to the ground.

Myra was firing her pistol up into the air by then, but the puny .38 caliber bullets had no effect on the ship that was hovering above, and seconds later she, too, was lying on the ground, her face contorted in pain. Without warning the light disappeared as the aircraft responsible for it veered to the east, and the thrumming noise began to fade into the distance.

Walker struggled to regain control of his body, and had just managed to sit up when a cluster of handheld electric torches came bobbing out of the surrounding darkness. One of them was directed into his face as a pair of Hybrids jerked him to his feet.

"I have no idea whether you want to live," a female voice said, "but if you do then don't resist." The voice was human.

Walker was still processing the words when the pack was jerked off his back and alien fingers probed his clothing. They found and removed the .45, two spare magazines, and his folding knife. But other items, including Walker's wallet, compass, and the recorder taped to the small of his back were left where they were. Whether that was intentional, or the result of a sloppy search, wasn't clear. Later, after they had a chance to talk, Walker would discover that Myra's experience had been similar. It was as if the stinks were after weapons—but had no interest in anything else.

And why should they? Anything that couldn't hurt them was irrelevant.

As Walker squinted his eyes against the bright light the torch came up to light the woman's face from below. She had short gray hair, haunted eyes, and a pointed chin. It gave her an elfin look. A metal collar was buckled around her neck—and a silvery chain led off into the darkness.

"My name is Norma," she said. "Norma Collins. I'm a fifth-grade teacher from Kokomo. You are to return to the road."

"You can speak with them?" Myra wanted to know.

"No, of course not," Collins answered, contempt in her voice. "No one can. But I know what they want. Now move . . . Or all three of us will be punished."

As he and Myra turned toward the road, Walker

caught a glimpse of what he would come to know as a Steelhead standing immediately behind Collins. The vehicle Twitch had spotted in his rearview mirror was idling below. It was a Lyon flatbed truck, and it appeared to be new—most likely it had been taken from a dealership.

A vicious-looking Hybrid snarled at Myra, who hurried over to the tailgate, where two men were waiting to pull her up. Walker was next, and he soon found himself wedged in amongst approximately twenty people, all standing, as the engine revved and the truck jerked into motion. For a moment he couldn't see Myra, and he panicked, but then their eyes met.

At that moment the lights that illuminated them were extinguished. There was a horrible clashing of gears as the Hybrid in the driver's seat missed second and Walker heard a voice in his right ear. "We call the stink behind the wheel Shit-for-Brains," the man explained. "He's still learning to drive."

Walker couldn't see the man's face, but he had the impression of a big bearlike body, and a forceful personality.

"Where are we headed?" Walker inquired.

"Beats me," came the answer. "But I'm in no hurry to get there. How 'bout you?"

Walker couldn't help but smile ruefully.

"Point taken. But why stay aboard? We could jump off."

"Take another look," the man replied. "Up at the cab." Walker turned, saw that the top half of a Hybrid was sticking up through a hole cut in the roof. The cab light was on, so the 'brid was lit from the bottom, and the weapon cradled in his arms was plain to see.

"My name's Burl," the man said. "Harley Burl. I can't say it's a pleasure to meet you, or any of these other folks for that matter, but welcome aboard. The good news is that we're all bound for heaven. Except for Norma Collins that is . . . She's going to hell."

Time seemed to stretch after that, as the truck rumbled through the night and the prisoners sat or stood huddled together for warmth. Night gradually gave way to day, as if the darkness was reluctant to surrender its power over the land and allow another day to begin.

The sun was victorious but was little more than a dimly seen presence off to the east where a layer of thick clouds filtered the sun and kept any warmth from reaching the badly ravaged landscape. Everywhere Walker looked he saw deserted homes, wrecked vehicles, and the unmistakable signs of defeat. The truck had bypassed Chicago and was headed toward Rockford when a battlefield appeared off to the right. Just one of the many places where the Army and the Marine Corps had attempted to make a stand. Something which Walker, as the former Secretary of War, understood better than most.

Wrecked M-12 Sabertooth tanks, LU-P Lynx All-Purpose Vehicles, and shattered Chimeran Stalkers stretched away into the distance, and Walker knew that thousands of dead soldiers lay below the shroud of snow. Eventually, when spring came, a vast boneyard would be revealed. Because the Battle of Rockford, like so many other battles, had been irretrievably lost.

Then the panorama was gone. Farmhouses blipped past, and the truck began to pick up speed. Myra, who was standing directly in front of him now, turned her head.

"The road, it's icy! We're going too fast!"

Walker agreed with her, and others did as well, but they were powerless to do anything about the situation as Shit-for-Brains took advantage of a long straightaway to make better time. Before long the Lyon was up to fifty miles per hour as it roared down the center of the highway.

As the truck topped a slight rise and fifteen or twenty crows took to the air, Shit-for-Brains swerved radically, probably to avoid something in the road. Prisoners screamed, two wheels left the ground, and the Lyon went over. Walker fell on Myra, and she fell on someone else as a loud crash was heard and the truck slid for fifty feet or so before finally coming to a stop.

Some of the prisoners had been thrown clear, but he and Myra were still in the truck, lost in the wild tumble of arms and legs. Walker heard a chorus of moans as people sorted themselves out. As they extricated themselves from the tangle of bodies, he was pleased to discover that none of his bones were broken, and a quick examination revealed that Myra was okay as well. Both had been lucky enough to fall on others, some of whom were seriously injured in the crash.

While the injured were pulled free, Walker heard a series of gunshots and turned to look for the source. That was when he saw that one of the prisoners was making a run for it, or trying to, although the calf-deep snow forced him to lift his knees especially high and was slowing his progress. The projectiles fell short at first, but quickly caught up, and ate the man from below. There was an almost universal moan from the rest of the prisoners as he fell in a bloody heap.

"That was Fuller," the man named Burl said bleakly. Burl had a broad forehead, dark eyebrows, and a three-day growth of beard. "Fuller said he'd run first chance he got, and he did. The man had balls," Burl added by way of an informal eulogy, "and I'll miss him."

The Hybrid who was responsible for Fuller's death

turned back toward the prisoners as Shit-for-Brains led Norma Collins around the front end of the overturned truck. She had been sitting on the passenger side of the cab, and was bleeding from a cut on the forehead, which she continued to dab until the stink jerked her chain. Gathering her wits, she addressed the group. "You will line up on the road," she said. "We're going to walk."

Burl muttered "bitch" under his breath, and some of the others had even worse things to say about Collins, as those who could shuffled out onto the road.

"This woman needs help!" Myra proclaimed, and she knelt next to one of the crash victims. "I think her leg is broken."

"She'll be taken care of," Collins replied coldly. "Do as you were told."

Myra was about to object when Walker took hold of his wife's arm and pulled her to her feet.

"There's nothing we can do, dear. I'm sorry . . ."

She glanced back at the injured woman, then allowed herself to be led around the truck to the road. The people gathered there couldn't see what took place, but they heard two shots. Myra began to cry, and buried her face in her husband's chest, as Collins appeared with Shit-for-Brains in tow. Three other Hybrids joined them.

"Start walking," the schoolteacher said grimly, "unless you want to die here."

As the group began to walk, Walker thought about the man named Fuller and the woman named Collins. Both seemed to demonstrate one thing: In spite of appearances to the contrary, the prisoners weren't entirely powerless. They could die whenever they chose. And death, all things considered, was looking pretty good.

Except for one thing—the recorder still taped to the small of his back. Walker had an obligation to deliver it to Freedom First, if he could just find a way to do so.

Determined not to fail, he put his head down and felt the wind sting his cheeks as the group plodded north.

Walker chose life—but life was hell.

What remained of the day passed slowly as the prisoners were forced to march up the highway, never pausing except to get a drink of water when their captors did. Like those around him, Walker was hungry, *very* hungry, but all entreaties to Norma Collins fell on deaf ears. Probably because she was as helpless to do anything about the situation as the rest of them were.

Finally, when darkness began to fall, the Chimera stopped in a small town. After a quick look around to see what sort of shelter was available, Collins returned and directed the prisoners into an old building. A sign that read "Antlers Hotel" hung out front, just below the impressive rack of moose antlers that had been nailed to the facade. It appeared to be the type of establishment that catered to traveling salesmen, long-haul truck drivers, and people with car trouble.

Collins led a Hybrid and the prisoners through a shabby lobby, into a dingy dining room, and down a short flight of stairs into a candlelit kitchen.

"I thought you'd like some light," Collins said, as if she was doing everyone a favor. "Make yourselves at home."

And with that she and the Hybrid left the group to its own devices. Once the door at the top of the stairs clicked closed the search for a second exit, weapons, and food began. Unfortunately there was no other way out. Cutlery—if there had been any—had been removed by Collins and their Chimeran captors, and the shelves were empty.

But there were lots of nooks and crannies, the looters had been in a hurry, and it wasn't long before the prisoners came up with a jar of red beets, another jar filled with pickles, and the best prize of all—an unopened container of peanut butter!

Burl took charge, and thanks to his size, no one argued as he portioned the precious stuff out. Everyone received two servings, plus a length of pickle, and a piece of beet. Each person also got a sip of beet juice or pickle juice to wash down their meager feast.

And that's what they were doing when Walker heard the door open at the top of the stairs. Collins appeared a few moments after, still on her leash, with two Hybrids following along behind. The stinks stood with weapons at the ready as their slave surveyed the room. Her eyes were like chips of coal.

"The hotel is a mess," she announced, "and the Chimera need someone to clean out a room they can sleep in.

"You!" Collins said assertively, as she pointed a finger at a woman in her early twenties. "Get upstairs."

The young woman's name was Betty. All of the color drained from her face as she stood, and her mother, a woman of forty or so, started to sob.

"Please!" the woman said. "Let me do it instead."

"There's no need to be concerned," Collins said woodenly. "Your daughter will be back soon."

All of them hoped it was true. But as Betty climbed the stairs, followed by Collins and the two Hybrids, they found it impossible to believe. There was no insulation between the floor and the ceiling, so it was easy to hear footsteps as the four arrived in the dining room above. Then came scuffling sounds, followed by a series of short screams, and a solid *thump*.

Betty's mother uttered a forlorn wail, and Myra put an arm around her shoulders in an attempt to comfort her.

"They're going to eat her," Burl said darkly, as he whispered into Walker's ear. "The bastards are going to eat her. With help from Collins. And who knows?" Burl mused out loud. "Maybe Collins will get some table scraps. I wouldn't be surprised."

There wasn't anything the captives could do except find spots to sleep and get what rest they could, knowing that the next day would be just as hard as the one before. Eventually Myra went to sleep, huddled in his arms for warmth, but Walker couldn't. Because even though the candlelight was dim, he was sure he could see the dark stain that was spreading across the ceiling above, and he knew it was red.

When morning came the prisoners were forced up the stairs, through the blood-splattered dining room, and out through the lobby into the cold light of day. Betty's mother had retreated to a place deep within herself by then, leaving her eyes empty and her face blank. If she saw the blood, or understood who it belonged to, she gave no sign.

The day was cold but clear, and as the column made its way northward, Walker saw three white contrails claw the blue sky. Sabre Jets most likely, flying at about 25,000 feet, and entirely unaware of the captives below. Not that the pilots could have done anything for the group other than put them out of their misery.

Fortunately for the Walkers they had been permitted to keep their winter clothing and sturdy hiking boots when they were captured, but not all of their fellow captives were so lucky. Some of the prisoners wore relatively light clothing and had been forced to supplement it with whatever they could lay their hands on. There were blankets that they wrapped around themselves, and rags which were bound around their feet in order to

combat frostbite. So it was a scraggly-looking group
that followed the highway past houses that stared unsee-
ingly at the road, mangled cars that had been destroyed
from above, and crow-pecked bodies clothed in suits of
glittering frost.

An hour passed, then two, before the column arrived
at a major intersection where another group of prisoners
stood waiting. Walker took notice of a sign, and realized
they had crossed into Wisconsin, having bypassed Rockford.

There was a momentary pause as the Hybrids communicated with one another via stink-speech, followed
by new orders from Collins, who seemed eager to assert
her dubious authority over the newcomers.

"Form a column, keep your mouths shut, and start
walking."

They weren't supposed to talk to each other, but it
was easy to get away with, so long as Collins was out of
earshot. So Walker fell into step next to Burl and kept
his voice low. "So what's your theory, Harley? Where
are the stinks taking us? And why?"

"I don't know," Burl admitted. "But you're the Secretary of War, so you tell *me*."

Walker was silent for a moment. They had been careful to maintain their false identities, fearing that if the
stinks knew who they had, they might try to take advantage somehow. But given how many times Henry's face
had been in the papers, he supposed the deception
couldn't last forever. He glanced at Burl. "How long
have you known?"

"Since last night," the other man answered. "Back in
the hotel. A newspaper was lying on a counter. It was
more than a month old—and you were on page two.
The reporter quoted you as saying that everything is

under control and we're going to win." Burl offered a sly grin. "Would you like to revise that?"

Walker winced. "Yeah, I would. Things aren't going well—but I still believe we can win. *If* we fight like hell. The only problem is that Grace might decide to give up."

Burl's eyebrows rose.

"Really? Please share."

Walker knew he should share. Because if anything were to happen to him, Myra would need help getting the recorder to Freedom First. So he told Burl the whole story, and once he was done, the other man nodded.

"You're right, Henry. Assuming what you say is true, the recording is important. *Very* important. You can count on me to help in any way I can."

That made Walker feel better, and the hours seemed to pass more quickly as the group marched through farm country. The skies continued to be clear and the sun actually helped to warm them. On one occasion Walker saw three figures stalking along the distant horizon. Thanks to the briefings received over the last year, he recognized them as Chimera-made Goliaths. The gigantic, four-legged machines were nearly two hundred feet tall, and heavily armed. The fact that the mechs could move around with total impunity during daylight hours was further evidence of the extensive footprint that the Chimera had been able to establish in North America.

Another column of human prisoners joined theirs about an hour later, which suggested that the Chimera were scouring the countryside for humans, and herding the prisoners to a central location of some sort.

Night was falling by that time, and as the column continued its way north, Collins was there to urge everyone on. "Pick up the pace!" she ordered sternly as a Hybrid accompanied her back along the column. "We're almost there. Or would you like to sleep out in the open tonight?"

None of them knew where "there" was, but none of them wanted to sleep in the open, so the prisoners kept going. And as they did, the Hybrids led the group past a sign that read "Hasbro Mining," turned right onto a well-churned secondary road, and toward a scattering of bright lights that lay ahead. Huge pieces of half-seen machinery loomed in the shadows to either side, as well as buildings that threatened to disappear into the gathering gloom and the dry snowflakes that were beginning to fall as the temperature dropped.

And then they were "there," being led around the edge of an open pit mine, which was lit by pole-mounted work lights. Walker could see an access road that corkscrewed down into the bottom of the depression, the shantytown that had been constructed there, and three flickering bonfires around which dozens of people were huddled.

"Well there it is," Burl said sarcastically, "home sweet home."

As Hybrids led them down into the pit, and the walls rose around him, Walker thought about the recorder and Chicago. Would Myra and he be able to escape from the open pit mine?

Walker wasn't willing to give up, but it was hard to feel optimistic, as the earth swallowed him up.

# CHAPTER TWELVE

# ANGEL OF DEATH

**Near Valentine, Nebraska**
**Monday, December 3, 1951**

William Dentweiler was wearing a snap-brim hat, a suit, and a thick topcoat, but the air blowing in through the VTOL's gun ports was frigid and it would have been nice to have a lap blanket. But there weren't any blankets, not that Dentweiler could see anyway, and he couldn't bring himself to ask. Partly because he didn't want to come across as a whiny civilian VIP, and partly because he knew the thin layer of warm air between his skin and his clothes would disappear the moment he stood up. Which he would certainly have to do if he wanted to address the helmeted crew chief who was slouched on top of a crate labeled "Cartridges, 7.62mm, Ball M5A2."

So Dentweiler remained where he was, gloved hands thrust deeply into his pockets, as the VTOL droned north toward base SRPA 6. Like President Grace, Dentweiler was of the opinion that allowing SRPA to construct and maintain its own bases had been a mistake, even if the need for secrecy seemed to recommend it. Because now, as the war continued to drag on, the SRPA hierarchy was starting to show an independent streak even though the officers in charge of the Army, Navy, and Marine Corps were typically cooperative.

But it was too late to strip SRPA of its bases at this point, and as long as Grace remained in control of the organization's budget, they would be forced to toe the line.

Dentweiler's thoughts were interrupted as the engines changed pitch, the VTOL communicated a different set of vibrations through the seat of his pants, and the aircraft seemed to stall briefly as the engines went vertical. Then, as Dentweiler felt his stomach flip-flop, the aircraft went straight down. Less than a minute later he felt a palpable bump as the VTOL's landing gear made contact with the oil-stained mech deck.

The crew chief came over to help Dentweiler release the harness that held him in place while the engines spooled down.

"Welcome to Nebraska!" the noncom shouted cheerfully, "and watch your step. The ramp can be slick."

Meanwhile outside the VTOL, and well clear of the windmilling props, a group of officers was waiting to receive the President's Chief of Staff. Major Richard Blake was in charge of the delegation, which included a scruffy-looking intelligence officer named Captain Bo Richards and Lieutenant Nathan Hale.

Having completed the mission into enemy-held Hot Springs less than a week earlier, Hale had been hoping for a three-day pass, and a chance to visit Cassie in Denver. A trip that would have allowed him to see Dr. Barrie as well—who was said to be recovering nicely.

But that plan had been blown out of the water when a so-called rocket arrived from SRPA Command ordering Blake to stand by for a visit from a VIP, and to prep a SAR team for a special mission. A mission that would involve both Richards and Hale.

So he felt mixed emotions as the battle-scarred VTOL

put down, the props stopped turning, and the cargo ramp grated on concrete. The civilian who strolled down the slanted surface paused to look around, and having spotted the group waiting to receive him, ambled over. Blake took care of the introductions, and when it was Hale's turn to shake hands, he noticed that Dentweiler's gloves were still on. A small thing, but he knew that life was comprised of small things, all of which typically added up.

Nevertheless, he showed the proper respect.

"It's a pleasure to meet you, sir," he said, and Hale noticed that Dentweiler didn't seem to be surprised by the color of his eyes.

"The pleasure is mine," the official replied. "Nice job up in Hot Springs by the way. President Grace wanted me to thank you."

A compliment from the President of the United States was a very special thing, and Hale couldn't help but feel a surge of pleasure, but there was something about Dentweiler's cold affect that prevented him from liking the man.

"It was a team effort, sir," he said truthfully. "I'll pass the message along."

"You do that," Dentweiler replied dismissively, turning to Blake. Together they led the way to the elevators with Richards, Hale, and the others following along behind. Though dressed in a rumpled Army uniform, the Intel officer had longish hair, three days' worth of unshaved stubble, and a weather-beaten face. Hale barely knew the man, but had already come to enjoy his irreverent sense of humor. "The only thing more dangerous than a Steelhead armed with an Auger, is a civilian carrying a briefcase," Richards said sotto voce. "God help us both."

The elevator delivered the group to the admin deck

and a smartly uniformed sergeant who was waiting to escort them through security and into the same conference room where the briefing for Operation Iron Fist had taken place.

But the maps, photos, and schematics were different now. The aerial shots didn't come as any surprise—Hale was expecting those—yet some of the pictures had been taken from ground level. That was unusual, since most SAR missions took place behind enemy lines where such photos were almost impossible to get. And even though he didn't know the city well, Hale recognized Chicago's war-torn skyline, and felt something cold trickle into his bloodstream. Because while an attack on a building in Hot Springs was a bit loony—a mission into stink-held Chicago verged on insane.

"Okay," Blake said, once all of them were seated and their visitor had removed his overcoat. "Listen up . . . Mr. Dentweiler is here to brief us on a top secret SAR mission—only this time we're going to bring back a person, rather than an object. Mr. Dentweiler, the floor is yours."

The Chief of Staff's white shirt, striped tie, and blue suit were impeccable. Light glinted off rimless glasses as his eyes passed over each face. "Thank you," he said levelly. "Major Blake indicated that this mission will be top secret, and he is correct. Under no circumstances are you to share any aspect of this briefing or the mission itself with friends, family, or the press. Is that understood?"

All of the participants nodded dutifully, and having received that assurance, Dentweiler began what appeared to be a carefully rehearsed speech.

"As you know," he began, "things are not going well. The Chimera have control of Canada, and are pushing south into the United States. However, thanks to the black eye that you and the 5th Ranger Battalion gave the stinks last week, plus the Liberty Defense Perimeter presently under construction, the President remains confident that we will not only be able to stop further incursions, but counterattack in the very near future.

"That's the good news," Dentweiler continued. "The bad news is that in addition to battling the Chimera, the government has been forced to cope with internal dissension, too. That includes organizations bent on overthrowing the elected government, all manner of whacko dissidents, and—I'm sorry to say—the occasional traitor. In this case a cabinet-level official who had not only given up on the war, but left Washington in an effort to contact the stinks and try to open negotiations with them.

"I know," Dentweiler said, even though no one had spoken. "It's hard to believe—but I assure you it's true. And, what makes the situation even more shocking is the fact that the official I referred to is none other than Secretary of War Henry Walker!"

The group had been silent up until then, but that was enough to elicit a heartfelt "Holy shit" from Captain Perko, who was there to represent the Air Corps.

"Yes," Dentweiler said solemnly, "that was my reaction as well. Frankly we don't know if such negotiations are even possible, given how alien the stinks are, but were Secretary Walker to find the means to communicate with the Chimera, it could be disastrous. Not only because of the possibility that he might claim to represent the United States government, but because he knows everything there is to know regarding the defense perimeter. That's why it's absolutely imperative that you find Walker, and bring him back. Or, failing that," Dentweiler said darkly, "eliminate him."

Blake had been silent up until that point, but the last comment caused him to frown and clear his throat. "I'm sorry, Mr. Dentweiler, but the charter under which SRPA operates specifically prohibits our personnel from participating in assassinations. However, if we can find Mr. Walker, I can assure you that we *will* bring him back."

For a moment the Chief of Staff was silent, and then he nodded agreeably.

"Yes, I'm sure you will. And that brings us to the question of where Secretary Walker is hiding. Based on information provided by the FBI and other sources we believe he's in Chicago."

Having already identified the photos on the wall, Hale wasn't surprised. Nor, apparently, was Richards—who was busy cleaning his fingernails with a switchblade. Hale wondered how he got away with it, but Major Blake hadn't seemed to notice.

"We tracked him from Washington to Indianapolis," Dentweiler continued, "and we damned near nailed the bastard, too, but two hours before our agents closed in on the hotel where Walker and his wife were staying, the two of them left town in the company of a so-called runner named Twitch. According to Twitch's common-law wife, he was headed for Chicago."

Richards sat up straight upon hearing that news and the knife vanished. "Twitch Saunders?"

Dentweiler raised an eyebrow. "I believe that was his name—yes."

"Then they had a pretty good chance of getting through," Richards mused. "Twitch is expensive—but he's the best. But *why*? What can the Walkers accomplish in Chicago? The city is crawling with stinks."

"There's no way to be absolutely certain," Dentweiler replied, "but we believe Walker plans to contact Freedom First and ask for their assistance. You're acquainted with the organization, I believe?"

"Yes," Richards answered. "I am. They hate President Grace, but they hate the Chimera even more, and fight the stinks every day. In fact, some people claim that something like five thousand 'brids are tied up trying to track the rebels down. If true, that's five thousand stinks who aren't headed south."

"I've heard that argument," Dentweiler responded, and his voice was strangely cold. "I might even buy into it if it weren't for all the lies they tell via their illegal radio station. Which, when you think about it, is probably why the Walkers were drawn to them."

Hale could sense the tension between the two men—as could Blake, who was quick to intervene. "In spite of the illegal radio station, it should be noted that Freedom First people continue to be a valuable source of intelligence," the major pointed out, "which they funnel to Captain Richards here. I'm sure his knowledge of the group will prove to be invaluable in determining whether the Walkers are in Chicago or not. In fact," Blake added, "I daresay we wouldn't be able to execute the mission without him."

The last was intended as a warning, which Dentweiler received loud and clear. He forced a crooked smile. "Yes, of course. Well, that's the essence of the situation, and I have only one thing to add. If you apprehend Walker—no, *when* you apprehend Walker—he may be carrying a diary or other materials. If so, bring them back. And such materials, should they exist, must be treated with the utmost secrecy. Under no circumstances will unauthorized personnel be permitted to read them, copy them, or share them in any way. Is that clear?"

"*Very* clear," Blake replied, as he directed meaningful glances at Richards and Hale.

"And *Mrs.* Walker?" Hale wanted to know. "Are we to bring her back as well?"

"Of course," Dentweiler replied harshly. "She's a criminal. Just like her traitorous husband."

The briefing came to a close shortly after that, Dentweiler was escorted up to the mech deck where his VTOL was waiting, and the junior officers were allowed to remain behind.

"So," Hale said as he and Richards made their way to the elevators. "You've been to Chicago."

"Yes," Richards answered grimly. "I have."

Hale glanced sideways. "How bad is it?"

"On a scale of one to ten, it's a fucking twelve," Richards said. "I know you were in England—and I know it was a freak show. But this is going to be just as bad, and maybe worse. Bring your A game, Lieutenant. There won't be any second chances."

The trip from SRPA 6 to the Chicago area was interrupted by two intermediate stops. One to refuel, and one to wait for a storm front to pass, because Echo Team had enough problems to deal with without flying into the side of a hill. Which, given the plan to come in low and fast, was a very real possibility, especially in the dark.

Except that, as Hale crouched between Purvis and his copilot, and stared out through the *Party Girl*'s badly scratched canopy, what remained of the city of Chicago was anything but dark. What looked like bolts of lightning strobed between half-seen structures of uncertain purpose, fireflylike blobs of incandescence floated here and there, and clusters of tightly grouped greenish blue lights marked the location of Chimeran fortresses. A convenience at least some of the stinks were about to regret.

"Okay," Purvis said tightly, "we're ten minutes out, so it's time to get ready. Good hunting."

Hale nodded soberly, "Thanks, Harley. Watch your six on the way out."

"Count on it," Purvis replied. "Now get the hell out of my cockpit. I have work to do."

Hale grinned, stood, and backed into the cargo compartment as Purvis spoke into his headset. "Hollywood to Eagle-Three . . . I'm eight out. Come on down and kick some ass. Over."

"Roger that," came the reply. "Stay low, stay slow, and we'll show you cargo camels how it's done. Over."

A few months earlier Purvis might have taken exception to the cheerful arrogance inherent in the fighter pilot's transmission, but he'd seen the latest stats. Chimeran fighters were three times faster than their human counterparts, more maneuverable, and better armed. In fact, the only edge human pilots had over the stinks was skill, because, good though their aircraft were, Chimeran pilots lacked imagination and were delightfully predictable.

Still, the life expectancy of a Sabre Jet pilot was even shorter than that of a VTOL cargo camel, so Purvis let the trash talk slide.

"I'll be sure to take notes," he promised dryly. "Hollywood out."

Cold air roared into the VTOL's cargo compartment as the twelve-man SAR team prepared to execute one of the most difficult evolutions any of them would be called upon to carry out. The plan was to rappel from a hovering VTOL into a stink-held city in the middle of the night. It was, as Sergeant Kawecki so eloquently put it, "a chance to do something really stupid."

Both side doors were open, the sliding gantries were extended, and the men were lined up ready to go as the

*Party Girl* made her final approach, and a series of explosions rocked the northeast sector of the city. Hale knew that a Chimeran tower was located up that way, but the real purpose of the Sabre attack was to create a diversion calculated to pull Chimeran resources away from the area where the SAR team was going to put down.

The strategy wouldn't work entirely of course, but it couldn't hurt, and he was eager to improve the odds any way that he could.

Both Hale and Richards checked each and every soldier to make sure their harnesses were clipped to a descender and that each rope was properly threaded. Once that process was complete Richards took his place at the head of the line and waited for Kawecki to check *his* hookup.

Hale, meanwhile, was at the tail end of the other line, so that if Richards was killed during the insertion, he would be available to take command. That was the theory anyway, although there was always a chance that *both* men would be killed, which would leave a noncom like Kawecki to take over.

All such thoughts ended abruptly as Purvis switched from horizontal to vertical flight and battled to keep the *Party Girl* steady. It was no small job, as gusts of wind hit the ship from the west and gravity did its best to pull her down.

Hale saw the green jump light flash, heard the VTOL's crew chief yell, "Go, go, *go!*" and watched his Sentinels exit, one after another. There were no signs of ground fire, and the ship was positioned above a so-called fresh point, meaning a set of coordinates that hadn't been used before. A precaution intended to lessen the chances of an ambush. But that didn't mean much in a city where they might be rappelling onto the roof of a stink stronghold if Purvis was the least bit off target.

Then it was Hale's turn.

As he threw himself out the door, he was conscious of the need to put a sufficient amount of space between himself and the drop ship's tubby hull, lest he smack into it. A very painful proposition indeed and one that would slow his descent in a situation where speed was everything, and mistakes could cost lives.

Hale felt a brief moment of free fall, followed by a spine-stretching jerk and a surge of fear as the VTOL lurched sideways, coming within half a foot of his dangling body. Frigid prop wash blew straight down and threatened to spin Hale around as he ran his right hand along the rope that curved around his right hip. By letting rope slide up through the descender, he was able to swiftly lower himself to the ground.

Things became a little easier as one of the Sentinels already on the ground took control of Hale's drop line and held it steady. A few seconds later he was standing on a city street, where he hurried to unclip his harness lest the *Party Girl* inadvertently soar upward and jerk him into the air.

"The last man is clear," Richards said over the radio. "Thanks for the lift, Hollywood. Out."

Purvis had been waiting for what seemed like an hour. As his crew reeled the drop ropes in and brought the extendable gantries inboard, he took the ship straight up.

Powerful searchlights and long necklaces of tracer fire began exploring the night sky, searching for the meat-things that had been so audacious as to invade Chimeran airspace. The Sabre Jets were long gone, having fled south, before the stinks could scramble their fighters.

Which was nice for the jet jockeys, but not for Purvis, who was still in the area.

The solution, such as it was, consisted of switching to level flight while fleeing south at little more than rooftop level. A very dangerous process indeed, especially at night, but one calculated to keep the Chimeran fighters off his ass. Because they were so fast that they couldn't ride the VTOL's six, and being unable to get under the ship's belly, they were unlikely to nail Purvis with their cannons.

So it was their heat-seeking missiles he feared the most, and the only defense against them was to fire white-hot flares to port and starboard as the *Party Girl* ran for its life.

Meanwhile, back at the insertion point, Richards was busy sorting everyone out.

This was his fifth drop into Chicago. That made him an Ace in the parlance of his Intel peers. How many more such missions was he entitled to before his number came up? Six? Seven? Or five and out?

There was no way to know.

But given that Hale and his men were Sentinels, and he wasn't, Richards knew he was the most vulnerable man on the team. An irony that he did his best to ignore as his subordinates went about creating a defensive perimeter and waited to see who would arrive first. Freedom First—or a heavily armed Chimeran response team.

It was a question made all the more urgent by the fact that they had been dropped into the center of a major intersection. It was too dark to see his surroundings clearly, but thanks to the photos he'd memorized, Richards knew that partially burned-out buildings surrounded him on three sides, with an elevated train station on the fourth. Any or all of them might provide protective cover, but if the Freedom First guide arrived *after* the team cleared the street, he might assume they had been compromised, and leave without them.

Then they would be shit out of luck.

So Richards was forced to settle for a wheel formation, with all the Sentinels facing out as precious seconds ticked away. The guide was *late*—five minutes late—and Richards was getting ready to retreat to the train station. He considered his alternatives. Should he leave a radio where the guide could find it? That might work, but if a Chimeran patrol happened by, it would signal the team's presence as well.

Suddenly a manhole cover popped up out of its metal collar, fell over, and hit the street with a clang. Richards yelled "Don't shoot!" and not a moment too soon as Corporal Vedka and Private Oshi swiveled toward the noise, ready to fire.

"Eyes front!" Hale ordered, lest the men in his sector take their eyes off the perimeter. He turned to see Richards kneel next to the dimly seen guide and exchange a few brief sentences. Then the group was on the move.

In keeping with pre-established protocols, the Sentinels armed with scope-mounted Fareyes, M5A2s, and Rossmore shotguns descended into the depths first, leaving those with Bellocks, rocket launchers, and the team's single minigun to provide security until they, too, were ordered below.

That was when Hale dropped into the hole, felt for the rungs with his feet, and passed the M5A2 down to Private Tanner. The biggest man on the team and the proud owner of the minigun.

The cast iron lid made a harsh grating sound as Hale pulled it over, pushed the chunk of metal up, and then lowered it into place. At that point the team could lay claim to a clean insertion. An accomplishment that boosted their chances of success from damned unlikely to the realm of the barely possible.

As Hale lowered himself into what appeared to be a storm drain, the first things he noticed were the dank, fetid air and the harsh glow of a flare which had been inserted into a crack in one of the brick walls. He hit bottom, and a layer of black sediment squished under his boots as Tanner returned his weapon.

The scene that greeted him was surreal, to say the least. The Sentinels were lined up with their backs to a wall as a young woman inspected them. Except that "inspected" wasn't the right word, since what she was really doing was looking each man over prior to sniffing him the same way that a friendly dog might have.

She had rough-cut blond hair, a pug nose, and was dressed in a leather jacket, tight-fitting jeans, and lace-up boots.

"They call her Spook," Richards explained as she moved from Cooper to Samson. "She has an extremely acute sense of smell—and that can be quite useful down here. By memorizing what each man smells like, she'll be able to sort them out in total darkness, if need be."

"I see," Hale said as the vetting process continued. "Is that why people call her Spook?"

"No," Richards replied, "that has to do with her tattoos."

That was when Hale noticed the tattoos on Spook's face, neck, and hands. At first he had thought they were a trick of the light from the flickering flare. Most if not all of them were symbols which seemed to have religious or occult value, including variations on pentagrams, crosses, triangles, sigils, moons, and at least one ankh, located at the very center of her forehead. "So they're for more than decoration?" he inquired.

Richards nodded as Spook subjected an embarrassed Private Perez to her strange form of scrutiny.

"Yeah. Spook believes that those symbols protect her from Chimeran energy projectiles, and maybe they do. You'll notice that she isn't wearing any body armor, yet there isn't a scratch on her. And that's saying something, here in Chicago!" The strange young woman completed her inspection of the men and turned to approach the officers.

"Stand by," Richards said. "It's your turn."

Hale stood his ground. Spook had very direct green eyes, and they registered surprise as she examined him. She was pretty, even with the facial tattoos, and exuded a strong animal magnetism. "You have stink eyes," she said artlessly. "And I can smell the virus on you. The others have it, too. But not as strong."

Hale didn't know what to say, so he was silent as Spook began to sniff his right arm. She followed the limb all the way up to his shoulder, where she paused for a moment, before licking his neck. That was something new, and slightly erotic, as Hale had the opportunity to smell *her*. Rather than the soapy fragrance he had come to associate with Cassie, Spook exuded a musky scent which was appealing, but in a different way. "You taste like they do," Spook said as she pulled back. "You're changing. Did you know that?"

Hale shrugged. "I've been immunized. That amounts to a change."

Spook stared at him thoughtfully, as if deciding whether to say more, then turned to Richards.

"The station is two miles away," she said. "The first mile and a half will be very dangerous."

"We'll be ready," Richards assured her. "Lead the way."

So Spook led the way, followed by Richards, Kawecki, Henning, Vedka, Oshi, Perez, Obo, Cooper, Samson, Dana, Tanner, and Hale.

The order of march had been determined by the type of threats they were likely to encounter, the sort of weapon that each Sentinel was carrying, and the need to place an officer at each end of the column.

The going was fairly easy at first, because the ceiling of the main tunnel was at least eight feet high, and it was wide enough for three men to walk abreast. Not that Richards or Hale would permit such a thing. Their challenge was to keep the Sentinels spaced out so that a single explosion couldn't kill more than one or two men.

Illumination, such as it was, came from the lights built into or taped onto their weapons. White blobs overlapped each other and roamed the ceiling, walls, and floor as the twelve-man column followed their young guide through her subterranean world.

Then the situation changed as Spook paused in front of a pipe that was about four feet in diameter. It opened into the larger drain at a point approximately three feet off the floor. After peering back, as if to make sure that the Sentinels were still with her, Spook entered the smaller tube and promptly disappeared.

Hale watched Richards and the rest of them remove the secondary weapons that were slung across their backs, and slip them into canvas drag bags which each man would tow behind him lest the barrels get caught on an obstruction of some sort. Tight spaces weren't good, but Hale figured that Spook knew that, and wouldn't have chosen such a route unless it was absolutely necessary to do so.

It took a full five minutes for the team to enter the

pipe. Hale went last, the M5A2 carbine dragging behind him as he elbowed his way forward with the shotgun cradled in his arms. The surface beneath his chest was dry, and would remain so until the snow started to melt and the spring runoff began.

Thanks to the light projected from under the Rossmore's barrel and reflected from one wall back to the other, Hale could see Tanner's drag bag and the soles of his enormous boots as the other Sentinel made his way forward. It was a slow, painstaking process and Hale hated the way the tube hugged him from all sides.

At one point it was necessary for him to pull himself over the corpse of a badly mauled rat. But he'd been forced to deal with worse—much worse—and he kept on going. He was in a rhythm by then, and starting to feel better about things.

"Leapers!"

Spook yelled over the radio Richards had given her, but the horrible screeching noise spoke for itself as the cat-sized Chimera dropped out of vertical drain holes to land in the pipe they occupied. It was just about the worst thing that could have happened at that point, since none of the Sentinels could fire forward without hitting the man in front of them.

So as one of the horrors landed on Tanner's legs, and turned to attack Hale, the only thing he could do was to thrust his shotgun barrel into the Leaper's gaping mouth, using it as a club. Fangs broke as the weapon went in, and the stink shrieked in pain as Hale drew his commando knife, and slashed at the beast. A good twenty inches separated the two combatants, but the Fairbairn Sykes was long enough to make contact, and the tip found a major artery.

Blood sprayed the inside surface of the pipe as Richards shouted over the radio.

"Fire up into those drains! Kill them before they can drop!"

Private Russ Dana was directly in front of Tanner. He was one of two Sentinels armed with an L11-2 Dragon, which he had already used to fry one of the Leapers. Samson's boots had been singed by the momentary belch of flames but there were no complaints as Dana rolled over to direct the flamethrower upward.

There was a subdued roar as a tongue of fire shot up through the vertical drain, found flesh, and cooked one of the falling Leapers. The body caught on an obstruction, another stink landed on top of it, and began to eat its way downward.

He and Henning sent blast after blast of liquid fire up to intercept the gibbering beasts even as one or two others managed to roll over and bring other weapons into play. Hale's Rossmore generated a deafening *BOOM, BOOM, BOOM* sound as he fired upward and empty casings fell back on him. They were hot, and therefore uncomfortable, but a lot better than the alternative.

Then, as suddenly as the attack had begun, it was over, and the team was free to elbow their way forward again. Those located at the tail end of the line had no choice but to drag themselves through the bloody remains of their attackers, and the stench typical of all Chimera combined with the throat-clogging odor of cooked flesh and the harsh smell of gunsmoke.

Finally after what seemed like an eternity of crawling, but was actually only ten minutes, Hale saw Tanner's boots disappear, followed by his drag bag. Then it was Hale's turn, and he stuck his head out into an open chamber, where the others were waiting to pull him clear.

As before a flare was inserted into a crack, and it produced a harsh blue-green glow as minor wounds were checked. Some of the Sentinels took long drags from their I-Packs, and others looked to their weapons. Hale slipped shells into the Rossmore, and he swung the shotgun up just as something *huge* materialized out of the darkness.

"Don't shoot!" Spook said tersely. "Ralf won't hurt you . . . Will you, boy?"

At that point Hale and the rest of them were treated to an amazing sight as a brawny lion-sized Howler padded over to stand on its rear legs while it licked Spook's face.

"Don't ask," Richards said as he appeared at Hale's elbow. "It was wounded, Spook found the beast, and nursed it back to health. But watch what you do . . . Ralf will attack *anything* that threatens her. Human *or* Chimera."

Hale had never heard of such a thing, much less witnessed it, but he was coming to realize that by living in such close proximity to the Chimera, Chicago's freedom fighters were finding new ways to adapt and survive.

With the fearsome Ralf ranging ahead, Spook led the team through a maze of interconnecting tunnels and passageways, slogging through ankle-deep water. All were deserted, but there were signs of habitation. As Hale walked along he saw graffiti, ledges where cooking fires had scorched the walls, and in one sad case a mound of broken bricks with a white cross painted directly above it. There were occasional signs of battle, too, including areas where the walls were pockmarked with bullet holes, empty casings littered the floor, and well-gnawed bones lay scattered about.

Eventually, having traveled the better part of two

miles, the team was forced to pause in front of a well-guarded steel gate. Based on appearances Hale concluded that the obstruction had originally been put in place to filter debris out of what was transformed into a raging river at certain times of the year. Twin ladders led up toward the surface, and would allow maintenance workers to remove accumulated garbage from the filtration system below the streets.

But modifications had been made—a pass-through door had been added, and two heavily armed men were there to guard it. They nodded to Spook, eyed the Sentinels warily, and kept their weapons handy as Ralf followed his mistress through the opening, followed by the SAR team.

From a point fifty feet farther on, a hand-excavated passageway led to a large subway tunnel that had originally been separated from the main storm drain by seventy-five feet of solid earth and rock. Tracks ran both ways and gleamed dully under the light cast down from fixtures above. Clearly the Freedom First rebels had some sort of power plant, and weren't afraid to use it. Still another sign of how resourceful they were.

A flight of stairs led up to a platform where Chicago's citizens had waited patiently for the trains to arrive. Posters advertising the merits of the city's public transportation system hung above the wooden benches lining the wall, and another set of well-worn stairs led to the street above. The stairway was blocked by a makeshift wooden barricade with carefully placed Chimeran-made land mines, and was covered by raking fire from a large-caliber machine gun.

The weapon was positioned at the bottom of the stairway, and manned by a boy-girl team, both of whom appeared to be about twelve. They waved to the Sentinels as they passed by, and shouted greetings to Spook, who raised a hand by way of reply.

She led the Sentinels along the platform, past a shoeshine stand and an empty newspaper kiosk to a glassed-in office where the local subway sector manager had once held court. It was furnished with a huge wall map of the transit system, a calendar that boasted a topless brunette, and a beat-up metal desk. Some mismatched chairs, a bookcase filled with binders, and a coatrack completed the decor.

That was where Richards called a halt and ordered Kawecki to put half the team where they could defend the station, giving the rest of the Sentinels a chance to grab a bite to eat.

While they pulled out their rations, Ralf licked himself and lay down next to a bench, and Richards and Hale followed Spook into the office. The person in charge of Freedom First Chicago awaited them there. He had been a big man once, well over six feet tall, but now he was missing both his legs. He had fuzzy red hair, a craggy brow, and a fist-flattened nose. The wheelchair that supported his torso had clearly seen heavy use, and was fitted with holsters on both sides.

"Welcome!" the rebel leader said cheerfully, and he eyed Hale curiously. "My name is Jacoby. Sam Jacoby. Pardon me if I don't get up."

Hale chuckled politely as he went forward to shake hands. It was probably an old joke, one Jacoby likely used to break the ice and put new acquaintances at ease.

"Glad to meet you, sir," he said as the other man's fingers nearly crushed his. "My name is Hale."

Jacoby took in the yellow-gold eyes, raised his bushy eyebrows, but remained silent and turned to Richards.

"It's good to see you again, Bo. So the lieutenant has

been immunized, I see. Do all the people you work with have Chimeran eyes?"

"No," Richards replied flatly. "Only Hale. But the rest have Hybrid-fast reaction times, they can take more punishment than you or I, and they heal quickly. *Very* quickly, so long as they don't take major damage. It comes in handy."

Jacoby nodded grimly.

"Good. I'm glad to hear that the Grace administration finally did *something* right. God knows we're going to need all the help we can get, if we're going to win this war."

"Yes," Richards agreed soberly. "That's something all of us can agree on."

"So, why the visit?" Jacoby demanded tactlessly. "As you know, the government hasn't given us piss-all since they pulled out of Chicago. Present company excepted, of course. So you must be here on a special mission of some sort."

"That's true," Richards admitted reluctantly, as he went on to describe the meeting with Chief of Staff Dentweiler, the government's case against ex–Secretary of War Henry Walker, and the evidence that pointed toward a trip to Chicago.

"I know you dislike Grace and his administration," Richards finished, "but Walker plans to open negotiations with the stinks if he can. And that would be bad for everyone—including the members of Freedom First."

Jacoby nodded slowly, as if still in the process of assimilating what Richards had said.

"You've got that right, Bo," he said deliberately. "But I'm afraid that you made the trip for nothing. Walker sent us a letter, via runner. He said he was on his way to Chicago, carrying something of importance, but he didn't say what.

"Then, a few days ago, we got word that Twitch, the runner who had agreed to bring the Walkers to Chicago, had been killed. Some people figure the Walkers are dead, too, but others think they got away and are headed for our base in Montana. Personally, I don't have a clue as to what happened to them. God help them if the Chimera got ahold of them."

Hale waited for Richards to respond, and when the other officer didn't, he cleared his throat. "No offense, Mr. Jacoby, but why should we believe you?" he asked, careful to keep his voice as neutral as possible. "Given your dislike of the government, you could be protecting Walker."

Richards frowned and opened his mouth as if to speak, but Jacoby raised a hand.

"That's a fair question, son . . . But suffice it to say that Bo's correct. If Walker showed up here, and tried to open negotiations with the stinks, I'd shoot him myself!"

Suddenly an Army-style field phone on Jacoby's desk rang. Jacoby picked it up, held the receiver to his ear, and listened for five seconds before slamming the device down.

He mashed a red button, and a klaxon began to bleat. He had to shout to be heard over the din. "A trainload of stinks broke through the barrier a mile south of here and is headed this way! There isn't enough time to run, so we'll have to stay and fight. Welcome to Chicago, gentlemen—and here's hoping you live long enough to get out again."

The rebels were well organized for civilians, but the Chimera had the advantage of speed and the element of surprise, so the humans were still taking up defensive positions when the first blocky car appeared. It was going way too fast, as if the Hybrid at the controls hadn't had much practice driving it, and sparks flew as the brakes were applied and the train came to a shuddering stop.

The cars' curved roofs came within inches of the arched ceiling and were painted yellow, with black stripes. The stinks had chosen to commandeer one of the work trains normally used for maintenance, rather than a regular commuter train. Dozens of Hybrids emerged and a hellish firefight began. Glass shattered as plasma projectiles fired from a Bullseye sleeted across the office, and everyone hit the floor. Everyone except Jacoby, that is, who sent his wheelchair rolling forward, and drew his .45s.

He fired both pistols in alternating sequence, swearing at the Chimera as he did so, careless of the projectiles that whipped around him.

Hale knelt two feet back of the shattered window, triggered two 40mm grenades from the M5A2, and had the satisfaction of seeing both of them shatter windows and explode *inside* the second car.

Fortunately for Jacoby and his freedom fighters, the Sentinels were present to absorb the brunt of the initial attack and keep a lot of stinks bottled up on the train as others fell to combined fire from a multitude of sources. The battle was far from one-sided however, as Corporal Vedka took an Auger round right between the eyes, Private Henning died in a ball of flame when a stray projectile struck the fuel canister for his Dragon L11-2, and Private Oshi was struck down by half a dozen spines from a Chimeran Hedgehog grenade.

Serious though the causalities were, they were nothing compared to the slaughter imposed on the stinks who were forced to perform a macabre dance as a hail of bullets jerked, spun, and even lifted them off their feet before throwing them down onto the oily ground. Even the children on the machine gun got into the act by swiveling their weapon around to fire on the enemy.

Hale should have felt jubilant, but as he put half a dozen bullets into one of the Steelheads, he felt as if something was *wrong*. Nothing specific—just a crawly sensation that caused the hairs on the back of his neck to stand up straight.

But why?

The answer came as a shock as a blast of mental energy hit every human within a thousand feet, killing four of them, including Private Cooper, and bringing the rest to their knees. A few managed to fire anyway, but most were incapacitated, as Hale struggled to stand.

"There's an Angel on that train!" he croaked. *"Kill it!"*

Many experts believed that Angels were in charge of lesser Chimera, capable of giving them orders via mental telepathy. If so, the Angel on the train might well have planned the surprise attack based on intelligence gathered by subordinate forms.

Hale's order went out over the team frequency, but the response was anemic at best, because so many of the Sentinels were incapacitated. As a second flood of stinks poured off the train, he staggered out of the office and onto the body-littered platform. Spook was there, face-down on the concrete, having been rendered unconscious by the mental blast. Ralf had positioned himself next to her body, and growled menacingly as Hale shuffled past.

Energy projectiles and plasma projectiles pinged, zinged, and whined around Hale as he staggered head-down, searching for a weapon that might make a difference. So complete was his concentration that he didn't even notice the loud *clang* as one side of a maintenance car dropped away to reveal the monster within. Finally he looked up.

The creature had a vaguely triangular head, glowing eyes, a mouth full of needle-sharp teeth, and multiple limbs. Leathery, parchmentlike skin covered its hideous body and rippled as the Angel floated out over the metal ramp. It uttered another scream, accompanied by a new blast of mental energy, and Hale brought both hands up to cover his ears—even though the sound was *inside* his head.

Spines flew off the monster, penetrating whatever they hit, including concrete.

But then Hale spotted what he needed, lying only feet from Obo's prostrate body, and he staggered forward to pick it up. The L210 LAARK was prepped with one round and ready to fire.

Hale swore as a projectile knocked his right leg out from under him. He hit the concrete hard, fought to roll over, and brought the launcher into position. There wasn't enough time to use the scope properly, to take careful aim, but the Angel was only fifty feet away.

So Hale pulled the trigger, felt the rocket leave the tube, and gave thanks for a direct hit. Judging from the horrible caterwauling noise it made, the stink was hurt, but he knew how tough Angels could be, so he struggled to reload as the Chimera spidered forward.

Meanwhile, Tanner had struggled to his feet and leveled the minigun at the surviving Hybrids. The weapon's multiple barrels produced an ominous whine as they began to rotate, followed by a throaty roar as the gun began to fire. Waves of advancing Chimera fell as he hosed them down, his teeth bared, blood pouring from a shoulder wound.

That gave Hale the time he needed to finish loading the LAARK and fire a second rocket at the Angel. There was a loud *BOOM* as it hit, followed by an explosion of blood, meat, and bone that sprayed the entire area.

The Angel was dead, but by some miracle a Steelhead had survived Tanner's barrage and gained the platform. Auger firing, it was advancing on Hale.

The Sentinel thought about the Rossmore, and realized it was back in the office. He was waiting for the stink to kill him when Ralf attacked. Because the Auger bolts were a threat to Spook, who was just coming around, the Howler went for the Steelhead's throat, tore it out instantly, and remained crouched over the body.

Jacoby wheeled himself out onto the platform. Broken glass made a persistent crackling sound as it broke beneath the chair's wheels. Coming to a stop, the Freedom First leader aimed a glob of spit at one of the lifeless Hybrids. It hit dead-on.

"Bastards," he said defiantly as Hale regained his feet. "This is *our* fucking city, and you can't have it."

The battle for the Adams/Wabash station had been won.

# CHAPTER THIRTEEN
## LIVE BAIT

It had been a clear winter's day in Santa Barbara, as the sun began to sink over the Pacific Ocean, and shadows gathered between the houses that lined Garden Street. It was a quiet neighborhood, in which people had a tendency to keep to themselves, so other than the elderly man watering his lawn on the opposite side of the street, there was no one present to witness the arrival of a black Humber town car in front of Hannah Shepherd's house.

The house was a modest affair, indistinguishable from the homes around it except for the gold star displayed in the front window, and the meticulously kept garden out front. The man watched expressionlessly as the car's driver got out, circled the town car, and opened the rear passenger-side door. Then, as a man in a gray business suit made his way up the walk that led to the Shepherd house, the neighbor heard his wife call him in for dinner.

It was Thursday, and that meant meatloaf, one of his favorites. So he turned off the hose, walked around to the side door, and went inside.

Life was good.

\* \* \*

Having arrived on the tiny front porch, Dentweiler switched his briefcase from his right hand to his left, straightened his tie, and pressed the button located next to the door. He could hear the distant *bing-bong* as a chime sounded followed by rapid *click, click, click* of leather-soled shoes on a hardwood floor.

As the door opened Dentweiler found himself facing a woman with shoulder-length brown hair, a narrow, almost patrician face, and an expressive mouth. Her eyes were big, brown, and warily neutral. He recognized her from the photos in her husband's voluminous personnel file.

"Yes?" Hannah Shepherd said, careful to keep one foot behind the door. "How can I help you?"

The ID case was ready and Dentweiler flipped it open to expose a picture of himself over a full-color presidential seal. "My name is William Dentweiler," he said. "May I come in? There's something important that I need to talk to you about."

Hannah looked up from the ID case and frowned. "Are you from the Department of Veterans Affairs?"

"No," Dentweiler said smoothly. "I'm from the Office of the President."

Hannah's eyes grew wider. "As in President of the United States?"

"Yes," Dentweiler replied matter-of-factly. "It's about your husband, Jordan."

"But he's dead," Hannah objected, as the color drained out of her face and her eyes flicked toward the star in the window. "He was killed in action."

"Yes, and no," Dentweiler countered mysteriously. "May I come in?"

She nodded and pulled the door open, waited for the man with the rimless glasses to enter, and closed the door behind him. There was no hallway—the front door opened directly into the small living room, the main feature of which was a brick fireplace and a highly stylized oil painting of Jordan Adam Shepherd that hung above it. He was dressed in an Army uniform, and judging from his expression, was determined to wear it with honor.

Dentweiler crossed the room to examine the portrait more closely. Even allowing for some help from the artist, Shepherd looked quite handsome. A far cry from the monstrous *thing* the innocent-looking soldier had become.

"The painting was a present," Hannah explained. "From Jordan's parents . . . after his death."

"It's nicely done," Dentweiler replied. "May I sit down?"

"Yes, of course," Hannah replied apologetically. "Where are my manners? Can I get you something to drink? Some coffee perhaps?"

"No, thank you," Dentweiler responded as he unknowingly sat in Jordan Shepherd's favorite chair. A contemporary-looking couch took up most of the wall across from him. That was where Hannah sat down, careful to sweep her housedress back under her thighs and keep her knees together.

Dentweiler had two categories for women. Those he deemed worth having sex with—and those he wasn't interested in. And Hannah Shepherd fell into category one. Partly because of her slim good looks, and partly because she came across as so pure that Dentweiler felt a perverse desire to bring her down. But that would have been pleasure, and he was there on business.

He cleared his throat.

"First, please allow me to apologize on behalf of the United States government. Simply put, most of the things you were told about your husband's death weren't true. Jordan, and hundreds of men like him, volunteered to take part in a top secret program that resulted in a serum which helps our soldiers survive wounds that would kill you or me. He wasn't allowed to tell you about it, nor were we, and the program remains secret even now."

"So, Jordan's alive?" Hannah inquired eagerly, her voice full of hope. "He wasn't killed in action?"

"No," Dentweiler allowed soberly, "he wasn't. But I'm sorry to say that as a result of the program, your husband underwent many mental, emotional, and physical changes. That didn't happen to all of the volunteers, but our experts believe Jordan was immunocompromised at the time of initial treatment, which produced some unanticipated results.

"It was the government's intention to care for him, of course," Dentweiler added quickly. "But all such efforts came to an end when he escaped."

"Escaped?" Hannah echoed. "How? And from *where*?"

"Due to all the changes he underwent Jordan could be violent at times," Dentweiler explained darkly. "He was undergoing treatment at a government facility in Iceland when he killed a number of the people stationed there, and disappeared."

"My God," Hannah said feelingly, as tears trickled down her cheeks. "Where did he go? What did he do?"

"I'm sorry," Dentweiler replied gravely. "But subsequent to his escape, your husband went over to the Chimera. He was recaptured later, but then freed by Chimeran commandos. Our understanding of the Chimeran hierarchy is iffy at best, but judging from the casualties the stinks were willing to suffer in order to release Jordan, they place a high value on him. We don't know why."

Hannah was sobbing into her hands by then—shoulders shaking as Dentweiler went over to comfort her. "I know this is difficult," he said sympathetically, as he took a seat on the couch. The pocket square he offered her was so immaculate it clearly had never been used. "I wish there was a better way to tell you, but this is the best I can do."

Hannah accepted the handkerchief and made use of it to blot her tears as she got up and excused herself. She was gone for a good five minutes, and Dentweiler heard the sound of running water before she returned, her eyes red, and her face still a bit damp.

"I'm sorry," Hannah said, as she sat on the couch. "It's all such a shock."

"Yes," Dentweiler agreed understandingly, "it is. And I wish I could give you some time to absorb the news, but there's a war on. Simply stated we need your help."

Hannah looked surprised. "Really? In what way?"

"We want to contact your husband," Dentweiler replied gravely. "In hopes that he can help us open a channel of communication with the Chimera."

Hannah frowned. "Like an interpreter?"

"Yes," Dentweiler agreed, "like an interpreter. But first we need to pull him in, and while he has undergone a lot of changes, we have reason to believe that the human part of him is still in love with you. And, because he has developed some very unusual mental abilities, it's possible that Jordan could communicate with you if conditions were right."

Hannah looked down at her hands then back up again.

"The *human* part? Does that mean what I think it means?"

"I'm afraid it does," Dentweiler admitted. "I haven't seen him myself, mind you, but I understand that he looks more Chimeran than human at this point, and will probably become more so as time passes."

Hannah swallowed, albeit with difficulty.

"I see . . . So what would you have me do?"

"There's no way Jordan could come *here*," Dentweiler said, "not without getting killed. So, if you're willing, we'd like to take you to a facility located just south of Chimeran-held territory. A place where Daedalus could come."

"*Daedalus?*" Hannah inquired.

"It's the code name we use for him," Dentweiler replied smoothly, "from Greek mythology. Daedalus was said to be a very skilled craftsman."

That seemed to satisfy Hannah, who was silent for a few moments as she wrestled with everything she'd been told. Finally, she nodded in response. "Okay, I'll do it."

"That's wonderful," Dentweiler replied. "Your country will be most grateful."

Suddenly there was the sound of engines, followed by the squeal of brakes and the slamming of doors. Hannah rose and went to the front window. The blinds were up, and even though it was now dark outside, she could see the military-style trucks, and the goverment agents who had taken up stations out front. There was anger on her face as she turned back into the room.

"You were going to take me anyway, weren't you? Even if I said no."

"Of course not," Dentweiler lied. "When we move you, we want to make certain you're safe, so the troops are for your protection. Now, if you would be so kind as to pack a bag, we'll depart in fifteen minutes."

Hannah Shepherd had never been on a plane before. So the trip north on the military DC-3 transport was not only exotic, but scary. The first part of the ride was bumpy, too, and at one point Hannah was afraid that she was going to be sick, but managed to keep down the box lunch Dentweiler had given her, and thereby avoided the embarrassment of barfing into a bag.

Things smoothed out after that. The plane was a fourteen-seater, and the only other passengers were Dentweiler and two agents, so Hannah had plenty of room to spread out. She tried to sleep, but was too keyed up, and was left to stare at the little clusters of lights that slid past below, all the while thinking about Jordan.

He had been funny in high school, and it was his quirky sense of humor that had attracted her to him in the first place. He had a serious side, though, which had included big plans for the future, and their life together.

"We have to defeat the Chimera," he used to say. "That comes first. But then, after I get out of the service, I'm going back to school. I want to start a company, a *big* company that will build houses for everyone who lost their homes during the war. And then I'm going to build a huge home for you, Hannah, and buy you everything you could possibly want, and we'll live happily ever after. What do you think?"

"I think I'd be happy with *half* of your dream, or a quarter of your dream, as long as I have you," Hannah had answered. And she had meant every word of it.

But that future had been buried, along with what she'd been told were her husband's remains, and Hannah had been forced to go on without Jordan. Something she had still been trying to adjust to when Dentweiler showed up at her door.

Now Jordan was alive, except in a different form, which Dentweiler described as "more Chimeran than human." *Could* she look at him? And still feel what she had before?

There was no way to know, so Hannah kept her face

to the window as the engines droned monotonously, and occasional groupings of lights passed below. They were like islands in a sea of blackness—visible at the moment, but for how long?

Sheridan, Wyoming, was far enough north that it was subject to occasional Chimeran air raids, so the airport remained blacked out until the DC-3 was on final approach. That was when two parallel lines of lights snapped on, the transport lost altitude, and Hannah felt the sudden jolt as the airplane's fat tires touched down.

Then the lights went out as the DC-3 taxied off the main runway and over to a hangar that was partially lit by the wash from a pair of half-taped headlights. A ramp was pushed into place as the copilot opened the door and cold air pushed its way into the cabin.

Dentweiler was on his feet by then, and waited while Hannah released her seat belt and slid out into the aisle. A couple of minutes later they were outside and entering a car as luggage was loaded into the trunk.

"It will be a short drive," Dentweiler informed her. "Then you can get some sleep. The program will get underway in the morning."

Once they left the airport it was pitch black outside so Hannah had no way to know where they were going. The car followed a two-lane highway for what seemed like about five miles before turning off onto a gravel road which twisted and turned between rocky hillsides, and eventually arrived at a gate guarded by a squad of Army Rangers.

IDs were checked, the gate swung open, and the car drove through. The gate swung shut with a sharp *clang*.

Hannah Shepherd felt like a prisoner.

\* \* \*

There was pain.

Not personal-pain, originating from the swollen body in which Daedalus was trapped, but *other-pain* being experienced by someone else. And Daedalus was an expert where pain was concerned. It had been a simple thing once, a signal that something had gone wrong with his body, and should be corrected.

But during the months they had experimented on him, Daedalus had learned there were different *types* of pain. Flavors really, like ice cream, each having its own individual taste, texture, and consistency.

Since his escape from the facility in Iceland, Daedalus had been free to deepen his understanding of pain by inflicting it on others, and vicariously experiencing what *they* felt, as both their real and telepathic screams echoed through the ether.

So as the first tendril of fear-laced emotion made contact with his mind, Daedalus sampled it in much the same way a wine connoisseur might try a new vintage, and wondered why this particular anguish was somehow associated with him. Especially since the world was so awash in pain that it constituted little more than emotional static.

Then he had it, because this particular cry of pain was not only "addressed" to him, but had originated from one of the shadow people who populated his previous existence. A time when he had been a part without a whole. A poor cast-off creature forever doomed to live alone, rather than within the comforting embrace of the vast virus-guided oneness that provided each and every Chimera with both a place and a purpose.

For the most part shadow people were to be ignored, and Daedalus would have ignored *this* searching tentacle of pain, had it not been for one thing: It was from Hannah. Something was causing her voice to be heard more loudly—and with greater intensity than all the other voices on the planet. Hannah was the one shadow person Daedalus still cared about, the woman he had promised to "cherish in sickness and in health, for richer for poorer, and forsaking all others."

There were no orders as such. Just desires that originated with Daedalus and were immediately translated into concrete actions by lesser forms who, had they been asked, would have been unable to distinguish between his objectives and their own.

The initiative amounted to wasted energy, insofar as the Chimeran virus was concerned, but the virus didn't have an individual persona, and was reliant on the overall success of its various forms to conquer Earth.

And *that* effort was going very well.

Dentweiler was expecting an attack, so when three Chimeran fighters swept in from the north followed by a shuttle loaded with Hybrids, only the officers around him were surprised. They had been openly cynical regarding the mechanics of the plan, especially the part related to mental telepathy, but were ready nevertheless. So everyone took cover as the fighters shot up the base, and even went so far as to fire back, although that was mostly for show. Because Dentweiler *wanted* the stinks to achieve their purpose, which was why Hannah Shepherd stood at the very center of a natural depression, where she had been tied to what had once been a telephone pole.

Hannah had been systematically tortured over the last thirty-six hours, and was only barely conscious as the Chimeran attack began. She stood facing the pole, her arms wrapped around it as in a lover's embrace, supported by the eyebolt to which her wrists were tied. Her bare back was covered with red welts where she had been whipped, no matter how much she pleaded for mercy. There had been periods of unconsciousness—albeit brief ones, because each time the merciful darkness claimed her a bucket of cold water had been used to bring her back.

"I'm sorry about this, Hannah," Dentweiler had said as the stinging water ran down her bare legs. "But Daedalus isn't likely to respond to anything other than genuine pain." Hannah told him to fuck himself, which produced an appreciative chuckle from the agent in charge of whipping her.

She didn't know how long ago that had been—she had lost all sense of time. All she knew was that she was alone now, and there was a roaring—as if some sort of machine was approaching, greeted by light small-arms fire. Two sets of hands roughly cut her free, and there was a horrible smell that made her want to retch.

Moments later, she was aboard a strange aircraft, and felt it lurch off the ground.

Dentweiler witnessed the raid from the safety of an underground bunker, and watched the shuttle take off and bank toward the north. "We're tracking it?"

It was a stupid question, since that was the whole point of the exercise, but the major who was standing next to Dentweiler understood.

"Yes, sir . . . The tracking device woven into her hair is working, a Sabre Jet is following the shuttle north, *and* we have it on radar."

"Good," Dentweiler said grimly. "Notify the recovery team. Let's grab that bastard."

Hannah was terrified and with good reason. The stench inside the shuttle was incredible; she was surrounded by heavily armed Hybrids, and they were even more hideous than they appeared in photographs. And the fact that most, if not all, of them would have been happy to eat her made the situation even worse.

But they didn't, which left her to sit with arms crossed over her bare breasts, shivering from both fear and the cold air. Her badly lacerated back felt as if it was on fire, and if she survived, Hannah knew she would be forever scarred.

The flight was mercifully short, and if Dentweiler was correct, Jordan would be waiting for her. Hannah felt something like liquid lead trickle into the pit of her stomach as the shuttle put down, machinery whined, and a ramp slid down to touch the ground.

One of the 'brids growled menacingly, which Hannah took as a signal to deplane, so she rose to make her way down onto the landing pad. The motion opened some of her wounds, and caused her to wince as blood began to flow.

The landing pad was located at the center of an enormous cylinder and was large enough to handle at least three aircraft. The purpose of the surrounding facility wasn't clear to Hannah, but as she looked up she could see circular galleries, free-floating drones, and the half-visible sun, which was split by the structure's curving rim. She "heard" Jordan's "voice" a fraction of a second before his considerable shadow fell over her. *Hannah.*

The single word flooded her mind. It was heavily freighted with love, sorrow, and anger. *They hurt you.*

As she continued to look up, an airborne grotesquerie appeared. Jordan, or the thing he had become, was about twenty times larger than she was. Its body consisted of overlapping lobes of translucent flesh, all bisected by spiny ridges that flared away from a tiny human head, to stream back and form a long whiplike tail.

Jordan.

Just below the head and a cluster of glowing yellow eyes were two tentaclelike tool-arms and, farther back, four spiderlike legs dangled, ready to support the monster's weight should it decide to land. The creature was breathtakingly horrible, yet some aspect of the presence that had invaded her head was recognizably her husband, and Hannah reacted accordingly. "Yes," she responded, too numb and too weary to feel the fear she knew she should have been experiencing. "They tortured me in order to get at *you*." At that point she wondered who the real monsters were.

"You're safe now," the disembodied voice assured her. But rather than feel better, the way she might have, Hannah experienced a sudden stab of terror as Daedalus pumped what she perceived as gibberish into her mind. Was Jordan communicating in Chimeran? To her or someone else? Yes, Hannah believed he was still talking to her, and began to suspect that the man she had married was no longer sane. Not in the human sense anyway, as the thing farted internally produced hydrogen, and began to lose altitude.

As Daedalus loomed above her, Hannah could see the last vestige of her husband's form staring down at her. It appeared that Jordan's head was slowly being absorbed into his tumorlike body, and she guessed that it would eventually disappear. The skin covering his scabrous skull was drum-tight, and his eye sockets were deep caverns from which he peered out at her. "Jordan?" she inquired. Can you hear me? They're using me as bait . . . They followed me here, and they're going to attack you."

At that moment explosions shook the ground and a

specially rigged VTOL appeared overhead. Men were visible at the doors, crouched behind a pair of harpoon guns—both loaded with what looked like huge spears.

The VTOL had been equipped with harpoon guns capable of firing specially fabricated darts, each carrying 2,000 cc of a fast-acting sedative. A potion developed by SRPA, tested on captured Chimera, and proven to be effective.

The starboard gunner saw his shot, took it, and sent a huge dart into the airborne creature that was floating below.

Daedalus "screamed" as the harpoon entered his flesh, and the woman below him was driven to her knees as the "sound" echoed through her brain, and the brains of everyone in the vicinity.

The VTOL's pilot was incapacitated, and when he took his hands off the controls to slap them over his ears, the aircraft ran into the curved wall that loomed in front of him.

There was an enormous explosion, followed by a momentary ball of flame, and a series of crashes as chunks of flaming debris fell onto the landing pad below. Some of the smaller pieces hit Daedalus, as he struggled to remain conscious, but was ultimately unable to do so.

Daedalus hit the landing pad with a loud *thump* not ten feet from the spot where Hannah was kneeling.

And as unseen troops battled with one another outside the massive cylinder, *another* VTOL appeared above. It, too, was armed with harpoon guns, plus a specially designed harness, which was slung below the aircraft's tubby fuselage.

Hannah's hair whipped from side to side as she stood and the VTOL lowered itself down to a point twenty feet off the ground. That was when a team of Rangers slid down ropes and immediately went to work passing straps beneath Daedalus's form.

Hannah, no longer conscious of her nudity, knew it was time to do something. But *what*? The problem was solved for her when a sergeant appeared at her side, threw a jacket over her shoulders, and pointed at the bosun's chair that dangled below the aircraft. He had to shout in order to make himself heard over the roar of the VTOL's engines.

"All you have to do is sit on it, ma'am . . . They'll pull you up."

Hannah wanted to thank him, was *determined* to thank him, but that was when she fainted.

There was light. But in order to reach it Daedalus knew he would have to make the long difficult journey up out of the black hole he found himself in. So he *willed* himself upward, and the light grew gradually brighter, until it was all around him and he could open his many eyes.

That was when it came back to him.

Hannah's pain, her warning, and the attack. Which—as he took a long slow look around—Daedalus knew had been conceived to recapture him.

A silly notion really, since it didn't matter where his physical body was located, so long as his mind was free to roam. The meat people didn't know that, of course, because they were captives of their own limited capabilities, and therefore unable to grasp the truth of the matter.

His prison, because that's what it was, consisted of a cube-shaped concrete cell which was approximately one hundred feet to a side. It was featureless except for the cameras that peered at Daedalus from every possible angle, the harness that held him aloft, and the rectangular drain below. A convenience that would allow the food things to hose his excrement away. Except none of the creatures were anywhere to be seen, and Daedalus thought he knew why.

In order to test his hypothesis Daedalus summoned a bolt of mental energy and let it fly. He knew the weapon was sufficient to render most humans unconscious, if not actually kill them. The result was a 900 kV shock, which not only hurt, but told Daedalus what he needed to know. An electrode had been implanted in his body, thereby allowing the meat creatures to punish him whenever they chose to.

Meanwhile, judging from what Daedalus could see, his captors were elsewhere watching him via the cameras. Far enough away that mental attacks would be ineffective. That theory proved to be correct when a voice boomed over speakers mounted inside the cube. "Greetings, Daedalus, and welcome back. My name is Dentweiler. We want to speak with you."

Daedalus offered no response. None that the meat person named Dentweiler could perceive. But his mind was working. Daedalus knew he wanted to exert more control over the millions of Chimeran forms currently converging on North America. Whether that was a personal choice, or something the virus wanted him to accomplish wasn't clear, and really didn't matter.

Because Earth was about to fall—and that was the only thing that mattered.

# CHAPTER FOURTEEN
## OUT OF THE BLUE

**Near Custer, Montana**
**Monday, December 10, 1951**

Gray clouds hung like a lid over Montana, as the VTOL swept in from the south with a beat-up four-wheel-drive pickup truck dangling below its belly. There was a lot of open country north of Hardin, so there wasn't anyone around to witness the moment when the aircraft lowered the truck down to a point just a few feet off the snow-covered road, and the crew chief pulled the harness release lever. The pickup bounced once, then came to rest, as a tangle of steel cables fell on top of it.

Freed from its burden the VTOL shot up, scooted sideways, and came back down as the prop wash hit a layer of light powdery snow and sent it swirling in every direction. Then, as the *Party Girl* touched down, a couple of crewmen went out to retrieve their harness and drag it inside the aircraft while Hale carried his duffel bag down the sloping ramp.

Once on the ground he circled around to a point where Purvis could see him. The pilot grinned, and gave Hale a cheerful thumbs-up. Both engines began to spool up as the ramp was retracted and the ship started to vibrate. Moments later it shot straight up again, turned to the south, and sped away.

Hale was on his own.

But unlike the recent trip to Chicago, Hale was well within government-controlled territory. So while he made his way over to the truck, the Sentinel felt none of the usual gut-wrenching fear that went with being dropped into what some of his peers referred to as stink land.

Still, there was some risk involved in his current mission, since Hale had been given the task of infiltrating a Freedom First training camp near Custer. The idea was to find out if Secretary of War Walker and his wife were heading there, since they weren't in Chicago. The Grace administration was still determined to find them, or confirm that the two dissidents were dead, either outcome being quite acceptable.

The pale blue truck had clearly seen hard service, and was equipped with muddy Montana plates. Hale opened the driver's-side door, threw the duffel bag onto the far side of the bench-style seat, and slid in behind the big black steering wheel. The key was in the ignition and the six-cylinder engine started with a throaty *roar*. Which wasn't too surprising since SRPA mechanics had gone over the vehicle less than twenty-four hours before.

The four-wheel-drive differential was already engaged, so all Hale had to do was put the pickup in gear and head north along the two-lane highway. Local ranchers had left tracks in the snow, but judging from the way they were partially filled in, it had been at least six hours since the last vehicle had passed.

As Hale looked to his left he could see snow-covered range land, the Absaroka Mountain range beyond, and a strip of cold winter light that divided the ground from the pewter gray sky. The heater was on, but hadn't made much progress warming the cab, since all of its strength was directed up onto the slightly foggy windshield. It was a familiar scene—and one that was reminiscent of Hale's childhood.

The truck was equipped with an AM radio, and it wasn't long before Hale was listening to "Long Gone Lonesome Blues" by Hank Williams and His Drifting Cowboys. The music carried him north past ranch houses set back off the road, barns shingled with snow, and bare-branched trees. He came to a gravel road marked only by a mailbox mounted on a rusty old plow and that—according to the instructions he had been given—was the point where he was supposed to turn right.

So Hale put the wheel over and soon found himself on a well-churned road that ran straight as an arrow along a barbed wire fence, and pointed toward the rise beyond. As the truck sent waves of slush rolling right and left Hale began to feel the hairs on the back of his neck rise.

He often played the part of a hunter, as well as the hunted, and knew the feeling well. Somewhere, perhaps from the pile of snow-frosted boulders two hundred yards to the left, eyes were watching him. And unless he missed his guess the lookout had a radio, and was already in the process of reporting the new arrival.

A discipline Hale understood and was respectful of.

As the truck topped the rise Hale saw a collection of buildings that lay beyond. Some were old and weather-beaten, clearly part of a ranch that had been there for a long time; others had the bright yellow-orange glow of new lumber. They looked like military-style barracks and that made sense, since even though government officials frowned on it, the property had been rededicated as a boot camp for Freedom First volunteers. Once trained, they would be sent north into stink land, or if Montana was overrun, the fighters would remain behind to carry out hit-and-run raids against the Chimera. Missions Hale not only approved of, but thought the government should sponsor, rather than playing defense so much of the time.

A pole-gate made from a freshly barked log blocked the road, so Hale brought the truck to a stop, as two men dressed in deer hunting outfits came out to greet him. Both were armed with Bullseye Mark IIIs rather than deer rifles, which suggested that they had other game in mind. One of the sentries kept his weapon ready as Hale cranked the window down and the other man sauntered over to greet him. He had a craggy outdoorsy sort of face, half of which was invisible behind a thick beard. A wisp of vapor drifted away from his mouth as he spoke. "Hey, bud, this is private property. If you're looking for Custer, then turn around, and head back. The first right will put you back on the highway."

"Thanks," Hale replied neutrally, "but I think I'm in the right place. Assuming this is the Freedom First training camp that is. I'm here to volunteer."

The sentry frowned. "You got stink eyes . . . Anyone tell you that?"

"Lots of people," Hale replied nonchalantly. "Yellow eyes run in the family. My father had 'em, and his father before him."

The man looked doubtful, but nodded anyway, and he pointed to a parking lot where about two dozen vehicles were parked. Some were covered with snow, and clearly hadn't been driven for a while, while others were bare.

"Put the truck over there, bud," the sentry said brusquely. "If you're carrying weapons, lock them in the cab. Follow the signs to the admin building. Ask for Mr. Munger. He's in charge of recruiting, and just about everything else around here."

Hale thanked the man, waited for the second sentry to push down on the weighted pole-gate, and drove through. Then, having turned into the parking lot, he chose a spot between a late-model sedan and an old flatbed truck. Hale was carrying nothing more than a .45 semiautomatic pistol, which was consistent with his cover story and small enough to put in the glove box.

He got out of the truck and crossed the lot, then followed a trail of hand-painted signs to what had once been a one-story log home, but now functioned as the "Administration Building." Somewhere off in the distance the steady *pop, pop, pop* of gunfire could be heard, suggesting that some of the trainees were on the rifle range.

At least he hoped that was what it was.

Two more men were waiting for Hale inside the admin building. Both wore wool shirts, faded jeans, and sidearms. One was chewing on a wooden match. His eyes were nearly invisible inside a convergence of wrinkles. "Mornin'," he said conversationally. "Please turn to the left and put your weight on the wall. Lester here wants to feel you up." It was an old joke, but still sufficient to elicit an appreciative guffaw from Lester, who ran a pair of rough hands over Hale without finding any weapons.

Having passed that inspection, he was ordered to take a seat in what had once been a spacious living room. It was still homey, with a dark green rug, worn overstuffed furniture, and a crackling fire in the river-rock fireplace. The walls were covered with a variety of black-and-white photos. All of them were of the same man who could be seen fishing for trout, kneeling next to all manner of dead animals, and sitting atop a succession of fine-looking horses as he looked out over some vista or other. The ranch's owner then? Yes, Hale thought so, as he took a seat.

Hale was scanning old copies of *Field & Stream* when a man dressed in a tweed coat, corduroy trousers, and highly polished brown cowboy boots came out to meet him. Hale recognized him as the man in the photos. "Hello," the man said. "My name is Munger. Homer Munger. And you are?"

"Nathan Leary," Hale replied. "Glad to meet you."

Munger had a thin, somewhat ascetic countenance. "We'll see about that, Mr. Leary," he said grimly. "Many hear the call—but few are chosen. Please follow me."

Hale followed Munger back into what had been the home's master bedroom but was now furnished as an office, complete with a large wooden desk, lots of bookshelves, and a military-style two-way radio that occupied most of a side table. An extremely detailed map of Montana covered most of one wall. Munger had circled the desk, and appeared ready to sit down, when he spoke. "Atten-*hut*!"

After years in the Army, then SRPA, Hale very nearly snapped to. It took an act of will to frown and look confused, straighten up, and assume the sort of sloppy brace that a brand-new recruit might. Munger nodded approvingly and smiled.

"Sorry about that, but the Grace administration doesn't approve of our activities, and they continue to send spies from time to time. Soldiers mostly, men who look the way you do, and almost always pop to attention." With that, he took his place in the chair. "Have a seat, Mr. Leary, and tell me about yourself."

So Hale told Munger about losing his parents, growing up on a ranch in South Dakota, and drifting from job to job. All of which was true as far as it went. The only lie being his failure to mention his time in both the Army and SRPA.

Munger listened intently, interrupting occasionally to ask questions, but allowing Hale to do most of the talking. Finally, as the narrative came to an end, Munger formed a steeple with his fingers.

"So, tell me, Mr. Leary, what makes you think you have anything to offer Freedom First?"

Hale shrugged, but when he spoke his voice carried an undercurrent of menace.

"I grew up outdoors, and I'm a pretty good shot, and I hate the stinks."

"Montana is full of good shots," Munger observed dryly. "My mother can bag a rabbit from a couple hundred feet away with a .22—and she's pushing eighty. What we need are *exceptional* shots. More than that, we're looking for men and women who are willing to go where the U.S. Army won't, and hunt stinks until they get themselves killed. Which is what happens to 90 percent of the people who work with us. So, tell me, Mr. Leary, are you *that* kind of man? And are you willing to make *that* kind of sacrifice?"

Hale looked directly into Munger's eyes. "Yes," he said unflinchingly. "I believe I am."

Munger was silent for a moment, as if considering what he had heard. Eventually, having reached a decision, he nodded his head. "All right, Mr. Leary, fair enough. We'll put you through the wringer and see if you can take the pain. Then, if you're still here three or four days from now, the *real* training will start. Take your gear over to Bunkhouse 1, find an empty bed, and make yourself to home. But get lots of sleep—you're going to need it."

\* \* \*

Bunkhouse 1 was empty when Hale entered, although half of the sixteen beds had been claimed, judging from the personal possessions on or around them. Were the other recruits being put through what Munger called the wringer? Yes, Hale thought so, as he put his duffel bag on a bare mattress and went about the process of making it up using the bedding piled on the foot of the bed. The result was way too Army, so he pulled the corners out, and let the covers hang civilian-style.

Having spotted the cookhouse on the way over from the truck, Hale ambled back to see if he could get a bite to eat and, more important, to look for the Walkers. Because the whole idea was to ascertain if they were present, and then get out. Which he could do by looking incompetent the next day. Then, if the Walkers *were* present, a SAR team would drop in to pick them up.

But when Hale entered the cookhouse, there was no sign of the couple. One table was occupied by three men and a woman, all of whom wore the weary look of combat veterans, and none of them offered him a smile. Having checked Hale out and filed him under "newbie," they continued their conversation.

A few other people were present as well, singles mostly—including an older man who was poring over some financial records, a youngster with his right leg in a cast, and a retired bird dog who welcomed Hale with a single *thump* of his tail.

There was plenty of coffee, and some of the best cinnamon rolls he had ever tasted, but no sign of the people he was looking for.

The rest of the day passed slowly, as afternoon faded into night, and the recruits arrived back at the bunkhouse. Some were triumphant, and some were dispirited, but all of them were exhausted. Having introduced himself, Hale listened with interest as the other men de-

scribed a hellacious obstacle course, a demanding exercise called hide-and-seek, and expressed the universal
hope that something really bad would happen to a man
named Anthony Puzo.

Dinner followed, but didn't last long, because everyone except Hale was bone-tired, and couldn't wait to
log some rack time. So Hale lay on his bunk, listened to
the chorus of snores all around him, and thought about
Cassie. He hadn't seen the psychologist since the trip to
Denver, yet he thought about her constantly, and was
hoping for a three-day pass once his current assignment
was over.

At some point he fell asleep. And when he awoke it
was to the sound of someone beating on a galvanized
garbage can with a baseball bat.

*Bang! Bang! Bang!*

"Drop your cocks and grab your socks!" a deep
booming voice bellowed. "You have forty-five minutes
to shower, dress, and eat breakfast . . . The last man to
arrive at the obstacle course will pull rock duty. So get
your collective asses in gear."

"What's rock duty?" Hale asked as he swung his feet
over onto the cold floor.

"It's something you don't want," the man in the next
bunk replied. "But better *you* than me!"

With that the race was on as the men vied with each
other to clean up, get their clothes on, and invade the
cookhouse. But Army veteran that Hale was, he knew
how to do everything in a hurry, and was among the first
to arrive at the obstacle course where the feared Puzo
stood waiting.

Having been an NCO prior to gaining his commis-
sion, Hale knew plenty of drill instructors, but had
never seen one like Puzo. He stood feet apart, with a
much abused baseball bat resting on his right shoulder,

and a sizable pot hanging out over his belt buckle. A fringe of black hair circled Puzo's mostly bald head, coal black eyes peered out at the world from beneath a single eyebrow, and a truly monumental nose probed the morning air as if sniffing for miscreants. "Well," he growled, as the recruits lined up in front of him. "Look what we have here! Some new *meat*. What's your name, stink eyes?"

Hale returned the hard-eyed stare. "Leary," he replied, careful to leave off the usual "sir."

"Okay, Leeeery," Puzo said, "you look like a smart-ass. And I don't like smart-asses. Give me twenty-five push-ups."

So Hale dropped down, hands buried in the slush, and was busy pumping out push-ups when the last man arrived. His name was Carty, and he was a slim lad, with the air of a librarian. He was out of breath, and obviously scared.

"Well," Puzo said fatalistically. "Here's our rock boy . . . Okay, rock boy, bring me six rocks."

Hale was back on his feet by then, and therefore in a position to watch as Carty went looking for rocks. It wasn't easy finding them under the blanket of snow, and by the time Carty came back with six egg-sized rocks, the rest of the recruits had already battled their way through an obstacle course that included parallel rows of tires they were required to stutter-step through, a narrow beam that spanned a half-frozen pool of muddy water, a nine-foot-tall wooden wall, a rope climb up to a tower from which a trolley arrangement carried them to a platform a hundred feet away, and a slimy crawl through a sewer pipe to the end point beyond. Which was where Puzo was stationed when Carty arrived with a double handful of wet rocks.

The DI examined each rock as if he was sorting

through the crown jewels, looking for only the best diamonds. He rejected one submission with a grunt of disapproval, and sent Carty to fetch another. Then, with the élan of a professional baseball player, Puzo proceeded to hit all the remaining rocks so hard that they disappeared into the lead gray sky, and fell for what would surely have been a series of doubles.

Then, as Carty returned with the replacement rock, it was time for the already tired librarian to run the obstacle course. A process clearly intended to weed him out.

"It's for his own good," the man standing next to Hale said bleakly, as Carty fell off the beam and splashed into the pond. "Ironically enough, he's going to survive—and *we're* going to die."

Sadly, that assessment was probably true, Hale realized as the group watched Carty wade out of the freezing-cold water. Because, having been dropped into Chimera-held territory himself, he knew how long the odds were.

Lunch was a brief but hearty affair, during which Hale had a chance to eyeball some of the more advanced recruits and members of the organization's small but dedicated staff. Munger made an appearance, but the Walkers were nowhere to be seen, and Hale felt increasingly sure that they weren't around. Chances were that both had been killed during the long trip from Indianapolis. Anything else would amount to a miracle.

So as Puzo led the group on a one-mile hike to the makeshift firing range, Hale had already decided to miss at least half of the targets, as the first step of a plan to get himself ejected from the training camp. The sporadic sounds of gunfire could be heard as they came closer, Puzo sent Carty out looking for rocks, and the familiar smell of gunsmoke rode the otherwise clean air.

The shooting stand was protected by a long slanted

roof, supported by six-by-six posts, all set in concrete. Beyond that a long stretch of open land could be seen, with a line of six targets at what Hale estimated to be a thousand yards, all backed by a mound of snow-clad earth. Wind flags hung limply at both sides of the embankment.

Puzo led his brood in behind the firing line—Hale saw that the person who was currently doing the shooting was armed with a Fareye. A military weapon she wasn't supposed to have. And the woman was good—*very* good, as became obvious when she squeezed off the final round and put the rifle down on the table next to her.

"Good shot!" the range master said approvingly as he peered downrange through a pair of powerful binoculars. "You scored five bull's-eyes out of six shots. Number four was just a hair outside, but still in the kill zone."

"That isn't good enough," the shooter responded matter-of-factly. "I need six out of six."

The sound of the woman's voice sent a chill down Hale's spine. *"Susan?"* he said. "Is that *you?*"

Susan Farley turned to look. It was the same face Hale remembered growing up with. She had the same high forehead, the same spray of freckles across the bridge of her nose, and the same determined mouth. Her eyes widened in disbelief. *"Nathan?* They told us you were dead!"

"This is all very touching," Puzo said sarcastically, "but it's a waste of time. Let's clear the line . . . We have some shooting to do."

"But she's my sister!" Hale objected.

"And he's in the Army," Susan interjected, as her features began to harden. "Or he's supposed to be. What did he say his name was?"

"Leary," Puzo replied, as his eyes began to narrow.

"He's lying," Susan said grimly. "His *real* name is Hale."

Hale tried to turn, tried to react, but the baseball bat was already in motion by that time. Hale saw an explosion of light, fell into a bottomless hole, and suddenly ceased to exist.

The rarely used interrogation center was located in the basement underneath the admin building, adjacent to a well-stocked armory. Hale was strapped to an X-shaped structure which was secured to a concrete wall. He had been stripped to the waist and was clearly unconscious. Two ceiling-mounted lights were angled to spotlight the prisoner, making his many scars clearly visible.

Three other people were present: Munger, Susan, and Puzo. They stood in a semicircle, backs to the door, as Puzo lifted a bucket of water up off the floor. Munger nodded. "Let him have it."

Puzo grinned sadistically as the cold liquid hit Hale in the face and splashed the wall behind him. Susan felt a moment of regret as the man she had grown up with jerked convulsively and opened his strange yellow-gold eyes.

They served to remind Susan that *this* Nathan was very different from the one who had gone off to join the Army. This Nathan was probably an enemy, rather than a patriot, gone over to the Chimera.

Even if he hadn't, he was a traitor. Because, generally speaking, those who backed the Grace administration and its efforts to rob American citizens of their freedoms were little better than stinks, insofar as Susan was concerned.

\* \* \*

Hale tried to move his arms, discovered that he couldn't, and blinked his eyes in order to get the water out of them. Then, his expression changing not at all, he looked from face to face.

"So," he croaked. "You're probably wondering why I called this meeting."

Puzo had an old buggy whip that looked as if it had been salvaged from the barn, and was preparing to strike when Munger raised a hand. The DI frowned, as if disappointed, but lowered the whip. Hale knew the good-cop bad-cop routine when he saw it and waited to see what Munger would say. "You lied," Munger stated flatly. "About your name, your background, and your reason for coming here. Now you're going to tell the truth . . . Or Mr. Puzo will beat it out of you."

Except for his desire to find the Walkers, the rest of the story was pretty damned obvious. So there wasn't much to be gained by denying who he was, and Hale figured that if he played the situation correctly, he might be able to further his mission.

"Sure," Hale said hoarsely, as he stared into Susan's eyes. "What would you like to know?"

"What organization do you belong to?" Munger demanded.

"The Rangers," Hale replied, which though not technically true, was close enough for government work. SRPA was still classified as top secret even though an increasing number of people were becoming aware of it.

"Good," Munger said grimly. "Now we're getting somewhere. Why did you come here? To spy on us?"

"No," Hale replied matter-of-factly. "We know just about everything there is to know about this facility. So, why bother?"

"This is bullshit," Puzo complained bitterly. "He's

jacking us around. Let me work on him for a while. He'll be calling for his mommy within fifteen minutes."

"His mother is dead," Susan put in bleakly. "She died defending her home with a twelve-gauge shotgun. I figure she killed ten, maybe twelve stinks before a Steelhead took her down, and I shot it with Pa's Colt Peacekeeper. Let him talk."

Hale was impressed both by the steel in Susan's voice and the way Puzo immediately backed down. As if her authority was superior to his.

"I came looking for Henry Walker," Hale explained, "and his wife, Myra. Are they here?"

Suddenly the interrogation flip-flopped and Hale was the one checking expressions. Munger looked surprised, Susan appeared to be intrigued, and Puzo was taken aback. "Henry Walker? Who the hell is he?"

"He *was* the Secretary of War," Hale replied. "A man who, according to authorities, fled his responsibilities in Washington, and wants to engage in negotiations with the Chimera. Something that Freedom First would almost certainly object to."

"You're kidding," Munger said.

"No, I'm not," Hale replied. "The Walkers were headed for Chicago. The government tracked Walker and his wife as far as Indianapolis, but lost them after that. I was part of a team that went into Chicago looking for them. We came up empty, so I was sent here on the off chance that they made it this far."

"Chicago?" Puzo demanded incredulously. "That's bullshit . . . Nobody goes into Chicago except for our people."

"You have a radio," Hale countered. "Call Jacoby, ask him if we were there, and who we were looking for."

Munger, Susan, and Puzo looked at one another.

"Okay," Munger agreed, "I will. And you'd better be on the up-and-up."

"Terrific," Hale replied. "In the meantime, I could use an ice pack, a handful of aspirin, and something to piss in."

In spite of the fact that the sun had parted company with the eastern horizon some three hours earlier, and was still rising across a bright blue sky, it was cold and crisp as Hale and his sister, Susan, followed a game trail toward a big pile of weathered boulders half a mile ahead. It felt good to walk together as their boots broke through the crusty snow and made squeaky crunching sounds. It could have been years earlier, when both of them were still living on the family ranch, and blissfully unaware of the terrible threat brewing in a remote part of Russia.

After radioing Jacoby in Chicago, Munger had been able to verify Hale's story, even if Jacoby claimed the team was part of some super-secret intelligence group, while Hale continued to insist that he was a Ranger. And while none were too pleased about the manner in which Hale had infiltrated the training camp, they had decided to release the spy, rather than run the risk that the government would raid the compound looking for the Walkers. *And* their agent.

But Hale was supposed to leave the compound by noon, which left very little time to spend with Susan. "So you went back to the ranch," she said, as the two of them descended into a gully and scrambled up the other side.

"Yes," Hale replied. "I went back. I saw your message on the wall and the grave out back. That must have been very difficult."

"It was," Susan admitted. "After battling the stinks

for the better part of a day, and seeing everyone else die, it felt strange to be alive. Strange and wrong, somehow."

"I know what you mean," Hale replied soberly. "I had the same feeling after everyone in my outfit was killed in England."

Susan glanced at her brother as they followed the path past an old tumbledown line shack. "You're not in the Army anymore, are you, Nathan? You belong to something else. Something no one is willing to talk about."

"Everything has changed," Hale answered evasively. "Including my sister. You were pretty close to being apolitical when I left home. Now you belong to Freedom First. Why?"

Susan took note of the way the question had been turned back on her and knew she was correct about her brother's job. "Making my way south from the ranch was difficult—as you know, having done it yourself. But after two weeks of playing hide-and-seek with the stinks, I finally made it. So with nothing more than empty pockets, and a couple of guns, I sought shelter at one of the Protection Camps.

"It seemed like a good idea at the time," she continued, "but it wasn't. The moment I entered the camp I lost all of my rights and liberties, because that's how the Grace administration wants it. As long as there's something they can point at as an external threat, they can justify the suspension of civil liberties and stay in power.

"Except now, with the Chimera on American soil, they've let things slip too far. Because there's a very good chance that the stinks will win. Walker's decision to leave the administration and join us is a good indication of how bad things are."

Hale thought about the man named Dentweiler, and wondered if he was typical of the people who surrounded the President. Listening to Susan made it seem all too possible.

They arrived at the pile of snow-capped boulders, and chose to rest on the east side of the formation, where they could sit in the sun. Hale scraped the snow off of a flat-topped rock and both of them sat down. "I don't know, Susan, maybe you're right. Maybe it *is* late in the game. But we can't give up. We've got to fight back."

"And we are," Susan responded, as she placed a gloved hand over his. "Each in our own way. I know you're part of the effort, even if you can't say how, and I am as well. There's a place for Freedom First in all of this, Nathan. Someone has to push back against Grace and his cronies—and someone has to fight the stinks in places like Chicago."

Nathan took Susan's hand and looked into her eyes. "So, you won't go back with me?"

Susan shook her head. "No, Nathan . . . I can't."

Hale was silent for a moment. He nodded as he released her hand. "I understand. We were both taught to stand up for what we believe in."

"Yes," Susan agreed. "We were."

At that point an eagle drifted into sight, its shadow caressing the land below as it glided over its traditional domain, searching for jackrabbits, ground squirrels, and carrion. Both Susan and Hale shaded their eyes in order to watch the big bird circle above. *There are so many predators on the loose,* Hale thought to himself, *that one of these days there will be nothing left to kill.*

# CHAPTER FIFTEEN
# A COLD DAY IN HELL

Escape Tunnel 1 was four feet high and two men wide. What little light there was came from improvised oil lamps positioned at regular intervals along the upward-sloping shaft. Each jar contained a wooden block that was floating on a layer of cooking oil supported by four or five inches of water. A hole had been drilled through each block so that an improvised wick could be pushed down into the fuel below. As Henry Walker turned to deposit a scoopful of dirt and rock onto a sheet of scrap metal called "the wagon," one of the lamps threw a monstrous shadow onto the opposite wall. Walker was in his sixties, and he had all sorts of aches and pains, but was determined to ignore them in order to do his share of the work.

Fortunately his one-hour shift was almost over and Walker felt a sense of relief as he added one last scoop of dirt to the heaping pile and jerked on the string that ran the length of the tunnel. Tin cans partially filled with pebbles rattled noisily, signaling for the "donkeys" to pull the wagon downslope to the carefully concealed entrance. There "spreaders" would take the material out and scatter it around the pit a few pounds at a time. It was an exhausting not to mention time-consuming process, but in the words of Walker's friend Harley Burl, "What the hell else have we got to do?"

And for Walker, who still hoped to get his recordings out to the public, the escape tunnels gave him reason to hope.

The wagon made a grating sound as the donkeys towed it away, and Walker followed, looking forward to the moment when he would be able to stand straight. The trip served to remind him of the need for more supports, which, given the amount of wood already burned for heat, were in short supply. And that shortage had been responsible for the recent collapse some forty feet upslope in Tunnel 3. A disastrous event that not only claimed three lives, but had to be concealed from both the Chimera *and* the ever-watchful Collins, who insisted on a head count every morning. The prisoners had been able to fool the ex-schoolteacher by having people yell "Here!" for those who weren't actually present, but there was no telling how long the ruse would work.

The entrance to Tunnel 1 was located immediately behind one of the four-hole outhouses the prisoners had constructed for themselves. The shed was about fifteen feet wide and made out of scrap lumber. In addition to blocking the cold winter wind and providing users with a modicum of privacy, the shitter had another purpose as well. And that was to conceal the escape shaft that Walker and the other tunnel rats had worked so hard to create. Which was why it had been constructed against the pit's west wall.

A twelve-foot-by-twelve-foot chamber was located directly behind the four-holer. That was where the donkeys could unload the wagon, the spreaders could fill sacks with dirt, and Walker could finally stand up straight.

Which he did with an audible groan. One of the donkeys smiled sympathetically. His hair was ragged where chunks of it had been hacked off with a knife—and a grimy face framed his bright blue eyes.

"It don't get any easier, does it?" the man inquired.

"No, it doesn't," Walker replied, as he brushed dirt off his already filthy trousers. "I keep hoping the stinks will find this thing and put us out of our misery!"

Dark humor was the order of the day, so those around Walker chuckled appreciatively. He knocked on the panel that separated the tunnel from Cubicle 2 inside the aptly named "shit shack." Then, having heard no response from within, he lifted the section of paneling out of the way and put it to one side. Once he passed through the hole one of the donkeys lifted the barrier back into place. That gave Walker an opportunity to pee before zipping his trousers and stepping out into the cold morning air.

Prior to the invasion, the pit had been an operating sulfide mine from which the owners had been able to extract 8.4 percent zinc and 0.7 percent lead. And that, according to the mining engineer who had been killed in the Tunnel 3 cave-in days before, was a very rich find.

Like most open-pit mines the "stink hole," as the prisoners called it, consisted of a groundwater-supplied lake at its center, and a circular roadway that rose corkscrew fashion up through the terracelike levels that had been excavated in the past.

Once removed from the mine, the raw ore had been fed into an assemblage of buildings up top, where it was systematically roasted, smelted, and converted. Except that rather than ore, the Chimera were feeding *people* into the former smelter, none of whom were ever seen again. The choice of which prisoners to take was left largely to Collins. That was why most people sought to avoid the collaborator in hopes of escaping what could be a fatal glance.

It also explained why most of the people who sat bundled in blankets, ambled about, or gathered around "the boil" were so dispirited. Because the odds of their being taken off to the processing plant were good, and even if they lived long enough to crawl through one of the tunnels to freedom, the prisoners knew that most—if not all—of the escapees would be caught and executed.

But depressing though the situation was, people were people, and with death only a whisper away, there were those who sought to advantage themselves by forming and being part of so-called committees. Groups that were very similar to gangs, all vying to control resources like food, medicine, and clothing. And they were very much in evidence as a shadow drifted over the pit and a loud thrumming noise was heard.

The cry of "Dump! Dump! Dump!" went up as the Chimeran ship slowed its sideways motion and a black rectangle appeared in the shuttle's belly. Walker knew what was going to happen next, and ran to the rally point where Harley Burl stood waiting. Others were assembling there as well, all members of the Fair and Square Squad, which was dedicated to dividing all resources fairly, rather than allowing the competing committees to take possession of them and therefore the entire pit.

Speed was of utmost importance as boxes of supplies began to tumble out of the shuttle. Some splashed into the slushy lake where they sank or floated, depending on what was in them. Others exploded on contact, spewing their contents far and wide. And a few made it to the ground intact. Those were considered to be the most significant prizes—even though the prisoners knew some would turn out to be nothing more than a cruel joke. Because there was often little rhyme or reason as to what sorts of things the Chimera chose to drop.

In the recent past the prisoners had been on the receiving end of crates that contained basketballs, auto parts, and luggage. But there had been big boxes full of cereal, canned fruit, and canned dog food as well. The latter being highly valued because of all the protein contained in the cans.

So every crate was worth battling for, even if the contents were uncertain, and as Burl led his squad out to do battle with the committees, makeshift clubs were swung, fists flew, and even teeth were employed as the melee got underway. Walker, ex-Marine that he was, sought the very center of the battle.

A man wearing a homemade eye patch took a swing at the Secretary of War, only to have his arm blocked as Walker hit him in the mouth. The committeeman's lower lip split open, blood dribbled down his chin, and he was forced to fall back, along with his cronies. The battle was over two minutes later as Burl's men drove the gang away from the booty they were trying to claim.

Then, true to their motto of "fair and square," the squad hauled the boxes to a central location where the entire community could witness their activities, and began the process of evaluating their haul. Once that effort was complete everything that could be logically distributed was, including three hundred pairs of socks, fifty tubes of toothpaste, and a hundred straw hats. Food, and anything that could even remotely be considered to be medical in nature, was kept together to be rationed out to the entire population, including the committeemen. Chimeran drones, which never took sides in such battles, hummed ominously as they crisscrossed the air above.

Once the work of processing the dump was complete, Walker was about to look for his wife, when Burl intercepted him.

"There you are," the big man said. "I'm glad I caught you."

"Yeah?" Walker replied. "What's up?"

"Porter tells me the guy you hit in the mouth—Tolly is his name—was seen talking to Collins."

"So?" Walker demanded. "The committeemen suck up to Collins all the time. It never does them any good. The bitch would sell her own mother for a stick of gum. She couldn't care less about them."

"That's true," Burl agreed soberly. "But Porter says that as Tolly was speaking to Collins, he was pointing at *you*. So keep your head down and stay out of sight for a while. We're all going to heaven—but why hurry?"

Walker laughed, promised Burl that he would be careful, and went looking for Myra. She wasn't hard to find. Almost from the moment they had arrived she had involved herself with the stink hole's meager medical facility. It was a rudimentary operation housed in what had once been the supervisor's pit shack—a wooden structure that sat on skids and could be towed from place to place as the mine deepened.

Sadly, the "med center," as it was called, had been set up and maintained by a succession of doctors, dentists, nurses, and in one case a pharmacist, all of whom had been marched up the spiral road to the Chimeran processing center on the flat land above. It was presently being run by a midwife, a retired Navy hospital corpsman, and Myra. She hurried over to give her husband a peck on the cheek as he entered.

The couple had always been close, but with death hovering all around, expressions of affection had become more frequent. Myra's face was thinner now, and there were perpetual circles around her eyes, but they still brimmed with life.

"You've been fighting again!" she said accusingly. "I know because the casualties show up here."

Walker grinned. "Who, *me*?" he protested as he looked around. There were fifteen or twenty patients crammed into the building—at least three of whom were dying of amoebic dysentery. The rest were getting treatment for cuts and bruises received during the recent dustup. A couple of committeemen were present and glowered at Walker as their injuries were tended to. He ignored them and turned back to Myra.

"Let's have dinner together," Walker said. "I'll take you to the best restaurant in town. To hell with the cost."

Myra smiled brightly.

"But I don't have anything to wear!"

"They're very understanding over at the boil," Walker assured her. "Dirty, blood-splattered clothes are in this year."

"Well, in that case, I would be delighted," Myra replied gravely. "Give me five minutes to finish what I was doing and I'll be ready to go."

Walker stepped back outside to wait for her, and watched as the sun descended below the western rim of the pit, and darkness settled into the stink hole. By the time Myra emerged from the med center, another freezing-cold night had begun. The sky was clear, so the couple could see a scattering of stars as they made their way over to the boil, where they fell into line behind a blanket-clad man and his ten-year-old daughter.

Each prisoner received three handcrafted tin tokens per day, which they were free to use as they saw fit. Some hoarded the disks for reasons Walker couldn't understand. Others used the tokens to pay for items of clothing, or personal services, sometimes including sex. But most people—the Walkers included—were happy to exchange their tokens for three hot meals per day.

Each meal was always the same, with a consistency of oatmeal, yet different because the ingredients varied. So as the line shuffled toward the fire-blackened cauldron, there was always a certain amount of suspense, not to mention rumors, regarding the contents of the occasionally noxious brew.

As Walker's stomach continued to growl, and he accepted a chromed baby moon hubcap from one of the volunteers, he wondered what sort of gustatory experience was waiting for him. The "glop masters," as they were jokingly called, were men and women who were willing to cook and serve for an extra token a day, and Walker knew the woman who ladled two dollops of glutinous "boil" onto his makeshift plate. Edith had a halo of gray hair, a broad face, and a big smile.

"Hello, Myra, hello, Henry," she said cheerfully. "You're going to like the boil tonight! A couple of cases of meatballs came in today. Most people are getting at least one or two."

And sure enough, consistent with Edith's prophecy, both Walkers found meatballs in their mush. A tasty brew that included oatmeal, canned peas, and a scattering of raisins. It was important to eat quickly, because even though the boil was hot, their metal plates were cold and the temperature was dropping. So the Walkers hurried over to the edge of a nearby terrace where layers of rock offered stadium-style seating. Once in place it was time to fish spoons out of their pockets and dig in.

By unspoken agreement there was no conversation during dinner, just eating, so as to consume the food before it grew cold. And even though Myra would have never considered doing such a thing in her Washington home, the former socialite didn't hesitate to lick her bowl clean once her food was gone.

"Not bad," Walker said as he put his empty hubcap aside. "Although my mush was a bit overcooked."

Myra laughed. "I'll tell the maître d'. Come on, it's time to get ready for bed."

Just about all the stink hole's prisoners went to bed early. Partly because there was nothing else to do, partly because it was easier to stay warm that way, and partly because just about all of them were bone-tired. There were no formal sleeping arrangements, just hundreds of improvised shelters, many of which had been constructed by people who had been marched up to the processing plant above. The Walkers' lean-to was no exception.

It consisted of a slab of steel that had once served as a bridge over a drainage ditch. At some point prior to their arrival it had been moved using muscle power, and tipped into position against the second-lowest terrace. That was as high as the humans were allowed to go without being shot by the Bullseye-toting Hybrid guards above. Backed by automatic weapons and mortars, they were in an unassailable position. The Chimera *liked* the cold temperatures, and glowered down from above as the Walkers ducked under their slanted roof.

Wood was too precious to be used as a floor, so their bedrolls rested on layers of cardboard, which offered a little bit of insulation from the hard frozen ground. One end of the lean-to had been sealed with a piece of raggedy carpet, cut to size. Once inside it was Walker's job to close the other end with a carefully crafted plug made out of canvas stretched over a wooden frame. An oil lamp similar to the ones being used in the escape tunnels provided what little light there was.

Having opened their slightly damp bedrolls, and climbed inside with their clothes still on, the Walkers were ready to sleep. Or Henry was anyway, because after kissing his wife good night, he soon began to snore. Myra knew the pattern well, and once her husband was asleep, allowed herself to cry. The sobs were muffled by blankets and therefore nearly inaudible, but they lasted for a long time.

Myra awoke to find her husband gone. That was no surprise since he always rose earlier than she did. Daylight was filtering in around the carpet and the canvas "door" behind her head by then.

She would have preferred to remain in bed for a while, comfortably cocooned inside her carefully maintained air pocket, but Myra needed to pee. So she steeled herself against the cold, rolled out of her slightly damp bedding, and remembered all of the steaming-hot baths she had taken for granted during her previous life. Long luxurious soaks that lasted for half an hour or more. But it was best to forget such things, to relegate them to the past along with the joys of clean clothes and hot tea.

After a visit to the nearest four-holer, Myra went to collect her tokens before making her way over to the boil. Myra knew most of her fellow prisoners, as a result of working in the med center, and said hello to them as she passed, but few were willing to do more than mumble a neutral response. And she knew why.

Because even though many of the prisoners had lost track of the calendar date, all of them knew that the Chimera came down into the pit to take people away every third day, which meant that today someone was going to die. So people found it difficult to look one another in the eye and exchange friendly greetings until a new seventy-two-hour clock began. Then it would be time to mourn those who had been taken, commiserate with whatever newbies had been brought in overnight, and try to ignore the horror of what was taking place.

Still, even with that understanding, it seemed as if people were especially taciturn that morning as Myra waited in the line, received her portion of the boil, and went off to eat it. The glutinous mess was almost identical to the glop served the evening before, except that there was only one meatball in her portion and kernels of canned corn had been added. Once she was finished, Myra took her hubcap over to the kitchen area where she turned it in prior to leaving for work.

The first thing Myra noticed about the Med Center was the absence of a line. But that wasn't too unusual for a three-day when most people did whatever they could to keep a low profile. So as Myra opened the door, and stepped inside, she was readying herself to face the usual chores, many of which were quite unpleasant.

But what awaited her was something entirely different.

A familiar stench hung heavy in the air, people were sobbing, and three heavily armed Hybrids were present. As was Norma Collins.

"You're five minutes late," the collaborator said accusingly, as if she was in charge of the clinic. "Turn around and go back outside."

Myra led the way, closely followed by her fellow staffers and all of the patients, some of whom were so sick they could barely walk, dressed in little more than street clothes, with nothing more than socks on their feet. A few complained, but doing so was pointless as the Chimera herded them onto the spiral road.

Myra felt liquid lead collect in the pit of her stomach and battled to control the sudden desire to go to the bathroom.

Judging from appearances the stinks had been waiting inside the clinic for some time. If so, that would explain why people had been unwilling to interact with Myra earlier, knowing as they did that she was marked for death. Some were sad, no doubt, but secretly happy as well, having been granted another seventy-two hours of life.

Myra's head swiveled back and forth as she looked for her husband, desperately hoping for one last moment of eye contact and a final wave, but he was nowhere to be seen. Yet that meant Henry would live a bit longer, and she was grateful.

That left Myra with nothing to do but trudge up the muddy slope and face what lay ahead. The air smelled clean and fresh, with just a slight tang of wood smoke. The weak, nearly powerless sunlight bathed everything around her in gold, and Myra could hear blood pounding in her ears as she and her doomed companions circled the pit like birds uncertain of where to land. She had regrets, but very few, and felt fortunate to be alive, if only for a short while longer.

As Walker left Escape Tunnel 1, made his way through the four-holer beyond, and stepped out into the well-churned muck, he knew instantly that something was wrong. An almost perfect silence hung over the pit, hundreds of people stood staring up at the road, and then he remembered. It was three-day, the stinks were making a withdrawal from their meat bank, and people were going to die. That was when the glop master named Edith turned to him with tears running down her cheeks. "I'm sorry," she said sympathetically. "Myra was a very nice person."

What felt like ice water trickled into Walker's veins.

"No!" he shouted, and began to run. If the stinks were going to take Myra, then he would go as well, and they would die together.

Burl heard Walker, saw him start to run, and knew what the man had in mind. But Burl was aware of the recorder, the recordings, and how important they were.

So he hurried to cut Walker off, threw his arms around him, and brought the ex–Secretary of War crashing down. Then, as members of the Fair and Square Squad hurried to help, Burl kept Walker from getting up.

That was when Tolly and a group of his cronies sauntered over. Tolly offered Burl an evil grin. "Remember this the next time a dump falls out of the sky," the committeeman said ominously. "And remember, it belongs to *us*."

That generated a chorus of agreement from the other committeemen, who slapped one another's backs, and left as a group.

Another day had begun.

There were lights inside what had been the mine's smelter, but not very many, because the Spinners wanted it that way. Like the rest of the forms to which the Chimeran virus had given life, the Spinners had a specific purpose, and an important one. That was to take human beings, and seal them inside a chrysalis-like cocoon, where a complex series of chemical reactions converted them into whatever type of Chimera was in short supply at the moment. Hybrids mostly, since they were the foot soldiers in the battle to conquer Earth, and were subject to a high casualty rate.

None of this was known to the Spinners, who were

little more than parts in a biological machine, the purpose of which was beyond their understanding.

So as Myra was forced to enter the long rectangular building, and gagged on the stench, she was unaware of the fact that the Hybrids urging her forward had once been human. And that was just as well, because knowing would have served no purpose other than to make an already horrible experience even worse. As she moved forward, scritching sounds were heard and hideous-looking monsters peered out from the compartments in which they lived. Cubicles which, judging from the layer of the fecal matter in them, hadn't been cleaned out in quite a while.

As Myra was chivvied down the main corridor, her knees felt weak, and her heart beat like a trip hammer. She knew the stinks were going to kill her, but she didn't know how. And not knowing was worse than any fate she could imagine.

Then she was there, standing in front of an open bay as a Spinner came out to inspect her. It was about the size of a large dog, and walked crablike on six claw-shaped feet. Myra screamed, and screamed *again,* as something hot and sticky shot out to make contact with her body. Then she was spinning, feet off the floor, as the goo wrapped her in a sticky embrace. Once the thick impermeable substance rose to encircle her chin, Myra knew how she was going to die, and uttered one last scream before hot sealer filled her mouth. Then she was choking, unable to breathe, as the newly formed chrysalis hardened around her.

Meanwhile, in the curing room a hundred feet away, a scabrous arm shot out of a cocoon. One of dozens that occupied that particular area. Pieces of rotting chrysalis fell away to land on the filth below as the Hybrid struggled to deliver itself. There was a ripping sound as the pod broke open and a scabrous thing staggered out onto the floor. It was clad in rags and the sad remnants of a pair of lace-up hunting boots.

Myra was dead by that time—and a Chimera had been born.

# CHAPTER SIXTEEN
# TALKING THE TALK

**Denver, Colorado**
**Saturday, December 15, 1951**

It was snowing beyond the large picture window that looked out over the Denver Federal Center. The flakes were big and wet, as if determined to reach the ground in record time, where they quickly turned to slush.

In spite of what he had repeatedly said to the press, President Grace didn't like Denver, Colorado. But given the intermittent spire attacks—like the one that narrowly missed him while visiting the Lincoln Memorial—it was the best place to be. The brush with death had been a very unsettling experience. It not only cast doubt upon his ability to protect the citizens of the United States, but it forced the government to flee inland.

And the incident left Grace with a knot of fear in his belly. Not just a fear of failure, but fear for his life, which had been threatened on that dark day.

Such were his thoughts as he turned away from the wintry scene that lay beyond the glass, crossed his recently completed office, and entered the hall beyond. The crown molding was up by that time, but as he made his way down the corridor painters were still at work, and it was necessary to thread his way between their ladders.

Rather than try to imitate the Cabinet Room in the

genuine White House, the decision had been made to create something entirely different under the cupola, which was positioned at the very center of the new residence. In keeping with the dome above, the table around which the President's advisers were about to gather was circular, symbolizing the collegial spirit that Grace liked to project as being typical of his administration.

The table rested on a round carpet that was large enough for all twelve chairs to rest on. Provisions had been made for aides to sit higher up, behind a low wall, where they could observe what went on below and participate if called upon to do so. That section was empty, however, partly because it was a Saturday, and partly because the gently curving seats were still being constructed.

In keeping with Grace's well-known penchant for punctuality, all of his subordinates were present when he entered the room. They stood as he strode to where his chair awaited, located at the eastern point of the compass-shaped inlay that was set into the mahogany tabletop. Vice President Harvey McCullen's chair marked the western point of the compass, Secretary of State Harold Moody stood with his back to the north, and newly named Secretary of War General Gregory Issen was stationed to the south.

The others, including Presidential Counsel Hanson, Attorney General Clowers, Secretary of Agriculture Seymore, Secretary of Transportation Keyes, Secretary of the Interior Farnsworth, Secretary of Commerce Lasky, and Chief of Staff Dentweiler, occupied the quadrants in between, with room to spare.

The room still reeked of fresh paint as Grace motioned for his advisers to sit down. The reports that followed were anything but encouraging: As Seymore spoke of persistent food shortages, Keyes bemoaned a lack of trains necessary to move critical supplies around, and Lasky reported that the steadily growing underground economy was a serious problem. The greenback was steadily falling out of favor as more and more citizens were choosing to use silver coins, gold pieces, and old-fashioned barter to settle their debts. All of which made for a very gloomy meeting until it was Dentweiler's turn to speak.

"So, Bill," Grace said. "What have you got for us? Something positive I hope."

It was Dentweiler's moment, and he planned to take full advantage of it, as all eyes rested on him. "Yes, Mr. President, I *do* have something positive to report. Simply put, Project Omega is poised for success. The first objective, which was to recapture Daedalus, has been accomplished."

That news was sufficient to stimulate applause, which made Dentweiler feel very good, and brought a broad smile to Grace's face.

"Well done! That's the sort of thing we need more of. Where is he?"

"Sheridan, Wyoming, sir," Dentweiler replied. "Our experts are trying to establish workable communication protocols with Daedalus. Once that effort is complete, we'll be able to open negotiations anytime we want to."

"So, Daedalus is cooperative?" Farnsworth wanted to know.

Dentweiler smiled tightly.

"No," he answered honestly, "I wouldn't go that far . . . But, thanks to the right sort of encouragement, Daedalus continues to grow *more* cooperative with each passing day. Let's put it that way."

A number of people chuckled, but the Vice President wasn't one of them.

"I think we're playing with fire," McCullen observed

darkly. "The last thing the people of the United States want us to do is negotiate with the Chimera. But, even if they did support the idea, we would be foolish to trust someone like Daedalus. He may have been human once—but he isn't any longer."

"Project Omega is an option, Harvey, and nothing more," Grace interjected smoothly. "And I think all of us want to have as many options as we can come up with. But enough of that . . . Let's move on to the Victory Tour. How's that coming?"

Some of the cabinet members, Secretary of War Issen among them, thought it was premature to call the upcoming swing through the heartland a "victory tour," given conditions on the ground, but Grace had persisted. After the Lincoln Memorial incident, the people needed reassurance.

"Preparations are well underway," Dentweiler replied confidently. "You're scheduled to give the first speech the day after tomorrow, here in Denver. After that it's on to Omaha, St. Louis, Memphis, New Orleans, Houston, Phoenix, and the West Coast. We'll be busing people in from the Protection Camps to enhance the crowds. I think you can count on some extremely positive coverage in all the major papers."

"It will boost morale," Lasky predicted enthusiastically. "I like it."

"So do I," Grace agreed, "although I can't say I'm looking forward to all those chicken dinners!" That produced a chorus of chuckles.

The meeting ground on, and the snow continued to fall.

It had been a long day, and Cassie Aklin was tired by the time she finally arrived home, and was able to close and lock the door. Her roommate had already departed for work by then, which meant Cassie had the apartment to herself, as she shed her work clothes in favor of a robe and slippers.

Then, with some Nat King Cole playing on the radio, Cassie made a simple dinner that consisted of scrambled eggs with small chunks of fried Spam mixed in, and a piece of toast. Though plain by prewar standards, the meal was special because eggs were hard to come by. The local grocer had been kind enough to hold two of them for her.

Later, after the dishes had been washed, dried, and put away, Cassie went into the living room, where a book titled *The Catcher in the Rye* sat waiting on the side table next to her favorite chair. She had just sat down, and was in the process of making herself comfortable, when she heard a knock on the door.

It was probably Elsie, the elderly woman who lived down the hall, but with so many desperate people flooding into town she took the moment necessary to peer through the peephole before turning the bolt. What she saw made her heart jump.

"Nathan?" Cassie demanded, as she threw the door open. "Is it really *you*?"

That question was answered in no uncertain terms as Hale stepped in to close the door with a backward kick and wrapped Cassie in his arms. Her lips were there waiting, and half a minute passed as they kissed and whispered private things to each other.

Then, when they broke contact, Cassie looked up into Hale's face and smiled.

"I missed you . . . Could you tell?"

Hale smiled.

"No, let's try that again."

So they kissed again, and it wasn't long before a trail

of discarded clothing led to the bedroom, where Hale laid Cassie on her bed.

"Let's take it slowly," she suggested softly. "Let's make it last until dawn."

"Yes, ma'am," Hale responded with mock seriousness, as he lay down next to her. "Your wish is my command."

Two hours later the lovers took a shower together. And even though they had fallen well short of Cassie's goal, neither saw any reason to complain as they helped dry each other off. Then, clad in nothing more than a pair of boxer shorts, Hale followed Cassie into the kitchen, where she made a grilled cheese sandwich for him.

"So," she said as Hale took his first bite, and she sipped some tea. "Are you on leave? I know you aren't here for a checkup . . . I would have heard about that."

"President Grace is going to give a speech in front of the state capitol," Hale explained. "And given how unstable the situation is, SRPA agreed to provide extra security. So, being a true patriot, I volunteered to take part."

The last was delivered with a mischievous grin and Cassie laughed.

"Liar! You wanted to mooch one of my world-famous grilled cheese sandwiches!"

"Yeah," he agreed lightly. "You have me dead to rights. It's all about your grilled cheese sandwiches."

Cassie smiled indulgently. "You are a very bad boy."

Hale's eyebrows rose. "Really? Does that mean I'm going to be punished?"

"Yes," Cassie answered gravely. "It's too late to send you to bed without your dinner . . . But I can still send you to bed early."

"Damn," Hale said regretfully as he took a sip of milk. "That sounds very strict. But, if I must, I must."

The sky was three shades of gray, the occasional snowflake twirled down from above, and a man in a red Santa Claus suit held the door open for Susan Farley and Anthony Puzo as they left Union Station. The Santa's bell made a cheerful clanging sound and was an audible reminder of Christmases past. So Susan put both of her suitcases down long enough to adjust the blue scarf she was wearing on her head, remove a one-dollar bill from her purse, and push it down into the pot that hung suspended under a metal tripod.

That was a lot of money for anybody, given the war, and Susan felt momentarily proud of herself. Then she remembered that she wasn't going to need any money, impulsively shoved a ten-spot into the cauldron, and bent to pick her suitcases up off the cigarette-butt-littered sidewalk. "Bless you!" the man said fervently. "Merry Christmas!"

Susan doubted such a thing was possible, but smiled anyway as she made her way out to the curb. Puzo had corralled a cab by then, and consistent with his normal manner, made no attempt to help Susan with her suitcases. Once the luggage was stowed in the trunk, and the passengers were sitting in the back seat, the driver pulled out into light traffic.

"We're staying at the Ridley Hotel," Puzo informed him. "It's on the corner of 14th and Lincoln."

The cabbie nodded obediently as he guided the car up 17th toward the home of the Colorado legislature.

It was a relatively short drive, but there was enough time for Susan to catch a glimpse of busy sidewalks filled with men in uniform, shabby-looking civilians, and brightly decorated shop windows. But no amount of red, gold, and green could win the war, and the sight of it left Susan feeling sad.

The Ridley was a popular hotel that was set up to meet the needs of state legislators and the lobbyists who besieged them. It was also a favorite with traveling businessmen who were fond of the hotel's masculine decor, high-ceilinged rooms, and spacious Buffalo Bar.

As the cab pulled in under the Ridley's elaborate portico, two bellhops, both attired in pillbox hats, burgundy jackets, and gray slacks, hurried out to remove the suitcases and haul them inside. A large fireplace dominated one end of the enormous lobby. It was surrounded by groupings of furniture—the emphasis being on leather chairs, brass lamps, and large side tables. They were littered with cast-off newspapers, empty coffee cups, and half-filled ashtrays.

The reception desk was located at the far end of the room. It was made of highly polished dark wood. Etched-glass panels separated each of the three well-groomed receptionists and Puzo chose to approach the one in the middle.

"Good morning," he said breezily. "You should have two reservations . . . One for my daughter, Mary—and the other for me. My name is Perkins. Horace Perkins."

The receptionist was a middle-aged man dressed in a black three-piece suit. He had the manner of an undertaker as he ran a narrow finger down the ledger in front of him.

"Welcome to the Ridley, Mr. Perkins . . . Ah, yes, here we are. Two interconnecting rooms on the third floor. Is that correct?"

"Yes, it is," Puzo confirmed. "I can't stand people walking around over my head. Your elevators are in good working order, I trust?"

"They are," the clerk answered gravely, as if anything

else would be unthinkable. "If you and your daughter would be so kind as to sign these registration cards, I'll have one of the bellmen escort you to your rooms."

Then, as if to signal the end of the conversation, the receptionist brought his hand down on a button which rang a small bell. Susan was still in the process of signing her fake name when a burgundy-clad bellman arrived to load their luggage onto a cart.

Ten minutes later the bellman was gone and Susan was in her nicely appointed room, looking out through one of two tall windows as Puzo entered through the connecting door. "So," he said, coming to stand next to her. "What do you think?"

She was silent for a moment as she looked out onto the wintry scene. The capitol was off to her right. It was an impressive structure of Colorado white granite. Topped by a round tower, it had a bell-shaped dome, reportedly made out of real gold. Ironically enough, it was intentionally reminiscent of the United States Capitol, which the Grace administration had been forced to flee.

Occasional flurries of snow made it difficult to see clearly but the range was reasonable, just as she had been told. "I can do it," she said simply.

"Good," Puzo replied. "Would you like some lunch? The Ridley has a good restaurant. Or so I hear."

Susan felt slightly nauseous, and had ever since leaving Montana, so she shook her head. "No. Thank you. I'll take a walk instead."

Puzo shrugged. "Suit yourself. Let's meet here at two P.M. We have lots of prep work to do."

Susan nodded, but didn't turn to look as Puzo left the room. She waited for the door to close, let her breath out, and was surprised to learn that she'd been holding it in. Then, standing on tiptoes, she reached up to turn the window latch sideways and free it from the catch. With that accomplished she bent over, took hold of both handles, and lifted.

Much to her relief the window rose smoothly, allowing a blast of cold air to enter the room. Susan stood there for a moment as the incoming breeze caused the curtains to billow, and directed her gaze to a point roughly a thousand yards away. That was where a crew of men were hard at work constructing a wooden platform. And that was the spot to which her future was irrevocably linked.

After many months of testing and inoculations Hale had come to detest hospitals. But after Operation Iron Fist, and the mission into Hot Springs, South Dakota, he felt an obligation to visit Dr. Linda Barrie to see how the scientist was doing. So having accompanied Cassie to the Denver Federal Center, Hale pried Barrie's room number out of the woman on the hospital's front desk, and went up to see her.

Thanks to her rank, Barrie had a room to herself. She said "Come in" when Hale knocked on the partially opened door. Her face was still a bit pale, but just as pretty as before, and seemed to brighten at the sight of him. She was out of bed, but sitting in a chair, and made no attempt to rise.

"Nathan!" she exclaimed. "What a pleasant surprise."

"You look good," Hale said awkwardly as he placed a small Christmas tree on a table. It had miniature ornaments and had been purchased in the gift shop downstairs. "Everybody says you're doing well, too."

What followed was an awkward conversation for the most part, since the operation that brought them together was over, and they didn't have much to talk about. So the visit didn't last long.

But as he got ready to go, Barrie motioned for him to come closer. Once Hale was close enough to touch she reached up to pull his head down. Their eyes were only inches apart when she spoke. "Thank you, Lieutenant Hale. Thank you for what you did for Anton, thank you for saving my life, and thank you for serving our country." And then she kissed him on the cheek.

Hale mumbled something incoherent, fled the room for the hall, and felt glad to escape the hospital. The interaction with Barrie had left him feeling confused. Fortunately Hale had work to do, and was already thinking about it, as he followed a recently shoveled sidewalk out to the parking lot.

The LU-P Lynx Hale had been given to drive was just like the combat model he was used to except the machine gun was missing and a fabric roof had been fitted over the roll cage. The vehicle boasted a heater, but it couldn't compete with the cold air that flooded in through the open sides, and made an impotent whirring noise as Hale started the engine, backed out of the parking slot, and followed the road to the main gate. Guards saluted the officer as he rolled past, turned onto Alameda, and followed the busy street toward Broadway.

The purpose of the outing was to visit the state capitol, which was going to be the site of Grace's speech the following day. The Secret Service had primary responsibility for security, with lots of Denver police to provide backup, but a contingent of Sentinels would be present as well, in case of a Chimeran attack. The chances of something like that happening were extremely remote, but no one had been expecting a spire to land next to the Lincoln Memorial either.

So as Hale took a left on Broadway, and followed it to

the state capitol, he was thinking about the stinks and what sort of damage they might do if a shuttle-load of them dropped out of the sky in the middle of the President's speech. He was scheduled to check in with the Secret Service, and wanted to make certain they had arranged for air cover, so he went looking for a place to park. There wasn't any, because the legislature was still in session and entire sections of the street had been roped off, allowing a succession of delivery trucks to unload.

A speaking platform had been built, VIP bleachers were in place to either side of it, and a temporary fence had been set up to control what was expected to be a record crowd.

Hale drove around for a while before locating a parking spot three blocks away. After walking back he had to show his military ID before being allowed onto the capitol grounds. The man in charge of security was a Secret Service agent named Mack Stoly. He was a natty little man who was dressed in a gray snap-brim hat, blue topcoat, and pin-striped suit. He was at the center of a discussion that involved two other men and Hale noticed Stoly was wearing shiny street shoes. As if the agent was unwilling to compromise with the elements.

Hale, who was dressed in a winter uniform plus overcoat and combat boots, paused a few feet away and stuck his hands in his pockets while he waited for the conversation to end. That gave him a chance to conduct a slow 360-degree inspection of the surrounding terrain. As he turned he saw the capitol, a variety of structures off to the right, the portion of Lincoln Street which had been temporarily blocked off, the Ridley Hotel, the Civic Center, a cluster of public buildings, and then back to the capitol. Hale was looking up at the golden dome, and blinking snowflakes away, when someone spoke to him. "Impressive, isn't it?" It was the man he'd been waiting for. "My name's Stoly. Are you Lieutenant Hale?"

"Yes I am," Hale replied, as he shook the other man's hand. Stoly had blue eyes, even features, and a cleft chin. If he thought the Sentinel's golden yellow eyes were strange, he gave no sign.

"Thanks for coming over," Stoly said. "With so many people involved in security, it's critical that we coordinate things properly. This is a good opportunity to agree on where your men will be placed—and what they will be responsible for."

"Sounds good," Hale agreed, as he stuck his hands back into his pockets. "From what I was told, our job is to deal with the stinks should some of them drop out of the sky."

"True," Stoly acknowledged soberly. "It's damned unlikely, but after what happened at the Lincoln Memorial, *anything* seems possible. So we've got to be ready. But you'll have a secondary mission as well—and that's crowd control. I'm told that the President's Chief of Staff wants a *big* crowd. So, contrary to our advice, he decided to bus people in from the nearest Protection Camps. The problem is that a lot of the people who live in the camps aren't very happy with the Grace administration. They aren't allowed to own guns, thank God . . . But that doesn't mean some whacko with a knife won't try to rush the platform, or worse yet, *twenty* whackos with knives! So you and your men will be a welcome addition to our security team."

Hale spent the next hour accompanying Stoly from place to place, chatting with various agents and police officials, and discussing how to best position his Sentinels. He remembered to ask about air support, and was relieved to learn that it had been arranged. Finally, once the tour was over, Hale was free to depart. Which was great, because Cassie was about to get off work, and he had promised to take her to dinner.

Hale was whistling as he crossed 14th and began the walk back to the Lynx. Maybe, had he been thinking about work, Hale might have noticed the young woman in the blue headscarf who passed not thirty feet away from him. Her name was Susan Farley—and she was there to kill the President.

God must have been listening to William Dentweiler's prayers—because the day dawned bright and clear. It was also cold.

*Very* cold.

Which would have made things difficult had it been necessary to draw a Denver crowd. But thanks to busloads of citizens from the Protection Camps, all equipped with identical overcoats, box lunches, and "Noah Grace" signs, a sizable audience was guaranteed.

Meanwhile, Hale had men stationed on the capitol's roof, to either side of the speaker's platform, and on top of the barriers that had been used to block off part of Lincoln Street. Above, carving white lines across the sky, two flights of Sabre Jets could be seen ready to respond should Chimeran aircraft venture from the north.

So the stage was set as a cheer went up and the Army band played "Hail to the Chief."

The Governor of the state of Colorado gave him a nice introduction, and President Grace was in an ebullient mood as he left the warmth of the capitol. He crossed the plaza and made his way down four short flights of steps to the platform below. He liked giving speeches, being at the center of attention, and hearing the applause. So even though his administration was beset by problems, here was a moment he could actually enjoy. As Grace stepped up to the bunting-draped podium, flashbulbs went off, the last strains of "Hail to the Chief" died away, and the applause began to fade.

"My fellow Americans," Grace said, mindful of the fact that millions would hear his words over the radio. "Darkness continues to gather all around us, but here in the heartland of our country the sun is shining, and we have reason to rejoice!"

It was an applause line, and thanks to the twenty shills Dentweiler had positioned in the audience there *was* applause, which Grace acknowledged with a nod as he waited for the noise to die down.

What followed was a stirring list of victories, accomplishments, and positive trends all strung together to lift the cloud of gloom that hovered above so much of the nation. As Hale listened, even *he* began to feel better, in spite of the fact that he'd been to Chicago and seen first-hand what life was like in that city.

But Hale wasn't there to listen. He was there to help provide security, which was why he kept his head on a swivel, his eyes scanning for any sign of a threat. There was nothing to see, however, not until he turned his gaze to the Ridley Hotel, and the dozens of windows that stared out onto the capitol grounds.

One of them was open, and that in spite of air so cold he could see his breath, and feel his fingers starting to grow numb. A guest perhaps? Determined to get a better view of the speech? Or something more sinister?

As Grace gave the crowd a somewhat embellished account of Operation Iron Fist, Hale brought his binoculars up to examine the front of the hotel. Try as he might Hale couldn't see into the room. But as he continued to stare Hale saw a momentary flash of light which served to backlight both the person at the window *and* the familiar shape that was angled his way.

A Fareye! But then the image was gone, leaving Hale to wonder.

He blinked, hoping to somehow restore what he'd seen, but the room remained dark. Assuming he was correct, and not hallucinating, it was as if a light had been turned on behind the rifleman. Or a door had been opened into a well-lit space.

But what to do? Evacuate the President from the platform? That would be prudent, perhaps . . . But if the marksman was a Secret Service agent, or a photographer with a long lens, or a maid with a mop, a lot of people were going to be very angry.

But he couldn't just let it drop.

Hale glanced around for Stoly, and saw him on the far side of the platform. The handheld radio he'd been given was for emergencies only, and therefore silent, as he brought it up to his lips.

"Hale to Stoly . . . Front of the hotel, third floor, open window . . . At least one person inside. Yours?"

There was a brief pause, followed by an emphatic reply.

"Hell no!"

Hale felt a sudden surge of adrenaline as he took three steps forward to the point where one of his soldiers was stationed. "Give me your rifle," he ordered harshly, as he took the Fareye out of the man's hands. "And stand perfectly still. I'm going to use you as a rest."

As Hale laid the rifle across the Sentinel's shoulder, and put his eye to the scope, Stoly hit Grace from the side. And when the President went down a projectile hit the Governor of Colorado—who had the painful misfortune to be standing directly behind Grace when the projectile was fired. The Governor made a grab for his shoulder as he fell, and the rest of the dignitaries scattered in every direction as the sound of the shot echoed between the surrounding buildings.

People began to scream.

Hale had the window centered under his crosshairs by that time, and even though he couldn't see a clean target, he fired repeatedly. Hale figured that if he hit the would-be assassin, then that would be good, but even if he didn't, the counterfire would probably be enough to ruin the bastard's aim. And that would be sufficient. Because within minutes, five at most, Secret Service agents and policemen would storm the room. To his credit the Sentinel whose gun he had taken stood perfectly still as Hale continued to fire, brass casings arcing through the air, and people continued to scream.

The window was open, the dresser had been moved into position in front of it, and the rifle was resting on a carefully arranged sandbag. Susan swore as someone knocked Grace down and her bullet hit one of the men behind him. Then, as she worked another round into the Fareye's chamber, some quick-thinking bastard fired at *her*.

Except that he missed, and Susan heard Puzo make a horrible gargling sound as the incoming bullet tore through his throat, and he brought both hands up in a futile attempt to stop the sudden spray of blood. Then he was falling, as another bullet whispered past her ear, and smashed into the mirror behind her.

Susan spent a fraction of a second analyzing the possibility of a follow-up shot on the President, saw that Grace was unreachable under a pile of protective bodies, and adjusted her aim. Secret Service agents would burst through her door within minutes, she knew that. But if she was going to die, why not take the man with the rifle with her? Because if anyone deserved to die, it was the army of assholes who supported Grace and kept him in office. Susan found her target, and prepared to squeeze the trigger. Then she saw the left side of the man's face.

"Nathan!" That was when a sledgehammer hit Susan's head, and the long fall into darkness began.

# CHAPTER SEVENTEEN
# YANKEE DOODLE DANDY

**Near Madison, Wisconsin**
**Thursday, December 20, 1951**

It was one-day down in the stink hole, which meant that another group of doomed prisoners had been led away, and the survivors were going to live for another forty-eight hours. Well, most of the survivors anyway, because Henry Walker was determined to kill the son of a bitch responsible for his wife's death.

Walker couldn't *prove* that Marcus Tolly had engineered Myra's death. And he was fully cognizant of the fact that *all* of the prisoners were going to die, the only question being *when*. But logical arguments didn't matter, because Walker had to kill Tolly, or lose his mind. So having named himself judge, jury, and executioner, Walker had made a study of the one-eyed committeeman's habits, and created a plan. And, as darkness fell over the pit, that plan was about to be implemented.

Tolly had finished his boil by then, and having returned his empty hubcap to the outdoor kitchen, he began to make his way over to the tent he had appropriated from a family of three. Tolly stopped every now and then to schmooze with his cronies, but Walker knew it was only a matter of time, and was content to wait within a recently abandoned lean-to located only yards from his quarry's tent.

But as he sat there, peering out through a hole in the wall and waiting for his prey to arrive, Walker knew it was the last thing Myra would want him to do. In fact he could almost hear her talking into his ear.

*Killing Tolly won't bring me back, Henry . . . There's been enough killing. We'll be together soon enough.*

And Myra was right. Walker knew that. But watching Tolly swagger around the pit, pushing people around, and taking whatever he wanted, was more than Walker could bear. That's what he told himself anyway, although deep down he knew it was about revenge, and a desire to strike back at the man he felt sure was responsible for Myra's death.

Finally, having completed the long circuitous walk to his tent, Tolly paused to look around. Then, having satisfied himself that it was safe to do so, he bent over to enter his shelter. A shadow appeared as Tolly lit the lantern within and began to prepare his bedroll. That was the moment Walker had been waiting for. The key was knowing exactly where the big man was within the tent.

Walker had been a Marine, and he had killed before, but never like this. His heart beat wildly and his hands shook as he rose, and emerged from concealment. Three careful steps carried him over to Tolly's tent. The homemade dagger was one of dozens of such implements that had been manufactured in the stink hole and passed down to the living from the recently dead. The weapon was in Walker's right hand, and it made a ripping sound as it sliced through the patchwork quilt collection of fabrics that had been painstakingly sewn together to form a serviceable tent.

"What the hell?" Tolly swore as a hole appeared above him. "God damn it!"

Walker poured the better part of a gallon of gasoline

onto the committeeman's head and shoulders. The fuel had been siphoned out of one of the mining trucks and stored in a rubber bladder made from an inner tube. It gave off its characteristic odor as Walker opened a Zippo lighter. He flicked the wheel and sparks appeared, immediately followed by a blue flame.

Tolly looked up, saw the flame, and screamed, "No!" He was kneeling as if in prayer, and a thin trickle of pus flowed out from under his leather eye patch as he stared upward. But the pitiful sight wasn't enough to stay Walker's hand as he dropped the lighter into the hole and was rewarded with a loud *whump!*

Walker took a full step backward as Tolly was enveloped by flames and a wave of heat hit his face. The air around them was extremely cold, so it felt natural to bring both hands up, and enjoy the sudden warmth.

The committeeman was on his feet by then, having stuck his head up through the hole Walker had made, and he began to scream as he beat at the flames. People came on the run, but when they saw Walker standing there, warming his hands over the fire, they knew what had taken place. None of them chose to intervene. And that was a wise decision, because Burl had arrived on the scene, by that time along with other members of the Fair and Square Squad, all of whom were ready to deal with Tolly's fellow committeemen, should that become necessary. So as Tolly flailed about, and his tent caught on fire, there was no one to help him.

The Hybrids stationed around the rim stared down into the pit and watched impassively.

Finally, having lost consciousness, Tolly collapsed in a smoking heap. Walker spit on the badly burned corpse and heard the liquid sizzle before he turned away. He felt sick to his stomach, and his knees were weak, but for the first time in days he knew he'd be able to sleep.

\* \* \*

"Tunnel 1 is ready!"

Those were the words that flew mouth to mouth at roughly noon that day. And, as Walker knew from personal experience, it was true. Because he'd been in the shaft, working as a donkey, when the long-hoped-for breakthrough occurred. He hadn't been there himself, up at the top of the steeply slanting tunnel where the patch of gray sky suddenly appeared, but he was among the first to hear about it as word of the accomplishment rippled down the line.

It was joyous news, but troubling as well, because with the next three-day only hours away *everyone* would want to scramble through the tunnel, even though they knew that most if not all of the escapees would be caught and probably executed. So it was all Walker and the other members of the Fair and Square Squad could do to try and impose some sort of order on the situation.

The key was to present not only the perception of fairness, but the reality of it, which was why all 278 prisoners were given an opportunity to pull a number out of Burl's hat. A process that had to be carried out surreptitiously lest the collaborator, Collins, or one of the Hybrids take notice.

There had been talk of more complicated systems designed to give tunnelers, medics, and kitchen workers some sort of priority in recognition of their service to the rest of the prisoners. But such schemes were deemed too difficult to manage in the amount of time available. Besides, as Burl pointed out, "The only reason Tunnel 1 exists is because people who knew they wouldn't get the opportunity to use it were willing to dig it anyway. We're going to die. Get used to it."

As luck would have it Walker drew the number 131,

which wasn't very good, since it was generally assumed that at least some of the earliest escapees would be caught. That would draw attention to the rest, which would bring the entire exercise grinding to a halt and a predictably bloody end.

Still Walker couldn't help but feel excited as he went to retrieve the tape recorder and the evidence that would surely bring the Grace administration to its knees. Then, mindful of how demanding an escape from Chimera-held territory would be, Walker went to his tent to sort through the few possessions he had and load his pockets with those that were likely to be the most important.

Once that chore was complete, the only thing he could do was lie down and wait for darkness to come. At 10:00 P.M., the first person would leave the tunnel. Walker tried to sleep, but couldn't, and was still wide awake when the time came to crawl out of the lean-to and make his way through pitch blackness to the point where the line had already started to form. Then, having located numbers 130 and 132, all Walker could do was wait.

Harley Burl had drawn number 23.

A very low number—and one that gave him a good chance of actually clearing the hole. What happened after that would be primarily a function of luck, although those who were smart and in good physical shape would have a definite edge. And Burl, who thought he was reasonably smart, had a plan. A crazy, audacious plan that was so counterintuitive it just might work. Especially against a bunch of stinks.

So when the appointed hour finally arrived, and a chiropractor named Larthy crawled out of the tunnel onto the snow-covered ground beyond the rim, Burl was tensed up and ready to go. And as the line began to jerk forward, and giant shadows oozed across the walls, Burl felt his heart bang against his chest.

Would one of the people in front of him make a stupid mistake?

Would someone get caught within a matter of minutes, leaving him trapped in the tunnel? All he could do was hope.

Time seemed to slow as the line crept forward—each passing second bringing additional risk of discovery—as those at the head of the tunnel forced themselves to count to thirty before leaving the relative safety of their burrow. The gap was supposed to space the escapees out in hopes that the thirty-second intervals would prevent the prisoners from bumping into one another in the dark. But each pause felt like an eternity.

Finally, as fresh air began to seep down into the tunnel, Burl was only one person away from freedom. Then number 22's bloblike body was gone, it was *his* turn to count, and a light speared down out of the sky a quarter-mile in the distance. One of the escapees had been spotted. There was only one thing Burl could do, and that was to *run*.

Walker was about halfway up the tunnel when all the people who were still inside Tunnel 1 had no choice but to turn around and return to the pit. What ensued was a desperate scramble in which people swore at one another, a support beam was knocked out of place, and dirt rained down from above.

There were voices of reason however, including Walker's, as he called on the people within earshot to slow down, and to be careful lest the entire tunnel cave in on them.

But most of the support beams held, which meant that it wasn't long before people began to leave the tunnel and exit through the four-holer set up to hide it. And as they arrived, one after another, about two dozen Hybrids were on hand to receive them.

One of the stinks gave Walker a shove, and another growled at him as he was sent to join the others. All of the prisoners were huddled under the glare produced by three Patrol Drones. They hummed menacingly as they circled the crowd. "Do you think they'll shoot us?" a woman wondered, her teeth chattering from both fear and the cold.

"Naw," the man next to her replied dismissively. "We should be so lucky! It's kinda like when some of my father's chickens would find a way out of the coop. Pa didn't kill 'em, not right away. That came later. When Ma had a hankering for fried chicken."

Walker wasn't so sure about that, but eventually the chicken analogy was proven to be correct, as the stinks left the prisoners unharmed but tore all of the four-holers apart looking for more tunnels. There were two additional shafts, both located on the other side of the pit, but went undiscovered because the Chimera couldn't generalize beyond the example in front of them. Tunnels went with shitters, and vice versa, that was the extent of their reasoning.

The escape attempt did not go entirely unpunished, however. Once all the prisoners were out of the tunnel, and explosives had been used to seal it off, Walker heard a now familiar thrumming sound as a Chimeran shuttle drifted over the pit from the north. The wind generated by its flaring repellers blew snow, flimsy shelters, and bits of trash in every direction as the ship put down next to the poisonous-looking lake. Multicolored running lights strobed the entire area as the shuttle settled onto its skids.

That was when servos whined, a ramp came down,

and roughly fifty prisoners were marched down onto the ground. They were newbies, all having been captured over the last few days, and completely unaware of the drama that was playing itself out around them. That wasn't unusual, because newbies arrived every couple of days, though usually on foot. What caught Walker's attention was the fact that rather than be allowed to take charge of the newcomers the way she usually did, Collins was being held in check, and judging from the expression on her normally impassive face she was terrified.

Then, once all the newbies were off the shuttle, two Hybrids took hold of the collaborator's arms and dragged her up the ramp, where they forced her to turn around and face the crowd. And there she was, still standing on the ramp, as the shuttle lifted off.

The aircraft rose to a height of approximately one hundred feet, and all eyes were still on the ship as it began to hover.

That was when the Hybrids pushed Collins off.

The schoolteacher was expecting it by then, and screamed all the way down. The noise stopped when her body landed on top of a piece of rusty mining equipment, and blood splattered the ground all around it. The stinks were sending a message—and everyone understood it. Even if they didn't feel any sorrow.

"Rot in hell, bitch," someone said. It wasn't much of an epitaph—but the only one that Collins was going to get.

# CHAPTER EIGHTEEN
# REMEMBER THE ALAMO

The Denver Federal Center had its own detention facility—and that was where maximum security prisoner Susan Farley had been held during the days immediately following the attempt on President Grace's life.

The transfer area was a drab space with green walls, slit-style windows, and furniture that was bolted to the floor. Ironically enough, the only decoration in the room consisted of three pictures: one of the Federal Center's head administrator, one of Vice President McCullen, and one of President Grace.

Before being allowed to enter the transfer center, Hale was searched, not just once, but *twice*. Two armed guards stood side by side with their backs to a cement wall as he waited for Susan to appear.

The chains on her wrists and ankles made a rattling sound, so he *heard* his sister before the steel door swung open and Susan shuffled into the brightly lit room. Her hair had been shaved off and the spot where Hale's bullet had nicked the side of her skull was concealed by a white bandage. Had the projectile been one inch to the right, she would have been dead. Susan was dressed in gray prison garb, including a coat with a hood that hung down onto her shoulders.

"You've got five minutes," the prison matron said sternly. "Don't touch, don't whisper, and don't exchange physical objects without permission. The clock starts now."

Susan nodded impassively as she looked into Hale's golden yellow eyes.

"So you came."

"Of course I came," Hale replied. "You're my sister. I hired a lawyer . . . He'll visit you in the prison."

"Why bother?" Susan replied bleakly. "I did it. Everyone knows that."

"You sure as hell did," Hale agreed soberly. "But who knows? Maybe we can get your sentence reduced."

Susan smiled grimly.

"All of us are under a death sentence. You—of all people—should realize that. The so-called Liberty Defense Perimeter isn't going to work, the Grace administration is more interested in holding on to power than winning the war, and anyone with the guts to oppose them winds up in a Protection Camp . . . or worse. The only thing I regret is the fact that I missed. That was *your* fault, Nathan . . . And you're going to regret it, too," she added bitterly.

"That will be enough of that," the matron said grimly as she noticed the prisoner's agitated state, and motioned to the guards. "Load her on the bus. And keep your eyes peeled. She belongs to Freedom First, and there are plenty of sympathizers in the area."

Hale wanted to say something comforting, wanted to make peace somehow, but couldn't find the words as the guards escorted Susan through the door, and into the cold light beyond. "Don't worry, Lieutenant," the matron said gruffly. "She'll be all right."

"Thank you," he responded, but he wasn't sure anything would be "all right" ever again.

\* \* \*

After days spent worrying about Susan, and being questioned by law enforcement officers of every type, Hale was happy to return to work. Even if the first thing he had to do was attend a meeting.

It was being held at the Federal Center, but on the far side of the complex, and Hale no longer had the Lynx. So he set a brisk pace for himself, and after a ten-minute walk, he spotted his destination ahead.

SRPA headquarters–Denver was located in an unremarkable four-story brick building, which, according to the sign out front, was home to something called the "Federal Land Acquisitions Agency." A very real organization that occupied half of the first floor. The rest of the structure served the needs of SRPA staff. They were an extremely hardworking group who were responsible for planning and coordinating SAR missions throughout the West.

The briefing center was located on the second floor, and after clearing a security check, Hale arrived five minutes late. As he entered the rather austere conference room Hale saw that Major Blake, Chief of Staff Dentweiler, and a man he didn't know were waiting for him.

"Sorry I'm late, sir," Hale said. "I had to hike in from the other side of the center."

"No problem," Blake replied. "We just sat down. Have a chair. You know Mr. Dentweiler . . . And this is Mr. Burl. He was a prisoner in what was almost certainly a Chimeran Conversion Center until just days ago."

Hale shook Dentweiler's hand, noticed that it was *still* cold, and turned to the other civilian. "Mr. Burl . . . It's a pleasure to meet you, sir. And congratulations on your escape. If you don't mind my asking, how did you pull it off?"

Burl had a firm grip and a direct gaze. "I was lucky," he answered simply. "The stinks were holding us in a big pit. We dug escape tunnels, and one of them paid off. A few of us got away."

"Mr. Burl was the last person out," Blake added. "The alarm had been given by then, so rather than run into the Chimera's arms, he found a place to hide not fifty feet from the tunnel. *So* close the stinks didn't bother to search it carefully enough."

"I damned near froze my ass off," Burl put in ruefully. "But I was wearing four layers of clothing, and that helped. The *real* break came six hours later when a snowstorm passed through. I made use of the low visibility to escape the area."

"He stumbled across a road, followed it to a house, and hot-wired a pickup," Blake said admiringly. "And there he was, racing south, when a VTOL crew spotted him."

"Nice work," Hale said sincerely. "Did anyone else make it out?"

"A few did," Burl answered soberly, as he looked down at his hands. "But there's no way to know if any of them are still alive. Hundreds of people are still in the pit."

"Yes," Dentweiler said, as he spoke for the first time, "and one of them is ex–Secretary of War Walker."

Hale's eyebrows rose.

"Really? The man we've been looking for?"

"Exactly," Dentweiler replied grimly. "It seems the stinks grabbed the bastard while he and his wife were on their way to Chicago. All we have to do is pick him up."


Burl felt a sense of foreboding. He'd been too trusting. That was apparent now. But his intentions had been good.

Almost from the moment the VTOL picked him up, Burl had been telling anyone who would listen that Walker was being held prisoner, in hopes that authorities would want to rescue the Secretary of War—and therefore all of the poor souls in the stink hole.

He hadn't mentioned the tapes, however, and wasn't going to—not until he had to. He cleared his throat. "Yes, well, you might want to remember that the stinks take people away every few days. So Walker could be dead by now."

"We need to know," Dentweiler put in vehemently, his eyes hard. "The man's a traitor!" He turned to the Sentinel. "I want you to go in and get him. More importantly, the *President* wants you to go in and get him."

"And the other prisoners?" Hale wanted to know.

"We'll bring them out, too," Blake responded hurriedly, as if fearful that Dentweiler would give some other instruction. "But it's got to be fast . . . So the Chimera won't have time to counterattack. Otherwise we could wind up having to rescue the rescuers."

Hale nodded. "Understood. How large a force can I have?"

The question was directed to Major Blake, but Dentweiler chose to answer for him.

"You can have anything you want," the Chief of Staff said flatly.

Major Blake frowned but remained silent.

"And one more thing," Dentweiler added, his eyes on Hale. "The thing with your sister . . . Good work. We kept your name out of the press—we had to, given the fact that you're officially dead—but the President is grateful. He'd like to thank you personally once this mission is over. And with Major Blake's permission, we're going to add a contingent of Sentinels to the President's security team, and put you in command of them."

There had been a time, only days earlier, when Hale would have been proud to play such a role. Now, after seeing how much Susan had been willing to sacrifice in order to remove Grace from office, he wasn't so sure.

But Hale was a soldier—and gave the only reply he could. "Yes, sir. I'll do my best."

The sun had just risen, and was a dimly seen presence off to the east, as the six VTOLs came in from the west. Though not especially fast under even the best conditions, these aircraft were especially slow because of the vehicle that dangled beneath each ship. And, as the wintry landscape seemed to creep past below, the officer in command of the mission was busy questioning his own logic.

Hale was in the lead VTOL, crouched between his old friend Purvis and the *Party Girl*'s copilot, the three of them eyeing the terrain ahead. It was flat farm country for the most part, much of which had been ravaged by the war, but some of the farmhouses, barns, and silos appeared to be intact under layers of gauzy snow.

Strike Force Zebra had been spotted by that time, Hale felt certain of that, so it was safe to assume that the stinks were organizing a response. And that was where the speed versus throw weight calculation came into play. By choosing to bring two M-12 tanks, plus four LU-P Lynx All-Purpose Vehicles along with his troops, Hale was betting that no matter *how* quickly they arrived the team might have to cope with a major counterattack. If so both he and the rest of the Sentinels would be glad to have some heavy weapons on their side.

Of course the flip side was that Blake fully expected Hale to bring the vehicles out, which would entail time spent rigging lift harnesses, and a slower exit from Chimera-held territory. It was important matériel, and Hale was extremely conscious of his responsibilities. Purvis spoke over the intercom, breaking into his thoughts.

"We're five out. Prepare to deploy all vehicles—and get ready to hit the dirt. Welcome to Wisconsin, gentlemen."

As Hale rose, Purvis turned his way. He flipped the intercom off so only Hale and the copilot could hear him. "Watch your six, Hale," Purvis said, "so we can come in and save it again."

Hale grinned, shot the other officer a one-finger salute, and went back into the cargo area.

In addition to carrying a vehicle, each VTOL was loaded with twelve men, for a total of seventy-two soldiers counting Hale himself. It was an unusually large command for a second lieutenant, especially since more than half the troops were Sentinels, each of whom was judged to be worth three Rangers due to their quickness and ability to recover from wounds.

But given Hale's combat record, and his familiarity with the Henry Walker mission, Blake had been willing to put him in charge, with Kawecki acting as platoon sergeant. Now, as Hale took his seat, he knew all the men were watching him closely. "Remember," he said as he looked around, "I hate paperwork . . . So don't get killed."

That produced some guffaws, and served to take the edge off as the *Party Girl*'s door gunners began to clear the landing zone of stinks. Then, as all forward motion stopped, the crew chief pulled a lever and Hale felt the ship rise suddenly as the tank dangling under the VTOL's belly hit the ground.

Having released the extra load, Purvis put the *Party*

*Girl* down about fifty feet away from the M-12, ordered the crew chief to deploy the ramp, and cut power. A lot of fuel had been consumed on the trip out, and he wanted to conserve as much of it as he could. The engines were still spooling down as Hale led his men out onto the flat area that surrounded the mine.

Two of the soldiers ran over to the tank, while the rest followed Hale toward the point where one of the enemy's automatic mortars was dropping shell after shell into the crater below. Gouts of mixed mud and snow rose into the air as explosions marched across the pit and the defenseless prisoners ran every which way, searching for a place to hide.

"Shut that weapon down!" Hale ordered. "Then turn it around. If the stinks counterattack, we'll use it against them."

It took the better part of five minutes to kill the Hybrids who were guarding the emplacement and take possession of the mortar. Once that was done, Hale left a team of three men to redeploy the weapon while he turned his attention to what was happening elsewhere. And there were lots of things to worry about, something Blake had warned him about earlier.

"You're used to leading small groups," the older officer had cautioned. "This mission will be different. It'll have a lot of moving parts—not the least of which will be Mr. Dentweiler. The trick is to avoid being pulled down into the tactical stuff, and keep your eye on the big picture."

That prediction was already proving true. The rest of the strike force was on the ground by then, and a number of brisk firefights had begun as various squads began to tackle the objectives they had been given. But rather than try to micromanage those conflicts, Hale knew it was his responsibility to focus on the main objective, as

two of the group's All-Purpose Vehicles came roaring up
to stop a few feet away.

The first Lynx was assigned to Hale, and the second
was reserved for Dentweiler and Burl, both of whom
wore Ranger uniforms minus insignia, and carried pistols.

Hale had argued against bringing the civilians along,
but without success, or much sympathy from his commanding officer.

"You want tanks?" Blake had inquired rhetorically.
"Well, you got 'em . . . Along with the guy who wrote
you the blank check. Enjoy."

"Come on!" Dentweiler shouted as he stood upright
in the Lynx. "Let's get down into that pit and find
Walker!"

Burl, who was seated in the rear next to the machine
gunner, looked worried. Hale wondered what the man
was thinking. Here he was, returning to his own personal hell only days after escaping it.

Hale lifted a hand by way of an acknowledgment as
he climbed in next to the driver. He was armed with a
HE .44 Magnum and a Bellock Automatic. Both weapons
had been chosen for close-in work if it came to that.

"Okay," Hale said to the driver, "take us past those
buildings and down into the pit."

The engine roared, wheels spun, and slush flew sideways as the Lynx took off, closely followed by the second unit. Hale barely had time to look at the yawning
crater off to the left and marvel at how large it was before a couple of Howlers came bounding out of cover
and the .50 caliber machine gun began to chug.

Both Chimera were knocked off their feet, and the vehicle bumped over one of them, forcing Hale to hang on
for dear life as the four-by-four skidded sideways and a
dozen Hybrids poured out of the buildings ahead. They

opened fire with Bullseyes, and as the gunner brought the .50 to bear, Hale triggered the Bellock. The combination proved deadly as half a dozen stinks went down.

The driver straightened the vehicle out, just in time for the second Lynx to hose the Chimera down as it followed along behind. Then the battle was over as both vehicles followed the circular road downward. They were about halfway to the bottom when the gunner shouted, "Drones at ten o'clock!" and began to fire.

Hale looked up to see that a swarm of the flying machines had been dispatched to intercept the incoming vehicles. So he fired the Bellock, and had the satisfaction of seeing one of the drones vanish with a loud *bang*. An instant later the gunner scored two kills of his own. "Yee-haw!" the Sentinel shouted as he smoked a third machine. "Eat lead, assholes!"

Then they were past the drones, leaving the second Lynx to fire on the surviving machines, as they made one last circle of the pit and came to a smooth stop next to the half-frozen lake. Within a matter of seconds a flood of raggedy prisoners surged out of their various hiding places, all yelling excitedly as some tried to jump aboard the vehicles.

That was when Burl stood up and shouted at the crowd: "Back off!" Burl got nearly instant obedience as members of the Fair and Square Squad recognized their leader and hurried to provide him with backup. Hale was suddenly grateful for the civilian's presence as he gave orders for the prisoners to form a column of twos and prepare to march up out of the pit as fast as they could.

Meanwhile, having exited the second Lynx, Dentweiler was shouldering his way through the crowd while holding up an 8 × 10 glossy of Henry Walker for everyone to see. "Have you seen this man?" Dentweiler demanded loudly. "If so, where is he?"

There were lots of garbled replies as Burl left the organizing task to the members of the Fair and Square Squad and hurried over to the spot where the Walkers liked to eat their meals. The carefully wrapped recorder and the recordings had been hidden there, in a crevice between two large rocks.

But they were gone.

Burl was disappointed, and started scanning the crowd for Walker, when one of his buddies hurried over. "Harley, you crazy sonofabitch! You made it! And you came back . . . Never mind that serving of glop you owe me. We're square."

Burl grinned. "Good. I was going to mention it if you hadn't." Then he resumed his search, and said, "Where's Walker? I don't see him anywhere."

"They took him," the man announced sadly. "Yesterday morning, along with twenty-three others. He'd been here a long time, Harley, you know that, and the poor bastard's luck ran out."

"Damn it," Burl said disgustedly. "Twenty-four hours. The difference between life and death. Do me a favor would you? Help the squad get everybody ready to go. I've got to speak with Lieutenant Hale."

The Sentinel was standing next to his Lynx, listening to the latest in a series of sit reps from the noncoms up on the rim, when Burl materialized out of the crowd.

"Thanks for the help," Hale said, as he eyed the area around him. "What's up?"

"It's Walker," Burl replied soberly. "I know what happened to him."

Hale's eyes came around to meet Burl's.

"Yeah? Where is he?"

"He's almost certainly dead," Burl answered. "But we need to find his body. He was carrying audio recordings of President Grace laying plans to open negotiations with the stinks. Can you believe that shit? I didn't, until he let me listen to some of them. That's why Henry and his wife were headed for Chicago . . . They were going to give the tapes to the Freedom First people, except the Chimera grabbed them the same day the bastards got me."

It took a moment for Hale to absorb the full gravity of what he'd been told. But once he had a chance to think about it, everything fell into place. Walker's decision to quit his job, the desperate attempt to reach Chicago, and Dentweiler's overriding desire to locate the ex–Secretary of War. That, coupled with Susan's parting words, helped Hale make up his mind. "So you think the recordings would be on Walker's body?"

Burl looked relieved. "Yes. They aren't where he normally kept them—so I feel certain he took them."

"Up to the Processing Center?"

"Yeah," Burl answered. "We didn't know what it was . . . but yes."

"Okay," Hale said thoughtfully. "I'll see what I can do. But keep it to yourself. Understood?"

Burl looked grateful as Dentweiler arrived. "Yes," he said. "Understood."

"The bastard is dead!" Dentweiler reported triumphantly as he took his place in the second Lynx. "Come on . . . Let's get the hell out of here."

Hale was about to reply when Kawecki's voice came in over his headset.

"Echo-Five to Echo-Six . . . We have trouble, sir. Two Stalkers and a Goliath are approaching from the east. There's plenty of ground troops, too. Maybe two hundred or so."

Hale swore silently. No matter what he did there wouldn't be enough time to load the prisoners and pull out without a fight. Never mind the Walker problem.

"This is Echo-Six . . . Establish an observation post out to the west and tell them to keep a sharp eye out. Once we pivot to the east, we don't want anyone sneaking in behind us. Put everything else in front of those buildings. We'll use them for cover and try to defend them. And don't forget those mortars. Put 'em to work. I'll be up in five minutes. Over."

Once again Hale was reminded of the complexities associated with a larger command as he thought about the Stalkers, the Goliath, the people lined up at the foot of the road, and the vulnerable VTOLs parked on the ground above. Time was everything, and there wasn't enough of it.

The Chimeran armor would be within striking distance by the time the prisoners made it up to the top of the crater.

Such were Hale's thoughts as Dentweiler yelled at him from the second Lynx. "What are we waiting for, Lieutenant? We have what we came for . . . I need to get back to Denver."

Hale glanced up at the gunner who was standing in the back of his Lynx. Pointing at the Chief of Staff, he spoke forcefully. "See the man over there? If he speaks without my permission blow his head off."

"Yes, sir!" the gunner said without hesitation, and he swiveled the big .50 around so that it was aimed at Dentweiler's skull. That caused the gunner standing *behind* the Chief of Staff to swear and jump to the ground. For his part Dentweiler turned pale and slid down into the passenger seat like a deflated balloon.

Having bought himself a moment in which to think, Hale turned to Burl. "Things have changed . . . Tell the prisoners to line up in alphabetical order. Then break them into thirty-person groups. There isn't much space next to the lake, so the VTOLs will have to land one at a time. Load 'em as fast as you can. Understand?"

Burl nodded grimly. "And the recordings? You'll look for them?"

"If I can," Hale promised. "But the prisoners and my troops come first."

"Thank you," Burl said sincerely. "Thank you very much."

"Time to go topside," Hale said as he took his seat in the Lynx. The driver put his foot down, the vehicle sped upslope, and Hale issued orders to Purvis. "Echo-Six to Bravo-One. The stinks are closing from the east. You'll have to land in the pit in order to load passengers. But there's only room for one bird at a time. Copy? Over."

"This is Bravo-One," Purvis replied. "I copy. How many passengers? Over."

"About a hundred and fifty, give or take," Hale replied. "Over."

"That won't leave room for all of your troops," Purvis objected. "Over."

"Roger that," Hale replied stoically. "So don't stop for a beer on your way back . . . We might not be here if you do. Echo-Six out."

The first VTOL was already in the air and in the process of lowering itself into the crater, when the two four-by-fours emerged from the pit and skidded to a stop. Hale was the first one out and immediately pointed a finger at Dentweiler. "If you want to live, keep your mouth shut and stay with me."

Then, turning to the drivers, he gave them fresh orders. "Head east, find those Stalkers, and take 'em down. The tanks will tackle the Goliath."

Both drivers nodded, and as Dentweiler's boots hit

the ground they roared away. The battle began as the Chimera sent salvo after salvo of high explosives arcing down on the cluster of buildings—and the humans answered with cannon fire from the M-12 tanks and hit-and-run attacks from the speedy All-Purpose Vehicles.

Thunder rolled as Hale and Dentweiler arrived on the east side of the big barnlike maintenance shed, and took cover in the grease pit Kawecki was using as a command bunker. Hale's first task was to get a grasp on the overall situation and assume command.

By parking a grader over the concrete pit, one of Kawecki's men effectively put a partial roof over the bunker and Hale could hear the steady *ping, ping, ping* of nearly spent projectiles hitting the machine as he brought his binoculars up and began a quick left-to-right scan of the battlefield in front of him.

The tanks were about a hundred feet apart and hull down behind piles of mine tailings. The mounds of dirt offered excellent cover as Chimeran missiles probed the area around them. Farther out, beyond the fall of mortar rounds, one of the Stalkers was out of action and on fire as three battle-scarred Lynxes harried the second machine. But killing the last Stalker wasn't going to be easy. Each time one of the four-by-fours took a run at the Chimeran tank it was necessary to deal with dozens of Hybrids before they could get in close enough.

The fourth Lynx was little more than a burned-out carcass that lay farther out and marked the point where its battle had been fought ten minutes earlier. The vehicle's driver or gunner, it was impossible to tell which, had taken cover behind the wreck and was firing his M5A2 carbine at the oncoming Goliath.

A futile gesture—but a brave one.

"This is Echo-Six," Hale said into his lip mike. "Foxtrot-Six and Seven are too close together . . . Six will pull back, break north, and prepare to flank the Goliath. Seven will pull back, break south, and do the same thing. Execute. Over."

He received two speedy acknowledgments as he turned to Kawecki. "Put all of the LAARKs toward the center of the line—but back far enough to move laterally. Once the Goliath is within range, I want them to fire, then run to a new location. They won't be able to bring the bastard down, but they can keep it busy so the tanks can get into position."

Kawecki nodded, said, "Yes, sir," and hurried to put the word out.

With that accomplished, Hale instructed a nervous-looking Dentweiler to remain in the bunker while he set out to visit the defensive positions that Kawecki had established. His guide was a Sentinel named Jenkins. "Keep a sharp eye out, sir," the soldier advised. "We killed a whole shitload of the bastards, but we didn't get all of them, and there are plenty of places to hide around here."

Hale checked to make sure the Bellock was ready to go before following Jenkins up out of the relative safety of the grease pit toward the admin building to the south. Pieces of rusty machinery, freestanding utility buildings, and a pile of scrap metal offered opportunities to take cover, and the men took full advantage as they dashed from spot to spot.

They hadn't gone more than a few hundred feet, and were crouched behind a storage tank, when Auger fire slashed through the cylinder, missing Hale by a hair.

Jenkins returned fire from *his* Auger as Hale circled the tank, searching for the stinks which had to be on the other side. There were two Steelheads, both of whom swiveled toward him as he fired the Bellock. They stag-

gered as a fusillade of explosive rounds went off around
them and Jenkins attacked from behind.

Both went down hard, weapons skidding on concrete.

Hale was running low on ammo by that time, and he
was on his way over to exchange the Bellock for an
Auger Mark II when he saw another weapon lying on
the ground a few feet away. The MP-47 Pulse Cannon
must have been taken from a dead Sentinel, and Hale
was pissed off as he picked the weapon up and followed
Jenkins over to the admin building. The structure had
taken multiple hits by then, and the south end was in
flames as the soldiers in an office to the north end continued to fire a captured machine gun into the open area
beyond. A wave of stinks went down as the heavy slugs
swept them off their feet.

Hale made himself known to the sergeant in charge
before turning his binoculars toward the battlefield
where the second Stalker was burning brightly, and the
surviving Lynx was on the run as the Goliath hurled
missile after missile at it. The two-hundred-foot-tall battle mech was armed with Gatling-style guns, plus multiple missile launchers, and it was close enough for Hale
to feel the earth tremble each time one of its feet hit the
ground.

Then the newly repositioned tanks came up on the
Chimeran machine from the north and south. They
forced the colossus to swivel back and forth and divide
its fire between two targets. Explosions could be seen
*and* heard as the humans poured round after round into
the construct, which still kept on coming.

Most of the captured mortars had been silenced by
then, but the LAARK-equipped Sentinels were hard at
work, and Hale could see flashes of light as their rockets
struck the monster's superstructure and articulated legs.

It wasn't going to be enough, however. That became

clear as the Goliath stepped *over* the command bunker and brought an enormous clawlike foot down on top of the maintenance building beyond. It went straight through the roof, and most of the structure collapsed. Then the battle mech took another gigantic step and fired at the *Party Girl* as she rose from the crater beyond.

Purvis had given himself the job of flying the last bird out, and he swore as a missile flew past the canopy, exploding against the west side of the pit wall.

Then with engines screaming, he made the switch to level flight and felt the VTOL lurch sickeningly as something hit her.

But she was tough, and the Goliath was already turning away as the *Party Girl* skimmed the ground.

Hale reached the admin building with Jenkins in tow. They dashed inside and metal rang under their combat boots as they raced up a set of interior stairs to what remained of the flat roof. The fire was still burning a hundred feet away, but the wind was blowing north to south, so they could see in spite of the billowing smoke.

There were two ways to bring a Goliath down. One was simply to batter it to pieces—which was a long and dangerous process. The other was to fire some sort of explosive down the exhaust ports located to the rear of the mech's superstructure. And as they arrived at the west side of the roof, and the Goliath began to turn back toward the east, that was Hale's intention. The MP-47 Pulse Cannon was on his shoulder by then, and he could see the glowing exhaust ports, but not for long as the colossus continued to turn.

Quickly, knowing that more of his men were going to die if he missed, Hale fired. There was only enough time to get two shots off, but both hit their marks and exploded within the mech. That wasn't enough to kill the beast, but the Goliath was still taking fire from the man-portable rocket launchers, and one of its leg actuators was damaged. The combination forced it to pause, so that as the rim gave way under its enormous weight, it fell over backward. There was the equivalent of an earthquake as the construct disappeared from sight and landed in the crater. Then, heart in his throat, Hale ran for the stairs.

Once on the ground he summoned the remaining Lynx, which carried him toward the pit. He knew the Goliath was still operational because he could hear the insistent whine of its powerful servos and the clatter of metal on rocks. So he fully expected to see the machine's lethal superstructure rear up at any moment.

But as the Lynx skidded to a stop at the edge of the pit, it was another sight that met his eyes. The Goliath was lying on its back and legs flailing as it struggled to right itself. That left its belly exposed, and Hale smiled grimly as he got out of the four-by-four and brought the Pulse Cannon to bear. The weapon jerked repeatedly as Hale fired his remaining rounds. All of them hit the target.

The result was a massive explosion with a pressure wave strong enough to knock Hale off his feet and send a fireball hundreds of feet up into the air. Flaming debris fell for what seemed like minutes, but was actually seconds, and kicked up gouts of mud-stained snow all around the bottom of the mine. "Nice one, sir," the vehicle's gunner said admiringly as he staggered to his feet. "That'll teach the bastards!"

It was tempting to take a moment to savor his victory but, as Hale was coming to understand, the price of command was endless responsibility. So he was already thinking about what to do next as Kawecki arrived, followed by a dozen battle-weary Sentinels. It was good to see the platoon sergeant, but something important was missing from the picture. "Where's Dentweiler?" Hale demanded.

"He ran," Kawecki answered grimly. "There we were, firing up at the Goliath as it stepped over us, and the bastard ran. I couldn't chase him without leaving my men. Sorry, sir."

"You made the right choice. Where did he go? Did anyone see him?"

"Yes, sir," one of the men answered. "I saw him run into that building over there."

Hale followed a pointing finger to what had originally been the smelter. Except that the Chimera had converted the structure into what the Intel people assumed was a Processing Center.

"Okay," Hale replied, turning to Kawecki. "I'll take six men over for a look-see. Meanwhile, I want you to pull everyone back to the LZ, establish a perimeter, and rig the surviving vehicles for a lift-out. And stay sharp . . . By the time the VTOLs come back for us, there may be another wave of stinks to cope with."

Kawecki nodded. "Yes, sir. Danby, you and your men accompany the lieutenant. The rest of you follow me."

Hale traded the empty Pulse Cannon for a shotgun, and led the squad toward the long narrow Processing Center. He was struck by the fact that the building was intact. As if the Chimera had intentionally avoided firing on it for some reason. And as he stepped in through the truck-sized door he knew why. The place stank to high heaven. A sure sign that a significant number of Chimera were in residence. "Keep your eyes peeled," he warned. "And let me know if you see anything that looks human."

It was gloomy inside the building, and almost entirely silent—except for the sound of breathing. Not by one entity, but by *many*.

The beam projected by Hale's Rossmore caressed the grimy walls and the feces-smeared floor. Then came an ear-splitting screech as a dog-sized Spinner darted out to attack one of the men. It was immediately put down with a volley of gunfire, but continued to snap its jaws futilely until Danby put three rounds into its brain.

"There's bound to be more of them," Hale warned as the group approached a wall and the opening at the center of it. "Put those Augers to work. Let's find *them* before they find *us*."

Two men carrying Augers came forward. By sweeping their weapons back and forth, they could detect whatever Chimera were up ahead, and they could shoot through walls if necessary. "Bingo!" one of the soldiers said, as his sight lit up.

"Roger that!" the other exclaimed. "There's at least three or four of them! They look like stinks!"

"Take 'em out," Hale ordered brusquely, and the Sentinels obeyed. A cacophony of screeching sounds could be heard as the Auger rounds phased through the steel wall and struck their hidden targets. And because the Spinners couldn't fire back, they were systematically slaughtered.

Finally, when all the Chimera were dead, Hale led the squad through the opening and into the chamber of horrors beyond. It appeared that at least six Spinners had been lying in wait for the humans, and all were dead.

Farther back, standing in rows like a crop waiting to be harvested, were dozens of man-sized cocoons. Each pod incorporated a small vent which allowed the creature within to take in oxygen and vent carbon dioxide. And that was where the rhythmic breathing sounds were coming from. "Check 'em out," Hale ordered. "We're looking for Dentweiler and Secretary of War Walker."

"Yes, sir," Danby responded. "But we don't have to open those pods, do we?"

"I'm sorry," Hale answered sympathetically, "but the answer is yes. And we don't have a lot of time, so let's get to it."

What followed was one of the most disgusting tasks he had ever been required to carry out. Having slung the shotgun across his back, he removed the commando knife from its sheath, and chose a row of cocoons. By starting the cut at the top of each fleshy pod, and running the incision all the way to the floor, it was possible to pry open the cone-shaped structure. That produced a ripping sound, a sudden gush of puslike fluid that splashed his boots, and a horrible, gut-churning smell.

But that was the least of it. Worse yet were the Chimeran pupae within, some of which looked like what they would eventually become, while others remained recognizably human. They were soft, mushy things for the most part, their glassy eyeballs staring out of faces frozen in mid-scream.

Hale had just opened his fourth cocoon when a soldier called from the other side of the room. "I found Mr. Dentweiler, sir! And he's still alive!"

Hale hurried over to where the soldier was standing. The light from the Sentinel's weapon was centered on the pupa's head. And while his glasses were missing, and his features were partially obscured by a filmy material, there was no mistaking Dentweiler's face. Or the fact that he was still alive, and attempting to speak.

Hale stepped in to make a cut in the membrane that covered the official's face and rip the filmy stuff away. That was when he saw the staring eyes, the goo that had been injected into Dentweiler's open mouth, and heard a very faint voice.

"Pleeaasse . . . Kill meeee."

The words were breathy, because Dentweiler couldn't open and close his lips, but they were understandable nevertheless.

"What's he saying?" Danby inquired from a few feet away.

"He wants us to kill him," Hale replied matter-of-factly. "He's already too far gone to be saved, and he knows it."

"So what will we do?" the noncom wanted to know.

"Grant his wish," Hale said levelly, as he drew the .44 Magnum. "That's what I would want. How 'bout you?"

Danby's throat was dry. He nodded. "Yeah, I guess I would."

Hale backed away. There was a loud *boom* as the pistol went off. But instead of passing *through* the cocoon, the bullet was absorbed. Then, much to his horror, he saw Dentweiler blink.

So Hale ordered his men to stand back, triggered the bullet buried deep within the cocoon, and heard a muffled *boom* as what was left of the man exploded. Chunks of flesh flew, goo sprayed in every direction, and one of the Sentinels swore as a glob of pus hit him. That was when Kawecki's voice was heard over the radio. "Echo-Five to Echo-Six . . . We have four birds ten-out and inbound. Over."

"Roger that," Hale replied. "Maintain the perimeter, but load the vehicles, and as many men as you can. We'll be there soon. Echo-Six out."

"All right," Hale said as he surveyed the chamber. "Walker's been here a lot longer, so he won't be as pretty as Dentweiler was, but we need to find him if we can. Let's get back to work."

That announcement produced a nearly unanimous groan, but the soldiers did what they were told, and it was Danby who made the gruesome discovery. "I think I found Walker, sir . . . But it's hard to be sure."

Once Hale was there, standing in front of the partially opened pod, he had to agree. Walker's features had begun to droop as the chemicals within the cocoon went to work on them, and were barely recognizable.

"Open the cocoon and search the body," Hale ordered. "And there's no need to be gentle . . . He's dead, and we're short on time."

Opening the pod wasn't a pretty process, and once the body was exposed, Private Quinn had to search it. His features contorted as he ran his hands up and down the slimy corpse, felt a bump, and announced his find. "I have something, sir . . . Hold on while I cut it out."

Two minutes later Hale was holding a package wrapped in layers of carefully sealed oilcloth. "It was under his belt, sir," Quinn explained. "In the small of his back."

"Good work, Private," Hale replied. "When we get back to the base, I'm going to buy you and your squad a round of beers. Now let's pull everyone out of the room, and throw every air-fuel grenade we have in here . . . I wish we could do more but there isn't enough time."

The entire Processing Center was on fire by the time Hale and troops arrived at the LZ, where one VTOL had already departed, and the rest were loading.

"There's a whole shitload of stinks on their way down from the north," Kawecki announced. "The pilots saw 'em on the way in. Plus some of our jets are playing tag with two Chimeran fighters at fifteen thousand feet. They're outgunned though, so we need to haul ass."

"That sounds like a very good idea," Hale said mildly. "Let's get the hell out of here."

Ten minutes later they were in the air and fleeing west. That was when Hale had the opportunity to cut the package open, fool around with the unfamiliar machine he found inside, and listen to the spool Walker had loaded. The recording was pretty boring at first, but it wasn't too long before the possibility of negotiating with the Chimera came up, along with the name Daedalus. A being with whom Hale was *very* familiar, and had strong feelings about. When the anger came it arrived slowly, like a fever that made his skin hot, and forced sweat out through his pores.

Images flickered through Hale's mind. Dead soldiers strewn about the streets of London, the look on Nash's face a fraction of a second before the bullet hit him between the eyes, the empty shell casings that littered the floor of his family's home, Old Man Potter sitting in his rocking chair, Barrie going down on the roof, Spook's tattooed face, Susan in manacles, and the smooth, self-assured man who had promised the people victory, but was preparing to betray them.

And that was the moment when all the pieces fit together, when the slow flush of anger achieved focus, and a new purpose was born.

Walker was dead, but his self-assigned mission was alive, and the man who had chosen to carry it forward was very dangerous indeed.

# CHAPTER NINETEEN
# FADE TO BLACK

It was a bright sunny day, and the Chimeran battleship that hung over the area north of Sheridan, Wyoming, threw a shadow to the west, as if pointing at the secret base where Daedalus was being held.

The ship looked like a floating island, with smaller craft darting around it, and Sabre Jets etching tracks into the sky far above. As Purvis sent the *Party Girl* skimming in toward the town's little airport, he knew that the enemy warship could destroy his aircraft with a single shot from one of its energy cannons.

So why didn't it?

There was no way to know as he called Hale forward.

"So," the pilot said, as the Sentinel crowded into the cockpit. "What do you think of *that*?"

Hale was speechless as he stared up through scratched Plexiglas at the monstrous ship hovering above. But what *he* knew—and Purvis didn't—was that Daedalus was being held at a secret facility just outside town. And that President Grace was present as well, supposedly as part of his so-called Victory Tour. His actual reason for being there was to communicate with Daedalus, if such a thing was possible.

More than that, to negotiate with the Chimera in a

last-ditch attempt to slow—if not stop—their inexorable advance. So odds were that the presence of the looming ship had something to do with those talks.

But Hale couldn't voice what he knew, so he made the only kind of comment he could. "That thing is *big*, Harley—so don't piss it off."

Purvis glanced at Hale, realized that the Sentinel knew more than he cared to admit, and produced a snort of disgust. "I don't know what's going on here—but I hope the brass hats know what they're doing."

"So do I," Hale said grimly. "So do I. But don't bet on it."

Once on the ground, he saw that a Lynx was sitting on the tarmac not far from the specially equipped four-engined bomber that had been used to slip Grace in the night before. A ring of heavily armed Rangers were on-site to protect the plane. The four-by-four's driver came to attention, and delivered a picture-perfect salute.

"Welcome to Wyoming, sir."

"Thanks," Hale replied. He returned the salute and placed his duffel bag and weapon in the back. "How long will it take to reach the base?"

"About fifteen minutes, sir," the Sentinel answered as he slid behind the wheel.

"Okay then," Hale replied, and took his place in the passenger seat. "Let's hit it."

The soldier's estimate proved to be accurate as the Lynx followed a two-lane highway north for roughly five miles before turning onto a dirt road. Meanwhile, the Chimeran ship not only blotted out a large section of blue sky but bled ozone into the air which crackled with static electricity. The driver made no mention of it, but continued to glance up occasionally as he negotiated the series of twists and turns that led to the base.

When the four-by-four came to a stop in front of the

main gate an M-12 tank and a platoon of Rangers were there to greet it. Both men were subjected to redundant security checks by Secret Service, Army, *and* some of the SRPA personnel who had been added to the President's security team.

Thanks to Hale's status as officer in charge of the SRPA detachment, he was cleared with a minimum of fuss, and allowed to proceed. Five minutes later the Lynx came to a halt behind a convoy of six heavily armored vehicles that had been used to ferry Grace in from the airport. They were parked in front of a low concrete building that extended back into the hillside behind it and was protected by a number of antiaircraft batteries.

Hale thanked the driver, took both his bag and carbine out of the back, and carried them to the front of the building where it was necessary to pass through security all over again. Once that process was complete, a Ranger led Hale through a maze of starkly bare corridors to the observation deck, which consisted of a long narrow room that fronted an open space beyond.

Roughly two dozen people were present, half of whom were scientists, the rest being members of the President's security team or personal staff.

Major Blake was present because in addition to the Sentinels assigned to help guard Grace, SRPA had been called upon to help secure the entire base. So as Hale entered, the major came over to greet him.

"Good work rescuing those prisoners, soldier . . . Too bad about Dentweiler."

"Yes, sir," Hale agreed. "I can't say I liked the man— but that was a horrible way to go."

Blake nodded. "Sorry to drag you up here so soon after a difficult mission, but this is turning into a circus, and I need your help."

Hale raised an eyebrow. He knew Blake pretty well, and could see the anger in the other man's eyes.

"A circus, sir?"

Blake made a face.

"Dentweiler used Hannah Shepherd to lure Daedalus into a trap and brought him here. Now the President wants to talk to him! Lord knows why."

Hale knew why based on the tape recordings stored in one of his cargo pockets. And he would have said as much if a klaxon hadn't begun to bleat, and most of those present went forward to stare out through the armored glass. "What's going on?" he wanted to know.

"This is it," Blake answered grimly. "Dentweiler's eggheads have been using the carrot-and-stick approach to gain Daedalus's cooperation. Preliminary talks have been underway for a week now, and according to the people in charge, Daedalus has been receptive to the possibility of bilateral talks. So much so that when Daedalus requested a show of good faith, Grace gave permission for a Chimeran battleship to enter our airspace. Now he's going out to meet with Daedalus face-to-face."

"Face-to-face? You've got to be kidding," Hale replied. "Doesn't anyone remember what happened in Iceland? He can't be trusted. You know that . . . You were there when Daedalus broke out."

"That's what I told 'em," Blake agreed bleakly. "But they won't listen. They believe the pain they can administer to Daedalus, plus the fact that they're holding his wife hostage, will prevent him from running amok."

"That's *bullshit*," Hale responded as both men went forward to look out through the window. He was just in time to see President Grace step out into the huge cell where Daedalus was being held.

\* \* \*

Although his physical body was in Wyoming, Daedalus's restless consciousness was elsewhere in the world, mind-jumping from a Hybrid in Padang, Indonesia, to a Howler near Fada, Chad, to a Grim outside La Paz, Bolivia, to a Titan plodding across a wintry field in Ukraine, to a Mauler exploring the streets of New Delhi, India.

In each case Daedalus was welcomed, because he was an expression of the wholeness to which they all belonged. That's what *they* assumed anyway, although Daedalus had reason to believe that he had risen *above* the Chimeran virus, and even taken control of it. Unless it was controlling him so thoroughly that he couldn't detect its presence, that is. A possibility that continued to plague him, but one he couldn't do anything about.

Such were Daedalus's thoughts as a jolt of electricity brought his mind back to the body that housed it. It was an ungainly thing that resembled nothing so much as an airborne tumor from which spindly legs dangled. The electric shock didn't hurt, nor was it meant to, although the humans could turn up the intensity if they chose to. No, the nip was their way of summoning him back, typically for the purpose of a long, boring communication.

As Daedalus opened his many eyes, he saw that a human had stepped out onto the concrete directly below him. The floor had been hosed down less than an hour earlier and was still damp in places. "The man standing in front of you is President Noah Grace," a disembodied voice informed him. "He wishes to speak with you."

The words echoed endlessly through Daedalus's brain and carried him away. He was a Steelhead, feasting on a human leg in Paris, when a stronger electric shock suddenly jerked him back. "Meat-speech," as he thought of it, required a great deal of concentration, more so all the time, and his first attempt produced nothing other than gibberish. "Meano pontha hyblom oraga."

\* \* \*

Noah Grace stood in the shadow thrown by the airborne monstrosity and looked up at it. With the exception of the spire attack at the Lincoln Memorial, this was as close as he had been to a Chimera. If Daedalus truly qualified as such.

But rather than the bowel-emptying fear that Grace thought he might experience, he felt another emotion instead. And that was a sense of power. Because the monstrosity hovering above him was *his* captive—rather than the other way around—and therefore subject to his will. The only problem was whether it was still human enough to communicate. The gibberish was *not* a good start.

Grace cleared his throat. "I speak for the people of the United States of America."

Daedalus farted gas and his body sank. Grace felt a sudden stab of fear, but forced himself to stand his ground as the fleshy horror came down to something approaching eye level. He could see the remnants of a human head that had been almost entirely subsumed by the lumpy body to which it was attached. Coal black eyes stared out at him from deep-set sockets as purplish lips began to move.

"What do you want, meat-thing? You're dead, yet you speak."

A horrible odor enveloped Grace then, and he felt his gorge rising. However, he knew it was important to take control.

"I was told that you are rational—and capable of communicating with the Chimera. If that's true, and you're willing to cooperate, then you will continue to live. Otherwise I will have you killed."

Daedalus felt what amounted to a pinprick as one of the scientists on the observation deck sent electricity coursing through the electrode buried in his flesh. It was meant as a reminder. An order to mind his manners. "I listen," Daedalus promised as his mind jumped to the battleship hovering above.

"Good," Grace replied firmly. "I have a message for the Chimera . . . A message I want *you* to deliver. I—that is to say *we*—have killed hundreds of thousands of Chimeran forms, and will continue to do so unless all of them withdraw from North America and leave us alone. But *if* the Chimera pull their forces out, we will not only agree to a truce, but allow them unfettered access to the rest of the world."

Daedalus had already begun to laugh—a hideous, mind-bending sound—when the steel door located behind Grace rumbled open and Hale stepped into the huge cell. As part of the security team, it had been a simple matter to walk down a flight of metal stairs and enter the huge cube.

"Like hell we will," Hale growled as he raised the carbine. "Traitors don't speak for the citizens of the United States. This is *our* planet and we plan to keep it."

Most of the shadow people looked the same to Daedalus. But some—like Hannah—were unforgettable.

"Hale?" Daedalus said, the words coming more easily now. "So you're still alive . . . Who are you going to shoot?"

The Sentinel looked from one to the other, made his choice, and corrected his aim. Grace's eyes widened in response, and the President's lips started to form the word "No" as Hale's finger squeezed the trigger. The sharp *crack* echoed off the walls and there was a sudden spray of blood and brains as the body fell. The empty casing made a tinkling sound as it bounced off the floor and rolled away.

Then Hale was swinging the weapon around, hoping to put a bullet into what remained of Daedalus's human brain, when a bolt of mental energy killed three people and brought every other human being within two hundred yards of the cell to their knees. That included the scientist who had her hand on the dead man's switch that had been installed for just such a situation. As she fell, 5,000 volts of electricity arced between the nearest wall and the electrode located inside Daedalus. He screamed, and the stench of burning flesh filled the air, until the circuit was automatically broken.

Hale was lying on his back, his mind still reeling as a powerful bolt of plasma struck the top of the cell and blew it open. Chunks of concrete rained down, some of which struck Daedalus as his body rose steadily upward. He—or more accurately it—looked like a gas-filled balloon which, having escaped a child's hand, was free to roam.

But a shuttle was waiting to receive Daedalus a few hundred feet above—and the Chimeran battleship was there to take the smaller vessel aboard.

All hell broke loose as a vengeful Daedalus must have given orders for the battleship to rake the area. Most of the base was belowground, so while it suffered some damage, the city of Sheridan soon ceased to exist. Then, having accomplished its mission, the huge ship sailed north, seemingly oblivious to the Sabre Jets that sought to bring it down.

Hale recovered enough to stand, locked his hands behind his neck, and stood impassively as Blake and two dozen security people flooded into the roofless cell with weapons drawn. Six of them were Secret Service agents, but the rest were Sentinels. A doctor knelt next to

Grace's bloodied body, and felt for a pulse, but knew it was hopeless.

He looked at Blake and shook his head. "The President is dead."

"God *damn* it," Agent Stoly said angrily. "What are we going to do?"

There was silence for a moment as Blake considered what Grace had been willing to do. Finally he spoke. "Get the Vice President on the horn. He has a country to lead. Do you have a problem with that?"

Stoly scanned the faces around him. There was a whispering sound as his .38 Special slid back into its holster. "No, Major," he said. "I don't have a problem with that."

Blake turned toward Hale. "As you were, Lieutenant. The stinks may *take* this planet," he said grimly, "but we sure as hell aren't going to give it to them."

Hale bent over to retrieve his carbine. It was, the Sentinel decided, the one thing he could count on.